# The King's Trap
# The Hidden Land Novel 2
# Peter Meredith

I0654377

Peter Meredith

# Fictional works by Peter Meredith:

A Perfect America
The Sacrificial Daughter
The Apocalypse Crusade War of the Undead: Day One
The Apocalypse Crusade War of the Undead: Day Two
The Horror of the Shade: Trilogy of the Void 1
An Illusion of Hell: Trilogy of the Void 2
Hell Blade: Trilogy of the Void 3
The Punished
Sprite
The Blood Lure: The Hidden Land Novel 1
The King's Trap: The Hidden Land Novel 2
To Ensnare a Queen: The Hidden Land Novel 3
The Apocalypse: The Undead World Novel 1
The Apocalypse Survivors: The Undead World Novel 2
The Apocalypse Outcasts: The Undead World Novel 3
The Apocalypse Fugitives: The Undead World Novel 4
The Apocalypse Renegades: The Undead World Novel 5
The Apocalypse Exile: The Undead World Novel 6
The Apocalypse War: The Undead World Novel 7
The Edge of Hell: Gods of the Undead A Post-Apocalyptic Epic
Pen(Novella)
A Sliver of Perfection (Novella)
The Haunting At Red Feathers(Short Story)
The Haunting On Colonel's Row(Short Story)
The Drawer(Short Story)
The Eyes in the Storm(Short Story)
The Witch: Jillybean in the Undead World 1(Novella)

# Chapter 1

## Aric

Three miles into the forest, with the dull grey mists swirling about their ankles and the sun only a dim circle in the southwest sky, Caslin son of Fostin died. He lay upon the soft ground and breathed his last and Aric could do nothing but watch and grieve for this unknown soldier. Unabashedly, he wept over the loss of the man, while beside him—crowding him—the other men-at-arms of the Den did not. It was not their way. Their eyes grew stony and their lips became thin lines. Each touched their own chest with the palm of their hand and then touched Caslin in the same way. This was their goodbye.

Aric turned away, finding it hard to breathe. Looking back, he saw the long, thin trail of blood the young soldier had left behind; it disappeared into the magical fog. How far did that trail extend? How long had Caslin stoically bore the ruination of his internal organs, saying nothing, slowly dying? When he had finally stumbled and could not go on, Caslin had urged the others to leave him. They would not, not in this horror of a forest. They turned to Aric, but the fey had nothing left. His magic—the power of his soul—was, for the time being, spent.

Beside him, staring down at the body, Furen sighed in the heavy way that dwarves do, as if sighing itself was work. "We should not tarry over long. We know not what sort of reception our demon friend might be planning for us on the other side of these damned mists."

"I doubt there will be one," Aric said, unmoving. "Had it not been for Eireden and the Den, the fey would be no more. It is unlikely that our enemy foresaw his coming, else he would have stopped him ere he reached the Feylands."

"Either way, my Lord Fey," one of the soldiers replied. "Caslin would not want us to sit about mourning until the whole maug army came down upon our heads. He would want us to look to our duty."

In all his long life Aric Anorian had never been so emotionally spun. In the last few hours he had seen death and blood to last him a lifetime. Inside him roiled grief and guilt. There was so much guilt within him that he felt as if he were choking on it. "What about your duty to him?" Aric demanded, flaring in sudden anger. "Do you say nothing at his passing? No words of loss? Do you leave him here to be fed upon? Is this what passes for honor among the Den?"

The two remaining soldiers bristled with anger at this. Furen stepped between them and Aric. "Unlike you, my friend," the dwarf said in a gentle voice. "The Den and I, we are mortals and know much about death. Not only that we are soldiers. We laugh loudest and drink the heaviest. We live big because we know that our lives can be gone, passing in the blink of an eye. And we mourn and grieve longer than any. Caslin will be remembered, do not worry about that. Twenty years from now, you and I will only vaguely recall this young man, yet every soldier in his company will be able to tell you where he fell and if he had a wife or sweetheart. They will tell stories of him and they will laugh and cry. They know him and they will remember."

"In one thing you are wrong, Furen," Aric said in somber reply, feeling the weight of his guilt grow. "I will remember him. His death and the death of all today were caused by my actions. Only in death can I forget that." He then turned to the two soldiers. "As for my words, please accept my apologies. I was being presumptuous. I know not your ways and still would think to dictate them. That is wrong and foolish."

The soldiers nodded to this but said nothing; neither looked to have the strength for anything more. They were battered and bloodied from the long fight in the valley. Furen arranged the dead man, placing his spear at his side and his shield across his body. "There; he will lie as he fought. Come and no looking back."

Aric allowed the dwarf to pull him along and the two Den kept very close. They were afraid of the forest. They were afraid to take even a step away from the fey. Having come through without one to deflect the illusions they knew only too well what horrors awaited them if they became lost in the mists. Furen led and had no trouble getting them out of the woods; a few thousand fey had gone before them and though they walked light, many were injured and they left an obvious trail. A blood trail.

The sight of the bright fey blood had Aric reeling and he clutched at the sturdy dwarf. "This is all my fault, Furen. I let love blind me," he said in the language of the dwarves. "I disregarded the danger to my people just for love." In his dream he had pulled Ella out of the Theater of Ancestral Concordance with her words, *I Love you, Aric* still echoing in his mind and he had felt the same back. He had prophesized his love for her. He had loved her even before they had ever met.

"Love?" Furen asked. "What love?" It was no surprise that Furen didn't know. Aric, after the manner of the fey had kept his feeling hidden.

"Ella," he replied. Simply saying the name and picturing her face in his mind helped to calm his turmoil. "I love Ella. She..."

The dwarf stopped in his tracks. "You love Ella?" Furen demanded in a whisper despite the fact that they were speaking dwarven. "How can you say that aloud? You know how Gada feels about her! And you know how she feels about him!"

"I know how Gada *felt* about her. I saw the Rea' Edaere collapse. I do not believe he lived through that and if he did, he would be trapped under tons of rubble with no way out. Besides, he knows it already. He heard Ella say that she loved me and I fear it drove him mad. I believe he sought his death in battle."

Furen began again to stomp along, blowing out angrily so

that his mustache lifted. "I don't believe it will be Gada's fate to fall in battle. He is too mighty a warrior. His end will come through treachery."

Now it was Aric's turn to stop, his hand going to the hilts of his sword. "What are you saying? Are you saying I was not true to him? If so you will answer for those words! I tried to warn Gada on numerous occasions. I told him it wasn't going to work between them, but he would not listen—not to common sense and not to my prophecy."

Furen grumbled under his breath and took Aric's arm. "Let us keep walking while you threaten me. I am tired of these mists and wish to put them behind us," the dwarf said. "I don't know what is right when it comes of love between the Den and a fey. The dwarf way is far simpler. The suitors present their flowers; the woman chooses and that is that. There is not all this back and forth, wishy-washy garbage. We stake our claim, loud and proud. It cuts down on the confusion."

"Well that's just it," Aric said as he was tugged along. It was a testament to his mental state that his hand dropped from his sword as if it had never traveled there to begin with. "There can't be love between a Den and fey. It's unnatural. But I don't blame Gada. Eleanor has a power to her—a grace that strikes the heart and leaves you...enchanted."

"Aye," Furen replied. "She is no Gargefrel, but she is as you say, enchanting. Even I feel it. Look! The end of the mists!" The two Den sighed in relief and even Aric felt a easing of his heart seeing the blue sky and the open flower-filled meadows beyond. A few miles away milled thousands of fey and in a long, thin, ragged line before them were the remnants of the Twelfth Guard. He did a quick count of the men: one-hundred-and thirty-eight. How many had died? Too many. And how many fey had died? Far too many.

Aric's green eyes swept over his people, searching faces, searching, not for loved ones—they were all his loved ones—but searching for those that weren't there. Where was

Aristoi? Medci? Where were the twins, Felis and Norsis? Who were those laid upon the ground? Why did they not stir? And the line of Hunfier? Why were there just six standing together so mournfully?

"Where are they all?" he asked without strength in his voice. His head swam and his throat closed. The meadow suddenly felt to tilt and Aric would have fallen to the soft earth in his sudden grief had it not been for Furen.

"I know," rumbled the dwarf in his deep voice. "Many are gone, but so many were saved. Yet they are in danger still. Why do they linger? And where is Lienhart? Why has he not sent them on?"

"I see him not," Aric answered. "Nor do I see Ella!" He spun to look into the forests. With the mists, visibility stood at only fifty yards or so and she wasn't in sight.

"Maybe they've gone on," suggested Furen. "They did have that great, black beast of Lienhart's. They could travel fast on such a horse. Let's go ask if they've come and gone." Furen began walking with Aric following. The fey dragged his feet and kept looking back. In his heart he knew she hadn't yet come out of the forest. But why? There were creatures in the forest, some quite deadly; however few, if any, would dare an armored knight on horseback.

"You there," Furen called to the first of the men-at-arms. "Where is your captain?"

"I would ask you this same question, Sir Dwarf," replied the man. "We have been awaiting him this last hour and the men grow nervous. Why *they* wait I do not know; we have told the fey to go on, but they dither and none can say which is the way to go. Has your king fallen?"

This last he directed at Aric, but the fey barely heard. The dreadful idea that Ella hadn't come through the mists occupied his mind completely. It just didn't seem possible. She had left before him on horseback. She should have come through long since. A second time he scanned the crowd of fey hoping that she had come among them from another direction. Yet Ella was nowhere to be seen.

"Sir, Fey?" the soldier asked again. "Where is your king?"

Aric blinked at the question. "The fey have no king. Each looks to themselves for wisdom and direction, for who can command another?" He turned to the dwarf with sinking heart. "Ella hasn't come through. Mayhap she has fled some beast or roaming band of maug. I must go back!"

He started for the forest, but Furen grabbed his arm and spun him around with ease. "Wait, Aric! Your people are leaderless. Their wisdom has not prepared them for such times. Who will they look to if not you?"

Aric stared back and forth from the milling fey and the desolate and seemingly empty woods. His own wisdom had not prepared him for this moment either. Which way to turn? To go after the woman he loved or help the people he loved. His guilt decided things. Ella would have to wait, if only for a little while.

## Chapter 2

## Eireden

Before sitting down on the marble floor of the Theater of Ancestral Concordance, Eireden gave the old fey the slightest of curious glances. In exhaustion he let his hands drop to his sides and he watched idly as a trickle of blood ran down his arm and began collecting drop by drop on the cool floor. He didn't really care who had named him. Not then. Just then he didn't care much about anything.

"What do you mean *you* named him?" Generai asked as she went to Eireden's side. "And who are you?" Out of training the Den scout began to look over her prince's wounds. They were many, yet none could be counted as life threatening. In a pouch on her belt she carried field dressings and bandages. She was just pulling one out when the fey stopped her.

"I am Garris-Unhi. You may put those away," the fey said. "I will heal him."

"Don't waste your time," Eireden told him. "You said yourself we were doomed. Better to let my life seep out of me. The sooner it does the happier I'll be."

Garris nodded to the request and then turned to the scout. "And you? Would you like me to heal thee?"

Generai backed away quickly from the fey with her hands out. "No...I mean yes, please. But the prince first. I would that he be healed fully and he has many injuries."

"I would, however he has indicated..."

"Do not listen to him on that, Lord Garris. That is depression only speaking. We need him to be whole whatever may come. We are Den, my Lord Prince," she scolded Eireden. "We will make a good showing of ourselves and perhaps there will be a chance at escape."

"Do as you will," Eireden replied, listlessly. "I live but never more have I wished to die. In what way does escape serve me? I will be forced to slay a kinsman—a boy I helped raise to manhood, and then as further reward of living I will have to stand by and watch as my love loves another."

"Never believe that you can see the ends of all things," Garris said kneeling in front of Eireden. "Even those of us that are far seeing can see but a little of all there is." The fey extended his hands and from them a blue light enveloped Eireden. Immediate relief swept over him. It did little to affect his mood.

"Now your turn," Garris said to the scout.

Generai was surprised. "You have strength left?"

"Indeed, my reserves are greater than many, but still less than some," the fey replied and again extended his hands. As the light covered her he added, "To answer your earlier question, I did not exactly name the prince. Rather a dream came to me and I saw the coming of the next Eireden as the son of Eirolden. Who knew how it would come back to haunt me."

"What?" Generai asked in surprise. "You can't blame Eireden for all of this! It was a fey who brought the maug upon you. Tell him it was Aric's doing, my Lord. Tell him, Eireden!" she demanded, incensed.

Eireden shrugged. "I blame not Aric. He was played by a demon, or so we believe. Well at least it's not some maug captain. Whoever our enemy is had a long-term plan and great patience. Ella wasn't in the Forbidden Lands by accident. She was planted there and many years ago. There is only one question: has she been enchanted? Can you tell by her blood?"

"No, however I know that she's not enchanted," the fey answered. "I checked her myself. Aric's vision and the oddity of her circumstances had me apprehensive. The most I can do with her blood is try to discover her lineage. Though how that will serve us, locked away down here, I don't know."

"Maybe we can dig out," Generai suggested. "Not through the rubble, but up through these walls. It might take some doing. Still it's our only chance."

"The walls are solid marble, a foot thick at a minimum," Garris said. "And then there would be a fifteen foot tunnel you would have to dig. You are welcome to try. I don't have any tools, but you can use my chair. My guess is you would do little but draw attention to us."

"I say we try," Generai said confidently, pulling back her blonde hair. She went to the chair and hefted it and as she did her enthusiasm wilted. The chair was too light. It would disintegrate against the hard marble at the first strike. She plopped down into it. "Or maybe we wait."

A silence settled on them. Eireden could wait. In fact he needed time to sort out his feelings. As he had fought the maug he had been so horrifically angry that he had seen Aric's face on each goblin he had killed. That wasn't right. Aric had done nothing wrong. If anyone had screwed up it was himself. How would things have turned out if he had been man enough to claim Ella for his own? This day would have been different that is for certain. But who knows? Maybe the horrible outcome would have been just put off for another time and how likely then that he would have five companies of Den at his disposal. Not very.

As dreadful as it may seem the day's results might be the very best they could have hoped for. And they had Generai to thank for it. Her unquenchable love had saved the fey, as well as Ella, or so he assumed. He could still feel her.

"You were great today, Generai," Eireden said. "The fey would have been annihilated if you hadn't acted...and I would still be a *gada*."

She smiled. "You are my Prince. Every day that you spent as a *gada* was a day I spent in pain."

"I was in pain as well," Eireden said. "And I fear it will only get worse. How do I face Eirowyth? I must slay a man that I loved. I still—even after all these years—can't believe that he said the things that he did. I just don't understand why."

"To gain the throne?" Generai replied. "It seems the most logical explanation. That or he actually believed you ran and his honor forced him to denounce you." She gave him a sharp look after she said this as if trying to see some falsehood in his countenance.

He shook his head sadly. "No. I didn't run. Even if I wanted to there was nowhere to run. The maug and the... and the other creatures were everywhere. I kept having to dash back to the rear guard to keep them from being overwhelmed. And then the van would slow to a crawl and I had to hurry to the front."

"Maybe in all this running around he thought you actually ran for good," she suggested. "Maybe he saw you run back and that was when he got cut off from the rest and he just assumed you had not returned."

"No, he was very explicit in his charge. He said I ran clear away and didn't come back." Eireden paused staring at the tacky little pool of blood that he had dripped onto the marble. Its color was maroon, but next to it was a brighter drop. One of Ella's. She was fey. Even her blood said so. How had his eyes so deceived him? How had his heart? Absently he touched it. The blood was still wet; he mixed it with the pool of his own. "I still go back to why? If you had known Eirowyth like I did you wouldn't believe that he would lie to gain the throne. His honor meant more to him than his life."

"That is what I heard," Generai said. "It's why everyone is so up in the air about this. No one can believe you ran and no can believe he would lie."

An idea struck Eireden. "Garris? Aric told me once that you had the ability to look into the unknown past. Could you look into the time when Eirowyth was in the Demorlaik and find out why he would say things that weren't true?"

Garris had been bent over a small dish that was red with the blood of Ella. He didn't look up. "There is a chance I could see some of that time, yes. However, I cannot look into his mind and know his motivations. So I don't think it would be much use to you. Now if you don't mind, this takes quite a bit of concentration. If you can hold your questions for a couple more hours, I would appreciate it."

"Sorry," Eireden murmured.

Generai raised her eyebrows at him and gave him a smile that said: *Touchy-touchy*.

They respected his wishes and the pair sat in a dull silence for well over two hours as the fey bent over the blood, whispering incantations, and jotting notes. It was not until the first of the goblins could be heard digging at one of the walls that they made any noise at all. And then they did little besides stand and stretch. Eireden worked his muscles and looked around the room to see how the battle would be fought.

For the moment the goblins were coming in from a single direction, which meant he would kill many of them before they wised up and dug a second entrance so that they could come at him from more than one direction. In preparation, Generai and he began arranging bookshelves so that they had an impromptu fort around where he figured the first tunnel entrance would open.

Then came a much longer wait as the goblins ran up against the marble and vibrations shook the walls. Suddenly Garris sighed and said, "I have discovered the line of the father, but the mother is a complete mystery to me. I have no records of her whatsoever. I am completely baffled."

"And the father's name?" Eireden asked. Just then the marble cracked under a series of heavy blows. Pieces began to chip away.

"His name would be unknown to you," Garris said.

"In truth I didn't expect it to be otherwise," Eireden replied, drawing his sword. It had so many notches in it he figured the blade wouldn't last much longer. "But humor me anyway will you please? Call it a dying wish." Immediately he regretted saying that. Generai had been tight lipped and nervous, but now she began to fidget.

"Her father is Darhmael of the line of Narvai," Garris said.

Eireden shrugged. "You were right. I've never heard of him. Is there any significance to the name?"

"Nothing that will help us now," Garris said with a calm air. "I've never killed anything before. I don't know if I can begin now."

The prince gave Generai a look but she was too preoccupied with her anxiety to appreciate it. "Are you alright?" he asked her.

"Yes...no. It's just that we're trapped. I hate being trapped like this. If they get in, there's nowhere to go. Always on the surface there..." The loudest crash yet interrupted her and now a small, black hole appeared in the wall.

"It'll be alright," Eireden said to reassure her. "No matter what happens, know in your heart that you have won a great victory today. Because of you we saved many, many innocent lives. The men of the Twelfth Guards know who made this victory possible and they will remember. And these goblins—they will remember as well! We will fight like lions, you and I. They will come to fear us."

The hole grew bigger. Eireden stepped to one side and Generai to the other. "I'm afraid," she said looking down, ashamed. "I'm not afraid to die fighting like a soldier of the Den. I've never been afraid of that. I'm—I'm afraid to live. As a woman. I'm afraid they will keep me alive."

"Oh," Eireden said in understanding. The maug would torture any prisoner they managed to take alive. Everyone knew it to be the worst death imaginable, but female prisoners were also raped in a hellish fashion. "Would you like me to make sure that you aren't taken alive?"

She wouldn't look at him as she answered, "Yes, please. Let me give a decent account of myself first and then...make it quick."

Now the hole was a few feet on the side and still no

goblin sprang out. They were making it good and wide before they came on. "I will. Fear no more about that. But first we will make them pay! We will have our revenge for all that died today."

She nodded and he was glad to see her grey eyes clear and hard as rock.

Just then the first of the maug burst in. He was a burly fellow still wielding the pickaxe that he had used to make the hole. Behind him, filling the low tunnel countless more could be seen. Eireden drove his blade at the goblin, thinking he would run the fellow through with ease, but unbelievably the goblin was quicker and stronger than he appeared and turned the blade aside with the pickaxe. Eireden had been sloppy and now he was open for a backhand move of the axe, but for some reason the goblin paused. Eireden didn't, he drove his foot in a hard front-kick straight into the goblins chest. It sent the thing reeling, his breath exploding out of him.

And then goblins were everywhere screaming and slashing with rusting blades. It was all he could do to stay near Generai to keep his promise.

# Chapter 3

## Ella

The mists were beyond dreadful. Every nightmare ever conceived came at them so that Lienhart and Ella ran from horror to horror, growing ever more weary and confused. Up became down. The imagined became real. The definition of sanity became stretched so that it lost all meaning and Ella stumbled along, fearing that her mind drifted on the edge of madness. To keep the horse from bolting Lienhart wrapped his cloak about its head and still it shivered and sweated and kicked out unexpectedly.

Even Whip-wip was affected by the illusions. Her face radiated pure terror whenever she looked from the pouch at Ella's belt. Out of sympathy for the poor creature, Ella took off the pearl she wore and gave it to the trembling fairy. Whip-wip took it greedily and, huddling around its light, refused to look any more at the world of illusion around them.

Ella envied the fairy's ability to escape the mental agony, and she had to wonder about her own state. How long could she endure this torture? How long could the captain? His face in his helmet was the color of paper and his eyes rolled wild. His head jerked back and forth with every sound, new or imagined—and there were so many that were imagined. For what seemed like hours, along with the bizarre images in the mists, the cries of babies could be heard, children screamed as if in great pain, the wail of the dead called for their loved ones and the moans of the wounded asked why?

*"Why Ella? Why did you betray us? Why did you let them kill us? You did this to us! You led the maug to our homes. You killed us! You! You! You did this..."*

*"My babies. The maug are feasting on them, devouring them, and their sweet blood runs down their tusks...*

"I didn't mean to!" Ella cried out unable to take it any longer. "It wasn't my fault!"

Lienhart grabbed her and shook her roughly. "Stop yelling," he hissed in harsh anger. "More of them will come. Is that what you want? Is it? You want them to find us?"

"No, please no," she whispered cringing away from the captain's raging face. Was he too one of the illusions? Had she become lost from the real Lienhart? "Get away from me. You're not real."

His grip on her arms tightened to the point of pain and then unexpectedly he relaxed his hold on her all together and she collapsed to the ground sending up a billow of the fog. "I'm not real?" he asked her, bewildered. "I don't feel real. I feel like I'm crumbling away. Nothing makes any sense. Why do I have this sword? What good does it do me? It can't hurt the mists. Nothing can. Nothing. We are fools to even try."

"*Throw away your sword. It is nothing but a burden to you. Feel how heavy it has become.*"

Ella blinked at the sound. That was her own voice! It sounded just like her, only she was sure she hadn't said anything. "Don't do it," she said quickly. "Keep the sword. There's something out there that sounds like me...it might even look like me. It will trick you. We have to kill it!"

Lienhart went in a slow circle, staring out of the fog, the sword shaking in his hand. "I don't see it. I don't see it. There's nothing...wait! There it is," he said staring down at Ella. "She's right here."

"*Kill it quick before she can attack.*"

Again the sound of her own voice came to them from out of the mists. Lienhart raised his sword and it was a moment before Ella realized he was just about to kill her with it. "No! Stop. Lienhart, it's me, Ella. The real Ella. You can't listen to what's in the fog. It's trying to get back at us. It thinks we killed all those fey. But that was an accident. How was I supposed to know the goblins could follow me? Aric said it wouldn't be my fault. He said I wasn't evil, but...maybe he was wrong. Maybe I am evil."

"How do I know what is what?" Lienhart asked, grabbing his hair in his fist. "How can I know what is the truth of anything with all these voices talking, demanding, screaming! Why do they scream like this? Why? How can I put anything to rights with all this screaming? Shut up! Silence in the ranks, damn you! I will have silence in my formations. You there, dress on the man to your right. Keep in line."

Ella turned to see whom it was that Lienhart was screaming at, but all she saw was fog and more fog. When she looked back to the Den captain he was stomping off, yelling at some imagined soldier. Panic swept her. Being with an insane Lienhart was a thousand times better than being alone. She leapt up and chased him down, only suddenly there were two Lienharts going in two different directions, and she couldn't tell which was which.

"Captain! Don't leave me," she begged. At this he stopped—both of them.

"Ella? There are so many of you. Which is real?"

"*I am! Don't leave me.*"

Her voice again came from off to the right. The two images of the Den captain took a step in that direction. Desperately, Ella screamed, "Please, Lienhart. Don't move. Just stay right there. I will come to you." The images stopped in place, only she was too afraid to go to either. They were separated by a bare twenty feet, but in the swirling fog the wrong choice would doom her. Which one did she choose? "Lienhart? What color are my eyes?" she asked.

"Blue—*blue*," both images said in almost the exact wavering tone.

The two answers came at once. She had expected the illusion to be more of an echo of the reality. She tried again, "What...what did you tell me not to call you in the woods when we first met?"

There came a pause and then one of the images said, "Lord."

Followed a fraction of a second later by, "...*Lord*."

Ella ran to the first and clung to him weeping; he was real. She could feel his cold armor and smell the sweat of his fear. For his part he practically crushed her in his embrace. The mists deepened around them and they stared about, alone. The black charger had disappeared. They could hear it whinnying from all directions as it wandered away still blinded by the cloak tied about its head. The horse would never come back. It would fall in a crevice and break a leg or be eaten by some creature...

That thought brought a hard truth to Ella. "I think there is something actually alive out there," she whispered to the captain. "Not just illusions trying to drive us mad, but something real. When I asked you about my eyes it was able to answer just as quickly as you did, but it took a moment to know personal stuff and so there was a delay. Did you notice? Your voice came like an echo."

"I did," Lienhart whispered back. "But I just thought I was going mad. I can't tell what is real anymore. I don't even know if I am."

She knew what he meant. "You are real and so am I. And so is whatever's out there. Show yourself!" she demanded suddenly. "Come out and face us you coward!" Her own voice came back to her out of the mists except instead of sounding angry it came back petulant and mewling.

"Are you sure it's just not the enchantments?" Lienhart asked. "They can be made to seem like anything."

"I'm pretty sure there's something real out there," she answered. "Was it like this when you came through with Eireden? There wasn't a fey with you, right?"

"There was no fey. And it's hard to remember what it was like...we...we closed our eyes and stuffed our hands over our ears. *He* led us through."

Ella thought about that. It didn't seem possible. When she had gone through with Aric, the forest had seemed relatively open, but it was still a forest. There were still hills and gullies and fallen logs and dense patches that had to be avoided. A blind man leading an army would have taken many hours, perhaps even days to get through. "Did Eireden close his eyes as well?"

Lienhart looked at his boots and toed the dirt of the forest floor. "No. He is brave. Braver than any...braver than me. He led us and somehow he was able see through the veil of illusions."

"Do you know how? Did he have magic?" Her own magic was slowly coming back to her, but it would be sometime before she could do more than float even a pebble.

"The men of the Den rarely have magic. We spend too much time training in war to develop magic. I think...I think Eireden just has a power of mind the like of which hasn't been seen in many years. I wish that I were as strong, but I am weak."

"*I am weak...*"

"*I am weak...*" came the echoes of his voice. The captain wilted under the shame of his own words.

"Listen not to these figments!" Ella cried aloud to bolster Lienhart. His fear was undermining what little strength she had left. "You are a Captain of the Den! Stand tall and we will ignore these phantoms just as Eireden did."

In mockery the mists formed themselves into the perfect likeness of the rugged, handsome prince. He sat atop Lienhart's black charger and he wore the clothes Ella had last seen him in: leather armor and dark cloak, save in his hand he held the elf-sword of Aric's.

For a time Ella stared and the image stared back with its steel-grey eyes; she turned away. "We should not go that way. It is certainly a trick." She pulled Lienhart directly away from the apparition of Eireden, but then before her stood Aric. He beckoned to her.

"This the way out of the forests, Milady," Aric said. Just like the illusion of Eireden, the vision of Aric was perfect in every way. Beautiful skin—golden hair—the wonderful, confident smile. It was Aric. And she half went to him.

"No!" Eireden cried. "You can't go with him. He cannot protect you as I can. I would die for you, my love." My love! The words Gada had used right before the first forest battle. Ella turned back to him. He was the real one for sure. The scar on the side of his face was exactly as she remembered. His hands were large, strong, but gentle.

"You told me you loved me," Aric said in the calm, assured way of his. "Sure he might die for you. It's all he knows, killing. What does he know of living? I would live my life for you."

This was too much for her. Ella reeled and Lienhart caught her. "What's happening?" he asked. "Do you see something?"

"You must choose," a voice hissed out of the vapors. At first the mists looked simply to be blowing, but then she saw eyes. They were large, the size of footballs, and pure white. Then a head formed from the mists, like that of a giant lizard and in its mouth it had rows of teeth two feet long. Her mind went numb at the sight and her knees buckled.

It was a dragon.

Ella tried to scream, but no air escaped her. She could only point. Now Lienhart saw and he fumbled for his sword.

"Choose the correct one and you will find peace and the way out of the forest," the dragon said, indicating Aric and Eireden. Ella looked from one apparition to the other. How could she make such a choice? Her insides were a chaos of thoughts, and memories, and feelings of the two men and just then she couldn't make sense of any of them. Eireden represented adventure and danger—perhaps the main reason she had followed him into the Hidden Lands. If she chose him she would live her life on the edge of his blade, perhaps always only one step from death. Aric represented laughter, contentment and a steady, beautiful love, something that she had longed for all her life.

How to choose?

She realized this decision would not come to her emotionally; it would have to be based in cool reasoning. Simply, Eireden wouldn't be able to get them out of the forest. Yes he could find her and certainly could protect her, but what then? They would be just as lost and stuck in this limbo of a world forever. Only Aric had the power over the mists. He was magic as was she.

"I choose Aric Anorian."

# Chapter 4

## Eireden

A blade, rusty and old, but still wickedly sharp, slid in at his belly. Eireden riposted, turning the sword away and laying out the innards of the howling goblin. Reversing the motion he blocked first one, then a second spear jabbing in toward his neck. He would have to get in a little closer. That would be no problem. The first spearman was a touch slow. The goblin had left his spear sit in the air for as much as half a second after his miss.

Lazy, lazy.

Eireden gave him an easy target and then when the goblin committed he ducked and again the spear was slow to come back to the ready position. The Den charged and before the goblin knew what was happening Eireden had plunged his sword four inches into its neck. There was no sense going deeper just to satisfy vanity. Yes he could have sheared the head clear away, but moves like that sapped strength and he pictured himself in a long battle. There were, after all, tens of thousands of goblins between him and safety.

To his left he saw the bright gleam of metal and the heard the sharp sound of battle from up the tunnel—the goblins were fighting each other! This was common enough with their kind, especially when they thought there was treasure to be had. Eireden took a quick peek to see what sort of mayhem was occurring, hoping there would be a bloodbath going on, but it was just a few of them going at it.

Probably one of them got over-excited, he thought as he slashed across the shaft of the spear of his next opponent. This was the problem with spears as defensive weapons; you could lose fingers. The goblin screamed in pain as three of his long grey fingers fell to the floor.

Eireden danced back and as frequently happened in battle he developed an open awareness of almost everything occurring around him: there were four goblins arrayed in front of him, none particularly eager to meet him head on. More were in the tunnel fighting each other. Garris-Unhi stood to the side, shouting and pointing at the burly goblin who had first come through the opening. It was just getting up, though it was having a hard time as it were entangled in a cloak that seemed far too big for it. A few feet to Eireden's right, Generai had killed a goblin and now was advancing on the one with the long cloak.

Something wasn't right. He felt it in his bones as he leapt at the goblins in front of him. Two quailed backwards while the other two thrust their spears at him. At some point in the short fight Eireden had picked up a goblin spear and he used it to parry the attack on his left, while with his right he brought down his sword on the helm of the other goblin. It cut through to the bone.

The blade snapped as he withdrew it and then something clicked in Eireden's mind. He realized that the burly goblin on the floor looked almost to have a beard. A thick beard it now seemed, not the scraggly black stuff of a normal goblin. And he was short; shorter than the other goblins by at least six inches. And beneath his cloak wasn't the nasty stitched up leather armor they usually wore; instead he had on a coat of rings.

"Stop!" Eireden bellowed. And stop is what exactly happened. Above the burly goblin Generai stood poised with her sword in both hands. She had a killing gleam to her grey eyes. The three goblins in front of Eireden stopped as well. They looked back and forth confused and wondering what it was they were stopping for, yet none moved beyond that. Even the fight in the tunnel ceased. Two of the goblins stood at the entrance to the tunnel and now Eireden saw that the gleam of sword he had seen before from that direction was more than it had been—more than it should be, in this goblin-invested valley.

The sword's gleam was too bright; it burned away at the illusion that had been woven about it. It was an elf-sword—

Aric's elf-sword.

"Don't kill him," Eireden commanded, Generai. "That's Furen."

She stared down and a second later she gasped.

This little noise marked a resumption of hostilities. Like a thrown switch everyone jumped into motion. The goblins saw that by some strange magic they were now outnumbered and broke towards the tunnel entrance. Without pity, Eireden followed and slew them one after another, while Aric, with a quick thrust finished his opponent before he could recover his wits.

"Is that all?" Eireden asked glancing up the tunnel. He almost sounded disappointed.

"There are more up above," Furen said as he got up from the floor. "Perhaps even more than you can handle."

Despite everything that had happened in the last day, Eireden couldn't help smiling at the dwarf. "Even with you by my side?"

Before Furen could answer, Generai blurted out, "What are you two even doing here? Why didn't you escape with the others? Wait...please tell me that most of the fey escaped?"

Furen looked to Aric to answer, but the fey was in a quiet discussion with Garris, so the dwarf said, "Aye. Most did escape, which was a miracle of sorts. We made it through the forest and...and," he paused and glanced up at Eireden briefly and then resumed, "And there were the fey. Just standing there, leaderless. It was a sad thing really. With so many hurt and lost, they seemed only to walk in circles asking each other endlessly, have you seen this person or that."

Eireden didn't like the look in Furen's eyes. "And?"

"Well Aric finally got them going. The fey are a strange people. They make great followers but terrible leaders. I had to keep pushing Aric to give orders. We needed you, Gada. I think..."

"His name is Prince Eireden," Generai said, stiffly. "You will not use the term *gada* again. It's offensive."

The dwarf gave her a small bow. "As you wish. I like Eireden better anyway. So Aric was frantic trying to get the fey rounded up and marching. And it was then that Prince Gamelling arrived with two-hundred knights. Very handsomely he ordered his men to dismount for the wounded and together he and Aric got the fey moving toward Hildoeven."

"What of Rhyoeven? Did they not send any men?" Generai asked.

"I know not," replied Furen. "They had not before Aric and I went back into the mists."

Eireden eyed the dwarf shrewdly. "What of Ella? You know she concerns me more than any, why have you not mentioned her? Did she send you back here for me?"

"She never made it out of the mists," Furen answered in a hollow voice. Eireden's chest drew in, but no air came to his lungs. He felt to be choking on nothing. His mouth worked like a fish lying at the bottom of a boat. Furen touched him on the shoulder and said, "I'm sorry, my friend. We don't know what happened. It should've been an easy ride out, seeing as she is fey. She went through with Lienhart and he is brave and capable. Can you feel her? We came to find out if you were alive and if you could sense her."

Now Aric turned and stared at Eireden with haunted eyes. "I can feel her," the Den said, pointing. "She is east and slightly north."

"We have to go! Gather whatever you need," Aric told Garris. "But be quick about it."

"I need it all," the fey replied, putting his back to one of the bookshelves as if to protect it with his thin frame. "This is our history! This is who we are. There are records here that date back over twenty-five thousand years. We can't leave it to be destroyed by the maug."

"Today we begin a new history," Aric answered him.

"We don't have a choice. Every building is being plundered and then put to the torch. I would let you stay and die as you see fit, only I need you. I barely had the strength left to cover Furen and myself in an illusion and now I am depleted. We need your help to escape and save Ella."

For a long time Garris stood with his head bowed and then he began to frantically run about gathering pages from different cabinets. Aric assisted. The others watched for a time and then Generai looked around at the dead goblins.

"I can see dressing as goblins to assist in the illusion," she said, taking a seat on one of the overturned bookshelves. "But why did you bring some of them with you?"

Furen grunted. "They saw us digging and thought we were after treasure. We couldn't exactly fight them or there would've been hundreds coming down on us. So we played along. They were so eager they helped to dig! Only they were too weak to get through the marble. Personally..."

"Let's go," Aric said breathlessly, his arms stuffed with folders and stacks of paper. Immediately he started for the tunnel entrance.

Eireden grabbed him—a little more rough than he meant to. "Sorry. It's just you are going out there without the illusion."

Garris, careworn and tired from his earlier spell work, performed a series of illusions on each of them, bending light to make then appear smaller and an ugly, grey color. They then threw goblin cloaks over their attire and picked up spears. Eireden fretted that the illusion wouldn't be near good enough to fool anyone, but Furen assured him it would be just fine.

Sadly, the dwarf was right.

Crawling out of the earthen tunnel Eireden stood transfixed at the world around him. Gone was the gay little village and the streams and flowers and ivy. Gone were the quaint homes, the beautiful trees, the singing birds. Gone was the innocence.

[28]

In its place was a world choking with reeking black fumes and burning ash. The sky above was hidden from view by billowing clouds of stinking, acrid smoke. All around them were bodies, some hacked into pieces, some torn apart and bearing great teeth marks, others were nailed to the stumps of fallen trees. Most were goblin corpses and these were left where they had fallen. Eireden was shocked at their number. There had to be thousands of dead maug— many more than could be accounted for by the battle.

Just then a sharp fight broke out to their right and six more maug were added to the toll. This explained the extra dead. The maug seemed leaderless. The strong took from the weak and killed at the slightest offence. Where was the demon, Eireden wondered? Aric tugged at his cloak.

"Which way is she? We can't just stand here," the fey whispered.

The answer came automatically. His heart was a finely tuned compass for his love. He nodded toward the east and began to march in that direction. The others followed, staring about them in revulsion. Garris had to be restrained from crying aloud—it was something no goblin would ever do. As they came to the place where Eireden last saw Ella, he spotted one of those horrid burnt-looking creatures that had chased him and Ella across the battle-plain of Rhyoeven.

It sat atop a horse directing goblins in that strange childish voice it had. The maug scurried quickly to do it's bidding, with many a fearful look up at the evil creature. They were looting homes, cramming anything that looked valuable into carts and already there were many stacked high.

"No...it can't do that," Garris said. Thankfully his voice was little more than a weak croak from all the ash in the air. "That's Stahrani's home. She made that..."

Quickly Generai clamped a hand over his mouth and whispered in his ear, "Now's not the time for complaining, my Lord. You can do that when we are safely away. Though

I wouldn't even then. Complaints never stopped a maug from butchering an innocent life. Look around you. You say you've never killed, well maybe it's time you started."

"You know not what you speak," Garris hissed out. "Dangerous it is for a fey to start down the path of death. You are Den. More than any you should know this."

Generai opened her mouth to reply, but Eireden cut her off. "Generai, as you said we'll discuss this later. Let's go." He knew the danger Garris spoke of. They all did. During the sack of Shefarlaik, the elves of old might have witnessed a horror similar to the one they were living. It had changed them for the worse, blackening their souls. Still, there was no time to contemplate this. Danger reared up on all sides as goblins, drunk on death and destruction, went about in a mindless frenzy. Ogres lolled everywhere and more of those burnt-looking creatures could be seen gathering treasure.

Eireden led them through the once peaceful valley and did not look back. His mission lay in front; in the Forest of Mists. The illusions there had not failed and would not either, perhaps for eternity. As they came close, Aric walked on one side of him and Generai on the other. She kept very near to Eireden and tried to hide the fact that her hands shook at the sight of the looming forest. Furen went behind with Garris, who needed to be helped along time and again as he stumbled constantly. His head refused to look forward. He walked looking back at the destruction of his homeland, weeping.

The forest was much different for Eireden and Generai than it had been. Gone were the horrors of sight and sound. Gone were the walking dead and the rivers of blood, now it simply looked slightly foggy and it was an easy trek. For half an hour they walked in an eerie silence. At his side the scout relaxed visibly, she even wore a nervous smile. Eireden however felt his heart racing. Ella was in trouble. With each step closer to her he could feel her fear mounting.

Suddenly what sounded like a woman's scream broke the

quiet. It was close. Eireden hefted his goblin spear and dashed ahead, but then a riderless horse galloped into sight. Its eyes rolled and it frothed with foamy sweat. Eireden knew the horse; it was Lienhart's black charger.

"Hey! Hey! Whoa...whoa," he called to the beast and it immediately ran to him, nearly knocking him over as it eagerly pressed himself close as if for protection.

"That's Captain Lienhart's horse," Generai said. "What does that mean? Do you think he's dead?"

"In this damned forest, there is no way to tell for certain. Look, blood!" The horse dripped blood, but as far as Eireden could tell they came from numerous gouges and scratches along its hide. Feeling his fear begin to escalate, he went over the animal from tip to tail, but there was nothing to indicate if the rider had been hurt.

"So what do we know?" Furen asked. "Is there..." he trailed off as Eireden unexpectedly leapt into the saddle.

"Aric, your sword!" Eireden demanded with his hand out. "I need it." His own had broken and he had not found a suitable replacement and just then the need to arm himself properly was an imperative. Whatever was happening to Ella was becoming desperate, her fear shook his insides. Aric didn't hesitate and handed over the pretty elf-sword. "South-south-east," Eireden bellowed. "Follow as fast as you can." And with that he raced into the gloom.

Almost immediately the charger tried to turn around—it had had enough of the forest—but the prince mastered the horse by dint of his ferocious will. Illusions came up everywhere. He ignored them, concentrating on the ground beneath the charger's flying hooves and the power that drew his heart onward.

And then there she was in a small clearing. Ella on her knees looking defiant but frightened. Behind her stood Lienhart on the verge of insanity.

"I choose Aric Anorian," she pronounced in clear tones just as Eireden burst into the open. Angrily she turned her head as if the sight of him bothered her. "I said I made my choice! Get this away from me!"

What was she talking about? "Ella! It is I, Eireden! I'm real."

"You—you are nothing," she said slowly. "And I have already chosen...so leave. Go away! I have chosen."

A hissing laughter came from beyond the clearing. Eireden turned and stared in amazement. A mist dragon of some thirty feet in length lay looped around a pair of trees on the edge of the clearing. "You have chosen incorrectly," it hissed.

"What?" Ella asked. "How? It's my choice. You said..."

She fell back into Lienhart as Eireden fearlessly charged the dragon with the blazing elf-sword held aloft. From its gaping mouth, the dragon shot out a huge white cloud of vapor and then seemed to disappear into it as Eireden slashed blindly at the thick fog. By the time it cleared the dragon had gone.

# Chapter 5

## Ella

The image of Eireden came through the white cloud of vapors and stared down at Ella. It wasn't real. It was only an illusion with pain in its soul. "Don't look at me," she said, putting an arm up to shield her eyes from the vision. "You will only hurt me."

"I would never hurt you," the image said. "You should know I would never lay a finger on you. That was a mist dragon. Even in a normal wood it strives to confuse and deceive in order to isolate its prey."

"It did not deceive," she replied uncertainly. "It didn't...the real Eireden did hurt me. He hurt me more than anyone has ever. But you know that, fiend! You can read my mind somehow and show me everything that confuses me and causes me pain. Lienhart, turn away. It can't hurt us if we don't believe in it."

The image slid from the horse and touched her on the shoulders, gently turning her around. "I am not illusion. I am real. I am here. I've come to save you."

"No...no...no," she said backing from him, her hands out to keep him back. Her mind could not come to grips with this new illusion. It was more real than the others; she could practically smell the man she had once loved so passionately. "I chose Aric! You can't save me, Eireden. All about you is danger and pain. What kind of life is that? Who would want that? No. If I choose you we'd only be lost together. I chose Aric. He can save me the right way, the safe way. Now go away and leave us alone."

"It wasn't all danger and pain," Eireden said quietly, more to himself. "What about the fairies I showed them to you because...wait, where is Whip-wip?"

At the sound of her name the fairy poked her head out of her pouch and upon seeing Eireden she leapt up into the air and raced to the man. Surprisingly she kissed him on the cheek and then hugged him all the while whistling and hooting in a relieved manner. She then went into a long description of all the fantastic and frightful things she had seen in the forest.

Ella stared, dumbfounded. What was going on? Had the fairy lost her mind? "She thinks you're real."

Eireden sighed. "She thinks I'm real because I am real. You're going to be ok, Ella. Look, there is Aric and Furen. They are real too."

Whip-wip dashed across the clearing to greet them as well. Each received a kiss, a hug, and their own in-depth recalling of Whip-wip's fright. Furen, who had no idea what the little creature was saying, only nodded along sagely and every once in a while said, "Really?" This seemed to satisfy.

Ella's head spun. Were these people real? Was Eireden? Shyly she reached out and touched his arm. He was real! Her mouth came open, but no words came, and she was thankful for that. She had spoken too much already. What had she said? What horrible things had she said to her rescuer? She wanted to apologize, but then Aric was there and he grabbed her in an embrace. He smelled of smoke and blood. He spoke soothing words that she couldn't hear. She was too preoccupied.

Eireden had turned away and cast his hood over his face. He was in pain and she had caused it; first in the Concordance and now here. Twice he had come through hell to save her and twice she had inadvertently crushed his feelings. Ella gave Aric a half-smile and then gently pulled away. She wanted to go to Eireden and apologize and tell him...what? That he was too late? That he had missed his chance with her, but she was sorry that he had heard what he heard? Or was there something else she wanted to say?

Ella didn't get the chance to say it. Generai and the fey, Garris came out of the mists then. Ignoring the others the scout went straight to Eireden and pulled back his hood, giving him a reproachful look. "You are the Prince of the

Den! Not a *gada*." She then turned and walked toward Ella. How tall the soldier seemed. How proud her bearing. She leaned down and hugged Ella. "I'm glad we found you, my friend." There was something in those grey eyes that Ella found disconcerting—it seemed Generai had grown in the last day.

When the Twelfth Guard had marched out of Rhyoeven the day before Generai was only a third echelon scout. Now there was a swagger to her walk and a hardness to her eyes that only another woman would notice. She was letting it be known that she had staked her claim and that she would not allow a rival.

The object of her affection stood in the center of the clearing, purposely not looking in Ella's direction. He stood as if in deep thought, but Ella saw how wounded in mind he was at her words. Lienhart, shaking still from the ordeal, limped to him and knelt. "I have failed you my Lord. I could not protect the Lady. The mists and the creatures...and...and the screams...and..."

"Say no more, Captain Lienhart," Eireden said, gently. "You did not fail me. The lady is whole and sound. And from what I hear you performed miraculously on the battlefield today."

"May I give you my report?" Lienhart asked, looking relieved. The battle, no matter how hard fought and bloody, was still something he could wrap his mind around. His enemies had been flesh and blood. What lingered in the mists had been simply nightmares that he was desperate to forget.

"As we march. Though I suggest that you ride, Captain," Eireden said. "Your wounds must be bothering you."

"I would not ride, whilst my Lord walks," the captain replied. "And besides there is a lady present."

Seeing as she was basically unhurt, Ella tried to protest, but the men would have none of it and Aric helped her onto the back of the charger. The horse was so large that she seemed silly up there alone, as small as she was, and eventually she insisted that Generai ride behind her.

In this way they went through the forest, which now was as tame as it had been on their journey inbound. Lienhart gave his report; Furen stumped along singing in his deep voice, which lulled Whip-wip into a sleep atop his broad shoulder; Generai chatted about the battle at the Concordance; and Aric and Garris spoke in low tones, but about what she couldn't hear. Only she and Eireden spent the time in silence.

For her part Ella hadn't quite gotten over her fright in the mists, nor could she come to grips with everything that had happened to her in the last day. It was all getting to be too much and she wondered if it wasn't too late to go back home to Seattle. Not an hour later she discovered that it was.

As they finally came out of the forest, with the sun beginning to set behind them, they saw a line of soldiers waiting in formation a mile or so away in the rolling grasslands.

"Aric?" Eireden asked. "Can you make out the standard? Is it black and gold?"

"Blue and silver."

The prince of the Den sighed. "It's the First Guards. They're from Rhyoeven. May I once again borrow your sword? I'm afraid there is still one more opponent I have to face today—Eirowyth. It is time to settle things between us."

Aric unbuckled the sword belt and handed it over. Lienhart offered his shield, while Ella and Generai wanted to give up the horse. Eireden refused only the horse. The poor creature was in no state for another fight. Whip-wip went to him and touched his chest for luck. And Furen offered up a never-ending string of fighting tips.

The soldiers were indeed of the First and Prince Eirowyth led them. He stood out from the rest as his horse was the purest of white and his armor glowed in the fading sun. Heroic and valiant Eirowyth seemed, especially compared to the man who only a day before was an outcast of the worst sort. After a hard night's march and a long battle Eireden had a ragged appearance in his leather armor, which was old and torn, and stained with blood. Ella worried for him, but because of the nearness of Aric she kept her shaking hands in her lap.

Eirowyth was younger and fresher. His armor was of the finest quality and he had been schooled in battle by the very man he would face. What's more he had an air of confidence about him. There wasn't a single hint of nervousness to his demeanor at all.

The young prince sat and waited in silence as the six of them came up and halted a good fifteen feet away. For a long span of time the two Den eyed each other and then Eireden said, "You are a liar, Eirowyth. I never ran."

"Arrest them," Eirowyth said, with a wave of his hand.

The knights of his guard came forward and Eireden yelled angrily, "Stop!" and so great was the power of his voice that they stopped as one. "I challenge you, Eirowyth. It is the right of all Den to challenge their accuser as you well know."

"A *gada* can't challenge a Den, as *you* well know," Eirowyth sneered.

"I am *gada* no more. I am Eireden, Prince of the E-den line and I call you a liar."

"Oh, so you choose to be a man now?" Eirowyth asked, making no move for his sword. "You are like a jackal that only fights if cornered. Arrest them...including the man who claims to be prince."

"Get down!" Generai ordered Ella in a tone of harshest anger. Ella hopped down and Generai whipped out her sword, spurring the charger to come between Eireden and the knights. "You are coward now twice over!" she cried to Eirowyth, brandishing the sword. "You think you can avoid facing your prince in this way? By some trick of the law?"

Eirowyth eyed her with thin lips. "For now I will

overlook your insult, *Scout*. I have precedent. A criminal cannot demand to face his accuser before a criminal proceeding has taken place. In the case of the murderer Sanoi, seven hundred years ago. The criminal challenged the witnesses of his crime, hoping to slay them legally before they could testify in an attempt to cause his prosecution to fail."

"What crime are you referring to? Eireden has committed no crime!" Generai said. "You accuse him of cowardice. Though this is a failing of mind and body, it has never been considered criminal."

"He stands accused of treason. I'm sorry to say that your Prince consorted with the enemy. He sought to have the First Guard ambushed and me killed. A fine way not to have to face me."

"What!" Eireden raged. "What ambush? Are you talking about five years ago..."

Eirowyth cut him off, "No! I'm talking about last night. 'Somehow' you just knew that the Feylands were about to be attacked? You knew well before hand. And you knew any such attack was a guarantee that the First Guard and I would come to aid them. The maug were in perfect ambush position on the East road—as if they knew for a fact where and when we were coming!"

"I did not warn them," Eireden said icily. "Whoever set this attack up could have guessed that you would come out."

"But not when," Eirowyth retorted. "Only your messenger from the Twelfth Guards triggered our reaction. Had it not been for him it might have been a few days before we learned of the massacre. No, the maug knew exactly when we would be coming and there is only one person responsible for that—you."

Now all eyes went to Eireden and the question on everyone's mind was: how did he know? For his part the prince stood staring at the ground as if waiting for someone, anyone to defend him. Ella glanced around unsure. She wanted to say something, but the laws of the Den were new to her and really the only thing she could say in Eireden's defense was that he would never do what he had been accused of—he was simply too noble.

"Aric, help him, please," she whispered. Their eyes met, and just like that, she knew he would help save the only rival he had for her love. He had his own nobility. The fey strode forward, and strangely went to the black charger and whispered something to it in the high tongue, calming the skittish beast. He then turned to Eirowyth with an easy smile.

"Your accusations are perplexing to me and to all of us. You ask how he just knew about the coming attack? The answer is obvious; Eireden is of the line of kings. His father is a man of powerful will, while his mother is renowned as a witch. So it is no wonder that he has vision and insight greater than mortal men. He is farseeing just as the Den of old. Yet for some reason you give him too little credit, as well you give too little credit to our common enemy. This attack on the Feylands was years in the making, decades even. This sort of plan isn't composed without contingencies. How little foresight would it take to assume that help would come from the Den? Here is the rather simple answer to your question and it requires no conspiracy on the part of any to achieve it."

The soldiers murmured to each other, half-won over by the graceful words of the fey. Eirowyth wasn't, however. He sat in his saddle with eyes narrowed. "Aric Anorian, you have no say in the matters of the Den. You are criminal by your own admission and your words are meaningless to me—you are under arrest. As are you, Eleanor Belmont and Furen Traganfel. It is against our laws to free a known criminal. And you Lienhart; surrender your sword. You will be held until we figure out what part you've played in all of this."

"Yes, my Lord," the captain said, his face sickly white.

"And what is my imagined crime?" Generai demanded icily. Her sword still sat in her hand and it shook with her emotion.

"Misplaced devotion," Eirowyth replied with a softer tone. "I will pretend I didn't hear your offensive remarks, for your sake. By tradition, common soldiers are assumed to have been following orders. You are free to travel back to your unit in Hildoeven. Take this other fey with you."

The scout opened her mouth, but Eireden cut her off. "Do as he says. You are too fine a soldier to be jailed for insubordination." He then turned to Eirowyth and said, "Look at that. You have made criminals out of anyone who would help me, so that now you can ignore their words. And we all know why. You are afraid that my father might actually believe them and then where would you be? Left to face me. You say I planned this ambush? If I had, you'd be dead."

"Drop your sword," the prince ordered, ignoring the words of Eireden. "All of you. Place your weapons on the ground and back away."

Suddenly Ella found her tongue. She had gone numb at being called criminal, but just then she realized what Eirowyth reminded her of. "You sound like a lawyer, and that's not a compliment. You even used the word precedent! And you dig up some seven hundred-year-old case so you won't have to face your accuser. Ha!" she sneered. "Hiding behind the letter of the law is still hiding. Coward."

# Chapter 6

## Aric

The soul of the fey feeds upon light and love and laughter. The fey heal themselves through songs and smiles. They grow only in joy and wisdom.

In the dark they fade, growing mortal, growing old.

After a week in his cell Aric felt his age: a few decades more or less over three-thousand years old. Every bone in his body felt brittle and his hands had begun to curl in like the claws of a falcon. The cold iron at his wrists burned and the skin there was red and raw. His feelings of guilt over what happened in the Feylands only added to his misery.

When the king finally called for him the guards washed him down. He could barely stand. When he fell, they didn't bother to hold him up to clean him, instead they dumped buckets of water over his shivering body.

The mood of the guards was more surly than ever. These were new guards; the last ones who had been charmed by Ella, had been relieved of their duties. The current crop weren't too happy about their assignment. Aric didn't blame them. The smell was atrocious, the rats huge and aggressive, and the honor of guarding prisoners nonexistent. There was no worse job in the army.

This would be Aric's second time to go before the king. The first occurred just after they had arrived in Rhyoeven. The king's mood had been atrocious and little had been accomplished besides the venting of his anger on the lot of them. Even Whip-wip had received her share of the screaming tirade. At Eirowyth's suggestion the fairy was to receive a punishment just as the rest of them and a small iron cage had been fashioned, much like one used to house a small bird.

After he was cleaned and dressed in a soft white tunic Aric was shown to a room adjoining the audience chamber where Lienhart, Furen, and Eireden waited in a pensive silence. A few minutes later Ella came in holding the cage. In it drooped the fairy and so glum was she that Aric forgot his own misery and whistled the brightest tune he could manage. Whip-wip copied it back and her wings glowed just the slightest. Ella tried to smile at all of them, but when her eyes took in Aric they went wide.

"How are you Aric?" Ella said coming to him straight away. Her eyes held so much concern that he had to wonder at his appearance. How bad did he look? Worse than the others he was sure. Ella looked essentially unchanged save for being a little pale. She occupied a cell on the first floor where there was light and a breeze and fresh air. Of those in the lower dungeons, Lienhart fared better than Aric, but only barely. His anxiety at what would become of him kept him from sleeping and his eyes were a dreadful red. Furen seemed basically unchanged. The dark and the closeness of his cell were nothing to the dwarf. He had spent most of the week trying to cheer up Aric, telling randy tales, and singing songs in his deep voice.

Strangely Eireden seemed to have grown in his week of confinement. Not a lot, but still he seemed bigger, stronger. This was due to his near constant exercising. All day in his cell he could be heard counting out push-up and sit-ups. He would use the bars of his cage for pull-ups and other odd exercises that Aric had never seen before. Eireden trained for a confrontation with Eirowyth, which seemed less likely to occur with each passing day.

"I am as well as can be expected," Aric answered. He stared long into Ella's eyes. Her beauty and love gave him strength.

"That's a non-answer if I ever heard one," she said, now trying to hide her concern behind a smile. "Here, watch over Whip-wip, while I pay my respects."

She went to the others and like an unexpected warm breeze on a winter day they each revived somewhat at her presence. Furen even blushed after he gave his bow and kissed her hand for she hugged him after the manner of an American. She hugged them all, Eireden included and he did his best not to show too much enjoyment. It was a wasted effort. Aric had never been jealous even when Eireden and been so blatantly courting Ella. Jealousy was an emotion foreign to the fey and besides, he had known how things would turn out in the end. At least where love was concerned. The rest of his future now seemed precarious indeed. He had to wonder if he could last a year in the dank hole they had him in.

"You, Milady are the very vision of loveliness," he said when she came back to him. Eireden had pulled the one couch in the room to the window so that Aric could get as much light as possible while they waited to be seen and now Ella sat with him holding his hands.

"Thank you. You are too sweet," she said and then leaned in close. "How do I heal you?" she whispered, flicking her eyes to the door nervously. "My guards don't suspect that I can do magic, which is probably why I'm not cuffed as you. I practice when they aren't watching, but I don't know much more than floating objects."

"Well it's easy," Aric replied. "Remember your special place? Your garden?"

"How could I forget? Sometimes...a lot of times, I wish I had never left it."

After everything she had gone through Aric could understand. "You start there. Close your eyes. Picture the garden. Remember the feel of the air there. Remember, even when you hadn't known you could use your mind the way you can you had created a place of healing. Now put out your hands and touch mine. There. Feel my pain, but don't dwell upon its negativity, instead will yourself to set it right. Keep in mind healing is good—this is a happy moment. Joy is strength. Draw upon that strength."

She tried, but he could tell that she was struggling with his pain and the hurt of his body. It was dampening her efforts. "Now, I want you to picture me as you first saw me," he said. "Do you remember?"

"I was outside my dentist's office," she said and then smiled. "You caught me with my mouth open and gaping like a hippo's."

Aric could tell the image was well set in her mind as he started to feel warmth spread up from her fingers. "It wasn't at all like a hippo's. More like that of a baby bird looking to be fed...there, you are doing it. Keep the image of me, as you want me to be, in your mind. This is visualization. Your mind can only order what it desires when it can picture what it desires." Her strength surged at his words and he could feel his body responding.

Aric slumped back on the couch a second later, while Ella sat staring at him with a great smile on her face. "I did it!" she proclaimed. She then turned to the fairy. "I did it, Whip-wip. Did you see that?"

"*Sis, sis. Ella ssp*," replied the little creature. "*Seary zooti*?" Translation: Yes, yes, Ella nice. Where's fruit?

"I don't know," Ella said, sadly to her friend. "They almost never give us fruit, Aric. I don't understand how they can ignore such a simple request. They treat their prisoners in such a bestial manner. I don't find that honorable at all."

Eireden heard this. "We of the Den are very black and white. You have honor or you don't. You are treated with great dignity and respect if you do and if not...you are nothing and are treated as nothing. As a culture it has served us well. No other society of man has lasted even a tenth as long as we have. And it's because we retain our customs through the force of societal pressure and through law."

"I'm amazed that you of all people are defending how we are treated," Ella said. "You, who were once a *gada,* should know better than any that this isn't right. Your system is bankrupt of any moral standing."

"In this you are wrong," Eireden replied in a quiet tone. "Our ways can be harsh for those that break our laws, but that very harshness, coupled with the rewards gained by adhering to them, keep the great majority of the Den in a relatively blissful state. We are a happy people. Ours is not a perfect system, but compared to every human culture, past or present, we cannot be called anything but moral. And that includes a comparison to your American system. You have freedom, but little honor and look at the crimes that are perpetuated on a daily basis. Personally I think it shows the merits of our system that Eirowyth had to go back seven-hundred years to find a case against me."

"Well, then I'm glad I'm fey...or whatever I am," Ella said. She paused in confusion and then added, "I'm just glad I'm not a Den. They do nothing for the *gadas*. And what of the children of the *gadas*? Are they not innocent of their parent's crimes? Yet they suffer as much as any."

"Like I said, ours is not a perfect system," Eireden answered. "Thankfully there are only a handful of female *gadas* and thus only a few children are born to the dirt-yards."

Aric saw that Ella was unintentionally hurting Eireden by being so dismissive of his culture. "I would not jump to the conclusion that the fey are any more moral than the Den, my dear Ella," he said. "Yes, crimes between fey are unheard of, however we are a selfish people, if you must know."

Her surprised look made him smile, though it was a rueful smile. "Yes, selfish," he continued. "We keep to ourselves and never really care what happens to other peoples. Even before the Demon Wars there was strife and deadly conflict in which good societies perished to a man. Yet we did nothing to help or hinder. In a very real sense we allowed evil to flourish. In no way can I see that as anything but immoral especially since we had the power to stop much of it."

"Oh...I never knew," she said. She gave Eireden an apologetic look. "Quite a fall from my high-horse it seems. I guess I should learn more before I speak."

"Be not sorry my Lov...my Lady, I mean," he said, tripping over his words. "Yours is not the first voice to raise concerns over the fate of the children in the dirt-yards. There have been..."

"Silence," a guard said stepping into the room. When they all turned in his direction the man-at-arms continued. "The king will see you now. Follow me and pray for mercy."

Ella trembled at this so Aric took her hand and stood, no longer feeling the slightest pain. He didn't care for the way the guard had looked upon them, for he did so with a cold sneer. It seemed to portend that their fates had been decided already and when Aric saw who it was on the dais, he knew that his death in the black cell beneath the earth was a near certainty.

Eirowyth sat ramrod straight upon the throne of the E-den and upon his lap lay the naked, black sword of Ag-Raumon.

"You dare to sit upon that throne!" Eireden said and fire was in his voice. "Where is my father—the rightful king?"

Eirowyth drew in a long breath before almost whispering, "The king is dead."

# Chapter 7

## Eireden

When Eirowyth choked out, *The king is dead.* The room erupted in a cry: "Long live the King!"

Eireden stood swaying in disbelief. His father dead? That didn't seem possible. Never was a man as tough as Eirolden...even now in his eighties his sword arm was like iron. How could this have possibly happened? And what did they mean by *Long live the King*? Were they talking about himself? Wasn't he supposed to be king? Deep in his heart he had always assumed it would come to pass one way or another.

"I'm sorry for your loss, Cousin. He was a mighty man and a great king," Eirowyth said. He fingered the runes engraved upon the black sword and did not look up. "And it grieves me doubly that now I must pass judgment upon you for your part in..."

"Wait!" Ella cried. "You have not heard us out. How can you call it judgment when you have not heard all there is to judge?"

"Because I do not wish to prolong this moment of pain anymore," Eirowyth said. "Yet if there is more anyone can say in his defense speak up now."

Lienhart stepped forward. "I sent out the messengers asking for assistance, my Lord. I did so in my name as Captain of Twelfth Guard. I take full responsibility for the ambush and any deaths that may have come about because of it."

The new king shook his head. "Your loyalty is commendable. However, your lack of wisdom is not. It is well known that Eireden attempted to regain his name that night and ordered you to send out riders. You will not be held responsible for the ambush, but for your lack of vision and ineptitude in leading the Twelfth Guard I relieve you of command. You may stay on as a Man-at-arms if you wish, and for that you should be grateful."

The ex-captain's chin dropped and he stared at the floor as if not understanding. His head went back and forth but he remained speechless.

"You know little of real battle if you consider Lienhart's command inept," Furen said, darkly. "Go on; pass your so called judgments. None can be any more of a joke than what has just been spewn from your contemptible mouth."

"Your insults are not unexpected, dwarf," Eirowyth said with a sigh, sounding tired. "For your part in the unlawful release of a prisoner, I sentence you to one year in the lower dungeon—minus time served."

Furen's large hands turned into rock hard fists. He turned to Aric and whispered desperately, "My flower. It will not last and it is the only one left on the earth. All your valley is burnt and there is no other. Can there be anything done? Is there any magic that can preserve it?"

Aric shook his head, no. Furen ground his teeth in anger as tears of despair popped suddenly to his beady eyes. Ella touched his arm and it was then that the king called her name.

"Eleanor Belmont," Eirowyth said, speaking robotically. "For your part in the unlawful release of a prisoner: one year in the upper dungeons. I would ask that you release the fairy and tell her to go back to her people. If she stays with you she will have to remain caged."

"A year..." Ella said breathlessly. "I...I...was just trying to help."

"But you didn't," Eirowyth replied. He seemed distraught at carrying out his duty. "You made matters worse, though none here blame you for the attack on the valley. You were a pawn, yet you still broke our laws. Now, release the fairy." The new king held out the small key to the cage and Ella took it. She went and stood beside Eireden and used his bulk for a touch of privacy.

"Go on back home, Whip-wip," Ella said. Her blue eyes

dripped tears and her hands shook so it took a few tries to get the door open. "They will put me back in that cage and I want you to be free. But you can come see me in a year, or I will find you. Go on now." But whip-wip backed into the corner and refused to leave.

"*Tin swir*," Whip-wip said. "*Sis zooti*?"

"She won't leave me," Ella said with her back to the king. She was embarrassed that she couldn't seem to stop crying. "Can we get her fruit?"

Eirowyth remained silent for a time and then finally said, "I don't see why not. I would that she wasn't even caged, but..." he trailed off, throwing his hands up as if it were out of his control. He then turned to Aric and sighed again, a long dragged out sound. "Aric Anorian. So much blame rests upon your shoulders, yet you have suffered much already. I see your sorrow and regret and I'm moved to reduce your sentence from what was originally suggested by my advisors. You will serve only a single year for defying your imprisonment...after you finish your original sentence."

Ella turned around quickly. Wiping her tears on her sleeve she hurried forward. "In the upper dungeons my Lord? It will be his death if you put him back in the lower ones."

"No. The lower."

Ella threw herself down on her knees. "Please have mercy," she cried, pitifully. "Let me take his place in the lower dungeons and he can have mine in the upper. Please! I beg of you."

"No, I'm sorry. Our laws are firm," Eirowyth said, quietly. His eyes then danced to Eireden's face and away again. All this time Eireden had barely listened to the proceedings. He was still caught up in the idea of his father's death and he was having trouble comprehending the words flying around him, but when Ella went to her knees, her desperation revived him and brought him to full awareness.

Ella caught the look that went between the two cousins.

"What?" she demanded. "What is it?" She then went to Eireden and pushed him back away from the dais. Whispering, she asked, "Can you save Aric? Is there anything you can do?"

"There might be," Eireden replied simply. In fact he was sure there was. He was the only claimant to the throne and the charge he was being accused of could only be called flimsy. However Eirowyth was now king and had power. He could jail Eireden for an eternity yet it was probably the last thing that he wanted: his only rival sitting in the dungeons year after year. There would be questions.

"You have to save him, please. Do whatever you have to," Ella whispered, clutching his shirt. "I'm sorry for what happened between us. I'm sorry that I wasn't good enough for you. I wish I had been then who knows how this would've turned out? But...but that's in the past, I've chosen Aric. If he dies...I don't know what I'll do."

Eireden raised his head and looked at the fey. Aric and nearly everyone else was pointedly looking away from them. Only Eirowyth watched with sad eyes. How would all this play out, Eireden wondered? After all, this was a game—a horrible game he had brought on himself by not killing Eirowyth right away five years ago. But still it was a game. Eirowyth may have stretched believability in arresting Eireden, but he had Furen, Aric, and Ella dead to rights. He could have made their sentences twice as hard and nobody would say boo about it. Yet he had been strangely easy on them. He hadn't gone for the over kill. Why not?

To appear magnanimous? To appear the good guy, though it would, in the end, mean the death of Aric and the destruction of Furen's flower. But why Ella's light sentence? So he could claim her when all his rivals were dead and gone? Maybe. If so Eirowyth didn't know Ella like he did. She was forgiving, but not that forgiving.

"It's not that you weren't good enough for me," Eireden said to her, seeing now his cousin's mind. He wasn't after

Ella. He was using Ella...and Aric and Furen and Whip-wip. He was using their pain. "It's that I wasn't good enough for you. Hopefully Aric will be."

"You'll save him?" she asked with her hands still balled in his shirt. How beautiful she was even in her misery.

"Yes, on one condition."

Her eyes flicked to Aric and she asked guiltily, "What kind of condition? I—I don't think you know that I'm a..."

"Shush," he said. "I only ask that you put your hand on my chest like you did in the river."

"Oh—ok," she gushed. "I was worried that you'd...that is, you'd want to, well never my mind."

She released his shirt from her grip and then gently she put her hand to his chest and all the world fell away. The connection was instantaneous, his deep booming heart was the slow metronome of an athlete in his prime, while hers was the soft patter of one of the higher orders—yet somehow they ran together in perfect harmony. He filled his lungs with her fragrance and memorized every detail of her startlingly beautiful face. Only when he had drank his fill of her, when his heart was near to bursting with his feeling did he step away.

On purpose he didn't look back at her. To do so would've stopped his feet cold. Instead he went to the dais and stared hard into his cousin's eyes.

"I would know why first," Eireden said in a whisper. "Why all the lies?"

Eirowyth ignored him at first and drank from a chalice as if time was his to spend freely. Finally he said, "We've gone over this. I saw you run. Look me in the eyes and tell me there is falsehood within them. I saw you run. After seeing that...it was my duty to denounce you and what's more it's my duty to keep you off the throne. A coward on the Den throne! Never."

As always he looked for the lie in Eirowyth's eyes but it wasn't there and as always Eireden had a moment of self-doubt. *Did I run? Was that possible? No! I fought through,* he said to himself.

"You see no lie in my eyes either," Eireden said. He knew they couldn't both be right only now it almost didn't matter, he had made a promise. "Here are my conditions. When the deed is done Aric, Furen, and Ella will go free immediately. You can say you uncovered new evidence or whatever. I'm sure you will be able to *come up* with something. And Lienhart will get his commission back. He's better than you know. Agreed?"

"Agreed," the king said lightly as if he had been expecting exactly that. Eireden went back down from the dais and gave Ella a wink. He then turned to the king, who stated, "Eireden, on the charge of treason, I sentence you to the time of your choosing."

Behind him Eireden could hear Ella ask, "What does that mean? He gets to choose how long he stays in prison? That seems...No!"

Just then one of the men at arms came up and threw a rope at Eireden's feet, one end of which had been tied in a hangman's noose.

# Chapter 8

## Aric

"What an ass you are!" Furen cried out from his cell for the third time. And just as before Eireden said nothing. Aric, whose vision in the dark was nearly as good as his vision in the light had a great view of the man. He sat in the muck of his cell with his head bowed, running the rope through his fingers. Every once in a while he would glance up at the high ceiling where an eyebolt had been drilled into the masonry.

Each time Aric glanced up as well. His own cell had a similar bolt, one through which a length of rope could run. It gave him the shivers looking at it. Suicide was not unheard of among the fey, and in fact more fey died of suicide than in any other fashion. Though it was never from a sense of depression or despair. Quite the opposite. It was in the joy of discovery.

The fey are immortal and can live endlessly if they so chose, but the mystery of the next life is a constant draw. When, after seeing so many thousands of summer blooms and winter snows, a fey would suddenly realize that they've sung every song there was to sing and danced every dance there was to dance. In short, life, even the perfect life of the fey, can become monotonous and they become eager for more. When this happens a party is thrown and gifts and goodbyes are given. Then the fey goes to his sleeping chamber and falls into a deep sleep from which he wills his spirit away, and his body dies.

It's a peaceful time.

This, what the Den was contemplating, dying in the dark by his own hand, forced by a conniving king, was wrong. But there seemed no way to talk him out of it. When the sentence had been understood Ella had clung to Eireden in her grief and had to be pulled away. Furen had snatched away the rope and had thrown it on the dais at Eirowyth's feet.

"Be ashamed for even suggesting this, *gada*!" he had roared at the new king. "Try it on. It looks like a perfect fit."

Aric had said nothing. Despite their whispering, he had heard all that had gone on between Ella and Eireden. His heart had ached at the conversation. Clearly Eireden still loved Ella, and why not, she was perfect. Eireden loved her so much that he would die for her happiness. It wasn't something that Aric could allow, however.

"I will not have you die on my account," Aric said.

"It's not your choice," Eireden replied.

"It is actually. A fey can will himself into death. If I so choose I can die at any time even without a noose. And then it would be up to you to protect Ella."

Eireden grunted at this. "You know, sometimes I don't think she needs protecting. Or maybe she uses us to protect her—not in a nefarious way, but sort of like a natural defense. I mean I can't seem to help wanting to throw myself in front of danger for her. Sometimes I feel I love her too much."

"I loved her before we even met," Aric said.

Furen nodded at the bars of his cell. "I felt the same for Gargefrel. Only a perfect woman could be named so exquisitely. And I envisioned this perfect blossom of a girl...what?"

Both Aric and Eireden were suddenly snorting, trying to hold back laughter. Aric was able to find his voice after a minute. "It's—it's just the name...Gargefrel!" He couldn't go on and sat with his shoulders shaking, while the Den laid on his back holding his stomach.

"It doesn't translate well!" Furen growled and then stumped to the back of his cell.

"Oh Furen! Don't be like that," Eireden scolded, but with a smile that kept creeping back onto his face. "We're just being juvenile. Come, make fun of me. Call me an ass again. You seem to like that."

"You are an ass," Furen said from the hidden depths of

his cell. This only brought out more laughter from Aric and Eireden both of whom grew weak from it.

"What kind of prison is this that the inmates laugh so?" asked a woman's voice.

In a flash the three prisoners were up and staring through the bars at a sudden light. Two women flanked by two guards came down the fetid passage toward them. One of the guards carried a tall stool while the other held a tray of food.

"Lady Harowyth, you are looking better than ever," Eireden said. "It must be the dungeon setting. It suits you. The dark so hides the corruption in your eyes that who could see the lies?"

The other woman with Lady Harowyth, arrayed in black from head to toe, said, "Do not speak to the king's mother so. It would seem unbecoming."

They all recognized the cold voice of the former queen, Ilenwyth. "Mother, are you ok?" Eireden asked.

"I don't know. One second I'm fine, the next..." she trailed off for a moment. "But what about you? I hear you are letting your heart lead you from one disaster to another. If only you had...never mind. Life is full of *if onlys,* who needs another?"

"I'm just trying to do the right thing," Eireden said. "Sometimes even knowing what that is can be very difficult."

Lady Harowyth came to the cell door. "Stand away, please," she said, and then murmured something in a foreign tongue. Just like that the door sprang open. After Aric's escape the doors were now magically sealed and only a witch who knew the proper password could open them. The two guards came in; the first placed the tall stool in the cell and the second set the tray of food on it. They left quickly and somewhat nervously. Eireden eyed the stool and his face looked a little green.

"Your mother thought it was important that you had your last meal right away. Though I think it was just an excuse to come see you," Lady Harowyth said. "I told her you weren't quite ready for it, but you know how mothers are. My mother for instance, hated to be kept waiting." When she said this her eyes went to the rope and then she nodded toward the stool.

"My time is of my choosing," Eireden responded. "And the more anxious you are for me to get on with it the more I feel I should drag it out. Come back tomorrow. We'll see what kind of mood I'm in."

"You say your time is your own?" Harowyth scoffed. "What about his time?" she asked pointing at Aric. "And what about the dwarf's silly little flower? Even in its fanciful box it won't last forever. I would say your time is hardly your own."

Aric saw Eireden bristling in wrath and, worried that he would say something to hasten his own death, the fey stepped in. "Lady Ilenwyth? Will this new king keep his word concerning fruit for the fairy? She won't survive without it."

"Of course he will!" Lady Harowyth said quickly. "His word should never be questioned. Especially by a bunch of criminals! Let's be out of this foul place. The odors and the company are making me nauseous."

They turned to leave, all save Ilenwyth. "I know you'll miss your father. But you'd be proud; he died in battle, just as he wished."

"I am proud of him," Eireden called as she walked up the passage. When the far door closed he added, "Damn. No one knows where to stick the knife like your own mother."

"What do you mean?" Aric asked. "She only made that one little comment about your heart getting you into trouble and she couldn't be more right."

"Hey, do you mind?" One of the guards hadn't left with the others. "Eat your food. I'm not supposed to leave until you're done."

"I'm not really hungry," Eireden replied.

Furen jumped to his bars and tried to crane his face around to see the plate. "Hey, hold on now. What have you got there? Is that soup? I'll take the soup if you're not going to eat it. Oh, and that bread too. No sense wasting it on the rats."

The dwarf ate noisily while Eireden picked at his food and explained, "It's not the heart thing. It was telling me that my father died in battle. All my life my father would say that for a warrior, death in battle was the final reward. That no other death was fitting. You see what she was getting at? She doesn't want me to use the rope."

"What else do you have over there?" Furen asked. "Any steak? I'm craving steak." For the last week and probably for the rest of their time in the dungeons they ate a thin gruel from dirty wooden bowls using dirty wooden spoons. Eireden's food had come from an actual kitchen and had been served on actual china plates with actual steel utensils. It was a last supper of sorts though it was only a formality and he would still be fed the gruel, until—some prisoners who choose the rope took weeks before they used it.

The guard came over. "That's supposed to be for him," he said taking the tray back.

"Fine," grumbled the dwarf, tossing the bowl onto the tray with a clatter. "See if you get a tip. The service here is lousy. Ha! Did you hear that, Aric? Lousy!" The dwarf broke into hearty laughter but what was so funny no one but he knew.

The guard stared for a moment and then left. Just like that they were cloaked again in the wet dark. Almost immediately Aric felt the suffocating closeness of the cell and the weight of the shadows press on him. And then Furen began to sing. Aric wished it was a peppy tune, full of life but instead it sounded like a dirge, slow and depressing. And he wouldn't stop.

All that day and well into the night he sang. It made Aric's job of keeping Eireden from using the rope all that much harder.

"You can't kill yourself, Eireden," the fey pleaded again. "If you think it will help Ella, think again. Your death will be an anchor about her neck that she will wear for the rest of her life."

"You don't understand, Aric. I am doomed no matter what. I will not leave this cell alive whether or not I do this deed," Eireden said. For a long while he sat in silence curling the rope around his arm, becoming used to its feel. "My opponents have out thought me at every turn."

"Be not so negative!" Aric cried. "Our enemy from the Demorlaik did not defeat you. He tried to, time and again but by your actions the fey were saved! And this cousin of yours, Eirowyth...we will figure out a way to defeat him. You just have to hold on. You have to fight for your throne."

"That is not the way of the Den. We don't bicker and squabble. We don't fight for the throne. It is the place of highest honor. Each individual who ascends it has to know in their hearts that they belong among the kings of old. That they would do nothing to demean their names. In that I failed already. Even if I escaped and killed Eirowyth who would accept a *gada* on the throne? That could never happen! Not even a former gada."

"I think you are wrong," Aric said. "Both Captain Lienhart and Generai eagerly welcomed you. And the Twelfth Guards followed you unreservedly through the mists. That should tell you something."

"It tells me they are fools," Eireden replied, leaning his forehead against the bars.

"Wrong. It tells me that they know who their rightful king is. Only you could have brought them through," Aric said. "But I'll be damned if I know how. I understand this connection you have with Ella, but even with it, the mists should have driven you mad before you made it halfway through."

"The Demorlaik prepared me," Eireden said in a whisper.

"There were things in the Haunted City that had my mind teetering toward insanity. I mean, things that couldn't be, but were nonetheless. Yes, the illusions were bad, but compared to the Demorlaik...nothing compares to the Demorlaik. Have you ever been to the Haunted City?"

"No I never have, and I don't want to either. My heart pities any who are forced to go."

Eireden struck his head against the bars and they thrummed. "Yes you should pity us...or maybe not," he said. "Pity stayed my hand with Eirowyth. I thought that the horrors he had witnessed had changed his perception of reality and I hoped, that given time, he would remember events as they really were. Out of pity I did not challenge him and for this I was called a coward and was forced to become *gada* to keep my family name unsullied. Now I am branded as criminal with no way to defend myself. So that is why I chose the rope. At least some good can come of my death."

"No! I won't allow it," Aric cried. "Furen! Stop that dreary singing. Our good friend is depressed enough without it. Such sadness should not be allowed."

Furen came to the bars. "What do you mean dreary? That was a love song I am preparing for Gargefrel. You would be wise to learn it, for it will guarantee results. Eh? You know what I mean? Come, sing with me."

Again he started in on the baleful sounding tune and when Aric winked at Eireden and began to sing as well, the Den smiled once again. For the moment the rope was forgotten.

All that day, all that week, Aric grew steadily weaker. More and more he had trouble standing, his eyes grew dim, and his chest rattled with phlegm that he could never quite cough up, but despite that he fought a heroic battle to keep Eireden alive. He told jokes and long stories. He sang songs of love and sunshine. He picked fights with Furen and teased the dwarf mercilessly—all to keep the Den's mind from the rope.

On the eighth day Eireden parked the stool under the eyebolt and the fey redoubled his efforts and on the ninth day Aric slept. He had barely slept before this, so worried he was over his friend, not only that the cold iron of his cuffs burned his flesh and were a misery. But on that ninth day he started to grow numb to the pain and he didn't drag himself up to the bars as he usually he did to banter with Furen or wheedle Eireden. He laid there in his cell and tried to think of something new to say. And then he fell asleep.

With the all-consuming dark he had no idea of the time when he woke. How long had he slept? And why was the prison so quiet. In their nine days it hadn't been quiet at all. Furen was constantly singing and Aric was always trying to keep Eireden's spirits alive. But now—it was deathly quiet in the dark.

"Eireden?" Aric cried in a little whisper. "Eireden?"

"I'm here, my friend," the Den replied and his voice was powerless as well.

"Oh good, I thought..." Aric said, not able to finish the sentence.

"You thought correctly, because the time of my choosing is soon upon me. I waited as long as I did so your honor could be satisfied. You have done everything in your power to keep me alive and no shame can be upon you. You will sleep again and when you arise I will be no more."

"No! Then I will not sleep. Furen..." Aric broke down coughing, bringing up masses of green globs. "...Furen come help me."

"What?" came the muffled reply. "What is this?"

"Our friend says he is close to his time of choosing and only waits upon me to sleep. Only...I'm so tired...I don't have the strength now."

"You have the strength to talk that means you have the strength to sing!" Furen cried with a touch of desperation to his voice. "Come, sing my song. You must know the words by now."

"Furen, please," Eireden said. "He can barely talk, let alone..."

"Sing!" Furen cried in sudden emotion. "Eireden you owe me one song before you go and it had better be loud and strong, if not I will curse your name. Now sing!"

The Den chuckled. "If this is what you wish." He then began to sing Furen's love song and at first he was quiet but the dwarf urged him on and the Den took up his last song with gusto. Soon the power of his voice ran along the bars and they vibrated gently. Aric put his head back against them and before he knew it eyes has closed again.

And then he woke from an abrupt silence.

His cell sat catty-corner to Eireden's and he could see partially into it but of Furen's cell, one door down, he could see nothing. And if he could have looked in it at that moment he would have seen exactly that.

"Aric," Eireden whisper. "You have to see this."

With a creaking of his neck the fey turned to look into Eireden's cell. At first his eyes centered on the hanging noose and the tall stool, but then beyond that he saw something that barely made sense. Furen's face! A large block of stone had been removed from the back of Eireden's cell and their stood the grimiest dwarf in existence.

"How?" Aric began, but Furen held up a finger to his lips to quiet him. He then displayed the spoon that had sat on Eireden's plate so many days before. It was so worn down that it was barely recognizable.

## Chapter 9

### Ella

It was eighteen days since the Forest of Mists and still Ella woke in the pre-dawn quiet in a cold sweat. As always she lay shaking and cuddling Whip-wip's iron cage to her chest and as always the fairy tried to coo her back to sleep. This only had the effect of lulling Whip-wip, who was soon snoring in that tiny way of hers.

The images in Ella's mind were too horrific for any chance for sleep and so she went to the little barred window and peeked out on tippy toes to see how far off the sunrise lay. The night was cloudy and she had hoped for rain. Nothing beat sleeping to the sound of rain. However now that it was morning she wished the clouds away. With the low angle of the window she could only count on direct sunlight until a little after ten and then her cell would grow in steady darkness.

With the clouds and the angle of her vision it was hard to tell the time, so she glanced across the room at the chair that sat just beside a weathered writing desk. With a small flexing of her mind it slid across the floor and ran up under the window. Thinking nothing of this insignificant display of her growing powers she climbed up on the chair and then blew out noisily. This better view told her that it was probably just after four in the morning.

"Now what do I do?" she asked the bars, running her fingers along them. Despite the question, she knew what she'd do. Ella would begin her mental exorcises and then do her physical ones. She would practice her magic, lifting her chair with her mind a hundred times and then she would struggle her desk up a few times, maybe ten or so. Then she would tackle her bed and if she were lucky, or strong enough she'd get it most of the way off the floor. What lay behind this near-masochistic ritual was Ella's fervent wish that when she was finally done with her ridiculous prison sentence she would be strong enough to be able to fly. How wonderful would that be?

And she would just fly away. Away from her problems. Away from the death and pain of the Hidden Lands. But would she fly way from Aric as well? And Eireden? No, not Eireden. He'd be dead by then for sure...or Aric would be or...she didn't know which. Her heart told her that Eireden wouldn't or perhaps couldn't die as a suicide. Yet if he didn't then Aric would die.

Suddenly she gripped the bars of the window in angry frustration and then sunk her head against the cool metal.

"I'll just fly," she said, when she calmed. Jailed as she was the idea of flying captivated her and she daydreamed while looking out of the tiny rectangle of a window. In those dreams it was Aric who flew with her. It just seemed natural. He had the body of a gymnast in his peak, trim and hard, while Eireden was just plain huge. She couldn't picture him flying.

The daydream reminded her that she had work to do and so she hopped down and began lifting the chair, concentrating on that odd unnamed bubbly part of herself. At eighty her head started to pound and by a hundred her breath came sharp and fast, still she pushed out five more—a personal best.

"Pretty good, huh, Whip-wip?"

The fairy had cracked an eye, a mistake she quickly realized. "Sis...sis...sssp," she said and then rolled over, tucking her pearl to her chest. She had at some point in the last week found a pearl. How, caged as she was, Ella didn't have a clue. This one she kept for herself and slept snugged up to it.

"Nice is all I get? That was a hundred and five," Ella replied mostly to herself. The fairy was already back asleep and would remain that way until the sun woke her and then, watch out. She'd be irrepressible for a good twenty minutes and then cranky for the next hour while she waited on breakfast. In the wild Whip-wip would sleep and eat off and on all day long, whenever the fancy would strike her. Life in the cage was a whole other story and she hadn't gotten use to living so regimented.

Ella was right there with her. The last eighteen days had felt like a year unto themselves and she didn't know how she'd make it through the next three-hundred-and-forty-seven! "By learning to fly," she said and then leapt in the air. Even with her magic helping her she only remained aloft half a second longer than she normally would. Still half a second was a start. "But not yet," she said touching her head where it pounded.

She began a series of stretches, letting her brain ease it's thumping. And then when she was relaxed, instead of going on to lift her desk or the bed she ran about the cell jumping as high as she could, trying to will herself into flight. The results were not impressive—all she managed to accomplish was to wake Whip-wip early and give her something to laugh about. Still she managed to stay up a full second after many tries.

The remainder of her day was just as dull as the previous seventeen. At about noon she had her daily visit from Ilenwyth. The purpose to the visits wasn't at all clear to Ella. Always the former queen would come with a warning in her eyes—*be careful what you say, they are listening*—the look said. Ella didn't need the look since Ilenwyth never came to the jail alone. Accompanying her were two witches, who watched everything carefully and listened in on their conversation, but why they'd care if Ella remarked how bored she was or how bland the food she never knew.

The witches were there on orders of Lady Harowyth. Quite a bit of suspicion had fallen on Ilenwyth's shoulders after Aric's escape, and for good reason, since it was she who had supplied Ella with the charm potions. At first Ella had been smugly satisfied at this. It seemed fitting that a person who had been involved with so much intrigue should be babysat, as it were. However, then Ella met Harowyth. Just as Ilenwyth, there were many calculations in her eyes, but unlike the former queen, Harowyth's eyes were deadly cold beneath a thin veneer of civility. Immediately Ella hadn't trusted her and hadn't needed the unspoken warning from Ilenwyth to be careful around the mother of the new king.

Yet even these warnings didn't endear Ella to Ilenwyth. What did was the news of the death of the old king. After the passing of Eirolden, Ilenwyth missed only a single visit and when she returned the next day she seemed to Ella much like an old teacup, chipped and cracked but painted over to hide the wear. A single misplaced word seemed all it would take to cause her to crumble and so Ella, always sympathetic to the least suffering, made sure to be as pleasant as possible. As the days passed Ilenwyth slowly healed; it was either that or she grew strong enough to hide the cracks in her soul.

Now, despite the fact that the daily visits were something to break up the dull monotony of her day, and the fact that with each she grew closer to Ilenwyth, Ella secretly dreaded them. Every day she waited on pins and needles fearing that she would finally see the news of Eireden's death in his mother's eyes. This was bad, but as the days drew out, she then started worrying about Aric. If Eireden didn't kill himself how long could the fey hold out? Aric had looked dreadful after a week in captivity—could he last a month? Or even two? And if he did, what kind of shape would he be in?

Ella didn't know. She didn't want to know. She couldn't hope for Eireden's death and nor could she hope that he lived. Neither could bring her joy.

That day Ilenwyth's eyes held no news of her son's death and as usual she spoke little of current events, despite that Ella pressed her on any word concerning the fey people. Since her imprisonment the only information that had come to the dungeons was that the fey had gone in a great body to Hildoeven. Whether they were still there or what they were doing or planning, Ella didn't know and any attempt at finding out had been politely brushed aside by Ilenwyth—and always with more warning looks.

Many subjects were off limits such as what happened to the Feylands and what was the maug army doing rampaging around the Hidden Lands, however one subject, the demon, was such taboo that Ilenwyth refused to even hear it.

"Is there any word on the demon?" Ella asked one day. Ilenwyth went so far as to pretend the word had never left Ella's mouth. Instead she acted as though Ella had said 'lemon' and had spoken at some length about different recipes she knew that called for lemon as an ingredient.

Magic was another subject not open to discussion. Again no warning looks were needed for Ella. Magic to her was too personal, it stemmed from the most private part of herself; it certainly wasn't something to show off or brag about. Even when she had been in Rhyoeven the first time she had only spoken of her abilities to Furen and Generai.

So, during Ilenwyth's visits the two women talked about the weather or about horses or about anything that didn't have to do with something. This was of course frustrating, but still the alternative for Ella was staring at the walls while Whip-wip slept, or when she awoke, having a one-sided conversation with the fairy who frequently moped. After eighteen days Whip-wip began to mope a lot—they both did. Nothing ever happened. Everyday seemed an exact replica of the previous and this eighteenth day was no different: six o'clock sunrise—seven o'clock breakfast served by the day guards who had just come on shift—noon lunch, then visit by Ilenwyth—six o'clock dinner served by the swing shift guards, and finally a midnight walk-through by one of the night guards.

The rest of the time was hers to do as she pleased. She exorcised her mind and body, but that only took so much time; after which she would try to engage Whip-wip but the fairy slept more and more. Therefore Ella stood, or sat, or paced. She couldn't nap; after exhausting herself in the mornings her magic kept her too keyed up—this was one of the reasons she didn't practice in the evenings, there'd be no sleep afterwards.

She basically did nothing except to brood and wait for her next contact with humanity. This didn't come from her jailors. The guards were surly; they detested their assignments and blamed her for their predicament at losing their men-at-arms status. When they brought her meals they'd glare with such animosity that Ella had taken to staring out the window at these times. Dinner that night was no exception. When the steel door creaked open from the guardroom, Ella took Whip-wip's cage and went to look at the light of evening sun as it reflected off the building across from her.

It wasn't much but it was better than seeing the look on the guard's face. It would only be sullen like the way he walked. The guard came down the hall slowly, letting his sword thunk against his armored thigh. The sound annoyed her. It had her picturing a slovenly soldier—something that grated against her idea of a proper Den warrior. Sure enough when Ella gave the man a glance from the corner of her eye she saw that indeed he wore his leather armor sloppily.

"Don't look at him, Whip-wip," Ella said—none of the guards cared for the fairy any more than they cared for her. But Whip-wip continued to stare. "What? Do they have strawberries tonight?" She turned, curious. They didn't have strawberries. The guard carried nothing. He stood leaning against the bars of her cage as if exhausted and he was more unkempt than she had first reckoned; his armor hung on his small frame and his helmet had slipped down and nearly covered the green of his eyes. The beautiful emerald green of his eyes.

## Chapter 10

## Aric

At first Aric felt a wonderful exuberance at the sight of the dwarf scraping away at the mortar that held the blocks of stone in place. Then an hour went by and another, and another, and still Furen made no discernible headway in removing a second block. By nightfall Aric's spirit's faded gradually until he found himself drifting in a deep sleep. It was so deep that he almost felt that he could fall away from reality for good. That he could just let go and explore the next life. It felt right to do so. There was so little in this life that held him to it.

He had failed his people—because of him they were now homeless, living at the whim of the Den. He had failed his friends—because of him they were jailed. He had failed Ella—where could she turn to now? To the Den, who considered her a criminal? Or to the fey? How many would welcome her with open arms? As his body further crumbled, succumbing to the dark, depression laid a hold of him, turning his thoughts against him, making that final trip to the next life so much more attractive.

"Aric! Wake up, damn you," Eireden barked. "I said wake up!" This he thundered using the power of his voice. It brought Aric around briefly.

"No. Why should I?" the fey said sounding somewhat like a croaking frog. His throat felt like he gargled with gravel. "You two escape. Go on and escape. Go on and leave me."

"I can't you nitwit. I promised Ella, remember? And besides, we need you."

How could they need him? Aric could barely lift his arms. "I can't dig. I can't do anything."

"You can keep an eye out for the guards," Eireden said. "Prop yourself up against that wall so you can see down the hall. Come on!"

It took much barking and ordering to get Aric to move and even when he did, the fey wasn't much good as a look out. His head would loll on his shoulders and his eyes would lose focus, but that didn't bother Eireden much. The Den prince kept a steady flow of encouraging words going, some of which sounded exactly like what Aric had been saying for the last few days to Eireden.

All the while Furen worked. The dwarf was relentless, scraping and chipping. Eventually, sometime after dinner, he removed a second block so that the huge Den could now wiggle through to a squat tunnel that Furen had dug by hand over the last few days. After this the pace of digging picked up immeasurably. They broke up the stool and used it to dig at the compact earth. They tunneled beneath the passage between the rows of cells and came up beneath Aric's. He could hear one of them through the stones beneath his feet.

"What good is this going to do?" he asked Eireden, later. "Why make a tunnel so we can crawl back and forth between us. Are you going to throw a tea party?"

The Den stood stretching to his full height and cracking his back—the tunnel had been made by a dwarf, for a dwarf—he was getting quite stiff. "No tea parties, not until we get safely away. I'm working on opening up a hole almost right between us." Eireden pointed at a spot in the passage. "And Furen is working on getting into your cell. Boy, can that dwarf dig! You have no idea."

"And I don't want to know," Aric replied. "I'm so tired of the dark and the wet earth. I'm so tired of everything...if it wasn't for Ella I would embrace the sleep. But she has no one." Eireden glared for a second and then turned away, heading for the hole in the back of his cell. "Don't be like that," Aric said, drumming up enough strength to grab the bars. "Ella is...Ella is not fit for a Den. Even you whom I most admire and esteem. She is of higher blood."

"I know what she is," he answered, incorrectly.

"Then you know the very idea is an abomination."

Eireden didn't turn. "Well it hardly matters now. She made her choice and I have to respect that," he said over his shoulder before he struggled through the small opening.

The Den didn't understand; the idea of mixing blood with a lower order was repugnant, not just to Aric, but to all the fey. In all their long history it had never been done nor even considered. Though at the moment Aric was having trouble caring. He was too tired to care. He could barely keep his eyes open for his useless guard duty. What was the point anyway? In eighteen days they had but the one visit, while meal times were as regular as clockwork. Who cares if he just closed his eyes...

"My friend?" Furen said gently, touching his leg. "Your magic has grown if you can keep watch with your eyes closed. That's a trick you're going to have to teach me one of these days." Furen had removed one of the stones in the floor of Aric's cell. He had just enough room to raise his head.

It was hard for Aric to focus on the dwarf as he was an exact match in color as the dirt around him. "How...did...you..."

"I've been digging, remember?" Furen said.

"Oh right. How is that going?"

"I'm here aren't I? Unfortunately the Den are no slouch when it comes to their masonry. At the same time this is still not dwarf work otherwise we'd never get out. I would have beveled all these stones, that way they would be utterly seamless. Ha! Think about trying to get out of that. Then I would've used...Aric. Hey Aric? Did I lose you?"

The fey blinked slowly at Furen. "A little I guess."

Furen looked concerned. "That's ok. I can go on sometimes about good stonework. How about you just keep watch and try to hold on. I should be done before dinner."

There was nothing for Aric to hold on to exactly. He felt his consciousness slip away with every passing hour. Just before dinner the floor of the passage between the cells seemed to just drop away and Furen's filthy head emerged grinning from ear to ear. He said something to Aric, but the fey couldn't make out anything but deep rumbling tones and in a second he was gone again. Then time became meaningless. At some point he heard a shout and then what sounded like baking pans falling to the floor. He thought, at first his dinner had been dropped, except that they were fed on wooden plates and so the sound made no sense.

Before he could puzzle it out he fell back into a stupor. Then he woke once again this time to the sensation that the earth was sucking him in to its inky black depths. Aric panicked and clawed at the stone but was dragged down nonetheless. The air was close and hot. He felt his lungs fighting to fill themselves, but he was too weak to draw in the fetid air. There was nothing around him but shadows and more shadows...but then there was light and a breeze.

Over him knelt Eireden and in his hands metal jingled. "Here it is," the Den said, holding aloft a small iron key. And then Aric was free. The hated cuffs were removed and Eireden lifted his limp body easily as though he were as light as a child. The man carried him down the passage and where before there were empty cells, now four of them held the unconscious forms of the men who had once stood guard over them.

Aric was carried up to the guardroom where he was given water and food—proper food, not the gruel of the prisoners, but the meat and vegetables off the guard's plates. Furen, still grimy from his tunneling, sat eating from two plates all the while staring at the box that held his flower. He had found it in the prisoner storage room along with all their other belongings.

"Where's Ella?" Aric asked. There was plate of food and next to it sat a smaller one laden with berries. It could only be Whip-wip's meal. "Is she gone? Did they take her away?"

Eireden stood at the door keeping guard and didn't turn at the question. Furen swallowed what had been a heaping forkful of potatoes and said, "She's still in her cell. Eireden thought it best if you free her."

"What? This is no time for gallantry, my friend. We have to get out of here before..."

Eireden held up his hand. "Calm down. We can't go anywhere until dark no matter what; it's our only chance. Sunset is in two hours and the shift change is in four. You have time enough to recover somewhat. So eat something and then we'll clean you up. Hopefully you'll be able to walk on your own soon." A half hour later, fed and cleaned, and wearing the armor of one of the unconscious guards—a suggestion of Eireden's just in case any visitors came by— Aric went to Ella's cell. She stood at the window and pretended that he wasn't there. The fairy, drawn by the fruit on the tray stared for a long time and then her blue eyes went wide.

"Hello Whip-wip," Aric whistled in her language.

Now Ella saw who it was and she rushed to the bars, jostling the fairy in her cage. "Aric...how did you...what are you...what? What are you doing here?"

"We're escaping tonight," Aric said, barely holding himself up. "At least Furen and Eireden are escaping. I won't leave without you."

"Then I'm leaving, too! You look...well you look worse than before. I didn't think that was possible and your wrists!" She set the cage down. "Let me have your hands; I'll heal you."

"No, not yet," he said, pulling his hands back. "There is something you need to do first. Can you tell me if your cell is being held magically? Can a normal key unlock this door?"

"I don't think so. There were two witches who..."

"*Zooti! Zooti! Zooti*!" cried Whip-wip stretching her tiny arm, trying to get at the plate of fruit that sat only an inch from her finger tips. Ella knelt and pushed a raspberry through the bars of the tiny cage.

"Sorry. Whip-wip has been going crazy here."

Straightening she said, "There were two witches, and both did a spell or something on the door. I felt it when they did it. The air sort of got warm and pushed back at me a little."

When Aric looked down at the fairy and then back up again, his head went light. "I need to sit," he said before sliding down the bars.

"I should heal you," Ella said. "Why can't I?"

"Because you will need all your strength to open this door. These walls up here are pure rock...at least according to Furen, and he seems to know a lot about this sort of thing. This means we won't be able to dig you out. It'll have to be the door and I'm too weak."

"I'm weaker than you," Ella said desperately. "You know all sorts of magic and I don't know barely anything."

"You can do this...easily," Aric said.

Ella laughed though her eyes held pain. "No I can't. You told me before that a spell can only be countered by a stronger witch. And there were two of them! Could you do it? If you were fully healed? Maybe that's the way to go. Maybe I should heal you and you can break the spell."

"No don't try," he said as her hands came back again for him. "I don't think I could. When witches band together they are stronger that they normally would be. One and one make three if you understand me."

"I do. That's why we have to find a different way. I'm not strong enough. Everyone says that learning magic takes years of practice and I've only been at it a few weeks. I can barely float my bed," she said pointing at the bed in the corner. "How could you possibly think I can do this?"

Weak as he was Aric still found the strength to chuckle. "You floated your bed?"

"Barely a second or two."

"Then you can do this. That bed probably weighs close to a hundred pounds. That's a hundred stones! At my best I could do maybe fifty and those two witches maybe twenty a piece if they're above average."

"Generai could only do five," Ella practically whispered. "How? How can I do so much more? It doesn't make sense."

"It will when you find out who your parents are," Aric replied. Ella's eyes went wide at this and he gave her a nod. "Yes, I know at least who your father is, Darhmael of the line of Narvai. Now this is something you cannot tell Eireden or any Den for that matter—Darhmael is an elf. *You* are elven. The Den are their sworn enemies. It is within their law to kill you on sight."

Her left hand went slowly to her ear and traced its outlines. She then felt her face perhaps expecting that some sort of transformation was taking place. "I'm an elf? And they'll kill me? Why...I mean the elves were all bad but that doesn't mean I am, right? After all it's not hereditary, being evil. No one is born bad."

"Actually they are." Her eyes went wide and he was quick to add, "Though clearly you are an exception. Even in humans you will see for the most part good children born to good parents and evil children born to evil parents, however humans are more a product of their environment. A good child raised among thieves will be more apt to steal than the same child raised among the law abiding. Yet with the fey we are born good—certain notions are so foreign to us that we have trouble even accepting them. For instance murder. We hear the word and know the definition but it's simply beyond our comprehension. No fey has ever murdered another fey...or another human for that matter."

"But what of the elves? What of Darhmael? Was he bad? Or my mom, maybe she was a good elf."

Aric felt a lump in his throat at how desperate Ella wanted not to be evil. He shook his head sadly. "No, Darhmael was evil. Very, very evil. It was thought that he perished in the battle of Shefarlaik, but clearly that was not the case. And as for your mother...there were no good elves. They began as good beings—the very purest, however the Demon wars changed them. After so much war, and killing, and bloodshed, and after all the atrocities they witnessed and committed, none among them remain untainted. Not the women, not the children. Theirs became a society dedicated to death. First they dedicated themselves to slaying the demons—good or bad it hardly mattered to them. Then they went after the maug...and then the humans. That was their ultimate goal: to slay anything that wasn't elven."

"Then how am I good?" Ella demanded. "I am good. Really, I am...ask any one. Ask Whip-wip; she'll tell you."

Aric struggled to his knees, panting as he did from even this minor exertion. "You are good. That's what's so miraculous about you, Ella. Your soul is as pure as any fey's, though how I don't know. Perhaps your mother was innocent, yet if she was then why would she suffer such a beast as Darhmael to touch her, or why would she allow a child to come of their union?"

She shrugged at this and said, "Magic? Maybe this Darhmael did something to my mom? Oh! I hate this. Why can't anything about me be normal? Of course Darhmael did something to my mom and he did something to me as well! He made me into some sort of beacon and put me in the Forbidden Lands—he probably planted that dream in your head too. What else does he have planned for me? Perhaps I'm a bomb as well. Maybe he plans for us to escape only to go to Hildoeven and then, boom! I go nuclear and kill all the fey once and for all."

"Nuclear?" Aric asked.

"It's like an explosion—a huge fire that can destroy an entire city in seconds," Ella explained, glumly. "And yes they are real. Remember Eireden warning you how dangerous the humans had become? He wasn't joking."

This hadn't occurred to Aric. Was it possible? Could the plots of Darhmael be this intricate? It would mean that he had to consider the possibility that his first plan, the destruction of the Fey, would fail—which it had, but only by a miracle. However the miracle was named Eireden, and that name had meaning. Even Darhmael as powerful as he was, would have to respect it. And perhaps this was why Eireden had been Gada at the time. Was Eirowyth in league with the elf? Aric put a hand to his head and groaned.

Ella saw the look on Aric's face. "Maybe I should just stay in my cell. You guys should just escape without me."

"*Shee!*" Whip-wip said around a mouthful of berry. "*Swirr zee, issa zuu.*" Translated this meant: No. We have to leave far away.

"She's right," Aric said. "But maybe we shouldn't go to Hildoeven. Not until we know it's safe."

Ella slumped. "That's just it, we'll never know. As an elf I'll never be safe."

"I think...or should I say I hope you are wrong about that," Aric replied. "However, we need time and space to figure this out. Come run away with me."

## Chapter 11

### Ella

The idea of running away appealed to her. She definitely didn't want to go to Hildoeven where there were thousands of fey made homeless simply by the fact that Ella had come strolling through their valley? What sort of tremendous collective blame would they hang on her head if she went? She was sure she wouldn't be able to take it, yet at the same time she wanted to go to each survivor and throw herself on her knees in front of them and beg their forgiveness. She had known about the prophecy after all. She knew, but she went anyway, and for what? Adventure? Romance?

Yes and yes; and neither was any sort of excuse.

"I don't feel as though I should leave, but all the same I know I can't stay here," Ella said with a sigh. One thing was certain to her: She would not allow Aric to rot and die here in these prisons on her account—"How do I get this door open?" Ella asked.

"It's simple," Aric said closing his eyes. He looked a shade of pasty white as if their little talk had wiped out what small amount of strength he had left. "Feel with your mind—feel the bars and the lock, but most importantly feel the energy surrounding them. You want to destroy that energy. It's not something I can explain, however your mind will know what to do."

"I hope so," Ella replied to herself to the vague instructions. Whip-wip reached out and gave her a touch for luck which brought a smile to her face. Then grimly she stared at the bars and felt with that strange part of herself. It wasn't a tiny bubble any more, it was a grasping wind that she could send out and control. She bent her mind on the lock and felt the strength of the two witches; they were definitely above average. Their spells wove around each other twisting like strands of a rope, making each far stronger than they would otherwise be. Her mind attacked the power and she felt herself the stronger; however she also felt like a gorilla trying to tie shoelaces. She had strength but very little control and the ropes of the spell binding the lock tore time and again however she couldn't break them all at once and those that snapped rebound themselves when she moved on.

"I can't," she said panting and shaking. "I destroy part of the spell then as I come up against another part the first repairs itself!"

"Yes," Aric said. "I should have mentioned that; more importantly I should have mentioned that you can't stop once you begin. The power of your mind and soul is not infinite and your strength is lost even if you fail. Now it will be even harder, but you must try."

"What about magic words?" she asked with sudden excitement. "Do you know any that will help?"

Despite his exhaustion he smiled at her. "Magic words...there is no magic in words per say, the words are a way to focus the mind on a particular spell in order to get the most out of it. You know how certain smells trigger memories? Words do something similar. Certain sounds trigger certain mental responses, however each person is affected in a slightly different manner and thusly a word used by one may not be of any help to another."

Ella slumped at this and blew out dejectedly. She was already tired and wondered if she had the power left to open the cage. Whip-wip gave her an encouraging look and touched her again, before pointing at the lock.

"Fine," Ella said. There were people...and fairies counting on her. She blew out again, though this time it was a steadying breath, and then bent her mind upon the lock. There were the strands of the spell. They glowed in her mental picture—they had the strength of steel, yet she was stronger. She knew it. She just didn't know how to break them all at once so that they wouldn't reform. Ella began by trying to grasp each individual strand, just to get a hold of it, only it was similar to trying to get a hold of spaghetti, and they kept slipping away. She then grabbed the entirety of the spells with her mind and began pulling it apart as she had before and again as before some strands would break and then repair themselves while she was at it with others. Ella felt her strength waning.

Yet she couldn't give up, she was too entwined already and there was too much riding on her. She began to pull her mind out of the spaghetti of the spell but then she found herself almost caught up in it. This gave her an idea and she sent her will entwining deeper—wrapping her mind back and forth between the strands of the spell. It was exhausting but when she was done she had an iron grip on each part of the spell and all at once she torqued her mind and the spell snapped.

There was a little click and the door swung gently open until it tapped Aric on the leg—waking him. "You did it," he said blearily. "I knew you could."

For a moment they just looked at each other both too tired to move. Whip-wip on the other hand went berserk spinning in her cage and shaking the bars. With the last of her energy Ella touched the lock of her little cage and the door sprung open. Like a bullet, the fairy was out and flying around, piping in excitement, hooting in glee, singing so fast that Ella hadn't a clue what she was saying. Then the little thing shot away, heading for the open door at the end of the passage to the guardroom.

Soon she was back and even sooner gone again. Whip-wip flew so fast that her wings glowed a golden color and she left a streak of light trailing behind. Then she was on Ella's shoulder, panting and grinning.

"Can you stand?" Ella asked Aric. "I would heal you but I've got nothing left in the tank. Maybe if I could rest for a few hours." She suddenly felt lethargic after exhausting so much energy.

"I can stand. It's everything else that may be a problem.

But don't worry about me," the fey replied. "I'll find a way. Besides I think we can rest for an hour until the sun fully sets."

She ate until Aric drifted off and then she went to the guardroom. "I knew you couldn't kill yourself," she said to Eireden. "Or at least I hoped you wouldn't."

The Den was trying, with Furen's help, to fit into one of the sets of leather armor. Despite the size of most of the soldiers none had Eireden's combination of height and breadth. Ella couldn't help but smirk as he turned red in frustration.

"We'll have to cut it at the shoulders and hope nobody notices," the Den said, breathing easier as he undid the clasps at his side. He gave Ella a look, one that was supposed to be stern however his eyes lit too brightly at the sight of her for him to pull it off. "You can wipe that grin off your face," he said. "You're going to have to wear one of these as well and you're going to look like a little boy trying on his daddy's armor."

"Maybe, I will, but I'm sure to look better than Furen," Ella replied. "How do you plan on getting him through the palace?"

No one knew the answer to this very important question. As a matter of course with nothing better to do they fitted their armor as best they could and then with about twenty minutes left before the sunset they went to fetch Aric who was still sleeping where Ella had left him.

He looked much improved though he still wobbled on weak legs. "I can do something for Furen. An illusion maybe but it will last for minutes only. I could extend that if we could make him up to look something like a guard. Try to get him in some armor and I'm afraid you won't be able to carry your hammer." As Eireden, Ella, and Furen sweated the dwarf into splitting armor Aric wasted precious energy laughing.

Whip-wip laughed along as well until she remembered

the new pearl she was working on during her long captivity. She sped off to get it from her cage. When she returned she took Ella's old pearl from her and this she gave to Eireden. In its place the fairy gave Ella the new one. It was pure in its whiteness and larger than Ella remembered. Whip-wip also made sure that the others had theirs on as well.

"It's right here next to my heart, dear Whip-wip," Furen assured her, pulling it out. This seemed to satisfy. The fairy then got down to business and her proper gay sythei attitude vanished. She knew her role in the escape and a minute before they were ready she flitted away to scout the route. Eireden had suggested using the gate closest to the dirt-yards to attempt to make their escape from since it was common for odd types to come and go at all hours through that gate.

When the fairy returned with news that the coast was clear the four left the dungeons, moving as quick and quiet as possible. Whip-wip went ahead; as always using her exceptional hearing to keep them from getting caught. Twice she went flying back to warn them of coming danger. Eireden, who had grown up in the palace knew just where to lead them in order to hide.

However the third time that Whip-wip came back whistling a warning that soldiers were on their way, they couldn't hide. Just as they turned, the sound of approaching soldiers from the opposite direction came at them. They were trapped.

# Chapter 12

## Ella

"Do the spell," Eireden ordered, pulling his cloak about his shoulders and tugging his helmet down to cover as much of his face as possible. Ella did the same though she had to be careful that the overly large helmet didn't just fall straight off. Whip-wip slipped into the pouch at her belt, keeping it open only enough to peek out.

Aric complied and performed his spell but when he finished his exhaustion was such that he fell into Furen—a strange tall looking Furen—who held him up by the back of his leathers. Eireden decided to go on and try to slip past whomever it was coming toward them. They were soldiers; men-at-arms and one, an officer of some sort, gave them a queer look.

"Excuse me," Eireden said in a low voice. He had purposely stepped in front of the men, using his bulk in an attempt to shield Aric and Ella from view. The illusion on Furen made him appear more or less like any other scout or third echelon soldier, but the other two with their soft complexions and slim builds seemed too young to be soldiers.

The officer did little besides glare, though he did step to one side only at that moment a new group headed towards them. Ella's blue eyes sprang wide and her throat went tight. It was Eirowyth accompanied by two knights in heavy mail. To turn around now and go back the other way wasn't possible. And to add to their problems at that moment a voice called out from behind.

"You there, scouts!" Ella turned mainly because she couldn't bear the idea of looking at Eirowyth. Sweeping up behind them was Ilenwyth. The four froze in place with Furen still holding Aric up. Eireden hadn't turned. His great fist sat wrapped about the hilt of his sword and he stared with a hard anger at his enemy, but the king ignored him altogether as Ilenwyth called to him.

"Are these your messengers, your Highness? I have a letter that I'd like delivered with your permission." The lady wore a gown of flowing purple with diamonds at her neck and in her silver hair. She was quite eye catching and sure enough the king barely glanced at the four escapees.

"Yes, I was waiting on them myself," Eirowyth answered, testily, releasing his gaze on Ilenwyth and looking at Eireden. "You're over twenty minutes late. You had better be able to give a good account of..."

"Your Highness?" Ilenwyth cut in, holding out an envelope. "If you don't mind, may I add this letter to those going to Hildoeven?"

Eirowyth swung back to her and his face held blatant suspicion. "You need a letter sent out now? That's a little odd with an entire maug army between us and Hildoeven. Perhaps you could tell me why."

"I have decided to leave the capital," Ilenwyth answered, stiffly. "After...after...you know, there won't be anything for me here. Though I'd prefer not to talk about this subject in mixed company."

Everyone in the city knew what the mother of a condemned man was waiting for and everyone in that hall cast their eyes down—all save Ella. She stared at the woman and their eyes met in complete recognition. Ilenwyth mouthed the word 'Pearl'. Ella's hand went to her chest and sure enough the pearl Whip-wip had given her sat exposed for all to see; it was hardly part of a military uniform. Hurriedly she stuck beneath the loose fitting leather.

"That's perfectly understandable, Lady Ilenwyth," the king said after an awkward moment. "Here, scout. See that these get through safely and take the Lady's missive as well." Eirowyth held out the letters to Eireden, but the great Den stood stiffly, looking to be with an inch of slaying the king on the spot. Furen couldn't grab them, both of his hands were in the process of holding the fey up, and Aric had gone well over his body's limit for endurance.

This left Ella with her slim delicate fingers and smooth unscarred hand to take the letters—but there was no other choice. Stepping forward she said, "Yes, Milord," in the very lowest and gruffest voice she could manage, and then she reached for the letters and stared. Her hand looked not to be her own. Instead of smooth skin her hand appeared rugged and hairy with knuckles that seemed huge. She was so surprised that she nearly dropped the letters.

The king gave her a warm smile, looking her right in the eyes. "Ride hard soldier and you'll be fine."

He hadn't recognized her! It was impossible. Ilenwyth knew her at first glance but the king had looked her square in the face and...

The queen! Or rather the former queen, Ilenwyth must have done something, a spell of some sort. Ella bobbed her head to the man who had put Aric under a death sentence and had casually tossed a rope to Eireden—the rightful king. She pushed that from her mind and watched as the king turned away with Ilenwyth.

When they were gone everyone breathed a sigh of relief, all save Eireden. "I should have killed him! I would have killed him if it weren't for..." his eyes, burning with anger flicked to Ella. He softened quickly. "We should get going. Whip-wip, please scout ahead. But we're not going for the north gate; we're going to the stables. We are king's messengers after all."

They made it the stables without incident and with the official seal of the king on the letters they picked out the four fastest horses and were gone in minutes. Prudently, Eireden had them walk the horses out of the stables before mounting them. It would have raised quite a few eyebrows for anyone to see Furen attempting to get on his horse, not to mention Aric was simply too exhausted to even stand. The great Den picked each up, one at a time and tied them in their saddles.

"That is so embarrassing when you do that, my friend," Furen said. "I would appreciate at least some warning." Eireden had started with the dwarf, picking him by the seat of his pant and his collar. Ella giggled from atop her steed. She had leapt up onto the mare, not only with ease, but with glee as well. Horses meant freedom, that is what the queen had told her once and it was never more true than at that moment.

"We don't have time for niceties," Eireden said, climbing onto his own chestnut. "Your illusion is fading; we have to hurry."

Aric rode through Rhyoeven, sagged over, using Eireden as a crutch. "I can't go on...the armor is too heavy. It's too much."

"A little longer," Ella said from just behind them. "Feel the breeze. It's a wonderful night, Aric and we'll soon be free, just hold on."

He did barely. They gained the heavily manned south gate and with Eireden doing the speaking and the letters in his possession the portcullis was soon lifted. "Good luck," cried some of the gate guards. "Godspeed," said others.

"Is it that bad?" Eireden asked the gate captain.

"How can you ask that? Everyone knows the maug army is still in the field," the captain said. He pulled Eireden aside as the other three escapees stopped just along the curving road of the plateau. "Don't take the South Stream road whatever you do. The maug have been thick by the thousands on it waylaying any who attempt to use it. They are trying to cut our communications with Hildoeven. Take my advice, go east on the prairie. You've got good horses. Let them run if you see anything."

"I will," said the prince. "Thank you."

With that he spurred his horse and the four rode at the fastest clip possible for Furen seemed to be shrinking back into a dwarf with every minute. Ella and Eireden road ahead crying, "King's messenger!" in order to have the lower gates opened for them so that the Aric and Furen could pass through without slowing.

When they gained the battle plain Eireden did indeed turn east for the prairie. He rode standing tall in his stirrups watching all about them. Quickly Whip-wip demanded to be freed from the pouch, but Ella held back until they were far out on the plain. When she finally relented the fairy exploded up and out with such a cry of relief that even Aric found the energy to smile. The little creature swooped all about, finally stretching her wings after so many days confined.

Now despite the danger from the maug and the very good possibility of pursuit from Rhyoeven, they rode slowly. Furen could ride no other way and Aric was slow to recover his strength and sagged in his saddle. By midnight he could go no further and they made a camp—each taking two hour watches, except for Aric and Whip-wip both of whom slept straight through.

Ella's watch was the last, which was good since her nightmares generally came just before dawn. She could feel her power returning and she resisted the urge to exorcise it as she had for the previous eighteen days. There was no telling what the day would bring and she wanted to be as strong as possible. She did feel the ground and she let her consciousness drift along the root network of the plain.

There were maug on the plain and riders both. They were miles away—the riders to the west and closing slowly, the maug strung out to their south and east. Ella let the men sleep. The danger was still far away, and not only did she want the others to rest she needed time to think.

She was an elf. There it was. It explained so much, but at the same time it explained so little. Her father was evil, but what about her mom? Maybe she had been raped after a long...twenty thousand year coma? Or maybe she had hid herself during the Demon wars and then met her dad twenty thousand years later and fell for the bad-boy routine. It happens. Some girls just like that bit of danger in a man. Look at her and Eireden. He was...

"Stop," she said to herself. "Your love for Eireden is in the past," she forced herself to say. Aric was her future. Her very long future—she was immortal! How crazy is that? Never dying, always young, and with powers. Oh, the powers! The powers of the elves must be great indeed. For a long while she thought about all the things she might be able to do. She would fly that was a definite and she'd learn that trick of Aric's where they turned invisible. What else?

Just then she noticed Aric's green eyes glittering in the predawn light. "Go back to sleep," she told him gently. "The sun isn't up and neither should you be. You need to rest."

"I have rested all I need," he said. "Besides the sun will rise in a matter of minutes and I wish to see your beauty in its light. The last time I had this chance we were travelling west and the light wasn't right. I want to see you with the sun coming up behind."

"Aye, that I want to see as well," Furen said, rolling over. "It will make sleeping on these itchy plants worth it.

"Don't do it, Furen. Don't look at her. Ella is more dangerous than you realize," Eireden murmured, still lying on the bed of wheat he had made for himself and still with his eyes closed. "She will ruin it for Gargefrel. When could you ever look at another sunrise and not think of Ella?"

In the growing light the girl blushed. "Stop it, all of you. I'm not all that special. And maybe we shouldn't wait about for the sun. I should warn you, there are horsemen on our trail."

Now Eireden cracked an eye. "You don't seem too concerned. How far are they?"

"Far enough away that we can enjoy the sunrise," Aric answered. "Though afterwards we should begin to think about moving on."

Suddenly Whip-wip opened her eyes and up she sprang,

whistling and going to each faster than they could follow saying her good mornings and then she was gone singing out: "*Zooti!*"

Then their little encampment was strangely quiet. Ella turned to the men and found them all staring. "Stop it," she said, covering her face. "You're embarrassing me." They each mumbled an apology and turned away all save Aric who went to her and stared as if committing her face to memory. The light of the new sun was in his face so that his eyes shined like gems. He found her hands and his were warm and gentle.

Eventually Whip-wip came back, making a face, ending the long moment when the early sun seemed to make everything perfect. "*Shis-ffis,*" she said holding up a couple of small strawberries that were still mostly green. One had a few small fairy bites out of it.

"I bet they are sour," Ella replied. "If you can hold on, the forest is only two hours away."

Aric sighed at the interruption. "You mentioned the horsemen on our trail, but did you feel the maug?" he asked and then shook his head. "Wait! Of course you did."

"I did but I'm more worried about the horsemen," Ella replied. She went to her mare and threw the light saddle onto her. Eireden was doing the same for Furen's horse. "Can you cover our tracks or lead a false trail away? And...can you show me how to do it?"

The fey went to his horse as well and saddled her. "I can, but we shouldn't dally. There will be plenty of time later on for teaching and learning. Don't worry about that."

Aric had them backtrack for a ways down the trail they had made the night before and then he had them lead the horses away south in single file. This, he explained, would make covering their tracks all the easier. They waited only minutes and then he came walking backwards and it looked as though the wheat was simply standing up again where it had been trampled.

"Let's go," he said leaping into his saddle. They rode at Furen's top speed, which wasn't very fast, but on the other hand it kept the horses fresh. Still Aric and Eireden worried. They coached the dwarf how to sit up straighter and how to balance. Neither seemed to work so Eireden showed him how to take great fistful's of the horses mane and hold on tight.

Their anxiety over Furen's riding had Ella nervous and so she had Whip-wip fly ahead. Sure enough the fairy came back to report goblins strung out for miles. The good news was that they were in little groups of twenty about a hundred yards apart, clearly acting the part of a screening force for the larger part of their army. The fairy flew to the midway point between two of the groups and they rode straight for her.

It was a horrible, fearfully slow ride. Eireden had to keep beside Furen so he wouldn't fly from the saddle, but even so they rode so slowly. When the goblins spotted them and began running, Eireden tried his best to hurry the dwarf, but very quickly it became obvious that they wouldn't make it; the goblins would close the trap. Aric whistled and point to the left he then pointed to himself and before she knew what was what he had spurred his horse off to the left traveling at break-neck speed. The maug on that side hesitated and then turned toward him. Ella saw his plan.

She then did the same on the right. With the wind howling in her ears and her hair, rich and dark, streaming out behind, she rode straight at the maug. Thinking that she was attacking, they immediately turned at her but just as they did she cut right and rode across their front. Now the maug had to choose between the big human and this beautiful girl to attack. They surged to the right after her and she had to slow down to keep herself just ahead of them. She was the bait after all. Ella let them get close, but then with a word her dappled, grey mare shot forward. A second group of the goblins were charging in front of her, but they would be too slow and with yards to spare she zipped between them, laughing. The closest goblin threw his spear at her, but Ella, using only her mind, swatted it aside with ease.

And then she was well past them. She rode easily, cantering to the left to reform with a sweating Furen and a smiling Eireden. The Den's steel-grey eyes watched her for a long time and she heard him murmur to Furen: "I can look. I have no Gargefrel, remember?"

Ella pretended not to hear though it warmed her insides. Seconds later Aric rode up from the other side, looking completely different from the feeble creature of the night before. He rode standing straight up in the stirrups and his green eyes swept the prairie before them. The early morning sun glinted in his hair so that the gold seemed to be alight.

After a few hundred yards they slowed and Ella slipped from her horse to feel the ground. Aric stayed in his saddle showing his faith in her. "We are two miles north and east of the main goblin army," she said. "We can keep going due south and miss them altogether."

This they did, moving deliberately and checking frequently the range of their enemies. Three hours later they were deep in the forest and the maug were well behind them. They stopped at a stream to water their horses and Ella sat letting the water run over her bare feet. Whip-wip had found a plum and was busily eating it, uncaring that she was covering herself in its lavender juices. Ella couldn't or perhaps wouldn't stop staring at her.

Aric tried to catch Ella's eye but she refused to do more than play with the fairy and splash the water. She knew what he wanted—it was time to leave. Not just the stream, it was time to leave Eireden and Furen. She and Aric weren't going to Hildoeven, that was already decided. And really as a criminal twice over there wasn't any Den city that they could go to. What's more, because of her, there were no longer any Feylands either and if there were, the fey wouldn't likely take her in now that it was known she was an elf. The fey had helped to destroy the elves after all. Which left the dwarves. Would they take in an elf that had some sort of beacon in her? Not likely and besides she didn't think Aric could stand to live in one of their caves for long.

What options did that leave her? Whip-wip's grotto or the Forbidden Lands? Neither was in any way a protection. How easily she could be hunted. And she was sure that as an elf she would be. Her best hope would be to move around a lot...see the world, travel. Suddenly it didn't sound like much fun, travelling or being an elf.

In frustration Ella kicked the water, which Whip-wip took to mean that it was playtime. The fairy hurled handfuls of plum at her and she allowed it to splatter her silly armor. She wouldn't be wearing it for much longer anyway.

"Ella," Aric said.

"I know. It's time."

Eireden shot her a quick glance. His keen eyes burrowed into her, into her soul. "It's time for what?" he asked, though it seemed obvious by the sudden flare of pain behind those eyes that he knew.

"It's time to say goodbye."

## Chapter 13

## Eireden

"Eh? What is this?" Furen asked.

Eireden dropped his head. He had known this moment was coming, but still it struck him a blow, so that his insides felt to turn inside out. To hide his pain he turned away and fiddled with the straps of his saddle.

"We...ah...aren't going to Hildoeven," Ella said in a small voice. "It wouldn't be safe for us there. No Den city is safe. In truth I don't know where on earth we *can* be safe."

"What about below the earth?" Furen suggested. "You can stay with me in Hanmar. You'll like it very much. Trust me when I say the city of the dwarves is far better than any Den city. There is light; do not worry about that, and it's open and spacious with tall ceilings and great columns. And the pools! I know how much you care for the water, Milady. The pools are crystal clear and they're heated from underground vents. You can be my guest and don't worry about me being put out in any way. I have not let on for it is considered ill mannered to do so but I am an important dwarf. It would be nothing but an honor to have two such guests as yourselves."

At first hope flared in her eyes, but then Ella gave a shake of her head. "Thank you very much for the offer, but I must put the safety of your people first. Remember, I'm still a beacon—a goblin magnet—as Eireden put it. Until I can change that I can't risk it."

Furen considered this. "The ways into all dwarf lands are secret...I suppose you have a point. What about you, my tall friend? Hildoeven can't be any more safe for you than it is for them. I offer you the same accommodations. We'll have a grand time. Did I tell you about the ogres or the trolls? What sport we can have hunting them."

"Sounds like fun," Eireden replied. "Only I can't. My lands are overrun by the maug and my throne is in the hands of a coward. Ella was correct, in denying my challenge, Eirowyth hides behind the letter of the law; not the intent of the law. It was one thing not to face a *gada*, but another to levy criminal charges against an innocent man. I can't rest until I challenge him again."

"What? Are you, mad?" Ella demanded. "He'll just jail you a second time, or worse put you to death on the spot."

"If there was another choice I would take it. Legally my only option is to challenge him and hope he accepts. What's more, morally it my responsibility to my people. It's a duty I cannot shirk or pass on to another."

"If that is what your heart insists upon then please take my sword," Aric said unbuckling the great elf-sword. "Your false king will have the black sword of Ag-Raumon. By all accounts it's a terrible weapon."

Eireden knew the black sword. He had used it to slay the infamous troll of Argen's Gate, a most vile beast. He had carried it in war and battle, as well as on his journey through the Demorlaik. It was a very powerful weapon. Eireden eyed the elf-sword with such eagerness in his soul that it bordered on greed, but then he shook his head. "No. I have two loves. I must take care of the first and you the second. Keep the sword; you may have need of it."

"Stop talking like that," Ella said angrily. "You act like I can't take care of myself. I'll have you know, Eireden that I'm growing stronger in my magic and it's because..." She stopped at a slight clearing of Aric's throat. "It—it's because I've been practicing so hard. My point is you should take the sword, Eireden. You are the rightful king."

She had been about to say something else concerning her magic. *What could it have been*, Eireden mused? "The sword does not make the man...or woman. I have truth on my side. I do not need a special sword to overcome a liar."

Ella breathed out noisily. "The truth is not a shield. It won't make you stronger or faster. Eireden you have to know that honest people die all the time at the hands of criminals and all sorts of evil people. What about the innocent fey or the men of the Twelfth? I'm sure they were honest and they were killed by evil goblins."

"Those were battles. What I'm talking about are duels of honor," Eireden replied. "It is a precept among the Den that an honest man cannot be slain by a dishonest man in such a duel. The power of his truth will win out eventually."

Ella wasn't mollified by this and Eireden didn't really expect her to be. She had been raised in a world where truth was a matter of convenience. In America an honest person was more likely viewed as a chump or a pushover and definitely someone to be taken advantage of. In that world dishonesty bred dishonesty, but it was not so among the Den. At least Aric and Furen understood and both wished him luck. Ella refused.

"What would you have me do?" he asked. "Have Eirowyth assassinated? Or would you rather I run and hide from my problems?"

"Sometimes if you can't change a problem or fix it then you must be the one to change," Ella said. "You serve no purpose dying needlessly. The maug army is out there. Who, but you can lead the Den to victory over them? You can't do that if you're dead. And then there is the...the demon..." Ella faltered, turning her face down and looking abruptly confused.

Eireden touched her on the arm; the skin was so soft and smooth...and compelling. Quickly he pulled his hand back—he had given up any rights he might have had to enjoy that silken skin. He too looked down and said, "All of that goes hand in hand with my gaining the throne. But worry not for me. My destiny is set. I must face Eirowyth again, for it is the way of my path whether for good or ill. It is your destiny that I fret over."

This caused her to smirk. "Oh, I do as well. I'm fretting enough for both of us. And I hate the idea of running, because I fear I'll always be on the run if I start. I'd rather stay to help in some way but I'm too dangerous. There are too many *what ifs* surrounding me. Where did I come from? Who is my mother ...what did the demon do to me? I know you understand about a nuclear bomb. What if there is something like that inside of me hidden by magic? How do I know there isn't one and how do we know the demon isn't waiting for the right moment to explode it?"

"It would have to be the smallest bomb ever," Eireden said, giving her a look. "Though I guess I understand your point. He made you into an impossible beacon, what else did he do, right?"

"Right. He could have done anything," she said and then shivered. Eireden wanted to go to her but it wouldn't have been right. Aric put on an arm around her shoulders. She gave the fey a warm smile and then turned to Eireden. "I guess—I guess this is good bye; we're going to head east into America."

"And for me too this is good bye," Furen added. "Gargefrel awaits me two days south—on foot. I give to you this horse. It..." Just then a crow fluttered into a nearby tree and Eireden put his hand out to quiet the dwarf.

"Speak no more of your plans," he said in a hushed tone. This was the same forest that they had been tracked through weeks before and just as before a crow had dogged their tail. Quickly he searched the stream for a good-sized stone. It didn't take more than a second to find a round one with good heft. He let it fly and saw immediately that it would miss to the right—but then like a curveball from a pitcher the stone's trajectory bent in its flight and, unbelievably as well as impossibly, it picked up velocity. The stone struck the crow just as it leapt into flight.

Black feathers rained in the forest and the bird thumped lifelessly to the ground. Ella turned her head. "Your magic has grown strong," Eireden said. He was impressed. It took some skill to grab a stone in flight and vector it into its target. "I'll worry less about you now that I know how strong you've become."

Ella shrugged at the compliment. "I've never killed an animal before. Is there any way to know if it was really possessed like that other one?"

Aric shook his head. "Not now. But in these times you can't take the chance."

"Would the demon really send another crow?" Ella asked. "I mean he can find me whenever he wants. Maybe I just helped killed some bird for no reason."

"Though the demon might know where you are," Eireden answered. "He doesn't know what you are up to. I think in his great game you have graduated from pawn status and now he must worry about your next move."

"My next move is hiding," Ella said glumly. "And I still feel very much like a pawn."

"Hiding is still a move," Furen added. "It can be a very cryptic one as well. In his mind you could be doing anything: gathering your strength, finding allies, creating a weapon. What's more you can come out of hiding at any time and disrupt his plans. My guess is that he'll want to try to keep tabs on you at the very least and by doing so he'll use up valuable resources."

"You make hiding sound almost heroic, my friend," Ella replied. She went to Furen and put out her hand. He bowed low and kissed it gently. "I will miss you," she said to the dwarf. Ella then looked at Eireden. He saw confusion in her eyes and it seemed as if she had much to say, but after a moment only said, "Good bye, Eireden...be safe."

It stung a bit that she didn't proffer her hand to him. He made his own bow, but couldn't say more than a hoarse, 'Goodbye' in return. He then gave a bow to Aric who returned it deeper. "I owe you much, Lord Den. You redeemed a great failing of mine and saved my people from extinction."

"Don't think on it like that," Eireden growled. "You did not fail. There was no way you or anyone could have known Ella was a beacon. You checked her for enchantments, remember? So don't hang this on your shoulders."

It was clear that Aric still felt responsible yet he gave the Den a nod anyway before swinging up into his saddle. Whip-wip said goodbye last. Though as was usual with her kind it wasn't so much a goodbye but a litany of things they would do when they were together again: they would tease fish, find the ripest peaches, drop some toads on the maug, and cut Furen's beard while he slept; things like that. As she whistled and chirped her words she pulled his pearl from the folds of his leather armor and set it alight with a touch. She then did that for everyone except for Ella.

Ella pulled her own pearl out but it would not light. "*Fises shee zosis*," the fairy explained: It's not ready yet. With her 'Goodbyes' complete Whip-wip was eager to move on. To a fairy the future was always preferable to the past.

Eireden watched them go with a heavy heart and a long sigh. Furen matched the sound with one of his own. "So, you let her go," the dwarf said when the Aric and Ella trotted out of sight.

"I had no choice," the Den answered. "Our ways are not so easy as plucking a flower. Tell me. What happens when more than one dwarf presents a flower to a lady dwarf?"

"It's always the first to present that wins the hand. It's assumed that whoever gets there first must care the most." The dwarf looked up, craning his thick neck far back. "When you slay this demon, come visit me in Hanmar and we shall renew our friendship over ale and ogre's blood. What do you say?"

"I say that I will, but for now it's goodbye."

The dwarf nodded and set his stumpy feet heading south. Eireden turned to the west, alone again.

## Chapter 14

## Eireden

When, after a time, the trees finally hid Furen and the sound of Ella's and Aric's horses no longer slipped past their leaves, Eireden said, "Now for the easy part." To him, fighting—whether he fought goblins or demons or even his cousin—was far simpler and less painful than dealing with Ella. Even then when he should have been concentrating on the forest, focusing his senses on the world around him he was instead thinking about the girl.

"Why hadn't she offered her hand? It was the least she could've done. Did she think I would cling? Did she think that I'd demand more? Hhmph! I should go back and tell her how far off the mark she..."

He caught himself just as he looked back. He would turn around and tell her what? That he was over her? That clearly wasn't the case. "Maybe she was right not to let me touch her. I'm acting the fool." To center himself he let a song run through his mind—it turned into a love song. "Damn!" A song wouldn't work this time he realized. Too many that he knew had to do with love or loss.

Eireden decided he would have to focus on the real world; the physical world. He directed his thoughts to the forest, breathing in the full aroma of the leaves, the wet banks of the river, the flowers, the birds...he was just beginning to focus when he caught sight of another crow. The black bird sat among the very highest branches of a fir tree; too far out of reach of a thrown stone. Was this an agent of the demon? Or perhaps just a bird.

Mounting his horse and holding on to the tether of the second, he rode off cantering south and west. He knew a rocky prominence a few miles away, one in which he would have the advantage in height. If the crow followed he would see it easily. He rode hard and gained the barren hill. Yes, there flew the crow, going from tree to tree. Coming on steadily, but attempting to remain hidden. This wasn't normal crow behavior. Was the bird guiding other foes to him?

"What about Ella?"

Were there other crows trailing after Ella and Aric? Should he warn her? He paused, sitting atop his horse in full view of the world. Which way to turn? Toward Hildoeven or back toward Ella?

"Damn!" Always there was indecision when it came to Ella. From the very start he had waffled over her: was she a fey or not? Should she come with him into the Hidden Lands or not? Should he love her or not? "Stop it...you've been indecisive long before Ella. It's been since the Demorlaik; since Eirowyth. Do not blame her," he said to himself.

So which way to turn? He put the question to the test that his father, Eirolden used to judge things: which direction was the easiest? He looked both east and west. To the west was death at the hands of his accuser. To the west lay thousands of goblins and a demon bent on his destruction. To the west lay a city cut off and alone in a sea of enemies. To the east: a girl who loved another.

It was difficult to tell which direction would be the easier path but eventually he decided the east—Ella—how simple it would be to traipse after her swooning at her every look. Thus, as his father would have, he spurred his horse west— the man never shied away from the hard road. His motto: *If it is easy then someone else can take care of it.*

This was definitely the harder road. Even from miles away the smell of goblin and ogre had the Den war-horse skittish and frequently Eireden dismounted to try to feel his enemies through the root system of the forest. The main army was, for the most part, far off, north and west of him, yet there were still elements of the maug between him and Hildoeven so he turned south.

After a few miles he came to the small pond and let the

horses drink. When he bent to the water himself he caught a sight in the reflection. High above him wheeled three long-winged vultures. Were they spies of the enemy as well? Switching horses to keep them both as fresh as possible Eireden decided to turn east. If the vultures kept pace he would know soon enough. They did, yet he didn't know exactly what to do about it. They were far too high for any stone and they made a perfect marker to let his enemies know exactly where he was.

Fearing that even then the maug were closing in, Eireden turned again south to put some distance between them. After a time he realized that all this detouring away from Hildoeven had put him closer to unexpected allies. Eireden just hoped that they would be allies he could trust. Cresting a steep hill, he looked down upon the grotto of the *Sythei*. He could see them happily buzzing about, enjoying life as only fairies can.

Would they listen to him? As far as he knew only Ella had ever commanded a fairy to do something that was against their desire. He dismounted as he approached and left the horses to graze, knowing this would be hard enough without having to deal with the fairies trying to spook the poor animals.

"*Tiffses sup snir* Eireden," he said: Hello my name is Eireden. This he basically said to the empty pond and the trickling waterfall; the fairies had disappeared before he got close. "I am Den," he continued in the chirping of the Sythei. "I am friend to Ella and Whip-wip." This brought some of the more courageous fairies peeking out from beneath leaf and branch. "I need help."

"*Shee*! *Shee*, *tay tee sif*," some cried out: No! No more tree spirits. The sythei remembered him and they also remembered the time they had saved him from a tree nymph.

A male—formidable at seven inches in height—flew out of the brush and waved Eireden away. "*Issa zuu.*" Leave, far away, he demanded.

The Den pointed to the vultures overhead. "*Tays tee sif, che-che.*" Spies of the maug, it meant.

Cries of shee and issa zuu rang out and then a berry of some sort flew out of the foliage and struck him on the cheek. In seconds many more came flying at him, pelting him about the face. "Stop!" he roared, in the way only he could and the power of his voice stopped them cold. They slunk back into hiding.

"Whip-wip really is exceptional," he said under his breath.

Glaring about at his now invisible foes, the Den stripped off the stained leather breastplate. He went to the water and after casting in a number of stones in order to scare off the water nymph that resided there he commenced to wash his face. When he straightened he saw that the vultures were still above him, high in the sky.

Just then one of the fairies cried out from the brush, "*Ssi meach!*" Translation: Look at that!

Eireden stared around him wondering what they were looking at. Then the big male came up to him and pointed at the pearl hanging about Eireden's neck on its invisible string. The Den touched it and its light sprang forth. Now all the fairies came out of hiding and flew in circles around him. Some swooped in to give the pearl a touch and then they flew off again just as fast. Strangely, none of them now seemed in the least bit afraid.

"My friend Whip-wip gave this to me," Eireden said. At this more of the fairies came in to touch either the pearl or the Den. Was the pearl some sort of token? Did it make him part of the family at least honorarily? "*Seary sup?*" He asked the male his name.

"Easa-see."

"*Che-che maug, issa zuu.*" Translation: make the maug spies go far away, please. Easa-see didn't hesitate. He whistled up a dozen of his fellows and up they flew. The vultures were no match for the speedy and magical Sythei and in seconds they were sent crashing into the forest beyond the ridge as feathers spun lazily to the ground. The fairies gathered them up and dashed about tickling each other.

"Thank you, Easa-see," Eireden said as the male alit upon a nearby branch. "That was wonderful. Whip-wip would be proud of all of you." Thinking of Whip-wip made him think of Ella and immediately a cloud settled over his suddenly light mood. "I should be going. There are many goblins between here and Hildoeven."

The fairy leapt up and began pointing and whistling: the maug were coming right at them. He had seen them as they had attacked the vultures.

"Of course," Eireden said, putting his hand to the nearest tree trying to feel them through the root system. Unfortunately the signals from the land had become mixed and confusing. This was the demon's spell work. He had lost his aerial spies and now was looking to keep Eireden in the dark as to where his minions were going to attack from.

"Were they coming from the north?" Eireden asked. "I don't want to ride right into them." The fairy abruptly called to some of his family and they streaked away, which was unexpected. Were they going to act as scouts? He hoped so since it would turn the tables on the demon and give Eireden a good chance at escape. With that thought in mind he hurried to where he left the horses; he couldn't afford to wait for the fairies to return to get out of the grotto; it was a readymade trap.

As he climbed the slopes a few of the fairies stayed with him, they seemed completely relaxed. Two even hitched a ride on his shoulder and chatted. Unlike him, they had little to worry. They could fly away from danger or simply hide, using their unique ability to camouflage themselves. They could practically disappear while a person was looking square at them.

He hit the crest of the ridge and paused to look to the

north and west. Hildoeven lay about fourteen miles away—not far when a man had two horses to ride. However there could be many hundreds of maug to slip past and the sun was westering to his left. It would be a near thing to get to the town by sunset and he didn't know if they would let him in after.

Just then Easa-see flew up to him, but instead of landing on Eireden's outstretched hand the fairy went to a tree, broke off a stick, and flew to the ground. There he began a quick sketch that was easily recognizable as a map of the area. The maug were all along his path. Easa-see drew a line in the map that squiggled south and west and then suddenly shot north.

"Got it," Eireden said. Another detour. Another chance to be pushed further from his destination. Just then he felt very much like a piece in another chess game. There were pawns strung out along his front, while somewhere out there a black king directed them. This left him to wonder where the rooks and knights were—where those burnt looking creatures were. He would find out soon enough.

"Thank you, Easa-see. You've been a great help." He was just turning his horse when the fairy pointed at himself and then pointed at Eireden's proposed line of travel. The fairy was going to help him! Interesting. "*Snipp snee*," the Den whistled in appreciation.

It wasn't just Easa-see who helped him; the entire family pitched in. Some of the fairies kept tabs on the maug, while others acted as guides and thus the journey around the south and west was wonderfully uneventful. He rode accompanied by two fairies: Tissa and Sooni. Both of whom chatted eagerly about their little adventure—at first. Then they grew hungry and ate fruit in abundance and then when their little bellies were swollen they became sleepy and curled up in the empty saddlebag on the spare horse. Eireden let them sleep.

Somehow, probably through the pearl that Whip-wip had given him, he had become part of their family. They called him 'Father Den' in their language and acted as though he were just a very large fairy. When they awoke, unmindful of the goblins hunting them, they asked if he wanted to nap. He declined, though he politely ate of their fruit, which they frequently offered.

As they turned north and the danger increased his 'family' grew tense. There were more goblins than any had ever seen before. So many that he was forced to detour ever westward. Soon it became apparent that the town itself was surrounded in a loose cordon of enemies. In the growing shadows of the forest they lurked in small groups within shouting distance of each other. Seeing this, the sythei wanted to turn back for home and they began pulling Eireden back the way they had come.

"No," he said, gently. "I need to find a way through. I'll go alone. Thank you for helping as much as you have. Now go back to your grotto my friends."

They frowned at this, and Easa-see would not hear it. He sent scouts to find a way through the goblins. One was discovered, though it was small indeed. Along a gully where a stream had cut through the forest floor ran a spidery trail. Two maug bands sat on either side of it, but because of the thick brush there was a good fifty yards between them.

With fairies darting ahead, moving noiselessly, Eireden slipped from his saddle. Keeping to the best cover he could find, he walked the two horses as silently as he could toward the break in the goblin lines. Unfortunately horses aren't at all silent. One kicked over a large rock and not a second later the other threw his head back and whinnied. Eireden knew he had been heard. Jumping onto the back of the fresher of the two animals he sped for the opening. One of the fairies hovered there bravely blinking his light, and the man made right for her at top speed.

The fifty-yard gap closed with frightening swiftness. The goblins saw him and raced to cut him off— but just as it seemed he would be caught, fairies started sending their bright lights right into the goblin's faces, while other goblins suddenly went down in heaps, tripping over invisible filaments that the fairies had set in their paths. This threw them into such confusion that Eireden roared through the gap with yards to spare on either side. Now there was just a short two-mile ride to the gates of the city and he would be home free. He rode hard while behind him horns blatted.

As he came to the plain that surrounded the city a horde of maug broke from the edge of the forest. It wasn't the main maug army, which was miles away, still there were thousands of them and they were closer to the gate than he was, however they were on foot. Without breaking stride Eireden leapt into the saddle of the spare horse and spurred it on. Ahead streaked the fairies and they blazed into the maug causing an uproar of confusion. Goblins shielded their eyes in fear or blanched away causing them to slow and soon those that had slowed were being crushed under foot as the tide of grey-green bodies rolled on.

The fairies tried again, but with less effect than before, yet still the goblins slowed a little. Now a shout went up on the wall of the town. Men were surging to their battle stations believing an attack was underway, and many, many bows were trained on Eireden. He was almost certain that if one young soldier let loose an arrow, a hundred more would follow. Someone yelled for the gates to be opened, however more voices clamored for them to remain locked. No one knew what to do and still Eireden raced on, the thundering hooves kicking up dirt and sod behind him.

"Look Sythei!" Someone had spotted the family of fairies. A few of the smaller, younger ones had come back from attacking the maug and were now flying over the Den rider lighting his face in the growing dark of evening.

"The gate! Open the gate! The king comes! Open the gate." Eireden recognized the carrying voice of Lienhart. And sure enough there was the once-captain in the simple garb of a man-at-arms standing atop the wall. His words and tone still held authority and the gate creeped back. The second it opened enough to allow in the horses Eireden dashed through and then came the cries.

"Shut the gate! Shut it! The maug are upon us!"

Then came a great croaking shout and the maug surged against the gate. Bows twanged and arrows whistled. The gate did not close in time and the mass of goblins struck it sending men reeling back. Eireden slipped from his horse and threw his weight against the gate and pushed. More men joined him and there came a moment when the gate stood in balance between open and closed. And then up came knights huffing under the burden of their plate armor; among them strode Prince Gamelling in a rage.

Gone was his kindly outlook. "Give me the name of the traitor that caused my gates to open!" he demanded. "Whoever it is will pay with his life."

Lienhart's eyes met Eireden's and before he could do anything Lienhart stepped away from the others. "I opened the gate."

# Chapter 15

## Ella

As Eireden had his every move hounded, Ella and Aric rode at their leisure out of the Hidden Lands and down the eastern slope of the Cascade mountains. All about them lay the beauty of fragrant vales, running rivers, and hills covered in the summer's last blooms. The land here held less in the way of forest and wasn't nearly so wet as on the western run of the Cascades. It held a certain beauty nonetheless: meadows and rolling hills, flights of geese and herds of elk, and warm breezes wafting through the cool blue sky.

They followed a stream of icy waters that merged with others along the way to become a fast moving river. In places it foamed and frothed white as it beat angrily against huge grey boulders. In other places it seemed barely to move at all and looked almost like a pond. Whip-wip loved the water, fast or slow and spent as much time as she could playing in it. She tied dragonflies together at the tail and watched them go forward and back until she couldn't breathe from laughter. She went fly fishing, using real flies, and ended up getting dunked when she misjudged the size of the rainbow trout that accepted her bait. And she 'rode' a bullfrog by poking it repeatedly with a sharp stick in its hindquarters until it squirmed under a fallen log and no amount of poking would get it to move.

That first night they camped within sight of Lake Chelan. Without the lease hint of danger about them, Aric started a fire and made a soft nest from long grasses. Though there wasn't the abundance of fruit trees as there had been in the Hidden Lands, Whip-wip was still able to find naturally growing grape vines, and she shared her treasure with them.

"It's strange, I'm not really hungry," Ella said, eating the last grape. "After all that riding, you'd think I would be. In fact, I don't get hungry much at all. Is that an elf trait?"

[107]

"Yes. We process food so much more efficiently that we require far less of it than does man," Aric answered. "And we have conquered cravings as well, so that we don't eat for the sake of eating."

"We? You act like there's no difference between a fey and an elf. Wait, is there?" Ella asked, leaning back and seeing the billions of stars overhead. Stars had never been this visible in Seattle.

"There are certain differences," Aric conceded. "Size mostly, they are much taller. And they have a marked advantage in spiritual strength as well. There were some elves of old who could lift five-hundred stone."

"Five-hundred, wow...if my father is that strong, we could be in great trouble," Ella remarked. "What am I saying? We are in great trouble." Though just at the moment, snugged up warm next to Aric she didn't feel it. Instead she felt a great contentment with only a slight nagging worry over Eireden marring the beautiful evening. He was a subject that neither had brought up that whole day.

Aric took her hand and kissed it. "You're father is not that strong. There hasn't been any elf since the demon wars who have had that kind of strength. It was those wars which turned us into a dwindling people. Always the strongest left to protect the weakest until the strongest were no more and the weak...well the weak became the fey. In this I do not say we are weak in a negative way. It's not weakness to abhor death and destruction, torture and pain. We care about truth and beauty, song and sunshine...though this star-shine is not without its charms. The stars are reflected in your eyes so that they seem to shine out of a deep ocean."

Ella appreciated the compliment but the thought of a 'deep ocean' within her gave her a chill. "I do not count the fey weak because they are good. I just worry that our enemy is doubly powerful because he is evil," Ella said sadly. "Evil is not restricted in their methods as we are. Oh! I'm scared, Aric. How am I not evil? That is what I want to know."

"I don't honestly know," replied Aric. "I'm just happy that you aren't. In fact I think it's a wondrous thing. What a chance for my people to grow again. We've been stagnating in our little universe, becoming smaller with every passing year. And now to bring in elf blood—untainted elf blood—good elf blood is fantastic." This was an odd thing to say, Ella thought. It made her feel like a prize cow at auction. "Not to mention it takes the pressure off of me," Aric added, further confusing Ella.

"What pressure do you mean?"

"Oh, just the pressure to bond myself with someone I'd rather not," he said easily as if it wasn't a big deal.

"They make you marry someone you don't want to?" Ella asked astounded. Her voice rose as she added, "The fey will make you marry someone you don't love?"

"Shush, you'll wake the baby," Aric said with a smile. He pointed to Whip-wip who had curled herself up on Ella's chest, snug between her breasts. The fairy had herself wrapped around Ella's new pearl and a light snore came from her. "No one makes a fey do anything," Aric continued. "There isn't an iota of outside pressure, but there is great internal pressure for each to do their part for the whole. Sometimes that means marrying someone when you'd prefer another. I was pretty much slated to bond with Alseya. You met her before the battle."

"She's very beautiful," Ella said, remembering the white haired fey with the opal eyes. "Why—why wouldn't you want to...uh...bond with her? I take it you don't love her."

"Then you take it wrong. I love Alseya very much, even as I love all the fey. It's just that when something is expected like that, it takes on friction. Small things get in the way and become bigger things. Hesitation becomes stalling. Reasons to put it off become excuses and justification."

"Is this all because she is the prettiest and you the most handsome?" Ella asked. If this was so, it sure seemed awful juvenile for such a 'Higher' race.

"No, not at all," he replied. "Though it is nice to know you think I am the most handsome. She is of the Bellesarus line and is the strongest in many thousands of years while I am of Anorian line. Everyone knows the power of the fey is on the wane and everyone knows there is only one way to right that."

"By having the strongest of both sexes mate," Ella said in understanding. Aric made a sour face at the word mate and so she added, "Ok, *bond* then if you prefer."

"I do," he said somewhat stiffly. "The term mate just seems so animalistic. I don't even like to use it with regards to humans. Though after hearing about the reason behind Furen's flower, I may be tempted to use the word with regards to the dwarves. To think they base their relationships on who's first to hand over a flower."

"They've turned survival of the fittest into survival of the fastest," Ella said with a giggle. "It's a wonder they aren't all built like cheetahs. Of course I don't know what dwarf women look like. They may not be much to hurry for. Who knows? Maybe half of them are named dandelion and are still waiting for their flower."

Aric laughed. "I've never seen a dwarf woman either and for the life of me I just can't even picture a beautiful woman, dwarf or not, named Gargefrel."

Ella began to laugh and then stopped abruptly. "I'm being uncharitable and quite the hypocrite. Perhaps I'm pretty on the outside, but who knows what evil lurks below my skin? Wouldn't you think my father would have wanted me evil since he is? Unless...unless I was an accident."

"An accident? I don't understand."

"You know, an unplanned pregnancy..." Ella stopped as Aric began shaking his head. "I take it there are no accidental births among the fey or the elves?"

"No, there aren't. Why would you want a child to come about by accident?" the fey asked. "Life for the lower orders is all about accident and happenstance. It's ill thought out and can lead to all sorts of dire consequences."

"At the same time it can be the start of a great adventure," Ella replied. The word adventure awoke within her that dreamy need that she had felt when Eireden and Aric had first come into her life. They had offered her something unattainable in America—true adventure, heroics, gallantry and, above all, magic. She had got all of that and more. Almost more than she could handle it turned out.

Almost, but not quite. There was still at least one adventure left in her. "I want to find my mother."

## Chapter 16

## Eireden

The evening was low about them, seeming thicker due to the cries of battle and the sound of metal on metal. Onto his shoulder the gate pressed hard and Eireden heaved himself against it but he did so with his head turned around. Lord Gamelling's mouth quivered in rage.

"You opened the gate!" he demanded of Lienhart. "Why? Why on earth...no. Don't answer that. Consider yourself under arrest. Go lock yourself away in the deepest dungeon. I cannot abide the sight of you."

"No," Eireden said. "Belay that order." Grabbing one of the knights he shoved him hard against the gate to take his place before going up to the prince of the city. "He opened the gate for me."

Gamelling seemed dumbstruck at the sight of him and his mouth hung open uselessly.

Lienhart nodded at Eireden and said, "I opened the gate for the King. I would not have done so for any other." Behind them the gate groaned on its hinges as more and more of the maug swarmed at it.

"Are you...king?" Gamelling asked, looking at him strangely. His eyes went to Eireden's fierce determined face, but also to his torn leather armor—the face was that of a king there was no doubt; the clothing that of an imposter.

"My father is dead," Eireden replied. "And I have renounced being *gada*. According to our laws I should be king, but I am not due to the coward who has usurped my throne."

"You were jailed," the old prince said without strength. "You were sentenced to the rope...the time of your choosing. What should I do? Do I arrest you?"

Eireden turned to Lienhart. "Form the knights in a semi circle around the entrance. Three deep. We can't risk losing the gate; they'll tear it down at this rate. We will let them in and then it'll be like shooting fish in a barrel. Get as many archers as you can on those walls." Eireden then turned back to the prince. "Cousin, my sentence was fabricated upon a sham of a trial but even so," he paused and smiled, "I was sentenced to the time of *my* choosing and I have not chosen yet. Until I do you will answer to me."

"I will, my Lord," the old man said. "Here, take my sword. Your grandfather, my uncle, gave it to me forty years ago and it is as sharp now as it was then." The prince unbuckled his sword and presented it.

Eireden took it up with a flourish and suddenly a cry went up, "The King! The King!"

Men who were running for the battle stared, while others wept and tried to kneel before him. "Form your lines!" he bellowed. "We'll let the maug in if they want to dine on steel so badly." Seconds later the lines were formed around the gate and Eireden called for the great doors to be opened. When they were closed they were as stout as any part of the wall, but when open they were only as strong as their hinges and these weren't strong at all, not with the forces straining at them.

The gate swung open and in rushed the goblins, but just as they did they were showered with arrows from every direction and their attack faltered. However those that wavered were pushed from behind and they came on again. Suddenly lights flashed and blasted all about them and the maug stopped a second time in fear. Everyone had forgotten about the fairies. They zoomed in and zoomed out again and right behind them came another wave of arrows. The dead maug were in piles that the living had to stumble over and when they did they met the cold steel of the prince's personal guard.

The Den lines held firm in the face of the weak attack and into the trap more maug came, fighting against those desperate to get away. It was a slaughter of frightful proportions.

"We should have done this the first time they attacked," Gamelling said. His mood was now downright jovial at seeing the death of so many of his enemies. Eireden gave him a look and the prince answered it. "Oh yes. Ten days ago we endured a frightful assault. I've never seen so many goblins in all my life. It was touch and go I have to say. They came at us from all sides."

"Then this tactic wouldn't have worked," Eireden said. "This wasn't a planned assault. They have no scaling ladders, no grappling hooks, no mantlets, nothing. This was wishful thinking on their part. They saw the gate open and they came on. I think it's time we mounted as many men as possible. When they begin to pull back we'll give them a charge or two, but don't let your men get out of hand. I'll..."

Eireden paused as he saw a scout nearby. She stood with an empty quiver and the bow in her hands shook. He couldn't help but smile at her. When he did she rushed at him and threw herself to her knees in front of him. "My king. I never thought..." began Generai through her tears.

"Stand, my scout," Eireden said. "One does not kneel on the field of battle, not even before a king."

"Command me," she whispered and gripped his hand with all her strength.

"Gather my horses. Those two by the trough. You may ride with me."

She was off in a shot and by the time she came back, forcing her way through the gathering knights, the maug were on the verge of retreat. After so much punishment it didn't take much but the specter of the mounted men to get the goblins already within the city clamoring to get out. The entire lot of them broke and forced their way past those still coming in from the forests. Bodies were quickly cleared and a lane made and out poured the knights on fresh horses.

The goblins fled shrieking before the bright mail and gleaming swords. Eireden rode across the wide sweep and slew without tire, but he made sure to keep his men in check.

Yes, they had won a terrific victory, but it was against only a small portion of the full maug army. He let them ride down all upon the plain but did not let them near to the forests which were dark with his enemies. He then formed ranks and rode back in stately lines of five to the cheering of the people and warriors of Hildoeven.

Already teams of men had cleared the gate of the dead and more were piling the maug in heaps out on the plain. These would be set alight to burn throughout the night—the smell would be atrocious.

As he approached the walls the word, "King" ran through the crowds and when he broached the gate cheers erupted. The people of Hildoeven had been besieged for two weeks and this one man was the first reinforcements that they had received. To some it didn't seem that they'd need more.

Generai kept to his side and her proud grey eyes flashed when some called to her. Though they dimmed somewhat when out of nowhere the family of fairies swarmed him, each whistling and going on about the part they played in the battle. Tissa, who had stayed out of much of it came up and touched the pearl around his neck and set it alight. Then for luck the family flew about touching him and the pearl.

"Where are Ella and Aric?" Generai asked, blinking and ducking a little as the fairies swooped in and out. "And Furen? Are they jailed still?"

"No. Furen is a master delver if there ever was one," he answered. "He dug us out of the prison and with a little help we escaped. Ella and Aric are somewhere in the Forbidden Lands and Furen has gone home to present his flower to his girl."

"Oh...then how did you get all these fairies to help you?"

Eireden laughed as he dismounted. "They think I'm part of the family. They call me 'Father Den'. Lord Gamelling? Please tell me that the Lady Norafin has another thirty or so pearls *laying* about." The prince was eyeing the fairies warily. The saying in Hildoeven concerning the Sythei was:

a single fairy was considered lucky—an entire family was trouble.

"I'll make sure that she does," he said swallowing audibly.

# Chapter 17

## Eireden

As Eireden went with Prince Gamelling to the modest palace he noticed some remarkable changes to Hildoeven. Where the buildings had once been humble little wooden affairs unadorned and unspectacular they were now beautiful, colorful, vibrant. Springs ran along the cobblestone lanes and emptied into glowing fountains. Music drifted down the streets—different songs on different streets and when they came together it became a wonderful mixture of notes.

Eireden paused at one intersection and leaned this way and that enticed by a new song in each ear. "What has happened here?"

"The fey," the prince answered. "They have been feathering their nests so to speak. They have been busy as beavers decorating and adding 'touches' to everything. I can't complain. The city has never looked as beautiful. And it keeps them busy. There is much sorrow among them."

"What were their casualties?"

"You don't want to say this too loudly, but it wasn't bad," Gamelling said in a whisper. "Certainly not as bad as it could have been. About eight-hundred dead or missing, leaving a good forty-eight hundred left here in Hildoeven. As I said, it could have been worse. It could have been worse for us as well. They are the perfect guests, especially in a siege. They barely eat and they've planted all sorts of trees that sprout fruit at the drop of a hat, so we don't have to worry as much about starving."

"I will need to speak to their leaders as soon as possible," Eireden replied. He then stared around him. "Where are all the fey? How come they weren't at the battle? Not that they were needed." The battle had been so one sided that the Den had lost only four men.

The prince rolled his eyes. "They won't fight. They decided that it is better to die with their souls intact than to live as little better than the maug."

"Is that how they see us?" Eireden growled. "No better than the maug?"

The prince could only shrug as they went into the palace.

Dinner was a lively affair, but only because the fairies started a food fight. Otherwise it was dull. Sieges had a habit of bringing out the worst in people and the captains at the table were quiet after Gamelling read his dispatches from Eirowyth which basically said they were on their own. This wasn't much of a surprise. The siege was a loose one, seemingly easy to break and it was clear that the demon was hoping a relieving army would try to force its way through. To Eireden the trap was obvious and he was glad that Eirowyth wasn't falling for it. A few bad reverses and the maug could threaten the capital even with its strategic position.

Gamelling thought that his only recourse was to shore up his walls and hold on as best as possible. Eireden had other plans. After the food fight—as much to keep them busy as anything else— he directed the fairies to fan out in search of the maug. He needed hard numbers on his enemy. His own numbers were slim indeed. About a thousand regular army troops and another two thousand reservists was all he had to work with, and these last were middle-aged men or teenage boys.

After dinner the fey came in led by two females that he had seen in the battle of the Feylands. They were introduced as Feylon Darania and Alseya Bellesarus. "Can you tell me where my son Aric is? Does he yet live?" Feylon asked immediately, not at all recognizing protocol. As he was introduced as 'The Rightful King ' she should have curtsied to him.

"He is alive, Milady. And well," Eireden answered giving

her an odd little bow.

The striking Alseya with her white eyes dropped into a proper curtsey and said, "Then I take it that he isn't still being held prisoner?"

"He was freed even as I was by our good friend Furen Traganfel. Aric is now in the Forbidden Lands with Eleanor Belmont." This news relaxed the two considerably. Eireden didn't give them too much time to relax however. "There was a battle at the gates this evening and not a single fey was present to lend a hand. I have to say that after all our sacrifices I was very disappointed at this. From now on all fey will answer the summons to battle. You will be given positions to man—battle stations as it were—and you'll be expected to stand shifts on the wall just as the Den are currently. Not only that..."

"Excuse me Milord," Feylon interrupted. "We are not your warriors to command."

Eireden looked at her coldly, disliking the interruption. "Not only that you will limit the use of magic to strictly military applications."

"Our 'magic' as you call it is ours to use as we see fit," Feylon countered, her gold eyes flaring.

"Not as long as you are within these walls," Eireden said. "If you wish to use magic do so outside of them, but don't expect to be let back in." This brought on a very uncomfortable silence and the men and fey looked around in shock.

"You cannot do this," Feylon said in a low tone.

"I can. The ancient oath made by the Den is broken. We swore to protect the world from the fey by keeping you within the Feylands. As well we swore to protect the fey by keeping others out. That oath is broken and for that I am truly sorry. However now that it is broken I will look to protect my own—and I will protect those fey that ally themselves with the Den and none other."

His words sounded harsh even to his own ears, but he

knew them to be a necessity. He had seen the numbers of maug during the battle of the Feylands, he had felt the power of the demon, and he knew the inadequacy of the walls of Hildoeven. They had been breached once before and the city had been put to the sword. That had been over a thousand years ago and the only additional defense in all that time was the construction of the dry moat. At least he wouldn't have to worry about the demon constructing rolling towers.

"Do you not realize what could happen if you have us fight?" Feylon said. "Have you honestly forgotten what happened to the elves? War will turn our hearts black. War will make us worse even than the maug."

"Are you asking if I know my own history," Eireden returned. "I do and it is why that I'm not suggesting that you actually fight. My men need healers. I need illusions to confuse our enemies and veil our movements. I need enchantments to restore vigor in tired soldiers and light to fight by. And I need reconnaissance. I need to know when they will attack and from what direction. Those of you who are unwilling to do these simple things will be asked to leave."

Eyes flicked around the room and the fey went stone silent, all save Alseya Bellesarus, "We accept your terms as just."

Eireden let out a breath. He had been bluffing. There was no way he could send out the fey to be slaughtered right in front of his own gates. "Good. I ask that every fey stand a shift once per day. You will need to sort them out according to their abilities. Where we have..." A sudden shout from outside the room stopped his words. "Generai, can you find out what's going on?"

The scout had dined with her lord and all through the dinner she had kept quiet, only casting furtive glances at the man she loved. Now she hopped up, but before she could get to the door a man-at-arms burst in. "Milord! There is an envoy of the maug at the gate. They are challenging the...the...you Milord."

"Is that right?" Eireden said calmly.

"They have no claim!" Generai said, turning back to her king. "The captain of the maug challenged already. He slew valiant Cassidor. You need not accept."

"He called our lord the 'False King'," the soldier said in harsh angry tones. "He has to accept! Who can refuse such an insult?"

Lienhart stood forth. "By your leave I will fight as your champion. You are fresh from battle and weary."

Eireden sat back in his chair, musing. First, a captain of the maug slew Cassidor? That seemed impossible on the face of it. Cassidor, though of lower birth, was a great man, strong and hard, very capable with the sword. Second, Lienhart wanted to act as champion? This was not unheard of. A king, especially one without an heir, frequently had another act as champion. However it was the look in Lienhart's eyes that gave Eireden pause. The man didn't think he would win.

"Tell the maug I will be down when I have finished my council and after a glass of wine." Generai began to protest but he held up a hand. After the soldier left he told the scout, "I have no intention of fighting tonight. So rest your worries for a time."

This did little to mollify her, and the constant biting of her lip had him wondering who this maug captain was. Perhaps the demon was leading the army in person. If so it would be unwise for Eireden to accept the challenge, at least not without some sort of knowledge as to the thing's capabilities. Eireden allowed Gamelling and Lienhart to wrap up the remainder of the meeting with the fey. They discussed numbers, stations, and logistics and all the while Eireden thought about this challenge.

Challenges almost always worked in favor of the Den. Usually when a maug army came boiling up from the hidden depths of the Demorlaik they were led by some fell beasty or a maug of greater than average size. Slaying this captain would demoralize the rest, frequently making the battle that followed a perfunctory and grisly repetitious slaughter. This did not seem to be one of those times.

After the meeting the fey were strangely nervous and hung around, accepting wine from their hosts. Eireden had little time to enjoy his one moment of relaxation. His new 'family' started to trickle in with word about the maug dispositions and only Easa-see understood the necessity of brevity when relating military matters. The rest would regularly intersperse their reports of maug formations and numbers with descriptions of interesting flowers that they had come across or the devilish pranks they had played—sometimes on the maug, sometimes on Eireden's own soldiers!

The worst of the lot were Tissa and Sooni. These two fell to braiding his short hair while they told him all about a coconut tree they had discovered. Clearly they had completely forgotten about their mission concerning the maug. When he finished his wine, the king blew the two away with a great breath, which they thought was the height of hilarity, and buckled on his borrowed sword. Unfortunately the news brought by the Sythei was as expected—maug as far as the eye could see heading along the South Stream road and thousands more already in the forest. All of this meant that Eireden couldn't ignore his challenger.

Generai pulled out the braids and wrapped around his shoulders a sable cloak. "There you look the part of king at least," she said. "How any accepts the reign of Eirowyth is beyond me."

"I'm very glad that you made it here safely," Eireden said, "It warms my heart to have someone so close that I can trust entirely. Now, I need to you to hold your tongue on certain subjects; Eirowyth being the chief of these. I am not King yet, not until he accepts my challenge. And keep your mouth closed while I am in parley with our unwelcome guests, the maug. You are too quick to overstep your bounds, Scout." He meant the admonishment, but he touched her cheek to let her know he wasn't truly angry.

"I'll try," she said. "Though on certain subjects I can't make promises."

Eireden gave her a stern look that was all sham and she pretended to quail before it. He summoned his entourage of fairies, set his pearl shining, and went out to the gate. Accompanying the king as he rode through the gates were the two fey women Alseya and Feylon; Prince Gamelling and two of his captains; and finally Lienhart, Generai and the fairies. "Are there any illusions about him?" Eireden asked Alseya.

"Only in the forest beyond," she answered. "He is trying to keep his full strength unknown. Would you like me to try to pierce those illusions? They are skillfully set and will possibly drain me of my strength."

"No. Just let me know if they move. It is a trap only that I fear."

Alone on the plain the maug captain sat atop a black horse. He seemed a pit of darkness in the night and no light glinted anywhere upon him. The Den stopped a dozen paces from the lone being. Eireden said nothing; instead he blew a gust of air at Tissa and sent her spinning and giggling. Having the fairies nearby was relaxing. They were so quick to laugh they made him want to laugh as well and what's more they reminded him of Ella in their innocence.

"I suppose I was wrong," the dark being said, making Eireden and those around him flinch. Despite its size, its voice was that of some sort of malignant child—high and sickly sweet. Eireden knew the voice. He had heard it the night he had first brought Ella to Rhyoeven. "I was wrong when I called you a 'False King'. You are a king. All hail the King of the Sythei."

Eireden said nothing.

The creature kicked his horse forward, coming under the light of the fairies and all could now see the charred and cracked looking face. His eyes were all a jet black. "Well Sythei King, I challenge you. I call you coward and usurper—false King of the Den."

"What are you exactly?" Eireden asked. "I know you are not a demon for there are others like you. I don't think that it would be right to accept a challenge until I know what you are. After all you could be feeble-minded. Your attack earlier certainly suggested I faced an adversary of limited intelligence and it just wouldn't be right to kill a simpleton."

"You would know what I am?" the creature asked. "You might call me the new Den. I am what will replace you when you and your people are long gone. And as for an attack...that was no attack. That was just a couple of my more excitable toys getting out of hand. You'll know when the real attack comes for my army will cover this plain and it won't be the gate only that you have to fear will fall. It will be all of it. We will attack every inch of your walls simultaneously in one great unstoppably wave."

"That sounds positively terrifying," Eireden remarked blandly. Inwardly he was hoping the battle would go just as the creature suggested. A straightforward attack with some scaling ladders would be to the Den's advantage. What would be more to their advantage was if he could kill this thing. It would send a message—a message of woe and despair throughout the maug. With their numbers he needed every advantage he could get. "I accept your challenge, sir..." Eireden paused, waiting for the creature to give his name.

"I will give you my name when I am standing over your dying body, Fairy King," the creature sneered in its high voice. "Send your minions back and you will learn it soon enough."

"No, I don't think so," Eireden replied as nonchalantly as he could—that voice was just too freaky for his attitude to be anything but faked. "We'll meet a week from today. I have a lot of catching up to do. Parties mainly, I'm sure you understand. We have time; your army is strung out half way across the Hidden Lands. We'll set it for nine in the morning. I'd like to get a good night sleep and maybe have some breakfast first." It wasn't uncommon in a siege to put off challenges. Eireden knew their situation was tenuous and he needed all the time he could bargain for.

The creature considered and then said, "Are you afraid of the dark, Fairy King? Or do you think that I will blanch and wilt in the sun? If so you think again. The sun will not avail you. Not a ray will light upon this grass and alas for you I will be at my full strength." The creature came even closer and Eireden's horse tossed his head at the aroma of it—a pungent acrid smell. "Oh, how I hope you are worthy, Den. Let me show you the honor I bestow upon those that I have found worthy." He pulled back his black cloak and upon his dark mail hung a necklace of teeth. Mostly they were troll fangs but a few were even bigger; huge even.

"You will find me more than worthy," he said to the creature. However just then Eireden didn't feel at all worthy and for some reason he had trouble pulling his eyes from the great fangs. Some were nearly a foot long and wickedly sharp. The only beast he knew with fangs like that was a dragon. *He has slain a dragon*! The thought would haunt the king during the sleepless nights that followed.

## Chapter 18

## Ella

Taking his eyes off the expansive heavens above Aric shot Ella a glance. "Why do want to find your mother?" he asked. "She's going to be an elf just as Darhmael and she'll be just as evil. There is no other way."

"You don't know," Ella replied, moving her toes closer to the fire; the night was beginning to cool. "She could have been innocent and maybe forced against her will to have me. Perhaps magically so."

"By that same rationalization Darhmael could be the innocent one," Aric said. "Magically forced against his will to...you know." He gave her a nudge with his shoulder and she felt a blush coming on which only grew worse when he added, "Though if your mother looked anything like you it wouldn't take much magic or much in the way of forcing."

She beamed at him and then sighed. "So will you come with me to find my mother?"

"Where you go, I go," he answered. "I never want to be separated from you again, even if it means adopting Whip-wip as my first child."

"First? How many children do you want?" she said with a laugh.

"I have no number in mind," Aric replied. "The majority of fey will have only one child, which is why there are so few of us left. We have a negative birth to death ratio. But I've never given it much thought. I want as many as you want. If that number is fifty then fifty it is."

"Hey! Slow down now," Ella said, shoving him away playfully. "You keep on your side of the fire. I'm not ready to push out a litter just yet. Wait, that makes me think of another question: how long do fey mothers carry their children inside them? Is it nine months like a normal...I mean like humans?"

"No. We like our infants as fully formed as possible,"

Aric answered. "So the average is only three years. We want them to be able to walk out..."

"Stop that!" Ella yelled so that the fairy shot up in alarm. "Whip-wip, he's trying to scare me. Get him!" Ella began throwing the grass of her bed at Aric and the bleary-eyed fairy was quick to join in.

When he was covered and the fairy glowed pink with the fun, Aric surrendered. "Ok—ok. I was joking. It's actually eleven months more or less, and even then fey babies are small. Only a few pounds, I think you'll be ok."

"Eleven months? That still seems a long time especially for such a small baby." Ella put her hands on her own flat stomach feeling suddenly broody for babies. She shook the thought off. She wasn't even married yet after all—or as the fey put it bonded. Though the term had such an eternal permanence to it that it Ella couldn't say she cared for it. *Bonded*...she preferred the human term: marriage. It just sounded more romantic.

"How are the fey bonded?" she wondered aloud. "Is there a ceremony? Does the bride wear white...and no smart-aleck answers. I'm serious. Is there a ring involved? Because I don't mind telling you that I would rather like a ring."

"If you want rings I will give you one for each finger and two for every toe," Aric answered. "I see you even have them for your ears. I will give you one for each and one for your nose as well." She swatted him. "Ok, no nose ring. As for being bonded to another, yes there is a ceremony and it is beautiful and quite literally magical. Our families and friends gather and there is light and flowers and music and love. It is a most wondrous time."

"Then all the more reason to find my mother, don't you think?"

"I suppose."

So it was decided and the next morning they rode with more urgency. If there were any clues to her heritage they either lay beneath the haunted city of the Demorlaik, with her father, or east in Idaho where she had been given up for adoption. Idaho seemed like a better and safer place to start; only it was three-hundred miles away.

It took six days of riding through hard lands just to get to Spokane and they were some of the best days of Ella's life. Each morning she greeted the sunrise in the arms of her new love and each night she clung to him for warmth; and found a great deal of it. They lived off the land and with a fey and a fairy with her it was no problem, though with her skills increasing Ella could have made it without them.

On that sixth day of their trip Ella flew. She had been exercising her mind every day, but had not tried to fly, afraid she would embarrass herself. Finally she felt her magic strong enough to give it a try and willed herself nine and three-quarters feet from where she stood. Whip-wip was beside herself with joy and urged Ella to do more, showing just how easy it was as she barely flapped her wings to stay aloft.

"But I don't have wings, silly!"

The fairy didn't care and suggest Ella flap her arms. Aric, too was excited and he had her practicing using her mind and body at the same time. With a strenuous leap her distance doubled. Whip-wip flew next to her clapping her hands and hooting encouragement.

Though her base telekinetic power grew both in strength and endurance, her actual spell ability was less than childish—it was infantile in its development. Most spells, Aric explained, took many years of study and practice to gain proficiency in. There were exceptions to this. Spells that involved the physical, such as healing, were far easier to attune the mind to and Ella's eyesight, hearing, and smell became fantastic.

She could spot a crow at half a mile against a forest backdrop. They were always on the lookout for crows, though after a few days the danger seemed less and less. Her ability to read the earth also grew. This became especially true in the forest where she could feel the lightest scampering of a shrew at distances over a mile.

Despite the fact that he was impressed, Aric had expected exactly these results. "Who knows how much power you will ultimately gain, you are an elf after all."

"Perhaps I should fear my power," Ella said. "There's a saying here in America: Power corrupts and absolute power corrupts absolutely."

"The power didn't corrupt the elves," Aric said quietly. "What they did with their power corrupted them. If you stay true to yourself, Ella, you won't have a worry."

On that sixth day they were forced to wait for nightfall—horses weren't the most common form of transportation in Spokane—before they stole into the edge of the suburbs and came to Ella's adoptive parent's home. She loved them and maybe loved them more now that she knew she was adopted. It took special people to adopt a child and raise her as one of their own. Yet despite that love, Ella kept her and Aric's heritage a secret. She had him cover himself in a slight illusion to hide his ears and golden hair. The Belmonts, meat and potato kind of people, would never understand.

Ella even had to hide Whip-wip, who grumbled mightily over this. Restrictions on a fairy never set well with them. "It'll just be the night. Here, you can pass the time working on my pearl. It still won't light." For some reason this seemed to mollify the fairy, which gave Ella a cause for concern. What sort of prank was Whip-wip up to by agreeing so readily to "fix" the pearl? Would it give off a skunk smell when pressed? Or maybe it would explode in mucus? There was no way to tell with the sly little creature.

"Be good," Ella warned. Whip-wip gave her the most innocent of looks. There would be trouble, no doubt about it.

The evening with the Belmonts was sweet and relaxing. Ella and Aric were fed to the point of bursting and then came the questions: Where was Aric from? How did the two of them meet? Was this serious, what they had between them?

"Yes, quite serious," Ella answered. "The most serious, you could say."

Dave Belmont gave her daughter's left hand a meaningful look and said, "It can't be too serious. I don't see a ring."

"If you want to know the truth, I've been promised...let's see, thirty-three rings." Ella couldn't help smiling when she said this. "Ten for my fingers. Twenty for my toes. Two for my ears and one for my nose. Hey, did you know that rhymes?"

"Is this what counts for human poetry?" Aric replied.

"*Human* poetry?" Dave asked. "That's an odd thing to say. What do you mean by that?"

Ella and Aric looked at each other in a slight panic. "Aric simply has very high standards when it comes to poetry," Ella stammered out. "There is normal human level and then there is a supernatural level, you might say."

This pathetic explanation seemed good enough and for the rest of the evening they dodged question after question. The Belmonts were so very excited as to this new man in Ella's life that they far over stepped their bounds by bringing out Ella's baby pictures and then worse, her middle school pictures. These had captured, for all time, how the end of the eighties had wreaked havoc upon her fashion sense.

Though she was mortified into a wide-eyed silence, Aric only smiled broadly and asked for more. He even kept his wits about him and asked to see what sort of adoption information they had for Ella. Unfortunately there wasn't much save for a few scraps of meaningless paper from the Adams County Department of Health and Welfare. None of which came close to giving the names of her real parents. This should have been expected, but Ella felt a letdown all the same. It meant another journey and likely another dead end.

## Chapter 19

## Eireden

Eireden slept little for the next few nights. Not only because of the strange black creature wearing the dragon teeth, but also because there was just so much to be done. Before his arrival, Prince Gamelling and the people of Hildoeven seemed almost resigned to their fate. They had stocked up on arrows and sharpened their swords and had done little else. This sort of passive defense wasn't at all to the liking of the new king.

He immediately set the entire town into motion. Women and children, as well as the very old and the very young were put to work. He had the streets dug up and the cobblestones were carried one by one and set in little stacks all about the walls. A ten-pound stone throne from eighteen feet up could kill more readily than an arrow. Wood was called for and people stripped their houses of flooring and interior walls, some brought even their tables and beds. From this hodge-podge of materials towers were constructed at weak points along the walls.

Every pick and shovel in the town were employed in the most arduous, and dangerous work. Outside the walls the sound of digging went on day and night. The dry ditch had been left untended for far too many years. Its sides had eroded into gentle slopes and its depth was far too shallow for Eireden's liking. For a dry moat to be effective it had to be deep and V shaped. Teams of soldiers traded shifts—half of them digging, turning their heads back every now and then to the long dark plain, half of them standing a wary guard as they recouped their strength.

The fey worked as well, more physically than magically. Surprisingly the restrictions on magic use had gone over without an argument. Part of this was due to the efforts of Alseya and Feylon who were able to impress upon their people the need to refrain from wasting their energies on frivolous things, but mostly it was due to Eireden. He had saved them before when things seemed beyond saving and now he had come again in a black hour. His very presence was an inspiration to them—an inspiration to live.

With their quick hands and dexterous fingers, the fey made excellent fletchers. Not only could they make arrows at a marvelous speed, they could do so turning out far superior quality, even compared to the best Den fletchers. They were superior bowman as well and they went about re-stringing and fine-tuning the bows of the Den making them deadlier than before.

The king even set the fairies to work. This was a minor miracle in itself, since the words: *work* and *fairy* went as well together as the words: *fire* and *water*. So he played to their strengths. The one area of expertise every Sythei excelled in was that of being a nuisance. He set his family upon the maug army with the instructions: Make them cry. It was a challenge that every one of them was up to, except Tissa. The fairy was tiny even compared to her brothers and sisters and Eireden couldn't bear the idea of her being hurt. He set her upon a new mission, one designed to keep her well away from the battle.

"Am I being silly?" he asked Generai six very long days later. He had chosen the scout to act as his second in the coming challenge. Lienhart or one of the other captains would've been a better choice but they couldn't be spared from their labors and not only that, Generai wouldn't leave his side. "That I care so much about that one little fairy? With all the death in the offing, I'm worried over her; it's strange."

"Or sweet," Generai replied, putting in another stitch to his armor. "You did say that they had adopted you. I'm sure you would act the same way with your youngest child. Or maybe...raise your arms." He was having a set of plate mail fitted for his coming battle. The seams were still too tight in the shoulders and she began to let them out. "Or maybe you look on her as one of your subjects. You are not a normal king of the E-den you know. The king has always held authority over the Den alone, maybe being Eireden...*The* Eireden you are king of more than just the Den."

"We both know I'm not even king of the Den," he said. "I will only be so if Eirowyth accepts my challenge and if I defeat him."

"Yes, well, first you still have to defeat that horrible creature...and then defeat an army of maug...and then there's the demon. We can't forget him. So after all that, Eirowyth should be a snap...if he doesn't just throw you in prison on sight."

"Thanks for cheering me up," Eireden laughed. He swung his arms back and forth. "Could you remove the plates behind my shoulders? They're too constricting. And those along my back as well." A challenge was a different sort of fight than a normal battle where he could be attacked from every angle. If the charred creature had an opportunity to strike from behind—for whatever reason—Eireden would be in trouble plating or no plating. Besides, as big and powerful as Eireden was, he was actually quicker than he was strong and he was strong indeed. In a challenge he liked to fight as light as possible using that deft quickness in place of heavy armor.

"Less armor! You should be adding more armor," Generai said. "Did you see that thing? It was steel, head to toe."

Eireden had studied the armor of his opponent closely. It was quality workman ship, but like all armor there were weak spots. "I am not likely to strike his toe, so I would consider that a waste. Trust me and remove the plates. I will wear a short cloak so it won't be obvious."

Generai grumbled a bit under her breath but did as she was told. Eireden let her grumble. He stared out of the window that looked over the east wall. Ella was in the east where the sun was still hours from coming up. He could feel her still, but she was far away. How far away did she have to go before he wouldn't feel her?

"Will she come back?" Generai asked in a quiet voice. She kept her eyes down to the armor when she asked this.

"Yes, I fully believe she will," Eireden answered. "She'll come back, but we may be long dead by the time she does. Or at least old and grey."

The scout shook her head. "Not if you win. If you slay this creature and kill the demon and regain your throne she'll be back sooner than that, and what then?"

"I don't know. She'll probably go with Aric into the Feylands—the new Feylands I mean. I suspect that they will want to rebuild their lands somewhere else. My personal opinion is that the forests just north of Varisgard would be suitable if they wish to try the same sort of illusions. Why do you ask? Are you worried that I'll go all gaga the second she comes strolling in, if so I think you are wrong."

"You accepted the rope because of her," Generai said. "That's what the rumor is. People say that she has some sort of power over you."

Eireden laughed suddenly. "People said the same thing about my mother! You can't listen to what the rumor mills put out. I took the rope not because of Ella but because of Aric. It was his life I was trying to save. And even then I took it because I saw no way out. I figured I was done and I wanted my death to have some positive outcome."

"Oh...I didn't know." She stood there quietly for a moment and then she burst out in a rush, "Will you have dinner with me tomorrow...at my house...with my father I mean and me too of course?"

"I don't know. I could be busy then," Eireden answered. "If I live through the morning I'll likely be fighting a horde of screaming maug in the evening. And I have a hair appointment."

"A hair appointment...what do you mean?" She looked bewildered for a moment and then broke into a nervous smile. "That was a joke. I'm sorry. I think I'm just too anxious to laugh at anything. Do you really think they'll attack in the light of day?"

"Only if this captain can control the weather and I'm worried that he can. Yet if I slay him, they likely won't attack until night and if so then yes, I will dine with you." Eireden had far more important people he could have dined with and the meal would likely start the rumor mills flying once again. All that being said, he owed this girl much. She was loyal when everyone else had turned their backs and she had loved him when his life was worth less than dirt. "Your father is the candle maker? He is a sweet old gent and never said a cross word to me when I was *gada*. Just be warned however, it will be a quick meal."

Her eyes gleamed wet. "Of course you've got so much to take care of. I'll make sure that it's something light...or heavy if you're hungry...I'll make sure there are both. I should go tell him. He'll be so excited." With that she rushed out leaving his armor unstitched. The king took up the needle. It wouldn't be the first time he stitched his own clothes.

## Chapter 20

## Eireden

Just before dawn a heavy bank of grey cloud descended upon Hildoeven and hung low on the battle plain surrounding the town. It sometimes mixed with a dark fog that lay swirling over the soft grasses. Every Den city lay encircled by smooth flat battle plains. They kept armies from "sneaking up" on the cities and they allowed easier use of cavalry, this being the strongest arm of any Den army.

From his window, Eireden stared at the clouds with worry. There would be no sunlight just as the creature had said.

In front of him sat a plate of eggs that he had picked at, and around him, scattered in little clumps lay his family of sythei; all of them sleeping off the exhaustion of their mission to irritate the maug. They had returned at about four in the morning, each too tired to tell their tales which meant they were tired indeed. Only little Tissa hadn't returned yet and strangely this was affecting him more than his upcoming duel, though he knew not why.

Eventually he gave thought to his breakfast and shoveled the rest of the food into his mouth, not tasting a thing but knowing he would need the calories. He would need his strength.

A knock at the door and there stood Generai in her leathers. She had taken the time to buff them into respectability. "It's almost time. You should get suited up." Her lips were drawn and her eyes nervous, yet she had never looked better. Her blonde hair lay plaited upon her back and she stood tall, strong, but whip thin. In all she looked the proper woman of the Den and Eireden threw off any lingering regrets at having her second him.

Eireden pulled on his armor over his simple white tunic and strapped it tight. Next he placed his helm upon his head. It was of simple unadorned steel with a sliding visor. His challenger had worn a winged helm. It had been artfully done; in fact it was striking in its beauty. It was foolish. What use the extra weight? What use the decorative wings? They would catch a blow instead of deflecting.

But those dragon teeth...

They meant he wasn't someone to take lightly. The heavy clouds also spoke of this. Was he a witch? Probably. How much of his power went into creating the clouds? Maybe none, but who knew?

When he was dressed, Generai unexpectedly woke the fairies. "Sythei come bid your king, good luck," she commanded and oddly they obeyed. Each hopped up and touched Eireden, most touching the pearl as well. They seemed to understand that some momentous situation was in the offing and so they settled about Eireden and Generai as the two went to the gate.

Lienhart stood with his black charger. He had armored the great warhorse in shining barding. "Your mount my Lord. You will not find a better in all the Hidden Lands."

"And your shield my King," called a Jeden, captain of the knights, holding a shield—a scarlet dragon embossed over bright steel.

"And my sword you may keep," said Prince Gamelling.

Eireden mounted the charger and took the shield upon his left arm and in his right, the prince's sword. Though he looked every inch the king, he felt like an imposter, or a beggar in his borrowed armor on his borrowed horse wielding his borrowed sword. He pushed the feeling aside. Now is not the time, he scolded himself.

"Whether I win or lose, you have your orders," he said to the men present. Each of them had two sets of plans drawn up depending on the outcome of the duel. Depending on which way the moral of the men and the maug shifted. "You may not ride upon me my little friends," Eireden said to the fairies as he and his second made their lonely way through the gates. "Nor may you take part in this battle. No matter what. Even if I lose you must stay with Generai."

Once more the fairies touched Eireden for luck and then they draped themselves over the scout and her horse. The sight made the king smile. "Try not to move," he joked. "You might squish one."

She couldn't laugh, however. "Win," she said.

Eireden dropped his visor and cantered forward and there was the creature, seeming fell and menacing in his black armor. His mount, the color of coal, was decked in black barding and it pawed eagerly, almost hungrily at the grass of the plain. Around the creature the mists tried to envelop him, tried to hide him, while the mists around Eireden gave way and he felt exposed in his scrounged up trappings.

No useless words came between the two opponents; there was just an empty silence save for the beating of Eireden's heart. This came to his ears as a steady thump that increased with tempo every second that he sat there waiting. Now the creature drew his sword and its glinting metal was a surprise to the king. He had fully expected a black sword to go along with the black dagger at his hip. Strangely the silver of the sword's edge was reassuring; it would be easier to pick up against the black backdrop.

Eireden drew his own sword in answer and kicked the charger forward, but there came a pause from the beast. This drew a high mocking laugh from the creature. The charger was indeed a fine animal but he was clearly unnerved by the sight in front of him.

"This is our duty," he said patting the charger's trembling neck. "Whether we live or die, we do our duty. Now go!" With that Eireden spurred the charger on, taking firmer control, and he rode the horse as only an expert could— straight to its death. The two opponents came at each other in a headlong charge, each with sword raised. The king easily tracked the silver sword of his enemy and brought up his shield in an effortless block, while with his own sword he looked to find the crease between the shield and horse of the black rider.

This was Eireden's element. Swordsman against swordsman; skill against skill, and so far, he saw in the black creature over confidence and minor deficiencies in capability. So far he saw no reason at all that he would lose.

However...

At the last second, just before the two came together in a thunderous crash, he noted that the silver sword of his enemy gleamed too much—there was more light upon its edge than was possible, except by magic. Too late to do anything he tried to get his own strike in first, but the silver sword smote his shield and the light upon its edge flashed down with a deafening crack—sending out an electrical charge that coursed in a burning wave down Eireden's left arm, through his left leg and into the barding of the charger.

And then Eireden went flying as his mount pitched forward and collapsed. The poor beast spasmed and jerked on the grass as its body burned and smoldered from the electrical charge.

The black creature enjoyed the death of the charger. It sat atop its mount wearing a nasty smirk; inadvertently or perhaps uncaringly giving Eireden precious seconds to gain his feet. The electricity had burned his arm and leg, but for the most part it had passed along his armor harmlessly. Still he struggled to get up—an act that he hoped would pay dividends.

A second later the creature charged again. This time the king was careful to keep an eye out for the sword; thankfully it gleamed dully under the heavy clouds and so he took the creature's heavy blow upon his shield. Though there wasn't electricity in the attack there was still magic. The sword crashed down as if it weighed a hundred pounds and not the ten that it really did. The unexpected power behind the blow bent his shield in and drove the king to his knees.

The power of the creature was unexpected, still the king didn't panic. From his keeling position he rolled under the horse where the armored barding didn't reach and with one vicious blow disemboweled the creature's steed. Now it was the creature thrown from his mount, but Eireden didn't wait to gloat as his opponent had. He leapt to his feet and charged. Unfortunately, his quickness was only equaled by the creature, who was up in a flash.

Eireden couldn't afford to pause even a second and struck hard and fast. His first blow should have cleaved the black helmet in two, but instead it only sheared off one of the decorative wings. His second attack slid beneath the plates beneath the chin and should have slit the black throat. Neither caused so much as a scratch. Magic had foiled both. Still it became quickly obvious that Eireden was the better fighter. His footwork put him in a more balanced stance so that his attacks came with his full might. His skill with the shield allowed him to deflect tremendous blow after tremendous blow. Though his arm rang with the vibrations and ached down to his bone and though his shield was rent in many places it kept him whole. And his sword work kept his opponent retreating making his attacks far less that they would have been.

"Enough!" cried the creature. He put forth his hand and suddenly the grass all about Eireden erupted upward becoming thick as vines and these reached out for him with a thousand arms. He turned only to find a wall of this bewitched grass behind him. His sword slashed low across them and machete-like he cut a swath through it only to be caught up short with the real grass of the plain just in front of him. The vines had him by the throat, while more had his left arm almost covering over the buckled shield.

Quickly his vision dimmed as his blood was cut off in his neck and the veins of his face bulged and pulsed. He was seconds from blacking out and came to the realization that he would have to lose his shield. He had time and strength for only one more swing and with a hacking blow he felt the vine loosen at his neck. This came at the cost of his shield as it became engulfed in the hungry, man-high weeds. Eireden chopped and forced his way out and was given all of a second to recuperate before the creature was on him again.

Hewing at him with devastating blows the creature forced him back and back.

Still Eireden wasn't panicked.

More to the truth he was sad. He knew he would lose this battle. The creature had a reserve of magic that was simply astounding, making Aric look pitiful in comparison. That sadness had him questioning who his people would look to? Who would take care of them? Who would save them? Eirowyth? Probably not.

The answers to these questions, if there were any, would have to wait because suddenly the creature's tactics switched gears and caught the king off guard. When his enemy raised his sword to level another of those bone-rattling blows Eireden raised his own sword, looking to parry as he had been but then without warning he caught a glint of metal sliding in at his midsection, and at the same time the blow coming from above disappeared.

His mind screamed: ILLUSION!

But too late. Torqueing his body to the left helped, yet still the gleaming sword sliced through his mail, split his skin, and ran along his ribs. The pain seared into him. He ignored it. He had to. There was no choice but to ignore the pain and go on and on. The illusion worked well the first time but not so well the second—though his neck came with inches of fully opening up—and the third was almost nothing—a chunk of flesh went missing out of his thigh.

To counter the illusions Eireden attacked with a fury that left him gasping but still alive. However he couldn't keep contact forever and when the creature finally was able to step back a light shot out of his hands and suddenly Eireden felt as though constricting bands had a hold of him. It was his armor. The metal seemed to be shrinking. The first thing that had to go was his helmet. He tore it off and it shattered like glass upon contact with ground. Then his gorget, the armor about his neck began strangling him; he flung it off as well. Then he was in a frenzy to get his cuirass off before it crushed his ribs.

Panting from their fight, the creature watched for a few moments. He had spent a tremendous amount of energy as well as a not inconsiderable amount of blood. The king had scored with many of his attacks but most were little more than scratches because of the creature's magic. "Your teeth I will proudly wear, King of the Den," the creature said before swinging his sword in an over hand chopping arc.

Unable to get the breastplate off Eireden barely got his sword up in time. It hardly mattered. The spell had affected his sword, as well as his armor, and it shattered like glass. The creature's blade then went through Eireden's armor and into his shoulder at the neckline though not deeply. In desperation Eireden grabbed the creature and clung to him, still fighting his own armor one handed.

"Get off," it growled throwing the king to the ground. Now this had the odd happenstance of actually freeing Eireden from the remains of his armor as it shattered. Despite that he laid there waiting the final stroke too exhausted to move. He hoped it would be downward strike right into his heart. It would be quick and relatively painless.

"Who are you?" the king demanded. "You said you would tell me if we found ourselves in this position."

To make that true the creature did indeed come to stand above him, but instead of holding the sword above Eireden's breast he held it above his stomach. The creature didn't want it quick and painless, just the opposite. It opened his mouth to speak and suddenly Eireden didn't care who he was. The creature's position was careless indeed. With a quick kick he saw that he could drive the creature's right knee backwards possibly snapping the kneecap.

Eireden brought his foot back and then paused, dumbfounded when the creature spoke.

"I am Dahrain, first son of Darhmael of the line of Narvai," it said, raising the sword.

The king knew that family line. He had heard it before in the Rea' Edaere—in the great Theater of Ancestral Concordance. It was Ella's line. "You are a fey?" he asked instead of doing the smart thing and breaking that kneecap.

Dahrain laughed in that wicked high manner of his, "No. The fey are pathetic groveling cowards. I am an elf."

An elf! The word bounced around Eireden's mind turning him numb. He is of the Narvai line...and so is Ella. He is an elf and that has to mean...Ella is one too. How was this possible? How could he love a woman with such evil running through her veins? How? How? How! Had she made a fool of him? Had she been in on this from the beginning? A Den in love with an elf. It wasn't possible. Nor was it possible that Ella was related to this...this thing. She was beautiful through to her soul. He had felt it when she had touched his chest. That connection had been honest.

This being of the Narvai line certainly wasn't beautiful or good. Dahrain enjoyed the confusion and pain in Eireden's eyes, but when that ended he decided to strike, only this time he was a hair too late. The King of the Den drove his foot square into the elf's knee sending it snapping backward. It was such a quick move that no magic could have caught up with the blow and the elf went down.

Eireden was on him so fast the elf barely had time to recover his wits. But he did recover enough to let out a blast of pure telekinetic power sending the Den flying. When he landed, Eireden rolled and was up again, far faster than the crippled elf and was on him, pummeling with his fists, tearing at his winged helmet in order to get at the elf. He was in a rage and sought to kill and to rend the elf with his huge powerful hands...only the elf still had his magic and before he knew it light blasted him and he was on his back.

The elf was atop him grinning madly through his bloody teeth. Strangely Eireden couldn't feel his legs. And there was a pulse in his body that beat slower and slower. What was happening? He looked down at himself and there was the gleaming sword of Dahrain. Only the hilts and a few inches of metal could be seen the rest had passed straight through him and into the soft earth.

"I have slain the great Eireden," Dahrain whispered before sending another searing blast of electricity down the sword and into the king's impaled body.

## Chapter 21

## Ella

As the impaled king lay bleeding to death and just seconds before the elf, Dahrain of the line Narvai sent a thousand volts of electricity straight down his sword and into Eireden's body, Ella of the line Narvai turned her left turn signal on.

Like Eireden she hadn't slept well the night before. She was inexplicably nervous about seeing the facility her mom had dropped her off in. For some reason she thought she would be recognized even after thirty years and that people would *know* about her. They'd know she wasn't human. They'd know she was an imposter.

"You seem worried," Aric said from the seat next to her. His green eyes smiled into hers reassuringly and then flicked to the few souls walking the streets of the tiny town of Council, Idaho, population fourteen-hundred and eight. "You should not be. These people cannot hurt you. They are only humans and you are so much more."

"That's not what I'm worried about," Ella said. "I just feel—weird. My life has been one big lie from start to finish, you know? And this is where the first lie began. Somehow an elf was dropped off in this dinky little burg and left on her own. It just seems so...so crazy. Why here? There's nothing here but cows and farms and pickup trucks. What did my father think would happen? He couldn't know who would adopt me. He couldn't know that I would move to Seattle, or that you would dream of me."

"First, I don't think it would have mattered where you were. I would have gone to the ends of the earth to find you," Aric remarked. "And second, I think he knew that I would dream of you because there is a strong likelihood that my dream may have been planted within me. The elves of old wove spells that could be of amazing power, but could also be quite subtle."

"How on earth do you plant a dream?" Ella wondered. "Subtle or not I would think that you would have been able to tell if an evil force was trying to manipulate your mind. If not, we both could have a spell on us right now. Do you think that's possible? Do you think we're running around Idaho simply because my father wishes it?"

"I don't think we're being controlled by Darhmael, not through spell use at least." Aric tapped his head. "I've been questioning all these possibilities just as you and I've come to the conclusion that we are giving too much credit to our enemy. Our fears have made him greater than he is. It is one thing to plant a dream in the unwary, but quite another to try it on someone forewarned. No, it is safe to say that we are here on our own volition."

That was something at least. Ella couldn't stand the idea of being controlled. It made life seem pointless. "There it is," she said, gesturing to a low brick building that had a sign reading: Adams County Department of Health and Welfare, on its side. It was a big sign for a small building. She parked her mom's Ford Escape right beneath it. "We'll let Whip-wip sleep," Ella added as she slipped from the car. The fairy had spent the night exploring Spokane and had come back in the morning looking hung-over.

Feeling jittery inside Ella gave Aric a quick once over. He had covered himself in a simple illusion to hide his ears and attire. Not knowing the correct look he had copied what her father had been wearing at breakfast—plaid shirt and stained khaki work pants. By accident he fit into the surroundings of the welfare office.

A woman, middle-aged and just starting to grow plump, sat behind the desk and greeted them in the natural, friendly way residents of small towns have. However her sweet greeting was offset by the judging look in her eyes. *Is she pregnant? Is he abusive? What trailer park did they just crawl out of?* Were the obvious questions Ella read there in those pale blue eyes. Perhaps this was universal to people who worked in welfare offices, Ella considered. Still the look bothered her.

"Hi. I'm wondering if you can help me," she began in a small voice. "I—I was put up for adoption through this office thirty-one years ago and I was looking to check if there were any records that I could see. I'm trying to find my mom."

"Thirty years-one?" the lady began. "You're thirty-one?" Ella nodded and shrugged at the same time. "Well lucky for you. I would say you don't even look twenty-one. But...I suppose it doesn't matter either way, those records would be sealed. Confidentiality you know."

"After thirty years?" Ella demanded, gaining strength in her words. "That seems unreasonable. Don't you think a mother's right to keep her identity secret is only trumped by a child's right to know who their parents are? I can't see how the one is more important than the other."

"As well the fate of two great nations are at risk," Aric added in perfectly serious tones. "There are thousands of lives in the balance." The woman had opened her mouth to reply to Ella but what Aric said caused her mouth to close with a light click.

Ella laughed suddenly and loudly. Wearing a fake plastic smile, she said, "Oh, he's kidding. Really he's such a jokester. But I do need that information. Do you know what sort of recourse I have?"

The woman still eyed Aric strangely but eventually shrugged and answered, "I'd get a lawyer if I were you since only a judge can help you. Is there some sort of medical issue that you have a question over? Because as far as I have heard it's about the only way you'll get to see those files."

"You could say it was medical. It's a question of genetics that's for certain," Ella answered glumly. She then brightened as an idea came to her. "Aric maybe you could suggest something to her?"

"Such as?" he asked reasonably.

"I don't know," Ella answered with a tight smile at his

reply. "I was just thinking that you are so smart and all and you might be able to come up with a *suggestion*." When he still blinked uncomprehendingly at her she gave him a slight *push* with her mind. It was just a gentle tickle of her telekinetic powers, but still it swayed him back.

The fey frowned at her but then his eyes went a touch wider. "Of course a suggestion."

Misunderstanding what Ella was hinting at, the lady shook her head. "This is matter of principal not of money. We all have a fundamental right to privacy in this country and you won't find me so easy to bribe."

"We are not offering a bribe, Milady," Aric said, gently layering his soft voice with power. "Clearly that would be wrong. I would think that it would be illegal as well. No, we don't want you to do anything illegal."

"Nothing illegal," the lady mumbled. Her face had gone slack and her eyes drooped.

"I find it wonderful as well as coincidental you mentioned that only a judge could help. It just so happens that I am a judge," Aric said, going lighter on the spell's power. The woman looked woozy, swaying in her chair, so Ella came around the desk and prepared to catch her if she fell. Aric went on, "My judgment is that you are good person. Am I right?"

A faint nod was all the answer the fey received and he spoke again going even lighter on the magic. "And a good person would want to help this young lady, I am sure. She is kind and possesses a beautiful soul and the law is designed to help people such as this. Surely that is so."

"Sometimes, your Honor," the woman whispered.

"Yes and sometimes laws are written by dull-witted bureaucrats who can't fathom how these laws hurt the very people who need our help," Aric said. "Thankfully there are judges, such as myself, who can interpret laws to everyone's benefit. This is one of those moments where the good of the many outweigh the good of the few. Now, please go fetch the records in question. Her name is Eleanor. She was adopted by David and Sarah Belmont in July of 1981."

"Eleanor," the woman replied as if she were about to fall asleep. She then stood, before reeling drunkenly out of the room. They both stared after the lady and Ella hoped there weren't any stairs in the small building.

"I might have come on a bit too strong," Aric admitted, sheepishly. "It's just that I'm not used to enchanting humans, or I should say I've never enchanted a human before. I tried with Eireden, remember? My full power wasn't enough, so I gave this lady a good strong dose."

"Will she be ok?" Ella asked. Anxiously she began tapping the desk with her nails.

"Of course. Don't worry about that. It might take a few hours to wear off and in the mean time she'll just be a bit groggy and not quite herself."

Ella took a deep breath. "Oh," she said and then sighed. She took to pacing while Aric eyed her. She grabbed her hair in both hands and asked, "Do you think they'll have any records? Any at all? And what if they don't? What if we came out here and there's nothing? I mean it was thirty years ago. You would think that no one would keep records for thirty years. It would all start to pile up."

Aric looked out the window at the sleepy little town. "I suppose I don't know about this sort of thing. The fey would never give up their children voluntarily. Only through an unexpected death are our children raised in another home. Are there many adoptions in villages such as this?"

"I doubt it," Ella replied. For some reason she didn't know if her answer was a good one or not. Was she even more of a freak because it was such a rare thing out in the country for a woman to give up her baby? Or should she be happy because it made the possibility of finding her mother easier? With her insides churning she clutched her stomach, not knowing if it was better to be hopeful or scared out of her mind.

"Fear not the future," Aric said. "And fear less the past." The fey went to Ella and put his arms around her. He smelled of lilac and cinnamon—a strange and beguiling scent and with his warmth she immediately calmed. She sagged into his lithe body and waited upon the social services lady.

"Here you are, your Honor," the lady said to Aric as she bustled back into the room holding a manila folder. It's very thinness had Ella worried all over again. The lady handed the folder to Aric and he handed it to Ella who looked at it in trepidation. Would this really tell her who her mother was? Would there be a picture of her? Would she have long tapered ears and diamonds for eyes? Was she really an elf? That was the true question: was her mom an elf? For the most part Ella simply didn't feel like an elf. Though she didn't know exactly how that was supposed to feel, she at least figured it would feel different.

A name jumped out at her the second she opened the folder: *Elleni Feyden*. That had to be her mother. There were other names—meaningless names—of bureaucrats and social workers and there was her own name: Eleanor. She had been Eleanor Feyden at one time. And there was Dave and Sara Belmont. She knew their signatures. She knew their address. They were real. The rest of the forms were almost useless; they were filled with bureaucratic jargon and endless legalese. Eagerly she read every line. This was her past. This was her history.

About herself there was little to the paperwork beyond a brief description that read like the sterile questionnaire of a hospital record—Height: twenty-six inches—Weight: nine pounds—Eye color: blue—Hair color: brown.

That was it. Of her mom there was even less. The only description of Elleni Feyden was: *Mother has been deemed mentally incompetent*.

"This part here can't be right," Ella said pointing at the document. "Mentally incompetent. There's no way my mother was mentally incompetent." She turned to Aric. "Right? There's no way a...a...one of us could be mentally incompetent. Have you ever heard of such a thing?"

"No," Aric replied taking the folder and reading it. His green eyes shifted back and forth so quickly on the page that Ella had to blink. "Are they suggesting that your mother was insane?" he asked. "If so, they couldn't be more wrong. Insanity is a human ailment."

"It's drugs, your Honor," the social services lady announced. "When they say 'mentally incompetent' they almost always mean drugs. That or the mother was retarded."

Aric stared at the lady trying to fathom her meaning. Ella had to explain, "Some people ingest or smoke different substances. They sort of alter your perception and make you feel relaxed. Or so I've heard. I have never had the desire to try any of them."

"Yes, now I understand," Aric replied, shaking his head. "No. This sort of activity is something *we* would never do. What did she mean by *retarded*? Is she meaning your mother was limited in some fashion?"

"I'm sorry, your Honor," the lady interjected. "I should have said developmentally disabled. Sometimes I forget what's politically correct."

Her words did little more than to confuse the fey greater than before. "Developmentally disabled usually means that a person was born mentally handicapped," Ella said.

"I see...or I believe so," Aric said. "However, again that isn't something *we* need to worry about. My guess is that your mother was enchanted in some fashion. As this sweet lady has demonstrated, an enchantment can bewilder as well as beguile." He flipped through the pages a second time and then sighed, "There is nothing here that will help us."

"We have a name and that's a start at least," Ella said. She took back the folder and stared down at her mother's name, *Elleni Feyden.*

"I'm sorry, but we don't even have that," Aric replied

grimly.

"What do you mean?" Ella demanded. "Her name is right there: *Elleni Feyden.* It can't be any more plain."

"It's not," Aric said. "Feyden is neither a fey name nor an elf name, it's a Den name. It was the name of Eireden's—the original Eireden's—grandson. He took the name to rule under in order to try to bring about a peace between the two peoples. In the beginning of the ban, fifteen thousand years ago, the fey weren't happy about being stuck in the Feylands. They felt they had been imprisoned for the crime of helping to overcome their own kin. And the Den weren't happy because they were forced to act as jailors rather than go back home to the lands that they had built."

"What about *Elleni*? Is that a name?"

"No, it's from the elvish *Elleney*," Aric said. "It means terminate or kill. Thus your mother's name translates to kill—Fey and Den. A joke of your father's no doubt, but true nonetheless. He used her to bring you about, my love. And you were supposed to be the weapon to end the fey."

"So where does that leave us?" Ella asked.

"It leaves us in Idaho with no clue where to go next," Aric stated.

## Chapter 22

## Eireden

The morning took on a timeless feel for Eireden. Seconds drew out like long shadows while minutes were beyond comprehension over a distant horizon. The blink of his eyes became the slow wave-like motion of a condor's wing and each beat of his great heart, the rhythmic *lub-dub*, betrayed him with the cadence of a watch desperately in need of winding. Each thump came slower and slower and he knew that soon—very soon—they would cease altogether.

There was pain. A haze of it augmented and distorted his consciousness, yet there was also a novelty where pain was concerned. He had never been run through so completely and now he could feel parts of himself—deep parts of himself—that he had never noticed before. The strangest of these ran up along the edge of the elf-sword. It was an artery and with every beat of his heart he could feel his blood course down the blade. Beneath him was pool with edges that grew and grew.

The elf Dahrain leaned over him, straddling the Den's body. The elf gloated. There was dark laughter in his eyes that pained Eireden worse than the sword. He tried to push the elf away, but his arms were losing their strength and the most he could do was paw feebly. With his left hand he felt the slick, blood drenched platemail and with his right he felt the leather of Dahrain's belt, the hilt of his dagger and the velvet of a pouch at his side.

"I have slain the great Eireden," Dahrain whispered. This was true. With his artery slashed open his death was an undeniable fact. This wasn't a small artery like the radial artery in the wrist, this was the descending aorta, one of the largest arteries in the body and was thick around as his thumb. Without help, he would bleed to death in half a minute.

Thirty seconds was too long for Dahrain to wait. With all

that remained of his magical energies the elf sent a great flash of lightening blazing through his hands and down the sword. Every muscle in Eireden's body went taut, galvanized not because of the electricity, but against the searing pain. His insides felt as though they were on fire and the smell of charred flesh came quick to his nostrils.

But amazingly he was alive and what's more, though he was weak, he would grow no weaker. The lightening had passed along the blade and had grounded itself in the earth doing only minimal damage to the Den. Moreover the heat that flashed along the blade, hundreds of degrees worth of heat, actually helped the man. The heat cauterized his wounds so that his internal bleeding stopped immediately.

Over him the elf leaned a second time with an expectant look. But this changed to puzzlement when he saw that the Den still moved and breathed. He came close so that his smell pushed aside the harsh aroma of burnt flesh and stared into the steel-grey eyes of his opponent.

"Why aren't you dead?" Dahrain asked.

"I can't lose..." he whispered this so low that even the elf leaned closer. This was Eireden's only chance. How the lightening spell had helped he couldn't understand, he only knew that he still had some breath in his lungs and just enough strength for one more attack. Eireden's right hand found the handle of the elf's dagger, while his left caught a hold of his opponent's armor. He drew out the dagger and slid it up under the neck plate of the elf and kept pushing even as his hand ran with a very dark blood.

At first Dahrain tried to use his magic to hold back the edge of the dagger, but he had gone to that well once too many times and he had nothing left. By the time he understood this it was too late to do anything else and the tip of the dagger was through both his carotid and jugular. He died right there and Eireden had just enough strength to push the dead elf off of him.

And then he faded into a haze of semi-consciousness

where images and sounds came to him as if from miles away. Above, the dark clouds broke up under a strong wind and there was the sun hot and high. Next a scream ripped the air and then he blinked as lights swarmed his vision. There was a chaos of bizarre keening whistles and beneath that the sound of horses. One seemed much closer that the rest and the sound of its hooves brought with it a sense of doom.

"Eireden!" Generai was there above him with grey eyes rimmed with red. She stared at the sword protruding from his chest as if such a thing couldn't be possible. Now Eireden saw the fairies. They hovered around crying for him, their lights blinking in alarm. Where was Tissa he wondered? He was on death's door and still he worried about the smallest fairy.

"What do I do?" the scout asked in a panic but just then the fairies shot away in a blur of light. Generai's eyes went wide at what was coming. The horseman was coming, and he was a dread horseman. He came with vengeance and it could be felt by all.

Generai's jaw set and her hesitation disappeared. Taking the hilts of the elf-sword she drew it out of her king. Eireden swooned. A dozen blood vessels opened up and again his life drained out. The scout knelt and fed her life into his, healing him to the fullest extent of her power—it wasn't nearly enough. Still he didn't die as he expected, all the same he wasn't able to help the scout as she stood over him and fought against odds well beyond her.

Just as Eireden had, Dahrain had brought a second but so confident was he in his victory that he kept him well back. Now the creature—another charred and foul elf came on to finish the job that Dahrain had started. Between him and his prey was a single scout and a family of fairies who buzzed about like angry hornets. They were little more than a nuisance, but the elf wasn't in the mood and from his hands a gout of flame erupted sending the fairies scattering. Two weren't fast enough and their screams were high and shrill.

Their death sent the remaining sythei into a frenzy and they so terrorized the elf's horse that the steed kicked and reared before it rolled to rid itself of them. When it did the elf leapt easily away. Generai was on him hacking with the elf blade before he was even fully up, but his skill was too great. With a deft move he turned her sword aside and, before she could recover, his steel ripped through her chest. She reeled back and went to one knee, blood running bright and wet down the front of her leathers.

"No," Eireden said. It came out in breathless misery. Ten feet away his scout would die. However the fairies attacked again fearlessly. Light shot from their bodies and they moved at such speeds that no flame could catch them. The elf had other tricks than just fire. A great wind, like a wall of a hurricane came up and blew aside the fairies, sending them tumbling away.

Generai tried to regain her feet. She pushed up, only her leg wobbled and then buckled completely. From her knees she brought the sword to bear. He swatted it aside and then casually walked past her as she fell face first to the turf. Now more flame shot from his hand. It came at Eireden, snapping and curling around itself like a hundred serpents of orange and gold. This should surely have killed him but the flames bent around his body as if a sphere of glass encased him.

What was happening? The heat baked him yet he lived. And then he heard the other horses, those that had been further away. Prince Gamelling and his personal guard attacked the lone elf—six against one—and they were losing badly. The elf was just too fast and too powerful. But then the fairies swept in again evening the odds, but still Gamelling went down with a great gout of blood erupting from his aged body. Then a second knight fell.

Just then Eireden felt a warmth spread from his insides and he could no longer care about the battle. The feeling was too wonderful. He turned his head to see the white eyes of Alseya regarding him. She knelt above him and a shimmer of blue came from her hands. "You have prevailed where none could," she said. He couldn't find anything to say to that so he just lay there enjoying the feeling. It was like being reborn.

And then there was strength again to stand. Conversely the fey slumped against him as he sat up. She wasn't the only fey there. Feylon was on the field of battle, helping Generai. As well several others were there either healing knights or helping to subdue the elf. Ina wrath Lienhart rode up on the golden palomino of Ella's. Scattering knights and fairies alike he rode down the lone elf, striking him a mortal blow before trampling him beneath the hooves of his steed. Just like that the battle ended and a strange silence came about.

Prince Gamelling as well as two of his knights lay dead upon the battle plain and seeing them hurt the king worse that any blade could. Nearby the fairies were fluttering above a scorched area of the grass, looking for the remains of their two dead kindred.

"Can you stand, Milady," Eireden asked Alseya. Her eyes were listless. She had given too much of herself in an effort for him to live. She nodded vaguely, but didn't make the attempt. Eireden, who had been so close to death only seconds before stood and then picked her up. He wasn't feeling a hundred percent, but she was feather light.

"Gather our fallen," Eireden commanded the remaining knights. "We will leave none to be despoiled by our enemies. And hurry, we should not linger." The maug were forming on the plain. Though they seemed uncertain for the moment, he didn't want to give them an excuse to attack any earlier than necessary. "Lienhart!" he called. The once-captain sat atop the golden palomino staring down at his black charger. The horse Eireden had ridden into battle seemed to have died in frightful agony. Its blank eyes were wide and full of fear, even in death. "Can you take Alseya before you?"

"Yes Milord," Lienhart said, though his eyes were still on his dead charger. Eireden walked over to him still carrying the fey, when he noticed that she too was staring. It was the dead elf, Dahrain that she gazed at.

"On second thought, Lienhart. Please take Generai on your horse," the king commanded. "I will take hers and be along shortly."

Lienhart agreed and after a quick look of reproach from Generai the two rode off as did the others. Purposefully Eireden had waited behind. Placing the fey on the horse he stooped and picked up the Dahrain's elf-sword from where Generai had dropped it. He used it to point at the dead elf.

"Do you know what that is?" he asked Alseya. She paused in answer and her eyelids came down, drooping. Eireden hopped up behind her and she leaned back into him so that her head was on his chest.

"I've never seen it before," she replied in a tired whisper. Now she didn't want to look at it. The fey kept her head averted from the corpse and snugged her face into him.

"You didn't answer my question," Eireden said sternly. "I didn't ask if you had seen it before, I asked if you knew what it was."

She let out a long sigh. "That is an elf, though why he looks like that I do not know."

Eireden nodded. "And Ella? What is she?"

Alseya dropped her chin and the king could feel her eyelashes flutter against his neck. "She is an elf as well," the white-eyed fey said.

Even though he knew this to be true before she had said it, his face still went hard and the muscles of his jaw clenched. "One more question," he said. His voice started strong but he finished in a whisper: "Are all elves evil?"

"Yes."

## Chapter 23

## Eireden

To say the least Eireden's mind was preoccupied with the discovery of the truth of Ella's ancestry. He dwelled on it all the way across the battle plain back to the town. How would he look her in the eye if he ever saw her again? And if he did see her again, how could he not kill her? The elves and the Den were mortal enemies after all. And what if someone else found out? What if there was a clamor for her death? That thought gave him the shivers.

Alseya noticed yet kept silent, in fact she was silent the entire ride back. Despite the formations of maug slowly forming up behind them, Eireden kept the horse at a steady walk. His injuries weren't close to being fully healed and a deep ached radiated out from his chest where every breath pained him. Regardless he let Alseya lean into him. She was in a veritable stupor, lacking the strength to even hold herself up.

"Thank you for saving my life," Eireden said to her as they crossed through the gate. She murmured something softly before she was gently laid in a stretcher by the other fey and carried away to where she was staying. Only time would allow her to recoup her strength.

Once inside the gate, the king was accosted from all sides. Hundreds of people jostled him and touched him. Most wanted to congratulate him on his victory, some looked for orders and others just wanted to be near and lingered close to him accomplishing nothing but getting in the way. A delegation of a dozen fey sought to heal him: "By orders of the Lady Generai," they said. This he allowed. They brought him to the closest barracks and one by one they came and laid hands upon him until he felt just as he had before his battle. While this went on Generai brought water and towels, and a fresh tunic and cloak so that once again his handsome face shone from beneath the dried blood.

"What is it with you and fey women?" the scout asked under her breath as she tied his cloak about his neck. She drew the string sharply so that he gagged. Every one of his healers had been female and all breathtakingly attractive. He could only shrug.

When they left him, the king wanted to prepare for the coming battle however he had to deal with two more groups. The first to come were a gathering of the most senior captains. "The Prince of the city is dead," Lienhart announced to all present, but especially to the king. "He lies in repose within the palace. As you all know it is the responsibility of the king to appoint the next prince. Normally this is a decision that takes time, but with battle in the offing, it is thought wise to choose a successor sooner rather than later."

Eireden eyed the captains assembled. They were all good men from the rustic, but noble families of Hildoeven. Having lived in the city for the last five years as a *gada*, he knew each of them very well, perhaps far better than they suspected. As a *gada*, a nobody, he had seen how they treated their inferiors, which was a telling indicator in how they would rule. Because of this he immediately narrowed the list to four names. Captain Elled was a cousin of Prince Gamelling and distantly related to Eireden. He was of the highest birth but haughty, like a star football player in some backwards cow-town. Captain Dorcen was a hard working man who balanced running a farm with his duty to his prince—smart and capable, he was a likely choice. Captain Jeden was probably the most renowned swordsmen the city offered now that the heroic Cassidor was dead. He was a great figure of a man, nearly as tall and broad as the king. And lastly, Lienhart. Of lower birth, he had made the most of every opportunity to get where he had and he was a man the king would trust with his life.

"The city needs a prince," the king declared watching the four closely. "However I am not fully king yet. Eirowyth must face me first and if he doesn't; if he proclaims me outlaw, he may also proclaim those close to me, including the Prince of the City, a traitor." Everyone glanced around at this news and began muttering—all save two of the captains. Lienhart, one of the two, stood ramrod straight, while the other, Dorcen dropped his eyes to the floor.

Eireden read their actions: those that muttered wondered how the title would affect them in the long term. Dorcen's actions told him that he would do his duty, but didn't relish the title. "Generai, the sword, please" the king said coming to a quick decision.

One of the Elf-swords that were recovered from the battle, Eireden wore on his hip, while the other he had entrusted to his scout to hold. She came forward bearing it in its sheath. He took it solemnly and drew the bright blade. "Lienhart, of the family of Olmastin, once captain of the Twelfth Guard, I name you Lienhart, Prince of Hildoeven." The new prince knelt in front of the king who added, "May your reign be long and bountiful. Stand."

Lienhart did so, taking the sword his king held out for him reverently. "Thank you for your trust Milord."

"It seems our fates are entwined, Lord Lienhart," the king said. "Now they are more so. Good luck."

The new prince begged his leave having many new duties to attend to, one of which was to inform the Lady Norafin of the loss of her husband. Eireden had his own painful duty. His family of fairies had been the last off the plains. They had cried over the scorched earth where the elf had killed two of their family and now they had returned looking angrier than any sythei had ever.

Easa-see pulled him away from the gathering of Den. The two, with Generai in tow, went to one of the fountains in the city where the fairy showed the king a pair of charred bodies sitting on the marble rim. How tiny and sad they looked. "Who are they?" Eireden asked not recognizing them. "What were their names?"

"Zizis and Sheesa," Easa-see replied. The other fairies hovered about the fountain not laughing or joking. At the approach of the king they grew more animated and came to greet him and then they flew in and touched the bodies giving a bit of their own light to the dead.

Eireden went as well, but stopped just short. "I don't have any light." Easa-see touched the pearl about his neck so that it shone brightly and then pointed to the two frail bodies. The king went and touched each. "Thank you," he whispered. The fairies had died fighting for him. It wasn't something he would not forget.

With that done he left the fairies to their mourning and headed for the gate with his head spinning a little. So much had happened in so short a time that he was having trouble coming to grips with it all. Thirty thousand goblins helped him to collect his wits. Going to the ramparts he saw the maug in a long arc around the city. They milled about and in Eireden's eyes they seemed uncertain.

"We need to get you new armor," Generai said coming to stand at his side. "You can't fight in tunic alone."

"Is there any armor even left in the city?" Eireden asked, "I've seen some of the reservists wearing layers of thick quilts about their bodies and one had a fry pan for a shield."

"Unfortunately there are three new sets that have just come available," Generai said gently. "The prince was the tallest. I'm having his mail altered for you even now. Don't give me that look, Milord. You know he would have wanted you to be protected with the best. And there is no way we are going to let three sets of armor sit idle when we have men in quilts or tunics."

"I suppose," the king said, staring out at the maug. He didn't like putting on a man's armor when he was still warm. It seemed disrespectful.

"What are they waiting for," Generai asked, nodding toward the maug.

"I think they expected me to lose," Eireden replied; he

then pointed up at the bright blue sky. "And that the sun wouldn't be shining. They probably had standing orders just as we did. If I had to guess, they'll slink back under the cover of the trees here before too long and not come out till dark." He based this guess on the fact that goblins hated the light. It made them dizzy and weak. The king turned from his enemies and gave a glance down into the inner yard of the city where his men were gathering. Half of all the able-bodied men would make a sortie outside the walls within the hour.

Eireden wasn't one for a passive defense, not when he had any advantage whatsoever. With the sun high overhead he would inflict as much damage as possible and then retreat back into the city. His main hope would be that this action would entice the maug into a general attack. One was coming sooner or later and he would rather it come sooner while the sun still beat down.

Just then he saw the rabble on the plain start to recede. "Damn! They're heading back already." The king looked down into the yard and spied one of his captains. "Dorcen, have the trumpets sound! I want the knights outside the gates in ten minutes. I'm sorry, Generai. I cannot wait on the armor."

"Then do not ride in the van. It's not safe," she begged grabbing his arm. There were others around, many others. He gave her a stern look until she let go. "I have to look to your safety. I can't help that I love you," she added in a whisper as way of an apology.

"Would you love a coward who slunk in the back, letting others die in his place?" he asked. She shook her head and then dropped her chin. "Look at me—I cannot falter now. Go. Find me a shield. That at least I will carry."

The two parted. Eireden went for a horse only to find the golden Palomino saddled for him. Eagerly he vaulted onto its back. The horse was just as eager. Bristling with energy it pawed at the courtyard, while the doors creaked back and trumpet blared. The king drew his sword just as Generai raced up with a shield. He gave her a smile that told her that he would be fine and then called out in a commanding voice, "Dorcen get your archers on the plains as fast as you can. Knights! Follow me!"

Straight away he shot onto the battle plain with his dark mane of hair swirling in the golden noon light. His face blazed with the lust of battle and his horse shone like the sun above. The elf-sword, long and nimble but deadly sharp, gleamed and above him Easa-see and four of his fairies appeared like tiny stars. Not long before, death had come for the king, but now he felt alive like he hadn't in years.

Racing at his enemies felt glorious, but then he heard a cry behind him and looking back he saw that he had far outstripped his heavily burdened knights in their steel armor. Laughing he brought up his steed short. "Come on slow pokes!" he called. "Before they get away." This was a bit of a joke since his knights numbered less than two hundred and the maug seemed beyond count.

His presence alone on the field did not go unnoticed and many of the maug had turned from the forest and were charging toward him. This only made the young king laugh all the more. He waited until they got within fifty yards and then he kicked his horse in an easy canter away, but he did not go too far. They came on again, and again he waited to the last moment before riding away.

This time they did not follow. The king's knights were riding up hard, but Eireden checked them. "Form up in a single line," he called. This was an unusual formation for heavy cavalry. They normally arranged themselves in a triangular shape which allowed them to penetrate a line of infantry in the shock of their first attack.

The knights formed and waited—again an oddity. The first rule of cavalry: lose momentum lose the fight. Still Eireden waited and the maug waited, fearing some ruse. They were smart to believe it since the king only waited upon the arrival of his archers. These four hundred men and women hurried up behind the line of horses and stopped in a double line two deep. Once in place the king had the knights break into two groups one moved off to the rear and left of the archers, while the other to the right and back. Again they waited.

Now the maug came on, thousands of them, but not the full might of their army. Most had high-tailed it under the eaves of the forest. Yet still, four hundred archers were nothing compared to the numbers that remained and so they charged. Captain Dorcen kept his lightly armored third echelon troops in place in the face of certain death. They twitched and fidgeted as their palms grew sweaty and their feet grew light, longing to run. The captain kept them there long enough for the maug to get well in range and only then did he allow them to fire three volleys of arrows.

The twelve hundred arrows, raining into the densely pack goblins did great damage, killing many and wounding many more, but the goblin were hell bent on destruction. They rushed on and Dorcen wisely didn't try for a fourth volley. With the maug bearing down on him he sounded the retreat, however this quickly turned into a rout as the men broke formation and fled back toward town as fast as they could.

The cavalry seemed too far back and too far away to be much help and the men ran between the two wings. Still, Eireden sat placidly atop his horse. Around him his men leaned forward in their saddles itching to go, but the king waited, looking for that moment when the maug formations would lose any cohesion.

Half a minute later the goblins had simply become a mob chasing the archers and only then did he kick the palomino into a thundering charge. The knights across the field from him took their cue and charged as well. Standing against a charge of heavy cavalry takes courage, training, and the right weapons. The maug had none of this. The two mounted forces caught the goblins in both flanks and shredded the

[165]

lead elements. So great was their attack that within a minute they had passed clear through the goblins.

Eireden didn't turn for a second charge. That wasn't part of his plan. Instead he took a position similar to where he had been only minutes before—on the flank of his archers. Like magic the scouts had stopped running, reformed, and even then they began firing arrows at will into the bewildered maug. Gone was the fear and nervousness of the scouts. Gone was their panic. It had all been a ruse to lure the goblins into a trap. Now they were cool and steady, raking the goblins with volley after volley, until those in front were pushing their way to the rear and those in back didn't know what to do.

This sort of mayhem was perfect and the scouts poured a deadly fire into their enemies. Eventually through frustration and anger, the maug came on again, desperate to get at the archers. However Captain Dorcen retreated again, and again the cavalry struck leaving bodies in their wake.

The combination of missile and shock tactics was working so well that Eireden saw no need to change a thing and his men formed for a third go round while the maug looked on unhappily. The goblins had the advantage in numbers; they just didn't have the strategy or the training to overcome their foes.

Unfortunately the elves did. Two of the black clad fiends rode to the front and reformed the goblins into something that resembled a military formation. Behind the maug, ogres could be seen pushing their way to the front. Their size would nullify Eireden's advantage in cavalry and that would leave the archers alone to face overwhelming odds. The king sounded the retreat for real, and within minutes his men crossed back through the gate to a hero's welcome.

## Chapter 24

### Ella

Leaving the tiny town of Council, Ella drove westward with the vague notion of seeing the ocean. Other than that simple plan her future didn't seem filled with endless possibilities. It should have. As an immortal it should have felt that way. She should've been able to picture herself in Paris or Moscow, watching the sunrise on the year three-thousand. Or taking a shuttle to the moon on a mini-vacation in 4250 A.D. Or perhaps even simply snuggling up in front of a fireplace at Christmas in a few months time.

Instead of seeing an endless future she saw an empty one. Her past was such a mystery that it made her future look dim. Her birthday wasn't even her own birthday. July 18, 1981 was the day she had been abandoned, not the day she was born. All the signatures on all the forms had that day written next to them, but under *Child's Date of Birth* it only read: unknown. Unknown. That was her. That was Ella Belmont/Feyden. She was the great unknown.

"Have you ever been to the ocean?" she asked Aric. As always he seemed perfectly content. She had noticed that about the fey. It was so rare for them to get worked up over anything and then when they did, five minutes later they'd be calm again.

"No I haven't," he answered, beaming at her. "I would very much like to. I've read every poem written by fey or Den about its vast size, its unknown depths, and its majesty. Would you say we are near?"

"It depends. Do you want to collect the horses first or go straight there? If we go straight on we can be there this evening."

"Then I say we go straight there. We will always have time to pick up the horses later," Aric said. His words struck a tone within Ella. That was what she was missing within her. She hadn't quite figured out this whole notion of *later*.

For the fey, everything could be put off for *later*. Living forever meant that there would always be time *later*. It was a concept that she would have to get used to...except she had a sinking feeling that *later* would not include her. "Then let's go now," she agreed trying to find pep to spice her voice. If there was no later for her then it made sense to live now. "Wake up Whip-wip! We're going to the ocean!"

The fairy, who had been sleeping snugged up in an old cashmere sweater of Ella's, shot up and pressed herself excitedly to the window. She stared out but when she saw the same dull farms they had been riding next to all morning and she grew cranky. Whip-wip hated the car with a passion. To her it was nothing but a moving cell. At the moment Ella had to agree. It sped her on to that unknown where *later* didn't seem likely.

They fell silent as the miles whispered past beneath them and after a while her mind slipped and she pictured Eireden. What was he doing just then, she wondered? The answer came easy: fighting for his life, knowing him. He was a man who was never all that engrossed with the concept of later. Even to his detriment. He lived in the here and now, no matter how dangerous. This was great on the veneer, but underneath it grew stale, or she supposed it would. She hadn't known him all that long, really. Not long enough for it to grow...

"I'm turning on some music if you don't mind," she said to Aric. Eireden wasn't a subject she wasn't supposed to dwell on, no matter how many times she pictured his face.

"What do you mean?" Aric asked looking puzzled. This made her smile. She flipped open the glove box and glanced at her mother's CDs, searching for something lively. She didn't like the gloom that had settled down about her shoulders. The ancient selection of old rock made her groan, but there snuggled in with *The Who* and *The Doors* was *Huey Lewis and the News*.

"Perfect," she said as *The Power of Love* came thumping

up out of the sub-woofers. She cranked the volume and sang along. Whip-wip was up in a flash, alarmed at first but then gyrating her tiny bottom to the beat as she went to the speakers to figure out where the sound was coming from. The fairy loved it—far more than Aric who was quite overwhelmed by the driving beat.

At the end of the song Ella switched it off, much to Whip-wip's annoyance. "Primitive, but strangely engaging," Aric said. "How does this work? How is sound captured like this?"

"I don't really know," Ella confessed. "I suppose science is a form of magic and..." Her words were cut off by the sudden blare of guitars. Whip-wip had been studying the buttons on the console. They had left her stumped and so she began hitting them at random. Accidentally she found the 'on' switch and before she knew it, *I Want a New Drug* with its grinding guitar intro erupted.

The music was shockingly loud, but Ella let it vibrate the wheel and the windows. It felt good to let the sound take her away and she danced in her seat as she drove. Aric did as well but it was the fairy's dancing that nearly had them in a crash. The little thing used the dashboard as her own personal disco. She boogied and shook her tiny self with abandon. Ella thought she was such a riot that she laughed until she cried.

The music affected each in a different way. Aric loved every song of every CD. He found something good about each—but that was Aric. He found goodness in the least thing. It was easily his best trait. For him the songs were truth. If they were sad, he grew sad. If they were inspired by love, he held her hand and kissed each fingertip.

Whip-wip was like this but in exaggeration. She was extra peppy and extra loving and extra sad. When Bob Seger's *Turn the Page* came on, with its haunting saxophone she leaned against the speaker and wept. Strangely she asked for it a second time and while it played she shot light into the speaker.

"Powerful," Aric commented. "The humans have really managed to capture emotion in their music."

The part of Ella that had been raised by the Belmonts in the All-American city of Spokane wanted to protest the word 'their' in Aric's sentence. Instead she nodded along. There was no sense lying to herself even in these little things. The humans were now *them*. And so too were the fey and the Den. She'd have to get used to the idea.

"I need more pep!" Ella said looking through the CDs and trying not to think too much on things. She loved Aric and she loved Whip-wip; after that she didn't really know what to think about anything. "I need more rock and roll!"

The twenty or so CDs didn't make it through the nine-hour trip and when they began to repeat, Whip-wip acted the part on mini DJ. She had long before conquered the controls so now she could jump to her favorite songs or pop out the discs at a whim.

The trip really could have been made in eight hours, but just east of Tacoma Ella had spotted a pawnshop. The garish building sent a series of mental dominos cascading through her mind. "I think we need to hire a private investigator," she said, and then quickly explained to Aric what one was. "In order to find my mother," she added.

"I'm not following you," Aric replied. "Can a private investigator track your mother into the Demorlaik? They are just human, correct?"

"They are, but what if my mother was really good? What if she was able to escape from my father and took me here to America and left me in safe keeping and then went into hiding among the humans?"

"And would she keep using the same name?" Aric countered. "Because that's all we have left to go on. If she changed her name to Joan we'll never find her."

Ella didn't want to argue about this, she just simply wanted her own way and she wanted Aric to agree with it.

But that didn't look like it was going to happen so she voiced the real reason she wanted to hire a private investigator. "Ok, what if my mom was really crazy? What if the Demorlaik drove her mad and my father didn't care what happened to her. The paperwork mentions only her. He might have set her free among the humans knowing that eventually she'd end up in social services."

Aric considered this. "Well, I'd hate for that to be a possibility, and I really can't imagine it. But for your sake let's talk to this fellow and hope for the best."

So the pair spent a good hour finding a qualified investigator, which was more difficult than it seemed. When they did, and with Aric's *goading,* the gentleman promised to make Ella's case his top priority. Armed with just a name he went right to work but suggested not to wait. "These sorts of things can take time," he said. "If we are lucky a day or two, if not a week or two. And if we have no luck, it just won't happen." He advised them to call daily for updates.

Ella had been hoping for more immediate results. She had imagined the man clicking away at a computer for a few minutes and then printing out her mother's address. To kill time, and because she had promised both Aric and Whip-wip they continued on to the ocean, reaching it just at sunset.

Whip-wip went crazy the second she saw the water from the road, but it was some time before they found a section deserted enough to let a fairy roam freely. The second the door was open she sped away—dashing here to grab some sand—and there to inspect a shell—and into the air to feel the soft under belly of a gull. She spread her wings and caught a gust of ocean breeze and went soaring away singing as she rode the air currents higher and higher.

Aric took Ella's hand and led her onto the fading warmth of the sand. "I imagined this moment," he said. "I pictured you right there with the fire of the sun in your face...just like that." The fey stared with the dazzling gems of his eyes and the pale of his face flushed. "This moment is why I still live.

In the dungeons I kept this vision of you in my mind and it kept me going when nothing else could."

"Just this kept you alive?" Ella asked, feeling a heat in her cheeks and at her neckline that seemed to be rising. He stepped in closer to her and she caught the scent of him and breathed it in, making it apart of herself.

"No it wasn't enough," Aric said in a whisper. He was so close that she could feel the breath of his words on her lips and then their noses touched like crossed swords and they sparred playfully with the gentleness of the breeze. "I lived for another reason. I lived so that I could do this." Now their lips touched. They had kissed once before, a quick kiss on the verge of battle and death. It had been spur of the moment with no possibility beyond that brief second.

But now there was endless possibility and they kissed with the eternal sun upon them and the ceaseless ocean wind in their hair. They kissed and Ella began to understand the nature of love immortal.

Peter Meredith

# Chapter 25

## Eireden

The king breathed a heavy sigh as the sun went down. He watched the fiery orb though it burned his eyes and knew a sadness that he couldn't understand. Though he knew its source. Ella. She stood south and west of him. All that day as Eireden had made his final preparations for the coming battle he had felt her moving. She was like the sun itself. From east to west as the day progressed she had moved steadily.

Why? What was in the west that called to her? The ocean? The sunset? If he had no other cares, that's where he would have taken her. He had seen the ocean once a few years before. He had tracked a wayward fey all the way to the water's edge and the two had stood staring as the sun had set. "That's all I wanted," she had said. "Thank you." She had thanked him because she knew he could have taken her before that moment. He could have taken her before that day, but he had held off and followed her only. And he was glad he had.

Eireden turned from the sunset and looked into the dark of the east where death awaited.

That lone fey girl was dead already. She was not among those that had made it out of the valley. Gamelling was dead. The kind, grandfatherly prince would never laugh that quick laugh of his. Zizis and Sheesa were dead—his sythei family had brought him their remains in a tiny box made of woven grass and insisted he keep them safe. And where was Tissa, the youngest? Her errand should have had her back way before this, but she had not been seen in days.

He shook his head at this. Of all the peoples under his care, Tissa was the least, yet he worried for her the most.

Generai's hand found his. "Don't turn away," she said. "The light is not gone yet."

He turned from the east, but did not look into the west. Instead he looked at Generai, scout and warrior of the Den.

Tall and stern she was—until she smiled and the fading sun struck her and then she was beautiful. "You should let your hair down more," the king said. "It's a very pretty blonde."

Her grey eyes went wide at this at first. She then gave a little shrug and said, "Maybe I will. Maybe when we aren't about to be attacked by a horde of goblins. Maybe when I have some *reason* to let my hair down. Could you think of one?"

"A reason to let your hair down? There are many. I was just..." His words were cut off by a sudden blare of trumpets. Men began rushing to the walls. "It's time."

He started out of the room, but Generai grabbed him, her eyes searching his. "You have time to give me one reason don't you?" she asked desperately. He knew what she was asking. However right before battle he couldn't say no to her even though his heart lay in the west.

"A reason? Because it will make me happy," he answered.

Her hair was in a bun to keep it out of the way but she released it and then ran her hands through it. It was very pretty, long and soft, and he couldn't help but smile. "That did indeed make me happy," he said. "However it's not regulation. You wouldn't want anyone thinking you were getting special treatment would you?"

More horns sounded and she pulled him from the room. "You're wrong! I want everyone to think that I'm getting special treatment."

They hurried to the walls and the king had to put aside all thoughts of love-struck Generai and what his feelings should and shouldn't be regarding her or in fact any woman. The plains teemed with goblins. He ran up one of his make shift towers and spied all around. They were coming from all sides, but as expected they were concentrating on the weakest points in his wall—the gate—the two low points along the east wall—and the rocky area on the north where the dry moat couldn't be run. The king, in his shining mail, came down from the tower and mounting the golden palomino he rode to each point and rallied the men leaving them cheering.

"We fought 'em off before," cried one soldier. "We can do it again!"

Eireden cheered along with the men though he knew in his heart that they hadn't been tested yet. The first battle in Hildoeven after the fall of the Feylands had been a ruse only, a way to draw out the forces of Rhyoeven. Nor was the pitched battle at the gate a test or even the little skirmish won by his archers and cavalry on the plains. In none of these was the little town ever seriously threatened. It was now.

Even with the fey acting in support, his men were outnumbered ten to one.

Yet the Den had advantages. The first of these was Eireden himself. His very presence buoyed the men, sending their spirits high and they battled with greater strength and tenacity when he was near. The second was the landscape on which they fought. Their enemy—the elf Darhmael—had gambled in allowing his captain to challenge the king. It was a smart gamble and Eireden would have done the same thing, but losing meant not only the loss of a valuable captain it also meant the loss of a week. That week before the challenge had been put to good use. The dry moat was dug deep and its sides were cut at sharp angles. The gate and walls were braced and in the weak spots not only were towers erected, secondary walls were built behind the first—just in case.

Perhaps the greatest advantage that extra week gave them was in learning and practicing tactics. Interspersed among the men teams of fey operated. Most worked to heal the wounded, but the rest created simple illusions to trick the maug. The chief of these were used where the walls were undermanned; the illusions made it seem that there were many soldiers instead of few. This permitted the king to concentrate his men at weak points. It also allowed him to hold back a reserve force which he used to bolster any point that appeared threatened.

Finally the king had created two assault teams whose main purpose was to engage Darhmael or any elf that dared to lead an attack. The first team was led by Captain Elled. With him were Feylon and Captain Jeden along with three knights and three fey. The second team was led by the king himself. He chose Alseya and Captain Dorcen along with two knights and two fey.

"What about me?" Generai asked defiantly. Her eyes were hard and her lips drawn tight.

"You are brave beyond your ability, Scout," Eireden replied. "Your place is on the walls where your bow is needed."

"But I..."

The king's stern glare stopped her mouth from moving. "It was you who asked to be command by me, remember? They can't be all easy commands, my Scout. You will be most effective on the wall and that's where I need you."

"Yes, Milord," Generai said, eyes drooping.

She started away when the king added: "Leave your hair down so I can keep an eye on you."

"Yes, Milord," she said again, but with more enthusiasm.

"Sooni, go with Generai," the king commanded one of the fairies. Then to the remainder he said, "The rest of you to your posts." The fairies were to act as messengers during the battle. Each company captain would have one in attendance in order to get vital information to the king quicker than a man could sprint. Although Generai didn't rank anywhere near captain, Eireden wanted her to have a little extra protection, as well Sooni was the worst when it came to hair braiding. During drills she had driven Captain Jeden to distraction by turning his blonde Viking mane into pigtails— "It's not worth it!" the captain had thundered which had only brought on more laughter.

Eireden kept Easa-see and two of his brothers with him. They rode upon his broad shoulders as he inspected the defenses and his men unashamedly called him the Fairy King. To them, the fact that he could command the sythei only added to his mystique rather than detract from it.

Having made a circuit of the city he went to the tower nearest the gate. From it he could observe two of the four weak points in his walls and with his stomach turning he saw the goblins surging to cover the final hundred yards as fast as they could. The Den archers fired as quickly as possible and the arrows came as rain, yet the goblins were like an ocean. Where one went down nine took his place.

Long ladders they bore to scale the walls and had it not been for the dry moat the walls might have been swarmed within the first few minutes. Yet the moat proved a puzzle for most of the goblins and many tried to stand their ladders up at the bottom of it which left them a few feet short of the twenty-foot tall wall. Those that climbed were easily shot down. Quite a few of the ladders were broken as the maug laid them across the moat and used them as a bridge.

Soon the king started to receive messages from his captains. One by one fairies flew up to relate exciting stories of goblins with swords, and arrows that flew as fast black clouds. "Tell me your number first," he had to remind them each and every time. The captains were to give the fairies a number from one to ten depending on their level of distress. A one meant that there was no serious threat to the defensive perimeter while a ten meant the wall had fallen.

Riecie, a fairy with wings trimmed in gold, reported a number five from Captain Haymar. "Are there any ogres or trolls?" he asked, cutting her off in mid-story—she had been going on about Haymar's horse who didn't care for her sitting between his ears and using them to steer.

"O-gah *sis*," she said and held up both hands. He interpreted this to mean there were many ogres.

The king flew down the stairs to the courtyard. "Captain

Elled! Get your team to Haymar quick. Go easy on the magic. Uldair move two of the reinforcement companies over to the north wall." The assault team raced away on horseback while the men double-timed it on foot. Eireden's hand itched to draw his sword and charge into the fight, but it wasn't his place. Not yet.

"You'll have your time," Alseya told him, seeming to read his mind. "And when you do, maybe you'll be not so eager for battle."

"You mistake me, Milady. I am not eager for battle. This morning's affair might have cured me of that for all time," Eireden shivered when he thought about the fight with the elf, Dahrain. On its own his hand went to his chest.

"Are you still in pain?" the fey asked with concern taking his large hand in her tiny one. Hers were soft as velvet.

"No, not at all, thanks to you," he said. "It just feels strange to take a deep breath. It's as though my body thinks that it shouldn't be able to. I don't know if that is normal."

"For *Eireden* there is no normal," she remarked. "You are unique. A Den and not a Den."

Suddenly he realized that he was still holding her hand and the memory of her against his chest as they rode back into town came strong to him. She had been soft and molded to his body perfectly. He pulled away blinking to see past the white eyes. "I'm just a Den...now, if you'll excuse me." The king gave her low bow and then went back to his place in the tower.

"What was that about?" he asked staring down at the unfolding battle. His walls were holding and the casualties among the maug were horrific, but in the distance another wave of maug was approaching and beyond that, a darkness so thick that it could only be magical in nature. Seeing it gave him the shivers. How would his men fight in that? They would be literally blind while the maug would have little problem seeing. This first wave was just to occupy him—to keep him busy until the real battle would begin. And then his walls would fall.

The king shook his head and sighed—this sort of negativity wouldn't do at all.

"Does Alseya like me?" Eireden asked Easa-see, looking for any reason not to dwell on that approaching darkness. "I mean it sure seemed that way. Didn't it?" The fairy shrugged. The king went to the other window which faced upon the gate. With her blonde hair he picked out Generai easily and for a while he stared at her as she fired her bow and then answered himself, "It did seem that way. I'm almost sure of it. And that makes no sense. She wasn't acting like this yesterday."

Easa-see began pointing and hooting. "I see them," the king told him. The second wave was fast approaching and it was clear that it would break full upon the gate. "Uldair! Move the remaining reinforcements to the gate. And see that they have all the arrows they need." The king then turned to Easa-see. "Go to Haymar. Get a number from him and if it's four or less tell him I want my reinforcements back."

The fairy shot away like a streak of lightening.

"That's just what I need," Eireden mused. "Another woman who likes me." He had to ask himself: why was he thinking about women at a time like this?

"Because I'm not in the fight," he reasoned. The battle was pretty much taking care of itself so far and that left him with too much time on his hands. He began pacing back and forth to the two windows. A minute later Easa-see came back to report Haymar still at a five. His men were holding their own, and that's what counted. The King went to the window that faced the gate and looked out at the battle. It was hard to see exactly what was going on. He would have to trust his captain and their messengers.

"But she's another impossible woman," he said suddenly, throwing up his hands. Ella was impossible. First she loved another man and second she was an elf. Alseya was impossible. She was fey and what did Aric tell him time and again about the pairing of fey and human? It was an impossibility. And then there was Generai. An impossibility? Yes...she was impossible. He didn't love her.

"Maybe I could though," he said aloud.

"Maybe you could what?"

Turning quickly the king watched beguiled as Alseya came toward him. Her light feet in their white fur boots made not a sound. "I was just...talking to myself. An old habit."

"From when you were *gada*?" she asked.

"Yes." He didn't like how she seemed to see right into his soul. As far as he was aware no one knew of his habit.

"It must have been lonely, this self-enforced exile of yours." She came to stand so close that their arms touched. What was she doing? Why was she so close?

Just then Sooni buzzed into the room and cried, "O-gah, o-gah!" She held up both her hands. For just a second the king was glad for the interruption but then he hardened.

*Why hadn't he been warned before this*, he wondered? What happened to Captain Urren at the gate? "Get back to Generai," Eireden commanded. He then grabbed the fey and together they hurtled down into the courtyard. Captain Elled wasn't back. "Dorcen it's our turn."

Mounting their horses the little team rode hard to the gate. It being only a few hundred yards distant they were there in less than a minute. A dull thump came to them and the gate shook and swayed back on its hinges. They were using a battering ram!

Eireden raced up the stairs to the wall. Below him was what looked like a long low building on wheels. It had a sloping roof that protected the ogres inside from missile attack. From the front of it a steel-headed ram protruded. Back it went and with a hoarse cry in the primitive language of the ogres it swept forward to smash against the gate.

The Den archers were powerless to stop it. "Archers! Keep the maug back." There were plenty of targets just beyond the ram where goblins milled waiting for their chance to attack. The first wave of arrows sent them reeling away. Eireden didn't hesitate, "Dorcen are you with me?"

The captain glanced down at the roof of the building not ten feet below and nodded. With a cry that shook the air like thunder the king leapt down from the battlements.

## Chapter 26

## Eireden

Back swept the ram again and then the king dropped in front of the opening to the surprise of sixteen ogres. There came a strange moment that sometimes happens in battle where everyone pauses and considers their situation. It wasn't a good one for the ogres. By necessity the low building was cramped and the ogres were each more or less trapped behind heavy wood handles that protruded from the sides of the ram. The ram itself was a tremendous thing that hung suspended from the ceiling; letting go of the handles would do nothing to help the ogres in their confined state.

At the same time the king was just one man and the appearance of Dorcen a moment later didn't do much more to worry the beasts. What did worry them was the light that flashed into being when Eireden swept out the elf-sword. Then all hell broke loose. They knew that sword and they feared it.

A panic seized them, but it was a useless panic that accomplished little besides turning everyone in the ram-house deaf for the time being. The king lunged in at the first ogre and was shocked at how easily the sword pierced the thick hide of the creature. The ogre seemed equally surprised and just stood there in shock with the blade through its heart until it toppled over. Then the king came on in earnest, playing the role of butcher in a slaughterhouse. The ogres were both weaponless and defenseless and they died one after another.

With his normal sword Dorcen was less effective and killed just three before the king had slain the rest. And then there came another silence—one that kept itself within the borders of the long house. Outside, there was great noise and commotion, but inside nothing.

It did not last. A heavy thump hit the ceiling causing both men to look up, reminding them that there existed another battle all about them. Climbing through the entrance the two saw that they were surrounded by countless maug that were kept at bay simply by the thin wooden shafts that rained down from above.

"Climb!" the king ordered Dorcen and the two scaled the sides of the house and came to stand with the rest of their assault force. The knights and the fey were fighting sword and dagger against a sea of goblins that lapped up against the building. They were holding their own but it would not— could not last long. Beyond the goblins the hellacious magical dark rolled toward them like a bank of dead fog.

From every direction rusting swords and jagged spears came up at the seven of them, but these were handpicked knights and fey of great ability. They hacking away hands and arms with every swing of their long swords. Those goblins nearest fell back afraid.

"Take the rope!" came a call from above. The men on the walls had thrown down ropes and were waiting to pull the team up. Eireden wouldn't take the rope, not if it meant leaving six others behind. The king reached over and grabbed one of the fey. She spun like a feral cat but stopped her blade just short of his throat.

"Go!" the king ordered, handing her the rope. The fey was hauled into the air as if she were lighter than the rope itself and then the next fey was hoisted up. "Alseya go on," he called holding the rope to her.

She ignored him and kept fighting. With the black coming he didn't have time to argue and so gave the rope to one of the knights. He was far less easy to haul up and it sounded like a bundle pots and pans smacking against the walls as he went up slowly. The rope came back down and Dorcen was just handing it to another knight when the entire building pitched at an angle and went over on its side.

The goblins had changed tactics. Instead of attacking they lifted one side of the building. Hundreds of them heaved and the building lurched over. Dorcen and the knight both fell, while Eireden and Alseya leapt forward so that they still stood atop the building, though they stood upon its sloped side. A crash of metal to their left caused the two to look over to see Dorcen being hauled up the side of the wall while on the ground the poor knight was being impaled on spear after goblin spear.

The building pitched again. The king gave the fey a quick look, sure to see panic in her eyes, yet she only studied his face with an unnatural calm. He wanted to question this but the building gathered speed as it rolled. Now the building lay upside down. There was no bottom to it and so they fell inside with the ram swinging about with bone crushing force. The two flattened themselves beneath it while all around them the maug cheered and the dark enveloped the far end of the building.

At the other end arrows still dropped goblins by the score, but one leapt up with an axe and cut one of the ropes holding the ram and the end of it crashed down nearly crushing the king's leg. Eireden climbed to his feet, yet he did so in the dark. That hideous magical darkness was upon them at last.

It lay thick and near complete around the two with the only light coming from the gleam of the king's elf-sword. It shone upon the white of Alseya's eyes and upon the wicked teeth of the thousands of goblins that surrounded them. The building pitched again, but in the dark there was no way for the two to climb or jump anywhere. It rocked over on its side and then again so that it was up right and the pair spilled onto the black grass of the prairie. Then the building was heaved again so that it disappeared into the darkness and Eireden and Alseya were without any cover whatsoever.

Around them capered and jeered the goblins, seemingly fearless now that the dark had come, but all the same they kept out of reach of the king. Alseya had lost her sword and now she clung to him and he held her. Eireden turned searching for the city, but it was as if it had disappeared. Not a light of it could be seen. Was it close? Was it far? What direction did it lay?

The two stood in a nightmare sea of utter blackness. But they were not alone. There was a presence in the dark; a malignant tumor of a being came toward the two. The goblins backed away at its approach.

Eireden pushed Alseya behind him and held out the sword while his eyes searched the black for anything. However there were no shadows, no movement, no nothing to indicate something was out there but it was there all the same.

"You disgust me," a voice said from the dark. It was low and beguiling. "With your filthy hands all over such a thing of beauty." Alseya shrank back and this caused the voice to laugh bitterly. "Not you, betrayer. The sight of you is repulsive. Your traitorous race is beneath hideous. I'm talking about the sword."

The sword seemed to come alive in Eireden's grip. It twisted in his hand, yanked him forward so that he lurched to his knees, and then shot away from him, flying out into the darkness. Without the sword the black was altogether complete. He could feel Alseya's breath coming rapidly against his neck, but even this close he couldn't catch the least glimpse of her.

"There, that's better," the voice said. It came so close that Eireden jumped.

"Darhmael?" he asked.

"You dare speak my name?" A blow coming out of the black struck him in the face and then another. When his hands came up to protect himself a strike to his midsection came with the force of a mule's kick. It doubled him over, but still he kept Alseya behind him. "How gallant of you to protect this whore," the elf said snidely. Another blow struck the king and another. Eireden began losing focus on his consciousness. "Don't you know that all the fey are whores?"

A final blow and Eireden crashed to the ground and then

there came light. One brief flash lit up their tiny world and in it the king saw the elf sword slide straight through Alseya. The sword went through her as if she were made of air instead of flesh. And then came dark once again. More endless dark. The king crawled to where he was certain the fey was and he did indeed find her. She lay sprawled upon the grass and her breath came in little hitches. He ran his hand up her lithe body until he found the wound just below her breastbone.

"Run...run away," she whispered.

There was nowhere he could run even if he wanted to. "No. I will not leave you," the king replied in his own whisper.

"How sweet," drawled Darhmael. "You wish to die with your traitorous whore. Too bad I won't allow it. You'll both die alone in the dark. Just as this whole city will and all the fey within it."

"No..." whispered Alseya.

Eireden knew what sort of terror the fey had for the dark. As well he knew that the fey could will themselves into death. "I have light," he whispered. "Enough, if you wish to go on."

Her shaking hands found his and she gripped them with the last of her strength that wilted from her. "Yes...please."

Kneeling beside the woman the king touched the pearl that Whip-wip had made for Ella and light burned into the darkness. It shone in a blazing circle around them but no further. At its edge something leapt back and hissed. Eireden looked down on Alseya and saw that somehow she was happy. A smile crept at the edges of her mouth and her opal eyes were warmer than they should have been.

She looked past him into the nothing and he was sure that she would die right there, but instead she said, "Firefly."

Eireden looked up and saw the firefly. It was small with distance and turned circles bearing down at them. Another came behind; and still more until they reminded him of sparks off a campfire. But then there came hundreds and then thousands and a sound rent the air. A screaming sound like an artillery shell and the dark began to burn with the light of these tiny beings and then they were there over Eireden and Alseya beating back the magical darkness with a light that was equally magical.

Then the king saw what they were. They were fairies. Fairies by the thousands churned the night air as they flew in a great mass and their light grew and grew becoming a small fiery nova above them. A cheering erupted, and squinting, the king could see the city not too far away. Laughing soldiers began shooting arrows into the goblins who stumbled about—themselves blind from the light and more soldiers came down from the battlements to slay their blind foes with impunity.

Of Darhmael nothing could be seen but his fleeing shadow. He had put much of himself into the magical darkness and with his goblins going in every direction being hewn down left and right; he retreated from the Den in their power.

The king turned from the butchering and the slaughter and the death. He stared down at the beautiful fey. It was life that he cared about. "Please, don't die," he whispered.

## Chapter 27

### Ella

The kiss lasted until the stars shone and the moon crept up. It drew Ella's soul from the depths of her chest. That gossamer part of herself was an invisible glow that ran along her skin, exciting her, warming her, making every sensation that much more. Making the night perfect.

There was no rushing that kiss. It was long and slow and endless. It came without the urgency of a human kiss. There was a need associated with it, but it wasn't a frantic need. It was a need that knew patience that knew there would be many more of these perfect kisses to come. Yes, the kiss was perfect and it might have gone on—though it couldn't have gone further—except Whip-wip never came back. She had flown away on a breeze and just plain disappeared. Aric and Ella went up and down the beach calling for her but to no avail. Eventually they built a bonfire which they kept fed throughout the night.

"You shouldn't worry," Aric assured Ella in the morning when she still hadn't come back. "Whip-wip is fine. It's not like she's in any danger; you know it's practically impossible to kill a fairy, especially one as smart as her. If I had to guess she's off somewhere stacking turtles or some such nonsense."

Ella allowed herself to be comforted but wouldn't allow them to leave the beach, not until Whip-wip came back—which she did about noon the following day.

"*Sis twiick? Sis zooti?*" the fairy begged as she came up slowly against the westerly wind. If she had looked hung-over the day before, she looked on death's door that morning. Her wings drooped and her blue eyes seemed washed out. In fact she curled up and fell asleep immediately and even if Ella had any fruit it wasn't likely that Whip-wip had the energy to eat.

Aric wrapped her in the cashmere sweater and then went

in search of fruit, while Ella went swimming. The Pacific was cold—stinking cold, but she figured that she was an elf and that she could overcome something so simple as a drop in temperature. And she did.

And she overcame much more than that. Ella swam to unheard of depths and then tested her lung capacity. Diving deep where the light began to fade she held her breath for over four minutes. She also discovered that she could swim at Olympic speeds almost without effort. Using her raw telekinetic power as well as three years of swimming lessons, she churned the water, turning it white in her wake.

Aric joined her. He swam with an easy grace with a practiced motion learned over centuries on the lake in the Feylands. Everything about his technique seemed so effortless that she was astonished how fast he could go. One other thing astonished her. She didn't notice until he flipped over to do the backstroke that he swam buck-naked. Unabashedly so. He wasn't the least bit embarrassed, while Ella, who swam in her bra and panties, turned away with cheeks gone pink.

"Are you ok?" he asked after a minute. "You suddenly went quiet and you won't look in my direction. I haven't angered you in some fashion, have I?"

"Oh no. Don't worry about that it's just...I'm just...it's just...you're naked!" Ella stammered. "It's not something that I'm used to. Where I grew up people wore clothes in the water. Swimsuits we called them." Aric laughed at this. He had a tendency to laugh at everything. Smiling and laughing were always his first response to nearly any given situation. She loved that about him.

"We wear swimming apparel as well," Aric said, treading water with a gentle waving motion of his hands. "However if the mood strikes us to go for a dip and we don't have a swimsuit on hand it's not considered improper to swim unadorned. If you would rather, I can wait for you on the beach."

[189]

Ella wanted both to tell him, yes and no. She had been raised to consider public nudity improper, at same time she had to get used to the idea that she was an elf. Things would be different. But how would they be different?

She had the sudden urge to be alone with her thoughts. "If you don't mind? I'll be just a few moments," she said. He gave her a wave and then slipped below the surface only to pop up over a minute later practically on shore. Almost too late she realized that she was watching him come out of the water and quickly she turned away again feeling her cheeks heat up.

How would things be different as an elf? Because of her "elfness" would she suddenly jettison everything that she had been taught to consider right and wrong? And if so, why? Because she was suddenly now better than human? Because she was magical and they weren't? Had she become enlightened with the discovery of her parentage?

No. In fact the opposite was true. Her parents were evil—as evil as evil got. Her father and maybe her mother as well, had conspired to kill off an entire race of people. It was like having Nazis for parents. The thought was depressing. Ella slipped beneath the water and swam to the bottom of the ocean, some fifty feet down. There she settled onto the sand and looked up at the surface. It seemed so big.

She wasn't in any way better than the humans. Nor was she better than the fey or the Den or the dwarves. She wasn't even better than the fairies. And she didn't need to be. Ella just needed to be herself. Whether she was an elf or not didn't change who she was or how she had been raised. Just then, sitting indian-style on the bottom of the ocean, she thought of her fat, TV loving, adoptive parents and smiled.

They were human and they raised her right.

Ella shot up to the surface with a splash that nearly drenched Whip-wip who had been hovering over the ocean. The fairy danced back from the water. "Zooti?" she asked.

"I thought Aric got you an apple," Ella said as she began

swimming into shore doing her own backstroke so that she could watch the pretty fairy dancing above the waves. Whip-wip whistled and hooted disgustedly: the apple had been wormy. "We can get you some fruit in town. You name it I'll get it for you. Blackberries, strawberries, peaches, tangerines, whatever you want."

"We're getting out of season for some of those," Aric said. He stood on the beach once again wearing the simple tunic of a prisoner of the Den. This he had somehow—magically was Ella's guess—kept clean and neat. "By the way, what exactly is a tangerine?"

"You don't know what a tangerine is? Ha! The circle is now complete. When I left you, I was but the learner; now I am the master," Ella said in her deepest voice.

Aric looked confused. "The master?"

"Oh not really," Ella said in a hurry. "It's a line from a movie...but you don't know what one of those are either, do you? Well, first the supermarket and then lunch—we'll see what you make of pizza—and then we'll catch a movie."

As she expected, Aric was up for anything. After a quick trip to a local branch of her bank, where a little help from Aric overcame her lack of ID, they went to see what sort of fruit was available.

Everything imaginable it turned out. Whip-wip was allowed to come along but only on the condition that she stay hidden and quiet. Hiding was the easy part. At every turn amongst the displays she let out a new demand for *Zooti*! First a bite of pear, then a blueberry, then she demanded a chunk of banana...and so on. She even tried a bit of avocado, but didn't care for the mushiness of it. When they exited the produce section she settled down, but Ella was sure that it was only her extreme exhaustion that kept her behavior in check.

The fairy did perk up again when they reached the candy aisle. Her blue eyes went wide at all the colors and she again started demanding *Zooti*.

"It's not fruit," Ella explained. "Even this stuff with the pictures of fruit on them isn't fruit. It's candy. How do I explain candy to a fairy?" she asked Aric.

"You'll first have to explain it to me," he laughed.

"You don't have candy in the Forbidden Lands? What about fudge...or ice cream?" He shook his head at these questions and she joked, "Maybe we should rethink our relationship."

"Or maybe you should tell me what these are."

"Naw. It's better to experience them," she said. "After all which is better, the description of a rose or an actual rose...don't answer that. I can see the poetry forming behind your eyes. Let's just buy this stuff and have a sample-fest in the car."

"Sounds like fun, but first, when you say 'buy' what do you mean exactly?" Ella wasn't in the mood to begin an explanation of a market-based economy, not right there in the store at least. Though she knew that if he stayed in America much longer he would have to learn.

Once in the car Whip-wip eyed the candy in their bright packages like a kid at Christmas. The thought made Ella remember her vision of snuggling before a roaring fire on a cold night. Handing Whip-wip a red M&M, Ella asked Aric, "Do you celebrate Christmas?" Right away she could tell that the word was new to him and she followed up with, "What about God? Do you believe in an all-powerful being that created the heavens and the earth?"

"We don't know how the earth came about," Aric answered peeling his tangerine. "But yes we believe that there are beings more powerful than the fey just as there are beings of less power."

Suddenly the red M&M smacked off the window and went skittering away with the fairy hot after it. When she retrieved it she stared at it for a moment and then raised it up in both hands and bashed against the dashboard. She was trying to break it open to see what was inside. Ella cracked the thing with her mind, revealing the chocolate. Whip-wip tore into it. She loved it, but after a couple of bites it became too rich for her and she moved on to the next candy...and the next...and the next until she seemed drunk, weaving around the car batting into things.

Though she liked the taste of chocolate, it was the gummy bears that had her enticed. She wouldn't eat them. Instead she placed them around the car like decorations. Some she had holding paws; others she seated around piles of candy as if they were at a picnic and other she stuck in the vents of the air conditioning like little guards. When they were all set out in some manner, Whip-wip fell asleep.

"I'll never understand her," Ella said, collecting the bears. They would melt or become sticky if she didn't.

"She is alive and happy," Aric remarked. "What more is there to understand?"

In a perfect world Ella was sure she wouldn't need much more than being alive and happy. However she didn't live in that world just yet. Before lunch she called the private investigator who gave her, a somewhat cryptic answer to her case's status: "I'm following up on some leads. Call me back tomorrow."

Ella dwelt on this during lunch. She drove north and east toward Tacoma and found a promising pizza place. "Whip-wip. I need you to wake up for a sec," she said nudging the fairy from her sleep when they had pulled into the parking lot. "Aric and I will be right in there, but you can't come in. I promise I'll bring back some pizza, ok?"

The fairy clutched her stomach and groaned, "No twiick...no twiick. No peesa."

"Alright, no pizza," Ella said leaving the fairy who lay rubbing her bulging belly. "Right now she isn't all that alive or happy," she added to Aric.

Ella felt pretty much the same way after her own lunch. She ordered three mediums pizzas each with different toppings so that Aric could try everything. Though she ate and smiled and laughed, there was still that undercurrent of nervousness over what the investigator would tell her. Sensitive as always Aric picked up on this and held her hand and was very much the gentlemen.

He did so again in the movies. She chose an

action/adventure movie based off a bestselling comic book and did so strictly for the sake of the computer graphics and not the silly plot line. Aric was very much impressed with the excitement it generated and enjoyed it immensely. Because they caught a mid-afternoon show and had the theater to themselves Ella invited Whip-wip along as well.

The fairy watched the movie as if it were real life. She screamed out warnings to the heroes and ducked and dodged during the battles. When the love interest went to kiss her man Whip-wip floated smack dab in the middle of the theater with her hands clutched to her breast—and then raced back expecting Aric and Ella to kiss as well. And in the final climatic battle the fairy joined in, swooping down on the villain shooting her lights at the screen and then cheering at his demise.

When it was over she wanted to go again.

Ella wouldn't let her. Instead they went back to the beach, this time with new blankets and pillows. Despite the fire and the warmth of Aric's body against hers, Ella couldn't sleep. She watched the stars overhead and fantasized about her mom. In every one of these she was normal, which turned out not to be the case. The next morning she went right away to the nearest phone to call the investigator. He had found Elleni Feyden.

## Chapter 28

### Eireden

Instead of growing dim the fairies spinning around each other seemed to gain strength and their light intensified, and the orb of radiance rose higher into the air, banishing the night and the magic dark completely.

Directly below it Eireden knelt over the dying body of Alseya Bellesarus. Ignoring the mayhem around them he touched her face, and her white eyes came back to his. "Last night...I dreamed...of this very moment," she said in a tiny whisper of a voice.

"Yet you came to fight nonetheless," the king said bending closer. "Now I need you to fight again. Fight to live, please. For a little longer until help comes." He looked up and all he saw were his men-at-arms going here and there slaying at will.

"In my dream...I fought to live...because...you promised..." she trailed off, fighting for breath. Darhmael's sword had run her through the chest and now her lungs were filling with blood.

"What? What did I promise? I'll promise it now, whatever it is."

"You promised...to kiss me," she said.

His mouth came open and he stammered for a moment, "And—and I will but hold on." He sat up straighter and yelled, "I need a scout over here! Give me a scout or a fey!"

"Their power...is gone," she whispered. Her voice was losing the little strength it had. "Even the...fey. It's all...gone"

She was probably right. Darhmael had thrown everything he had at them. Eireden looked around. His men seemed to be filled with a bloodlust and none came near. Brave Alseya was going to die. She had stayed behind when she could have fled from atop the ram house despite knowing how it would end for her.

"Why? Why do you want me to kiss you?" he asked. She

seemed so vulnerable this near to death. So delicate.

"Because...in my dream...it was...nice," she answered haltingly. "Never been...kissed before."

At this, many thoughts exploded in his head, but he ignored them all. Alseya would be dead in a minute and he would not deny her this simple thing—not for one so brave. He kissed her then and softer lips he had never felt. When he broke the touch of their lips she smiled and then her eyes rolled back.

"Alseya!" Eireden screamed feeling a burning in his eyes. "Scout! I need a..." he stopped in mid-sentence. Generai was there gaping at him. In her hand was a bloodstained sword and across her back was an empty quiver. "Generai, come heal her now before it's too late."

The scout took a step back and her eyes went hard. "I've got nothing left. No one does," she said. "Let her be. Let her go and look to your men. There is battle still to be fought."

The king gaped at her hard tone and harder words. He then took in the battle plain in a long sweeping glance. Men were still streaming down from the walls and there was no 'battle' that he could see. There was only death. Though it was necessary death to be sure. No goblin would be suffered to live. However he was done with it. His sword had been taken from him and he could deal no more death that day. Not when he thought about the ogres trapped in the ram house and how he had killed them despite their awful begging.

"I have slain all that I will today," he said. "I look to life. If you can't heal her I will find one that can." The king lifted the fey as if she weighed nothing and clutched her to his chest protectively. He made to go to the city, but another fey came running up. Covered in blood as she was the king only recognized the gold eyes of Feylon Darania. "Help her," he begged.

In reality the gold eyes were only a dim yellow. Feylon saw whom he carried and her face sank. "I don't have the strength left. Captain Jeden, when the dark came there was an elf...and the Captain's injuries..." she left off looking horrified at whatever had happened to the first assault team.

There would be no help for Alseya.

The king glanced down at the limp form in his arms. She was nothing; so light compared to his great strength. How easily he could crush this tiny slip of a woman. Even then after those harrowing moments confronting Darhmael he was barely winded, yet this girl was leaking her life down his chest and there was nothing he could do. His biceps bulged in impotent fury and then even as the thought struck, he said, "Take my strength. Heal her with my strength."

"That's not something I can do," Feylon said miserably. "I mean I don't know how."

Eireden went to his knees in front of her. "Just do it!" he commanded in the tone of a king.

With Generai watching, Feylon went to the king and placed her hands upon his shoulders and then closed her eyes. For a second nothing happened and then a gold light appeared where her hands touched him. She screamed in pain and pulled back staring at her hands.

"It didn't work," she gasped looking at her palms in horror. "Your body resisted. It—it attacked me."

The blonde scout pursed her lips at this. "Let me. You're not Den. You don't know what our lives are like, and life is exactly what she needs. Lay her down," she ordered the king. When he did she knelt next to him and said, "What is life, but love?"

"What?" he asked confused.

"Close your eyes and don't move."

He did and was surprised when Generai kissed him. Softly at first, and then with growing fierceness. In seconds she crushed herself to him and then he could feel something swelling up inside him. It was an energy that came up out of his soul and it did indeed feel just like love. A powerful love that grew as they kissed—like a fire. No more wonderful feeling had he ever experienced, but then there was something else within the love. He could sense it on the strangest level. It was greed. Generai was taking his love and she wanted more and more. Greedily she wanted it all, every drop of it, and she wasn't going to stop until she had it. And what would happen to him when she got it all? The answer scared him.

He shoved her away and there on her face was raw animal emotion: anger, jealousy, and that awful greed. Then she blinked and swayed. The look was gone. "Lift her," she said in an odd voice. Still kneeling Eireden picked Alseya up and laid her against his chest; he clutched her from behind. And then Generai again surprised him. He thought that she would lay out her hands as healers did; instead she kissed Alseya gently on the lips.

For seconds nothing appeared to happen but then Alseya's hands came up and gripped Generai's arms holding her with surprising strength.

She had done it! Generai had healed the fey...but still they kissed. The blonde girl began to struggle. Eireden realized that she was dealing with the same greed of life and love that he had, and so he pried them apart. At first Alseya's hands were like claws on the scout's leather armor, but then she sank back against the king.

"You live," the king said, barely believing it.

"I didn't dream that kiss," she whispered.

The scout blinked at her dully and then crumpled to the ground to stare up at the great mass of fairies. "It's growing dark," Generai said. At first Eireden thought she was losing consciousness, but then he too saw the light dim slightly.

He stood and looked over the battlefield. The corpses of the maug carpeted the plains as far as his eye could see. Men were slowly coming back, walking in twos and threes, and all seemed whole. The king spun in place, searching for dead Den among the thousands of goblins. From where he stood he couldn't see a single one. He knew there had to be some—

the knight for instance—the one from his team, Peroda something. Lienhart had spoken of him highly. Only a glint of polished steel could be seen where he had fallen before the gates.

Now that he knew what to look for he searched again. There was more steel, but not much more. A helmet by the gate tower. A shield propped at the base of the wall. A broken sword clenched by a mailed hand. Where were the rest?

"We won," he said slowly as realization came over him. The impossible had happened. That which could not be done had been done. "We won. Sythei! We won!" he roared. At the words the great glowing orb began to break up as the thousands of individual fairies began flying here and there hooting in excitement.

"The firefly," Alseya said, pointing to a small streak of light. There was Tissa whistling with joy at the victory and then the rest of Eireden's family came up to mob her and this included the fairy Whip-wip who dashed from the pack long enough to go to the king and plant a kiss upon his face.

She made to fly back but he caught her in a gentle hold. "Is Ella ok?" he asked her.

"*Sis! Sis ekees.*" Translation: Yes she's happy. She then bit his finger sharp enough for him to let go.

Whip-wip left him and flew back to rejoin her family only to be replaced by the smallest fairy, Tissa. "This was not what I asked for," the king said with a smile. He had asked her to go find a *few* more fairy families to help out. Part of this order was strictly to keep her safe, but the other part was in earnest. The fairies had proven valuable fighting companions against the maug before and they certainly proved it again.

"Your highness? What are you going to do to keep ten thousand fairies occupied?" Generai asked, looking up at the swarm nervously.

"Oh, think of the poor cats of Hildoeven," Feylon added.

"You're going to need more dishes when they're gone," Alseya remarked. "You might want to think about that."

## Chapter 29

## Eireden

Outside the walls Eireden gathered his men. He formed them into companies and then, with a retinue of an uncountable number of fairies, he marched through the gates in triumph. Deafening cheers went up and the fairies scattered in excitement at the sound. Prince Lienhart, who had been directing the battle in the north part of the city and who had come within an ace of being overrun, greeted him, bringing him his mount.

"Hail Eireden, king of the Den, Lord of the Sythei," he cried out. A chant began: "Eir-Eh- Den! Eir-Eh- Den!" The sythei, electrified by the tremendous volume, spun in a glowing vortex over the courtyard and every face looked up. Thinking that the king had caused this, the chanting grew even louder.

The king let this go on longer than he really wished. He didn't want the adulation; however his people needed a champion to rally round. They needed to be able to celebrate. While they cheered he walked the golden palomino around the formations of men. He made a show of acknowledging his captains and waving to his soldiers, but what he was really doing was counting and recounting his men. To his amazement they filled the courtyard just as they had all week.

When the cheers died down he rode again to the front and smiled at his men. They were battled hardened men but just then he felt more like their father than their commander. "You chant my name, but I did not win this battle. You won this battle..." More cheers stopped him in mid-sentence and he had to wait almost a minute to begin again. "It's right that you are cheering yourselves. You fought like heroes, from the greatest captain right down to the tiniest fairy." Again more cheers. "From the scouts with their nimble bows, to the sturdy men-at-arms, to the healers among the fey, you are what made this victory possible. It was your hard work building these defenses, your diligence in training and your single-minded dedication to protecting your city and your loved ones that turned the tide. You are the reason behind this victory."

Again more cheers erupted. He allowed it to go on and as it did he turned and saluted the prince. "I leave the defense of the city in your hands, Prince Lienhart. If you'll be so kind, I'll need a casualty list as soon as possible." Next he saluted the fey, and, in a quieter less, bombastic tone, thanked them for their contribution to the fight. For some reason, as he spoke, his eye kept catching Alseya's. He tried to wrap up his comments as soon as possible. Generai had come with him and he could feel her watching his every move.

The king then called on the fairies, but they weren't all that interested in hearing what he had to say. To them a speech was a form of torture. Instead they were conducting what looked like a cross between a convention and a mass-family reunion. His own family came for him. Led by Whip-wip they brought him once again to the quiet fountain. There, on the marble lip was another body.

"Oh no," the king breathed feeling a dead aching depression come over him. He didn't need to ask who she was—he could see the gold of Riecie's wings as plain as day. This time he didn't wait and he walked up first. Touching his pearl the king bathed the broken body in its light and then touched her. She was very cold, but still so soft. Tears came from his eyes and he let them come freely as his family came to give the dead their light. Even Generai came up and touched Riecie's body.

"She was my favorite," the scout said with a little laugh that ended in a choked cry. "She—she was always so elegant and sweet...and..." The girl couldn't go on and Eireden pulled her in close and hugged her.

"I know. The sythei have such innocence it's as though a child has died," he said. "Come on. We should leave them.

[202]

They have some sort of ceremony they do in private." The two left the family singing dolefully and went to their quarters in the palace. His men would work throughout the night, stabilizing the walls that were damaged, reinforcing the gates, clearing bodies away and counting the dead. The one great perk, perhaps the only great perk to being king was that he could go to bed and leave the mess of cleaning up to someone else.

Besides he was too exhausted to be of any help. He hadn't slept at all the night before, and it was only that very morning that he had been a few heartbeats from death. Generai helped him out of his armor and bathed his wounds—there were more that he realized—and then she put him to bed with a kiss on the forehead.

Right before she left, she turned in the doorway. "What is it with you and fey women?" she asked for the second time that day. He couldn't tell her, because he didn't know. "Why did you kiss Alseya?"

"Oh that. Because she was dying," he answered. "And because she asked me too."

"So that's all it takes," Generai said with a laugh. "If I had known that simply dying would get you to kiss me I would have fallen on my sword a long time ago. No—don't argue. For one it was a joke and for two you're too tired."

He was indeed. She left him and before the door had shut he was fast asleep.

Just before sunrise the king awoke with a fairy standing on his pillow. It was Whip-wip, she had come to say goodbye. Though there wasn't a word for it in their language he understood anyway. She pulled him to the window and he tiptoed gingerly—his room was carpeted with lightly snoring fairies. There, she pointed away south and west. She need not have. He could feel Ella without any problem.

"Could you tell Ella...tell her that," the king paused. What words would she want to hear? That he had won a great victory? No, that sounded like bragging. That he was thinking of her? No, it was no longer his place. "Don't tell her anything. Let her be happy. And you be happy as well."

The fairy smiled at this, but then turned somber. She pointed to the table beside his bed and there sat another little grass-woven box. Inside, he was sure laid the remains of Riecie. Whip-wip began whistling in her simple language: *Keep her safe. Keep her near your heart.*

"I will," replied the king. Whip-wip flew and planted a kiss upon his lips and then was gone. He watched her until her tiny glow faded in the distance and then he went to the box. Picking it he went to put in his pouch with the other one when he noted that something in Riecie's box moved. Quickly he put it down and worked the clever little latch. Inside he saw the dead fairy curled up in the fetal position. It smote his heart to see her again. He saw what had moved. Someone, likely Whip-wip, had put a pearl in the box with her.

Sighing, the king closed the lid and put Riecie in the pouch with Zizis and Sheesa, but not before feeling the same little movement in their box. He didn't need to open it to know that Whip-wip had added pearls for them.

*Keep her safe. Keep her near your heart.*

He would. He would keep them all close.

The king put the pouch beside his bed and slept again and he dreamt of the great ball of light that the fairies had created with their—love? Had it been love that created the intensity of the light? He didn't know and the dream didn't help. There was a great swelling of love in his dream but whether it came from the light or the three women that haunted him he didn't know. He just knew that when he woke with Alseya sitting beside his bed he had a sudden guilty feeling.

"Good morning," she said as his mouth came open at the sight of her. "You are need of healing. It is not right for the Sun King to go about bruised and bloodied as you are."

"Sun King?" he exclaimed.

"That is what some are calling you," she replied. "And I

for one would say that the title is fitting. You summoned a light more piercing than the sun and banished evil with it."

Eireden didn't like it. After having lived as a *gada* for five years anything that seemed too grandiose made him uneasy. "In truth I am not a king at all just yet, and 'Sun King' I am definitely not. And second, Darhmael wasn't banished, he was simply driven away and third there are others with injuries far worse than..."

"Shush, my king," she said stopping his words with a simple touch of his lips. "Those that are in bad shape are being attended to and even the most injured of them all demand that you be healed first."

Before he could say a word a blue light spread from her light and the relief he felt was instantaneous He slumped back with an embarrassing moan of pleasure that reverted to guilt the second Generai walked in with a hard look to her grey eyes.

"Your presence is being requested my lord," she said coldly. "Perhaps you should be *dressed* before you receive any more visitors." The scout stood in her leathers, tall and haughty, in anger she looked down her nose at the small fey woman. Alseya didn't seem to notice.

"I will leave you to your valet, for now," Alseya said. She stood and left in such a fluid easy grace that she seemed to ride upon an unfelt wind.

"Valet!" Generai exclaimed as soon as the door shut. "Is that what I am to you? A servant?" The scout advanced on him angrily.

The king put his hands up, palms out. "I don't think that at all. If I had to give you a title—it would be chief lieutenant, or maybe lead advisor. Generai you should know better. You are the one person in this world that I can trust wholeheartedly."

This mollified her somewhat and the fire of her anger burned low, though he could see that it still smoldered in her eyes. "I don't trust that fey," she said. "She's been asking about you all morning. And now I find her in here when you aren't even dressed. That seems hardly befitting to me."

Eireden thought it wise not to point out that Generai was also in his room in his current state of undress. The scout began pacing, which left him trapped beneath his bed covers. "She is strange don't you think?" Generai asked. "It's her eyes. I don't like them. Without any pupils you can't really tell where she's looking. Don't you think that's strange? I think it's strange and not very attractive, despite what some lunkheads around here think. You know why all this came about, don't you? It's because you kissed her."

"Why all what came about?"

"Oh, never mind," Generai said. "What are you doing just laying there? Half the city wants to see you this morning. They've been pushing to wake you since the first light of dawn. Everybody wants to know when you're going to challenge Eirowyth. Some are even looking to make a parade out of it. We've never had a victory in Hildoeven like last night's."

"There will be no parade. I want you to make sure you cut that sort of talk off as soon as possible. Were I going to the capital for a simple coronation, then I would allow it, however I go to slay my kinsmen. There will be no parade for such a thing."

"Don't be so quick!" she replied. "Your victory last night almost guarantees that your cousin has to face you—almost. He could still hide behind the law. But with all the city behind you, Eirowyth will be shamed into accepting your challenge."

"It will be enough to take only a few," the king answered. "Now, if you don't mind. I have to get dressed."

She started to leave but stopped in the door. "Will you take me to the capital?"

This wasn't a simple request. Generai wasn't just asking to go to witness the challenge. She wanted to stay in Rhyoeven. More to the point, she wanted to stay in

Rhyoeven with him. After all of her intense loyalty, he couldn't say no, yet at the same time he didn't want to lead her on and say yes. He was in an awkward position: hurt her now or hurt her later.

*Maybe I could love Generai—if I tried,* he thought.

Yes, or maybe he'd always be in love with Ella. And what about Alseya? He suddenly pictured her face—beautiful, exotic, entrancing. The king blinked away the image. He couldn't dwell on this, not now. "Yes, of course you may come. I still need my chief lieutenant," he said, putting the hurt off for later.

# Chapter 30

## Ella

"I have discovered the whereabouts of your mother," the investigator said. Through the archaic pay phone he sounded very far away and Ella began to get nervous that her mother was in another country.

"You did? That's wonderful. Is she...is she here in America?"

The man paused long enough for Ella's anxiety to mount but then there came the sound of rustling papers and he answered, "Yes she is currently in a facility north of Seattle called..." More shuffling of papers, enough for Ella's mind to hang on the word facility. Nothing good ever came along with a word as sterile and unhappy sounding as facility. "Here it is: Puget Sound Behavioral Health. There is patient there named Elleni Feyden."

"A patient? Is she sick?" Ella asked, afraid of the term 'Behavioral Health'. What sort of behavior did that encompass?

"I don't have a diagnosis on her, not just yet. They keep that sort of information very tight under wraps. What I can tell you is that the facility is for chronic mental patients...what we used to call a loony bin back in the day. I'm sorry."

"Looney bin," Ella said breathlessly. The word came with pain associated with it. What would Aric think? The fey all seemed so perfect—she was certain that he would never understand. Would he look down his nose at her mother or at her? Ella took a quick peek out to the car and saw Aric staring right at her. She turned away feeling her skin ripple in goose bumps.

"I only used that term so you would understand what sort of place this is," the investigator explained. "It's not a place for people suffering with depression or addiction. I've looked into it. It's a place for people who cannot cope in the community. You understand what I mean by that?"

Ella thought she understood. "Is she dangerous? Has my mom hurt people?" Her back and shoulders spasmed with a sudden case of the shivers. *She's an elf; of course she's hurt people.*

"That I don't know," the man replied. "Like I said I don't have a diagnosis. Would you like me to look further into her situation? Given the right resources I can find out everything there is to know about her."

"No. You've done all that I've asked. I think...I think if I want to go further into this I can do it on my own." After getting the address to where her mom was being held, Ella hung up. She then stared at the scrap of paper: Puget Sound Behavioral Health. The words looked so harmless while the image in her mind was so torturous. Was her mom in some rubber-room? Did they have those still? Was she under restraints—in solitary confinement? Had she killed many people?

All of this kept her trapped in the phone booth, afraid to step back out into the real world. Eventually Aric came for her. He tapped on the glass and smiled in at her.

"Does this booth have a secondary function?" he joked. "Or have you forgotten how to work the door and are just trapped in there?"

Ella gave him a large fake grin and wondered how on earth she would tell him about her mother. Maybe she shouldn't. Maybe she should just take Aric back to the beach and forget about her. After all the lady had abandoned her, why couldn't she do the same thing? Why couldn't she just drive off down to Mexico and spend the rest of her very long life drinking margaritas on some white beach?

*Because I'm not evil*, Ella reminded herself. "D-do the f-fey have...uh...problems sometimes, you know, relating among each other in a way that one would consider abnormal? Or maybe very abnormal, or even bizarre? Does that happen? Like...uh, drooling or seeing things that aren't there, or talking to yourself?"

"Drooling? Only when one is very young. I'm sure that I drooled once upon a time," he said. "Hopefully you can still respect me?"

"I respect you. It's the other way around that has me nervous," Ella said. Aric began to protest this but she held up a finger to his lips and stopped him. "Let's get in the car. I'll explain while we drive."

As she had expected, chronic mental illness was an unheard of phenomenon among the fey. They could become depressed, as Aric had in the dungeons of Rhyoeven, but it was usually a fleeting thing. Never before had he heard of an institution like the one they were driving too.

"Humans are such fragile creatures," he said when she finished describing what they would likely find at the end of their journey. "How they have managed to last as long as they have, I'll never know. I think the Den are as capable as they are simply because they have lived out their existence so close to us."

Ella felt the urge to defend the people she had once claimed to be hers but didn't. What they would find at the institution would undoubtedly be worse than what she had described. It would be humanity at its most pathetic. "Just remember, it's not their fault. They weren't lucky enough to be born fey like you. Instead they were born with some malformed gene that left them susceptible to mental illness."

"I understand the term genes but what is a 'malformed' gene?" he asked.

"I don't know how to put it other than to say a birth defect. Unfortunately humans carry bad genes within them that can cause physical or mental deformities."

"Deformities," he said with a shiver. "Those poor people. But I have to wonder how your mother is mixed up with them."

In her mind a giant billboard appeared with the words: CRIMINALLY INSANE written across it in bold letters.

Who had her mother killed? Or maybe the question was: how many had she killed? "There could be reasons," Ella said meekly. "If she started talking about elves and fairies and goblins they might put her away. Remember, for us...or I mean for them those are make-believe creatures."

"They would lock away one of their own just for that? I know you were raised with them, Ella, but I find humans repugnant at times."

Ella did as well, even back when she thought she was a human. "How about we listen to some music?" she suggested. "Whip-wip, could you pick something out?"

The fairy was delighted to and she kept a three-hour dance-a-thon going until they made their ways onto the grounds of the Puget Sound Behavioral Health Treatment Center. Dull grey rains had come which made the grounds even more depressing than they would normally have been. Every window was covered with bars and every door locked.

Aric, again covered in a subtle illusion, got them past security easily with a simple suggestion and it wasn't long before they were seated in a conference room waiting on one of the staff doctors. Aric, at least was upbeat. "It's well lit and clean, which is good. I was worried we would be heading down into some sort of medieval dungeon. And she has her own doctor, so she must be healthy."

"What do we do if she's evil?" Ella whispered. That old question ran through her mind: how many people had her mom killed? She must have asked herself that a hundred times. "Can you fight an elf?" she added.

"Perhaps the very weakest elf...and even then, I doubt it," Aric replied. "I don't think you need to be worried all that much. If the humans can control her then she must be in chains. Or her cell is of cold iron. There is a lot of it in these buildings. Can't you feel it?" She could. The deeper into the building they had gone the more on edge she had become.

"Yes, I can. I've...hold on, someone's coming." She could hear the footsteps clacking down the hall and in half a minute the door opened and in walked a balding, middle-aged man. He wore a very crisp white coat and coming from underneath it Ella could smell fading *Polo* cologne.

"Hello, I'm Doctor Levin. Nice to meet you," he said shaking hands all around as Ella introduced herself and Aric. "And you are Ms Feyden's daughter? We didn't know she had one."

"I didn't know either...I mean, up until a few weeks ago I didn't know I had been an orphan at one time."

Dr Levine sat up straighter. "Interesting. It's very rare to find an adult who learns late in life that they had been adopted. I'm sure it's brought up many questions that you'd never thought you'd be asking yourself."

*How many people has my mother killed?* "Yes I suppose it has," Ella said putting on a thin-veneered smile. "But I'm not here to learn about myself. I'm here to learn about my mother."

"So you are saying you aren't in need of a shrink," he asked with a twinkle in his eye. The doctor waved his hand. "I can't turn it off even when I try. It's why I don't tell people at parties what I do for a living. If I do I get two types: those that clam up in fear of saying something that might be construed as 'crazy' and those that want to find the nearest couch to lay down upon." He laughed at this and Ella politely laughed along. Aric only looked curious.

"Who would want to be shrunk?" the fey asked. "Is this an illusion you are referring to or an actual corporeal reduction?"

Ella laughed loudly at this, hoping her nervousness didn't come through. "Corporeal reduction...ha-ha! He's such a kidder," she said and then patted Aric's hand, giving him a look that suggested he zip his lip. "Now about my mother. Has she, uh, hurt anyone? Is that why she's here?"

"Ms Feyden hurt anyone?" the psychiatrist asked. He had with him an inch thick chart that he began flipping through it. "Not to my recollection. No...no, I don't see anything in here concerning violence. There's nothing even before my time."

"Before your time?" Ella asked. "How long has she been here?"

Since 1981," Dr Levine said once again consulting his records. "The first document dates back to July of that year. She was admitted with two diagnoses...Delusional Disorder and Catatonia. A third diagnosis of schizophrenia was added...uh, six years later."

"And these disorders are what?" Ella asked. Of the three she had only heard of schizophrenia and like most people she didn't quite understand it fully.

"Delusional Disorder is a psychosis in which the patient expresses an idea or belief that simply isn't a fact," the doctor said, sitting back in one of the comfortable chairs. "Frequently a person will live in a fantasy world of their own making and in her case she believes that she is someone of great importance. Ms Feyden also suffers from Schizophrenia, which is a sort of catch all for a multitude of symptoms. It is usually characterized by a breakdown of thought processes and by poor or negative emotional responsiveness. She has auditory hallucinations, paranoia, and bizarre delusions. Her speech is disorganized and her thinking is significantly dysfunctional."

Ella felt hollow inside. Despite the fact that her mom was in a 'loony bin' she didn't believe she would have an actual diagnosis, let alone three. "And the last one?"

"Catatonia," the doctor said. "Is a state of neurogenic motor immobility, manifested by extreme stupor. This is her most severe diagnosis. There are days when she won't bat an eye or move an inch, despite all the meds we pump into her system."

"You pump meds?" Ella asked quietly. "Why would you do that?"

"In a vain hope of trying to help her," Levine answered with a shrug. "Our only chance is to reach her when she's lucid and try to come to grips with her underlying emotional issues then. Though I have to say in all honesty that we won't win this battle. We've tried every drug known to man and nothing works at least for very long. Your mother is simply beyond our ability to treat."

"If I understand correctly, these medicines are a crude form of healing," Aric said. "Since they haven't worked maybe I should take a look at her."

"I can allow the daughter of the patient in to see her but without proper authorization I can't allow..."

Ella gave Aric a knowing look and dipped her head toward the doctor. Aric picked up on this easily and interrupted Levine, "I am a healer much like yourself. I may be her only chance." This he said with an easy push from his mind. "You will let us see her."

Levine's eyes came open a bit wider as if he had just thought of a new idea. "Why don't you come down to the ward and see what you can do?"

"I think I will," Aric replied with an easy smile.

They followed the doctor to another building—one which had guards both inside and out—and then down a long hall. Heavy metal doors sporting tiny windows were set left and right, checkerboard style. Ella hurried after the doctor with a growing fear squirreling in her belly. What would her mom be like? Was she going to be beautiful? Was she going to be evil? Were all the diagnoses a front, a disguise so that she could remain hidden? Ella had to hold Aric's hand to keep from biting her nails.

"She's right in there," the doctor said, point to the fourth door on the left.

Ella went to the window. She stared in at Elleni Feyden for well over a minute and in all that time the lady didn't budge a muscle. For as much as she moved she could have been a manikin. "I think there's some mistake," Ella said, turning from the little glass window. "That's not my mother. That lady is human."

## Chapter 31

## Eireden

The king strapped on his armor, noticing that it had been polished to a shine. He also found the elf-blade that he had given to Lienhart in a gold and silver gilded scabbard. He paused before buckling it about his waist. The sword had been a gift to the prince—one that had meant to be a badge of his new rank. He knew better than to try and give it back, not until he won the duel at least.

Looking resplendent, Eireden set off for a tour of the city. It was not a lonesome walk. Generai awaited him just outside the door trying to make her wishes known to a small gathering of fairies. Easa-see perched with them. He immediately went to the king and alit upon Eireden's shoulders.

"What's the problem?" he asked his scout.

"I don't think there is a problem," she answered. "They were worried about you, I think. I believe they thought you were sick and in need of healing."

The king laughed. "It's because I slept in. If I'm not up at the crack of dawn they think there must be a problem. But I'm alright, my friends," he said, letting the fairies come and touch him to reassure themselves.

Draped with a dozen fairies the king met Prince Lienhart and the two made a circuit of the walls. As he passed, his men waved and cheered though they seemed dog-tired after a battle and a long night's work. The hardest part of this work was in relocating the dead goblins. There were many thousands of them and all ready heaps of their corpses were burning out on the plain. The king stared out and counted thirty of the piles on this side of the wall alone.

"Do we have an estimate of the dead yet? Ours and theirs?" the king asked

Lienhart pointed. "Those piles hold a hundred goblin each. So far we have over a hundred piles and we're not even halfway done yet."

"Twenty thousand!" Eireden said astounded. "I had no idea...and our side?"

"One-hundred and twenty-eight Den and thirty four fey," Lienhart answered and then laughed at the kings look. "That's how I felt when I heard. It was the training...the fey and our men worked together seamlessly. Unless a man was instantly killed he was healed by the fey in a snap. Now for certain not all were healed completely and some like Captain Jeden died anyway, but on the whole it was a miraculous combination."

"About Jeden. What happened on that north wall?"

"Oh my," Lienhart said, losing the look of satisfaction that had come over his face. "It was an elf. Just like on the plain all burnt and nasty. It was powerful and we were weak. The attack began with just goblins and then up came a company of ogres. I think our fey expended themselves too quickly and when the elf arrived he mowed through us so easily. Jeden and Elled fought heroically but they were overmatched."

Eireden sighed and looked at the haze in the air. "Did the elf get away?"

"No. All the fairies—I mean these ones here—not the ones that showed up in that ball of light, they attacked enough to distract it. I came late to the fight, and my guard and I were just enough to slay the thing, but it still took eight of us. Those elves are deadly."

They were and by his count there were at least four more of the burnt looking ones to deal with and then there was Darhmael. How many men would it take to defeat him? Perhaps more than they had. "They are deadly, my good prince, but so are you and so are your men. As always we shall overcome," the king said as cheerfully as he could, hiding the worry in his gut. The two men then went to the palace where the remaining captains awaited them. With the men were two women, Feylon Darania and Generai and not a few fairies. The town seemed covered in them.

"Our little friends seem to be behaving themselves, at least," the king said after receiving and giving the proper courtesies from all but Feylon who seemed distracted and worn. "I would know the status of our wounded, Lady Darania?"

"Oh...sorry, your Highness," the fey said as if coming awake. "The wounded? There are four-hundred and six who still await us. We could see to these men but we are still under the command of the Prince and his orders are for the fey to retain at least half of our strength at all times. In my opinion this is unnecessary. The sythei have reported the remnants of the maug army fleeing north."

Eireden considered this. "We will put you at a quarter strength and I will need twenty volunteers at full strength to accompany me to Rhyoeven tomorrow."

A murmur went through the men and Captain Dorcen spoke up: "You should not go to challenge Eirowyth, Milord. Make him come to you. That way you will have no fear of being jailed."

"I am sure the King has no fear of that now," Generai said with ice in her voice. "You know him not if you think there is any fear in our lord."

Dorcen's eyes flashed but before he could retort Prince Lienhart put out a hand. "I am sure that our lord is not afraid, but the good captain has a valid point. What is to stop Eirowyth from jailing you a second time. He jailed you on a whim once before?"

"I will answer this," Generai said before Eireden could even open his mouth. "I don't mean to over step my bounds but you, my King speak with less than perfect honesty on only one subject—yourself. The reason why your cousin will fight you is that you have proved yourself the rightful king. Who but the rightful king of the Den could have defeated that elf in single combat? And who but the rightful king of the Den could have destroyed that maug army so completely and at such little cost in life? Eirowyth will face you or he will face a revolt."

"She's right," Captain Dorcen said. "Only a fool would call you coward or traitor now." This was greeted with loud cheers and many whistles from the fairies who grew excited without knowing exactly why. Eireden and Lienhart did not join in.

When the men quieted Lienhart said, "Prince Eirowyth has proven himself a fool already. Is it known whether there is any precedent at all concerning this sort of thing?" The men all looked around nonplussed.

The king had already thought on this and had come up empty. "Not in living memory...but perhaps there is a way to find out." Eireden turned to Feylon. "Could we consult with Garris-Unhi on this matter? It's been mentioned that he has some skill in discerning the past."

"Garris? He's...uh...busy with Alseya on another issue altogether," Feylon said uncomfortably. "Besides his skills require some sort of starting time and ending time, which you don't seem to have." The fey were dreadful at telling lies or even keeping secrets. She wasn't lying about Garris' abilities but there was sure something concerning Alseya that had her nervous. Eireden wanted to pry since he had hoped that Alseya would be one of the twenty fey accompanying them to Rhyoeven.

"Well then, it's settled," the king said. "I will leave at first light and take a guard of a hundred men and fey with me. Those of you who come will act as witnesses only to the duel. If Eirowyth attempts to jail me then you will let him. Prince Lienhart, you will stay in Hildoeven."

The prince did not look happy about this and was about to protest when a deathly pale looking Lady Norafin called to Eireden. "My lord, King! Come do your duty." He knew his duty. The body of Prince Gamelling lay in state in the main audience chamber where he was being honored by the people of the town.

"Come, I will lead you to the front of the line," the lady said, taking Eireden's strong right hand in her soft grip. She then turned to Generai who had trailed after and said, "Know your place, Scout. It is the prerogative of a grieving widow to have the king to herself once in awhile." Chastised, Generai slunk away, but not too far away. "That scout never used to be so forward, but I suppose she does have your ear these days."

"That scout is very special to me," he replied, walking solemnly up the main aisle. Hands reached out and touched the king as he passed. He did not mind, though every once in a while someone would touch one of the fairies riding about on him and they would leap in the air, whistling.

"I hope not so special that there will be tears when you are made rightfully king. We both know how your mother is! There has never been a more conniving, under-handed woman ever to grace this earth—oh, how I miss her." Now they arrived at the open casket and a great sigh escaped the lady. "This is your fault," she said, pointing at Prince Gamelling.

He could not argue with that. "It seems a great many things are my fault."

"When you showed up last week he was days away from an ignoble, dishonorable death," the lady said staring down at her husband. "But you came and rescued him from that. You may not know it, but he hated growing old. It was always his wish to die in combat...and to be slain in mortal combat with an elf! He died a hero and I know he is very happy about that. I just wish I could be happy. I'm happy for him, and sad for myself."

Tears started to come down the woman's wrinkled face and the king held her. "Your prince fought for his king, his people, and for you, his love."

This cheered the lady. "You are so much like your father, which is a good thing. That mother of yours...did I mention how underhanded she is?"

"You did indeed," the king replied with a smile. "Though I have to tell you that this isn't news to me."

"Is it news to you that she is trying to start a rebellion?" Lady Norafin asked. A second later she added, "I suppose by that expression that it is news to you."

Eireden put a hand to his face, wondering what sort of expression he was wearing. He found his mouth hanging open. "How? How is she starting a rebellion?"

"This very morning I found a stack of unopened letters. They were from your mother and each was addressed to one of the princes of the five cities. They outlined the very flimsy evidence against you and hinted that military support could be needed. I thought that they were very compelling."

"Were compelling? Where are those letters?"

"I sent them on of course, as your mother intended. It wasn't easy, but after taking all of my pearls those fairies owed me many favors. I'm having that sweet, little Tissa deliver Prince Lienhart's even now."

"It seems my mother isn't the only one who is conniving," the king laughed. "But all for naught. I will not fight a civil war. I will fight a single man and even that I do not relish." The Lady Norafin kissed his cheek and said nothing else. The king left her to visit the wounded, the number of which was already far less than the four-hundred reported. The fey disliked suffering on any scale and those that were allowed to use their energies to heal had hurried to the task. By the next morning when the king prepared to leave there were less than fifty wounded.

"I'll never understand the Den," Feylon remarked after giving her report. She sat atop a dun mare wearing a cloak of gold that matched her eyes. "Your men do not complain before they are healed. They only do so afterwards."

"I so doubt that," Generai shot back. "The Den are not only stoic but gracious as well."

"Oh, they are gracious enough," the fey replied as the host rode out upon the battle-plain to a great cheering from the men on the walls. "It's just they think we are too good at healing. There was one soldier who was in a fury when his healer cleared up his old scar tissue along with his new injuries. It made him far more palatable to look upon."

"We are a war-like people, Milady," Captain Dorcen said. "Our scars we wear proudly. They are badges of honor. For some old veterans they are a map of their lives. They could tell you exactly where each came from and what sort of opponent they faced that day."

"I had no idea," Feylon said. "I will be sure to alert the rest of the fey."

Eireden checked the golden palomino so that he dropped back a bit to be near Feylon. "Speaking of alerting the fey, where is Alseya? I had expected her this morning."

"She was under the impression that you meant it when you said this was a volunteer mission," the fey replied. "She has left Hildoeven with Garris on an errand of her own."

"I suppose I should have asked her personally," the king said. "After Aric she is the most powerful among you and there are elves still left to be fought. We are vulnerable on the road, yet I could take no more and still leave Hildoeven properly guarded. No matter. We shall look to ourselves."

The hundred men and fey of his guard were augmented by an equal number of fairies who flew about chattering with excitement. They were supposed to be acting as advanced scouts, but instead they played tag, or had acorn wars, or slept, or ate, and some—Sooni and Tissa—even braided hair. The king did not begrudge them their antics; instead he had the fey check the woods around them frequently. The land was clear of enemies for as far as their minds could search.

Strangely, this bothered the king. Had he been in Darhmael's shoes he would have anticipated this showdown between the two rivals for the Den throne and certainly would have done something about it. An ambush being the most obvious stratagem. For this reason the king alternated between riding upon the road and taking to the forest in odd spurts. This accomplished little save tiring their mounts.

Just before sundown the king and his escort rode upon the battle plain of Rhyoeven and there set up camp with pendants flying. It was not long before there came a response from the capital. Down from the plateau rode a host of men in shining mail. Along with the swords at their hips they carried long spears each flying the blue and silver colors of the First Guard. They were resplendent and perfect in every way and very much the reason why Eireden would never consider a civil war.

The captains that came down from the city were the greatest the Den had to offer while only a handful among those that had come with the king from Hildoeven could come close to matching them in might or skill. A civil war would be a massacre. Rhyoeven held every advantage in men and material. Besides it was not the Den way. There had never been a civil war in their long history and Eireden wasn't going to be the first to start one.

"Form up!" he ordered. "Three ranks. Fey to the rear...all save you Lady Darania. You and Captain Dorcen to the front." The king mounted his golden horse and with Generai beside him he awaited his enemy.

Eirowyth looking tall and dashing even compared to his captains rode without hurry until he stood just paces from Eireden. The two looked upon each and seconds ticked by in near silence. As was his custom the king held his tongue placidly. Eirowyth also remained silent, gravely looking his onetime mentor up and down. How long they would have sat there is anyone's guess, but Sooni flew off the king's shoulder and fluttered in toward the men of Rhyoeven. She whistled her curiosity.

"What did she say?" asked Eirowyth.

"She is curious why we are all so silent," Feylon answered. "And I for one am equally so. We are here to speak, yet no one does."

The two rivals glanced at each other and still the king

remained mute. Eirowyth answered: "It is a practice of Eireden's that I have adopted. In a negotiation the first who speaks is usually the most anxious and thus in the weakest position. But...having broken my silence I will take the moment granted to congratulate you, My Lord Eireden on your victory. Word has come that you have shown your usual cunning and have destroyed a large part of the goblin army that has been menacing our lands."

Eirowyth's words were gracious and clearly heard. Those behind the king felt the tension ease, while the king did not. He was close enough to see the look in Eirowyth's eyes. His eyes held sadness and resolve; he would not relent. "I only serve the Den to my fullest ability," Eireden replied bowing his head to his cousin's compliment.

"And now you return to Rhyoeven as champion?" Eirowyth asked.

"As king!" Generai cried out.

This caused murmuring among the men, but Eirowyth smiled. "Ah, the fiery scout. I see that you haven't lost your touch, Cousin, when it comes to instilling such loyalty and...love in your soldiers. Be careful my good scout. The more you love this man, the more he'll disappoint you."

Generai opened her mouth to reply, but the king stepped his horse between them. "This is between us, Eirowyth. You will leave her out of it," Eireden ordered. "Do you still insist on naming me coward and claiming that I ran?"

This was the nub of the issue between them; what had caused so much unhappiness for five years. "I do." Behind the king his men grew tense and angry, yet Eireden had the opposite reaction. He felt relief. Eirowyth would accept his challenge.

"Then upon my honor I challenge thee," the king said in a dry voice. "You will take back your words or suffer my blade."

## Chapter 32

### Ella

"Of course she's human," Doctor Levine said. He gave a glance into the cell perhaps to reassure himself. "What did you expect?"

Ella ignored the question. She stared at the woman with a growing feeling of revulsion. "Why is her hair like that? Where is it all?" she asked, but didn't give the man a second to answer before she went on. "And why is she so skinny? You can see her bones under her skin...and her face..." Long scabs and scratches ran grooves up Elleni Feyden's face. There were more all over her arms as if she had attempted to peel her own skin away.

"Unfortunately, when Ms Feyden is not catatonic she is self-abusive," the doctor replied. "She'll tear out her own hair and scratch at herself. Because of this our protocol is to restrain her. And she is so skinny because she won't eat. We try to keep her fed through a naso-gastric tube, however she will try to choke herself with it."

Despite her revulsion Ella couldn't stop staring at the withered old woman. She was tiny and wrinkled. Her hair, where she had any, was grey and limp. She stood stooped in the corner gazing with dull, vacant eyes at the floor of her room. Her hands were hooked into claws and upon each finger were bandages— Ella didn't want to know why.

"She's not my mother," Ella repeated. "But we should help her nonetheless. Aric please."

She stepped away from the door and watched as Aric's face grew grim at the sight of the woman. "My goodness! You say this lady was born this way? How utterly horrid."

Doctor Levine's brows came down. "I didn't actually. It was likely a traumatic event which triggered this reaction."

Aric let himself into the room with a touch of his telekinetic power, while Ella took the file from Levine's hands. "May I see?" she asked perfunctorily. Starting at the back she began flipping through the pages, reading about the different diagnoses and their treatments. One jumped out at her: Electroconvulsive therapy. "Electro-shock!" she gasped. "You did that to her? How many times? How many times did you try that?"

The doctor tried to take the file from Ella, but she held him off with a strength that was far beyond her small size. He blinked in surprise at her power. "What's going on here? Those records are confidential. You can't just take them..."

"*Go to sleep*," Aric told him and instantly the man slumped over. Ella caught him with her mind and laid him gently down.

"They electrocuted her brain," Ella said coming into the room where the old woman remained motionless. Aric's lip curled in disgust. Before he could ask why, she said, "It's supposed to help some mental problems, but for the life of me I can't understand how."

"It's barbaric is what it is," Aric said, trying to raise the woman's head up. "You should be glad that we didn't find your mother among these humans." When he couldn't get her head up, the fey laid the woman down. She remained in her exact position remained only in a horizontal posture. "This is so bizarre. It's as though she has been petrified. Does that saying anything about paralyzation? Or maybe spinal injuries?"

Ella's eye caught on a picture in the front of the file. "No...there's nothing," she said slowly as her mind began to rebel.

"What is it?" he asked.

"Just heal her, please," Ella asked. The picture couldn't be. It wasn't possible. It was of a girl with clear pale skin and bright blue eyes. She had long dark-auburn hair, a slim nose, and a sharp chin. The picture could have been of Ella taken with a polaroid in another time.

Aric put his hands out and the familiar blue light spread out from his palms to cover the woman. She jerked once and then relaxed altogether. They waited for a few moments for the woman to do something, but she just laid there relaxed and apparently asleep.

"Mom?" Ella asked, coming to kneel next to the woman.

"Mom?" Aric repeated, his lips curled. "What do you mean by that? This isn't your mother, Ella. This is a human."

"Look for yourself," Ella said handing over the picture. Aric took his time studying the picture. He even turned it over and touched the back with his long fingers.

"She does indeed look like you," Aric said, handing the picture back. "But it can't be. You don't understand, the mating between an elf and a human is not possible and even if it were possible it would be..." He paused in his sentence just long enough to keep from saying something mean. "...it would be impossible."

"Yet I'm right here," Ella countered. "Explain that."

The fey took a deep breath and said, "I can't without coming across terribly bigoted. An elf would never mate with a human. Don't take this wrong, but the elves hated the humans. Remember, this was part of the driving force that turned the elves to evil. They saw humans as little more that monkeys. "

"What about the fey," she asked icily. "What do they think of humans...honestly?"

He leaned back from her in surprise. "Ella, I have always been honest with you. There is no reason for you to think otherwise. I don't speak for all the fey. We aren't like that. I can only speak for myself. In my view humans are a lower order. They have impressive potential, but they rarely live up to it. They have a penchant for villainy and pettiness, though there are those among them that are truly great. But I am not alone in this. You yourself expressed disgust over the low born actions of the humans."

"Yes...well that was then," Ella said not liking the reminder of her hypocrisy. "And just because I said that doesn't mean I think the fey or the elves are any better...or maybe they are. I don't know." In her heart she knew the fey were better. On the whole they were happier, nicer, more civilized. She glanced back down at the woman. That same heart told her that she was her mother.

Ella touched her hand. Though it was slim, it was hard. The woman's eyes flew open and with a boundless scream of terror she kicked herself away from the two and crawled to the corner using her feet to keep them away.

"Mom! Elleni, it'll be ok. Please, please calm down," Ella said desperately. "We're here to help you. Look at me. We can help you."

Elleni wouldn't or couldn't calm down. She thrashed the air with her limbs and screamed until orderlies came. Afraid of what they would do to her mother, Ella had Aric put each into a deep sleep. And still Elleni shrieked.

"You feel great calm," Aric said to her with magic in his voice. "You are no longer afraid." Elleni did calm, unfortunately she went right back into her awful catatonic state she had been in. They were both afraid to move her.

"Why wasn't she healed?" Ella asked. Suddenly she noticed that Elleni's skin was clear of the scratches and scabs. "Wait, she was healed. Look at her arms. It was only her mind that wasn't. Can't you fix brain injuries?"

"I can," Aric replied.

"You have magic," Doctor Levine said from against the wall. He sat bug-eyed but also slack jawed. "I saw you put those men to sleep. And I felt it when you told her to calm. It made me want to be calm too. I am calm. I felt it when you healed her and you did heal her, except her mind was never injured to begin with. Not in a sense that there were wounds or damage. What you see, the catatonic state is her mind's defense mechanism. She has experienced something so dreadful that this—this horror that you see in front of you is preferable to it. I see now what a mistake it has been to try to bring her out of this state. Don't wake her...ever."

A fierce desire to help her mom sprung up in Ella. "Can

you do anything for her, Aric? Can you erase her memories?"

"No, I don't think so. Memories are an integral..."

"What about another fey?" she insisted. "If you can't help her, what about your mother, or Alseya, or Garris? There has to be some sort of spell." Aric shook his head, no. Ella turned on the doctor. "Is there any medication that might erase her memory...make her forget who she was. Maybe we can start over, like she was just born."

"No drugs will help in that way. Not for long term memories," the doctor answered. "You don't want to hear this but Electroconvulsive therapy will cause memory loss. Though how many treatments it would take to completely eradicate the memory of her trauma I don't know. In this case the cure could be worse than the disease."

"What do we do then? I can't leave my mom like this."

"You really think this is your mother?" Aric asked, amazed.

Gently, Ella reached out and took her mother's hand. "I know it in my bones, Aric," she replied. "I'm some sort of cross-breed. The elf made me. He designed with the specific intent to destroy the Feylands."

"Destroy the Feylands," Elleni said in hoarse whisper.

"She spoke!" Ella cried. "Mom...Mom? It's Ella. Eleanor, your baby."

"Baby," Elleni repeated.

"Do not get your hopes up, young lady," the doctor said. "This is a response only. There is no active thinking behind those words. It's an echo in her mind only."

"What do we do?" Ella asked after a time. She had been secretly wishing that her mother would speak again without her saying anything. But it wasn't going to happen. Aric could only shrug at her and the doctor was even less of a help and sat there with his bug eyes unblinking. "We take her back to the Hidden lands," Ella decided. "Magic caused this and magic can fix it."

## Chapter 33

## Eireden

At sunrise the twittering of fairies woke the king. He scrambled up, excited to see the sunrise for the first time since...it took him a moment to recall the last time he was so excited to see a sunrise. It was the morning he first brought Ella into the Hidden lands in his old red truck. He had wanted to show her everything there was to see, certain that she would fall in love with the magical land just as he. That hadn't turned out so well.

Rising he oriented himself on the girl. She had moved the day before to the north and now was southeast of him. "She sure gets around," he murmured, taking a grape offered to him by Easa-see. What was she doing, he wondered? Showing Aric the wonders of America? "I wonder what he would make of a mall." For some reason this struck him as funny and he laughed his booming laugh, setting the fairies spinning in a tizzy.

"What's so funny?" Generai asked coming into the tent. A few berries were thrown her way and she deftly caught them.

"Oh just thinking about...never mind. I'm just happy is all," the king said. "For the first time in five years I can look to the future. I mean really look without worrying. It's refreshing. Win or lose I'm done with the past."

"You will win, don't worry about that," Generai said. "Especially since Eirowyth chose to take the lance off the table instead of insisting on his choice of swords."

"That was a smart move on his part," Eireden remarked. "I trained him, remember? And not once had he ever bested me with the lance. What good would the sword of Ag-Raumon do him with his shoulder impaled on a spear fifteen feet long?"

"I'm just happy you don't have to face that sword," she said with a shiver down her back.

"You're not the only one," he said, working his shoulders

in circles. His mind started to dwell on the upcoming battle, the moves he would make, and the moves his opponent would as well. Eirowyth was a very good fighter, perhaps only second to the king. He was meticulous and perfect in his execution and oddly his very strength was his weakest point. Eirowyth did not like to deviate from a preordained plan of attack, and if he did he was slow to regroup. Eireden was the opposite and fought best with only the vaguest of plans.

The king began warming up in earnest now under the watchful eye of the scout. When he noticed her staring he said, "You could be doing something useful, while you're waiting. Getting some breakfast perhaps."

"What I'm doing now has its uses," she countered wearing a broad grin. He pointed to the tent flap and she left still grinning, yet she came back with two plates of eggs in minutes. "Your men are on top of things," she said in answer to his look.

He was done eating too soon, which meant he was done getting dressed too soon, which meant he had a half-hour to kill. Easa-see helped fill the time. They played a modified version of catch which kept him loose. He would throw grapes far out onto the plain and Easa-see would zip after them, always catching the fruit just before it hit the ground.

"It's time," Generai said. "Fairies! To your stations." The scout had briefed the sythei on the nature of the duel and how they weren't to take part under any circumstances. They flew to the king and touched him for luck and then they went to the knights to settle among them.

Fifty yards away Eirowyth and his second waited on horseback. Everyone sat on horses, all save the king. He walked, feeling the earth beneath his feet, smelling the early air, listening to the horses stepping and the faint murmuring of the men. Mostly he watched his opponent. The man was as cool and calm as the morning and sat back relaxed as the seconds went through their ritual. When all was complete

Generai and her compliment remounted and rode off to the side where they would observe the action.

Only then did Eirowyth slide from the saddle and smack his horse on the hindquarters. "Was I right to keep my men from relieving Hildoeven?" Eirowyth said conversationally. "It's been bothering me for days whether I did the right thing."

Eireden walked to his right, putting the sun behind him— at least at first the light would be in his cousin's eyes. "It depends why you kept them back."

"It was their dispositions mostly. The numbers of maug gave me pause, but they were positioned by a person with military knowledge. They were so spread out that it practically dared me to attack, but I had the suspicion that destroying a relieving army from Rhyoeven was their main goal."

"It was," Eireden agreed. "I believe that's why they gave me a week to 'prepare' for my challenge. They were hoping to draw you out. And in case you don't know what sort your enemy is, they are elves. Very powerful elves. I would advise not to accept or offer any challenges against them."

Eirowyth drew his sword in a flourish. "You act like you know you are going to lose our duel."

"No. I act like a man who loves his people and will not put his needs before theirs." His own sword—a fine blade borrowed from Captain Dorcen—came out of its sheath with a song. "I truly wish this wouldn't have to go this way. Take back your words."

"I cannot," Eirowyth said saluting his cousin. Feeling slightly sick to his stomach, the king returned the salute as was custom. He then went immediately on the attack. He was slightly bigger, slightly stronger, and slightly faster than his opponent. However what counted most was that he had years more experience. The king had seen every variation of every attack ever to be used. He could tell a feint from an attack by the smallest clues: a shift in body weight, an open step instead of a closed one, a sharper than normal breath.

His sword work was unparalleled. He could turn a blade aside with such ease that he didn't really need his shield and he could find the weak point in a man's armor so that it almost seemed better not to where it at all. A minute into the duel the king drew first blood. A simple pivot had Eirowyth over extended and the king snuck the tip of his sword through the open space in the armor beneath the armpit.

"Well struck," Eirowyth said with a grimace. The king wiped sweat from his eye and nodded. He seemed oddly fatigued for how little he had worked and didn't want Eirowyth to notice his heavy breathing. The king scored again a minute later with his favorite riposte, cutting a jagged line just under the jaw of his young cousin.

There was no compliment this time, just a fierce prolonged attack. *The best defense is a good offence* had been drilled in Eirowyth's head from the moment Eireden had taken up training the boy. Ringing crash followed ringing crash and quickly Eireden realized that something was wrong. He was moving too slow in his ungainly armor and his sword felt as though it gathered in weight with every swing. His muscles began to burn from exhaustion and his breath came panting out of him. More and more he looked to his shield to save him until it throbbed and vibrated with a steady thrum from the blows.

One wobbly placed foot and the king stumbled. Eirowyth bashed aside his shield and then sent a hacking attack into Eireden's side, cutting a deep wound into the back of the king's left arm. The injury made hefting the cumbersome shield even more difficult and a second later he discarded it.

"Wait," Eireden tried to say, but his cousin came on again too fast. With his arms like dead weight the king began to rely on speed and cunning, twisting and turning so that mortal blows became glancing ones instead. Quickly his armor became damaged; indented from the force of the blows making it difficult to move in and his weariness increased so that his legs began to shake. Astoundingly, Eireden realized he was going lose the duel.

Not long after, Eirowyth realized that he was going to win also and stepped back. As was custom, he allow his opponent a final word before death.

"You cheat!" the king rasped out, he had never felt this way in battle.

"I can't believe you!" Eirowyth cried, throwing down his sword. It stuck point first in the soft earth and gently waved back and forth as Eirowyth glared in anger. "Where is the man of nobility and grace who helped to raise me? Where is the champion that won the battle of Hildoeven? Where is that man? Why am I forced to fight some mewling child who cries cheater when he is overmatched?"

Eireden swayed almost in rhythm to the sword; he was close to passing out, while Eirowyth only looked slightly winded. "You've done something to me. Magic...you've drained me of my strength. That's...that's no way to win. You can't cheat your way to the throne."

"I have not cheated!" Eirowyth roared. He came stomping up and with ease threw down the king. "Look into my eyes—you who can read men better than any. I did not cheat. Do you still see a lie?" Eireden shook his head. His cousin was being truthful.

He had lost fair and square. The last of his strength left him he laid back feeling his blood leaking down the insides of the steel cage that encased his body.

His cousin went to get his sword for the *coup de grâce.* Standing above him Eirowyth paused and asked, "Do you have any final words more fitting for a man of the Den?"

Eireden took off his gorget, exposing his throat. His hand touched the pearl hanging there and it let off its light. He yanked it off and threw it at his cousin's feet. "It'll help you control the fairies. You may not be able to win without them."

Eirowyth kicked it aside. "The Den protect the weak, not

the other way around."

The king looked beyond his cousin with his upraised sword and stared into the clear blue sky. The morning was perfect—the air had just the right amount of crispness to it. His last thought before the sword flashed down was: *It's a good day to die.*

# Chapter 34

## Ella

"Sit her up, will you please," Ella asked as she drove the Ford between two illusionary pine trees. The trees marked the boundary of the Hidden Lands. In the back seat her mother laid in her catatonic daze, her hands still hooked into claws, her eyes half-lidded seeing nothing. "Maybe the pretty forest will help her."

Aric did as she had asked, but not before she saw the look on his face. It was the same whenever he touched the old woman: pity, sadness, revulsion. She didn't question the look. The fey were so used to perfection that anything outside that standard bothered them. A few minutes later Ella slowed the car in front of a deep gorge between the mountains.

"This is where Eireden was attacked by those wolves," she said, remembering that day as if it was long in the past. "Do you think we'll be ok?"

"I'll check," the fey said, sliding out of the back seat with a simple grace. He was back in seconds. "There is nothing to fear around us for miles. It seems that the focus of the world is far away."

"I wonder why," she said driving down into the gorge. "A battle probably, though I hope not." Despite Aric's reassurance, she kept her eyes wide and the car in the center of the dirt road. They made it through and beyond without an issue. "I wish there was a way we could help, but since we're fugitives, I don't see how."

"We can't help," Aric said. "I wonder if we can even help this one lady...your mother, I mean. It feels as though we are only prolonging her suffering and putting you in useless danger."

Ella said nothing to this. Aric was being his honest self, but it still bothered her that he didn't think 'this human' as he thought of Elleni Feyden was worth the effort. When Ella had told him that she wanted to take her mother out of the hospital and back to the Hidden Lands he had said, "She's too far gone. Besides I've never heard of a spell that erases memories. We cherish ours too much to wish them away."

Out of pity he wanted to help Elleni onto her next life. For now Ella refused. She told Aric that she wanted to speak to Garris-Unhi, the most learned of the fey, before she went down that path.

*Can I kill my own mother*, she wondered? Sadly the answer was yes. Every time she looked back at the twisted and gnarled old woman it made her want to cry and do something, anything to help her. If that included putting her out of her misery she would, or if that including going to the ends of the earth she would do that as well.

She drove in silence, trying to put her despair out of her mind. "Look, the truck," Ella said with forced cheer as they passed Eireden's dead truck. It sat rusting beside the road and looked suddenly to Ella like a metal corpse. She forced the image away. "That's where I performed my first magic," she said to Whip-wip, who had lifted her head from Ella's lap long enough to look at the vehicle.

The fairy had seen enough trucks on her expedition in the Forbidden Lands that this one didn't do much to hold her attention. She yawned at it, showing her tiny teeth and settled back down for her second nap of the morning. Normally Whip-wip liked to sleep in the back seat—the movement of the steering wheel being too much of a distraction, but the fairy didn't care for the body of Elleni Feyden any more than Aric did. It was just too sad and fairies, as a rule, kept well clear of anything sad.

"We will be near your grotto soon," Ella said, stroking Whip-wip's ultra-soft wings. "Would you like to visit your family? I'm sure they would love to hear about your adventures." The fairy shook her head and warbled and sang which Ella translated: *No family home. They are in Den city.*

"Which city are they in?" Aric asked. "And why did they

go? Were they in danger?"

Whip-wip's answer surprised them both: *Go to save Hill town. Sythei big heroes. Win battle. Time for sleep.*

"Is that where you were the other night?" Ella asked. When the fairy nodded Ella poked her. "You could have said something! We were worried about you and now I suppose we weren't worried enough."

"By that she wants you to know that she's glad that you are safe, Whip-wip," Aric added. "I wonder which city she means by Hill town, Hildoeven or Rhyoeven? I for one hope it was Rhyoeven that was attacked. Their walls are very stout and their men strong and capable. Hildoeven has always been the weakest of the Den cities."

"We will know soon enough," Ella said. "For now it's just one more thing to worry over." They wouldn't have long to worry, however. The South Stream road was hard packed dirt in fine condition and they made good time. By noon they had come within the eves of the forest just shy of the battle plain. They stared in amazement at what lay before them.

Charred mounds of goblin dead dotted the plain. Some still smoldered while others were even then being added to by teams of men. The smell was atrocious. None of the fumes ran toward the city. By fey magic the reeking smoke pushed out toward the forests. Holding back their nausea, Ella and Aric moved around to the south where the mounds were fewer, while Whip-wip flew above the stench. The fairy was on a mission to find Garris-Unhi.

By no fault of her own, Whip-wip failed in that mission. Instead she brought back twenty fairies whom they had never seen before and a fey by the name of Archera.

"What joy to see you again, my Aric," the fey said, coming to grasp Aric's hands. His eyes, the blue of lapis lazuli, he turned on Ella. "And you Eleanor, I am happy to see are whole. Is the rumor true? Are you the good elf?"

Ella hadn't expected this question and she stammered, "I—I am an elf that is true enough. And I try to be good—as good as a person can be if that's what you mean."

"No one can say that Ella is anything but good," Aric said. "But what about you? And the fey? What has happened here?"

"There is much to tell," Archera said. "Would you rather we speak within the city. The aroma out here is undesirable." When they informed him of their continued fugitive status he demurred and told them of the battle. When he did the fairies flew about mimicking the action, including what they obviously considered the best part. Spinning about themselves as fast as they could, they created a glaring light. "And that is what banished the dark," he said pointing up at them.

"And where is Eireden now?" Ella asked. "Do you think it will be alright if we go into the city?"

Archera's handsome face drooped and the fairies came to rest from their antics more glum than Ella had seen a gathering of Sythei. "We've just had news. The Sun King has fallen in his quest for the throne. Yesterday at the break of dawn he left to challenge his cousin in combat and now a scout has just returned with the news that he has lost his duel."

When Archera told Ella about the death of grandfatherly Prince Gamelling she had felt a touch of nostalgic sadness but at the news of Eireden's death it was as if a spike went into her chest. "Fallen? Lost his duel? You mean he's dead? Is that what you're saying?" she asked, through tears she wasn't even aware were falling from her eyes. "You're wrong. He can't be dead—I would know if he was. The scout is just wrong. They're third echelon nobodies and don't know up from down half the time. I'm sorry but it's true. Eireden is not dead!"

"The scout is not at fault," Archera said, coming to touch Ella's hands, calming her. "It was Generai, a favorite of the Sun King's and she is inconsolable. I'm sorry, sweet cousin. Your loss is our loss as well. He championed the fey when no one else would or could and saved us twice."

"Maybe Generai was under a spell," Ella said in a small voice. "Illusion maybe, or some sort of charm that could..." She stopped in mid-sentence, her words pathetic to her own ears. "Suddenly I don't know what to do. What do we do, Aric?" Ella didn't wait for an answer; instead she poured herself into his arms and cried.

With gentle hands and a soft voice Aric soothed her. Ella stared at nothing as his words slipped into her mind as if in a foreign language that had to be translated before being understood. After awhile she felt like a spell had been put on her; she felt numb from the eyebrows down. "I liked it better in America. People died all the time back in America but they were never anyone I knew or cared about. I...I feel lost and—and maybe I should go check on my mother." Ella started to go but then turned abruptly. "Where is Garris-Unhi? Please, Archera, tell me he is alive."

"Aye, he lives yet...or so I assume," he answered. "He has gone back to the Feylands, though I don't know why."

"And my mother? And Alseya? Where are they?" Aric asked.

"Your mother went to Rhyoeven as part of the king's guard. And Alseya journeyed with Garris, perhaps acting the part of guard as well, though again that is just speculation."

"Well I wanted to know what we were going to do," Ella said, ignoring the hollow feeling in her chest. "Now I know. We are going to the Feylands also. After all we can't stay here. Just as before every Den city will be off limits to us. Thank you for your time, Archera." She started away, but noticed Aric lingering. "What is it?"

"It's the Feylands," he said softly. "I can't imagine what has become of my land, my home. I'm not sure that I want to know."

He looked back and forth between Ella and Archera as if in indecision. *Is he going to abandon me, now?* Ella asked herself in disbelief. "I'm going, with or without you," Ella said angrily. "My mother needs my help. And I need yours, but I will go alone if I have to."

"Do not talk so," Aric said, taking her hand. He waved goodbye to Archera with the other, before turning back in the direction where they had left the car and the catatonic woman. "I will accompany you. Our fates are entwined...then again I thought my fate was also entwined with Eireden's."

At the sound of his name her insides screamed: *Oh Eireden, why did you have to die!*

No...no she couldn't think on him. Especially now. To do so would set her crying again and who knows if she could stop? She forced him out of her mind, just as she had for the last week. To change the subject to something less painful she remarked, "Did we inherit all twenty of them?" All the sythei that had accompanied Archera were now flitting about the branches above them each trying to talk to Whip-wip simultaneously.

"It seems so. Though I doubt they'll keep with us when we go through the Forest of Mists. Even brave Whip-wip had trouble with that part of our road last time."

The fairies left them much sooner than that. When they got to the car the sythei marveled at it and explored every inch of it, however the body of Elleni Feyden made them nervous and when the doors were closed, those that were still in clamored to get out. This made Whip-wip very sad and she pressed her tiny nose against the window.

"If you'll be happier with them, Whip-wip. You can go. I won't be...actually I will be sad, but you can still go. I'll understand." Ella tried blinking as fast as she could but tears came at the very idea of losing Whip-wip so soon after losing Eireden. The fairy didn't even bother to think it over. She went to Ella's face and kissed her. "How about I do this for you?" Ella suggested.

She rolled down the windows and then blared her stereo into the forest. For several seconds the sythei were mesmerized by the Bee Gees, *Staying Alive*. Some even went invisible in alarm. But then Whip-wip was up dancing, boogying like she never could, trapped in the car. The hood of the Ford was her disco and the silver of her flower petal dress flared and sparkled. She was a sight. Pure unadulterated joy came off her in waves and for a time she danced alone but then all the fairies came down to join.

The sight of them, so happy, had Ella crying again, though she knew not why, for she smiled as she cried. Two songs played before a sadness started to creep in on the fun. The Sun King had died. She sighed, wishing she had been there to see the light of a thousand fairies raining down on him. It must have been a sight.

"It's time, my sweet," Ella said at the last song finished. The sun was nearing the mountains in the west. The possibility of more music enticed some of the sythei, however the body repelled them, and only Whip-wip came along as the car began to wind among the trees. Despite her hurting heart Ella played peppy tunes until the fairy tired an hour later and then she turned it off altogether.

"He was a great man," Aric said. These were the first words he had uttered since leaving Hildoeven.

Ella drove for a while without replying. When the sun was just a gold rim atop a mountain she killed the engine. She could have driven on to the Forest of Mists and beyond, but that meant spending the night in the Feylands. It was something she didn't think she could stomach.

"You are a great man, Aric," she said.

"No, I am fey. There is an important difference."

Ella gave him a quizzical look. "It's no matter. You are still great. The greatest of the fey that now live. Do you deny that?"

"Sometimes I wish it were not so. My life would be so much easier. My choices simpler. My fate kinder. Were I like some of my fellows I could look on you with love, unencumbered by the future."

# Chapter 35

## Ella

Eireden haunted her dreams that night though when she woke she could only remember flashes: the king on the golden palomino that had been a gift from Ilenwyth—the king fighting sword to sword with his cousin—the king standing beneath a blazing orb that beat back an unholy night—the king kissing the fey Alseya—and the king kissing the fey Alseya—and again.

She woke in her blankets needing a drink of water; she had a bad taste in her mouth. Unbelievably she had been jealous in those dreams. This she thought strange. Were he alive she would honestly wish him every happiness and that included kissing Alseya.

With her head nestled on Aric's shoulder she had to wonder what she had to be jealous of. She loved Aric and he loved her just as strongly, it was something that he could not hide. As a boy friend, and she did consider him such, he was attentive to her every need and put her wants above his. The truth was she couldn't ask for a better one. Not even Eireden could match the love this fey showed her.

He had tried of course, however it wasn't in his nature. Eireden had loved her in his way, but he had lived for his people. Whomever he would have married would have married The Den as well. "I suppose that's the way of kings," she said under her breath.

Ella glanced at her watch and then to the eastern sky; it was just beginning to go from black to navy blue. For once Ella had beaten Whip-wip awake. In a moment of 'turnabout is fair play' Ella poked the fairy a couple of times. Whip-wip raised her head an inch, cracked an eye at the skyline, and then immediately went limp again. Ella had to hold back her laughter. She poked the fairy again—and Whip-wip bit her!

"Jeez!" Ella exclaimed, sucking her wounded finger.

"What is it?" Aric asked in a voice so clear she had to

wonder if he had been asleep at all.

"I was just bit by a wild animal, no thanks to you," she said playfully. When he sat up and looked around in confusion Ella pointed at Whip-wip. "She did it. Never try to wake a fairy before their time."

"I could have told you that," Aric replied. "Here, let me see that." He took her finger and kissed. Like the magic it was the pain disappeared. "Good as new. Should we get an early..."

At that moment the sun broached the horizon and just like that Whip-wip leapt up with a song on her lips. She was happily surprised to see her companions awake already and began a long one sided discussion which revolved around two thing *zooti* and her dreams. Ella couldn't follow either end of the conversation.

"Thank goodness," she said when the fairy finally flew off to scrounge for her breakfast. "How do you pack so much energy in one tiny being?" When Aric made to answer she stood and said, "That was a rhetorical question. Will you help me exercise my mother?"

Ella did not like how horribly her mother resembled a statue now that they were allowing her to remain in her catatonic state. With Aric calming her Ella worked her scrawny body through a series of exercises and stretches trying to get the blood running. Similar to the fairy, Ella kept up a running conversation while she did this.

"*Zooti*?" Whip-wip asked holding out some berries.

Ella thanked her and then popped them into her mother's mouth, as an automatic response the woman chewed and swallowed. Encouraged by this Whip-wip went for more and when she returned she began pushing the berries through the wrinkled lips of the old lady.

"*Sis zooti ssp*," Whip-wip said, feeding Elleni: Yes, fruit is nice, it meant. The fairy said much more than that, but for the most part it was fairy nonsense.

When the fairy came back after fifth berry run, Ella said,

"That's enough for now. I don't think she's eaten this much in years, judging by how skinny she is."

After their own breakfast they took to the car and worked their way through the thin forest heading north and west until they saw the grey mist ahead of them. Whip-wip crawled into Ella's shirt pocket at the sight and refused to come out. The Forest of Mists was even less dense than the surrounding land and thus Ella made better than expected time driving the five miles through it. Aric knew the forest well and steered them clear of any actual ravines or gullies. Only once did they get stuck in a shallow bog of mud and water. Before Aric could get out to push, Ella gave a tremendous thrust with her mind and the car bounced forward spraying mud behind.

"Impressive," Aric said, simply.

"Darn tootin' it was," she answered back.

"I don't know what that means."

Impressive or not her head split with a sudden headache. Rubbing her temples she said, "It means I strongly agree." For the next half hour, until they cleared the mists, she kept her magic use to a minimum. The only time she used it was to feel the ground in front of them checking for more swampy areas.

And then they were through the trees, and above the sky was a robin's egg blue and below that the peaceful valley was a place of death. Clearly nothing was alive in the Feylands and likely nothing could ever live there again. The air was choked with foul smells. A few were somewhat expected like that of the suffocating ash that swirled in the air or the sickening stench of the decomposing bodies that littered the ground, but along with those smells was a bitter reek of harsh toxic chemicals.

The land had been purposely polluted. Where there had been fields of green and flowers of every color imaginable now there was only black and shades of black. Even the lake was like ink, dark and sludgy. Ella and Aric stared in horror at the scene and both cried, though neither was aware of it.

"You can feel the hatred," Aric said, touching the skin of his arm. "It's in the air."

Ella nodded. "It's everywhere. How does someone do something like this? What drives them? Look, every house has been destroyed. Every tree uprooted and then burned. And—and the earth it looks..." she stared at the befouled ground and for the first time noticed that it looked wet. "That's oil. He covered every square inch, every mile of the Feylands in oil. Who does that? Is my father insane?"

"Darhmael is not insane," Aric replied grimly. "Insanity is a condition of the lower orders. Darhmael is an elf. He is evil, consumed by hatred that has been growing in him for over fifteen-thousand years. He hates the fey. He hates the Den and humans in general, but he hates the fey with a greater passion and this is its evidence. We are race-traitors. That's how he sees us. He will hunt us forever."

That notion made Ella's stomach go queasy. No one was easier to hunt than her—she could be tracked anywhere. And whoever was with her would be doomed as well...Aric, Whip-wip, anyone. She felt sweat break out on her forehead while her breakfast started a slow roll within her. The smell and her fear were getting to her. "I'm going to be sick. Whip-wip, get off me..."

The fairy hopped out of her pocket just as Ella opened the car door. The smell outside the car was like a slap in the face. Her senses reeled or rather all of them reeled but her hearing. There wasn't a single sound coming from the Feylands. It was deadly silent. Ella leaned out of the car and vomited onto the black earth again and again.

When there was nothing left inside her, she shut the door and sat there trembling. Aric stared at her as if he had never seen such a thing before, while Whip-wip tried to hide in the jumble of items in the glove compartment. "I'm done Whip-wip. I'm sorry about that."

The fairy came back and crawled into her pocket. "*Swirr*

*zee, issa zuu,*" she sung: We have to leave far away, danger.

"We will but first we have to find Garris," Ella said. "Will he be at the Theater of Ancestral Concordance?" she asked Aric. When he nodded she drove the Ford further into the hell that had once been the Feylands. With her mind she checked and rechecked the road in front of them and strangely found it the least affected by the upheaval and destruction of the lands. The elf would have had need of it. Moving his army as well as transporting all the oil needed to coat the land would have required a good road.

The road meandered as it once had but now it ran twisting around slag heaps that rose to great heights, or curving along dangerous sludge swamps which appeared able to suck a person down into their vile depths. In the seat beside Ella, Aric looked to be on the verge of a catatonic state himself. He stared with huge eyes that refused to blink, while his mouth hung open.

"It's destroyed...forever," he whispered. "I had thought...I had hoped that we would be able to come back one day and fix whatever mayhem had been wrought, but this isn't mayhem. Darhmael has turned the land evil. It kills. Just being here is killing me. I can feel the poison in the air. We can't stay too long. It will kill us."

"We'll find you a new home," Ella said. "It'll be just as beautiful as it was." Determinedly she drove on looking for any sign whatsoever of the low building that housed the Concordance. There wasn't any; however she did see footprints in the sludge. "There! Those tiny prints have to be Alseya's."

"Whip-wip, you can stay in the car. The air is better in here," Ella said. "I'll leave it running, ok? Just don't touch anything. You wouldn't want to accidentally drive into one of those bogs." The fairy nodded and for once Ella was sure that Whip-wip wouldn't attempt any mischief. With a deep breath, Ella climbed out of the Ford. Immediately her eyes began to sting and her lungs burned.

"Let's...go." Aric choked out the words and then followed after the prints. Ella came right behind, wondering if they would even find Alseya and Garris alive. "This is the tunnel Furen and I dug, come on." He led them down into the tortured earth where the tunnel ran slick and more than once they slipped and were forced to claw at the walls to keep from sliding all the way down.

Ella was dreadfully afraid that they had come for nothing. Footprints led downward but there were none coming back up and below all was dark and silent. She was sure that they would find two lifeless bodies, overcome by the fumes. At the bottom of the tunnel, the dark was so complete that Aric touched the pearl that hung about his neck to give them the least light. When he did something came at them from the shadows with sword in hand.

"Aric! Eleanor! My loves..." It was Alseya. She came forward weeping in desperation and fright, seemingly on the edge of panic. "We feared it was someone else...or something else." She clung to them, shaking.

A new light was struck and by it they could see Garris—dirty and afraid—holding a lantern. He seemed so old. "Why are you here?" he asked, his fear and the shadows from the flickering light made him seem suspicious of them.

"I've come to seek your help," Ella answered. "I've found my mother and she is not well. She is in need of a certain type of healing that is beyond the average fey."

Garris' eye narrowed at this. "You will have my help but not before I've completed my task here. Alseya has a question concerning lineage that we are trying to unravel and I..." he paused looking about. The room was a shambles. Papers and scrolls were everywhere; some covered in filth, some burned beyond recognition. "And I am here to save what I can." The fey pointed to an overturned cabinet. Stacks of papers had been laid within it.

"If you help we can be done soon," Alseya suggested eagerly. "We've been here for hours. It's horrible. Don't you think so? The air and the ground. My soul feels like it's dying within me. I don't know if I can..."

Aric took her by the arms to calm her. "It's going to be alright. We'll help, both of us. Right Ella?"

"I can help," she answered surveying the room. Reaching out with her mind she began sending papers at Aric. They came slowly at first but as she got the feel for the action they came in such a blur that the dexterous fey couldn't keep up and Alseya jumped in to help. Minutes of this went by and then the cabinet was full.

"You two are in luck. We have an automobile from the human world with us. All we have to do now is get the cabinet up the tunnel," Aric said, going to the opening and peering up. "It's not going to be easy since it's so awkward and the tunnel so slippery."

"Just give me a moment. I just need a few minutes to rest," Ella replied, sitting down. With the use of her powers, her headache had come back and was now a dull thump in her temple. Grimacing from the pain, Ella asked, "So, what sort of information are you after, Alseya. If you don't mind my asking. I'm only curious what would bring anyone back here."

"I came in search of an answer on lineage." Alseya said. With the tedious work finished and the prospect of leaving at hand she had relaxed considerably. "It's odd that you should show up when you did. Part of what I'm searching for concerns an ancestor of yours, Aric." His eyebrows went up in question and Alseya answered, "Darania. The other part has to do with lineage of the Sun King."

Aric shared a look with Ella and she felt that pain in her chest again. Alseya caught the look. "What is it? What's going on?"

"Eireden...the uh, Sun King is no more," Ella answered. "He died yesterday morning in a duel with his cousin."

Alseya looked thunderstruck by the news. "Did you see this happen?" she demanded in a harsh whisper. "Were you there?" Ella started to shake her head and before she could even finish the simple movement Alseya proclaimed, "Then you don't know. He is alive. He has to be."

"There were witnesses, dear Alseya," Aric replied. "His death is a blow to us all."

"He is not dead!" she cried, heading for the tunnel. She scampered up it, her white clothes, filthy to begin with, became even more so as she slid and slithered up.

Garris watched in silence until she was gone from sight. "Eireden was a good human and a strong ally. He will be missed. You have my condolences. Now if you'll please help me with this cabinet." His manner was extremely cold and bothered Ella.

"I'll get it," she said. Grunting with the psychic effort, Ella hefted the cabinet and floated it up the tunnel. Her head banged painfully with the effort, but it was worth it to watch Garris' eyes go wide. No fey had the power to lift the wood cabinet. Theirs was a dwindling people. There were precious few with any real strength left. Ella understood this on a gut level and on that same level she felt contempt for the fey.

Normally she would have been shocked by such a feeling, but with her head thumping and the stink of the Feylands only adding to her bitterness, she dwelled on it instead. "Whip-wip, pop the trunk!" she called and in a second the trunk lifted. The fairy new every button and lever in the car—she loved working them. The trunk would never fit the cabinet so she dropped it in the muck and with Aric's help began to lift the stacks into the back.

"Did someone else come with you?" Garris asked.

A rider in black approached. With the swirling ash and the fumes that stung their eyes it was hard to make out who it was that rode so tall in the saddle. Closer he came and the elf sword hanging at his hip became more obvious.

"Is that...?" Alseya said

"Eireden," Ella whispered. She remembered the night of the battle on the road to Rhyoeven—how he had appeared out of the night dressed in black. With his undercurrent of power and violence he had been a menacing figure on his black horse. "That's Eireden!" she yelled and in her exuberance she raced forward to greet him.

# Chapter 36

## Eireden

The flash of Eirowyth's sword in the morning light was bright indeed and Eireden turned away as it swept up—then came the song of the metal splitting the air, but suddenly the song turned angry. More lights flashed and Eireden, as if slowed by a great weight, turned back to his cousin. The fairies were attacking the man. And then Generai was there, sword in hand, slashing at Eirowyth, driving him away. "Stay back!" she screamed at Eirowyth's second, a captain of the knights named Rudyid. The towering captain stayed just out of reach of the sword...and the fairies. They hummed an evil sound as they swarmed in a cloud above the scout.

"Generai, you can't do this," Eireden said from the ground. "I have lost. Let the new king do his duty." There was too little strength in him to even think about running, besides that wasn't his way.

"You are my king!" she thundered. "I will have no other."

"Scout! Call off your sythei," Rudyid ordered. "You are embarrassing Eireden. Let's have this be done with, no one wants this moment dragged out any longer. Say your goodbyes with whatever dignity you have left and be gone."

She ignored him. "Why did you lose?" Generai asked, raining tears down upon him. "Why? You couldn't have lost. You beat the elf in single combat. No one else could do that. No one."

"I just lost," Eireden answered. Inside him the question came: *Did you run away in the Demorlaik? Were you indeed a coward as your cousin pronounced you*? If he had it would go a long way in explaining why he lost the duel: the karma of the swords coming back to give victory to the weak, but righteous over the strong and ignoble. Belief in that karma was why he been so confident against Eirowyth. Now lying there, barely able to breathe from the weight of his armor he had to wonder: was Eirowyth right?

"I don't know why I lost," he told his scout. "But I have and now you must show your respect to the new king. Go—go and proffer your sword. To do otherwise is beneath us. You are Den and you are my scout. Now go."

She didn't, not right away. Instead she knelt and kissed the king as he laid there. "I love you. I have always loved you. And I will always love you." He had no answer to that, none that was honest. He did love her but not in the way that she loved him and to say anything would have been wrong. However she wasn't looking for an answer. She kissed him before he had a chance to think—a soft wet kiss—and then she was up, striding toward Eirowyth with face made hard in her grief.

Wiping her tears on the back of her hand she knelt in front of the new king. "I am your s-scout...c-command me."

The new king looked down upon her in pity. "I cannot command you Generai," Eirowyth said loudly enough for all to hear. "Love and loyalty command you. I know these can be greater than a king's order so I will not even try to counter them. But I give you leave to depart if you wish and spare yourself further misery. Do you wish to stay and act as witness or would you leave."

"I can't watch this."

"Then go, with my blessing," Eirowyth said.

Generai staggered up and looked around at the men on their horses. None would look her in the eye for she was grief itself. Taking her horse she shrieked in a voice that tore men's hearts, "I love you, my king!" and then she was gone riding like a storm across the prairie.

The fairies did not leave with her. "Easa-see, you must go with her," Eireden said. "Take our family and go." They ignored him and remained hovering over the fallen man. "Easa-see, go!" Still nothing. The pearl! Eireden stretched out his arm and snagged the invisible filament that held the pearl. "Easa-see, it's time for you to go," Eireden said in English and when that didn't affect them in any way he tweeted it.

"Why aren't they leaving?" Rudyid growled. His sword rested in his large hand, but he knew it would be useless against the fairies.

"Because they know what will happen if they do leave," Eirowyth answered with a long sigh. "Nothing is ever easy with you, is it cousin? Sythei! Hear me. I will not harm Eireden. No blade of mine will touch him," he announced in a loud voice. He then turned to Eireden. "You will have to do it yourself and I think it is only fitting. I still have the rope from the last time. Help him up."

The fairies wouldn't let Rudyid close until he sheathed his sword and even then they kept very near just in case. The honor guard from Hildoeven was dismissed and they made their gloomy way back south, while Eireden tottered along on foot, still barely able to carry the weight of his own armor. The morning sun seemed to bake into him, cooking him within the metal

"A drink, cousin?" he asked.

On a deep brown stallion the new king rode next to his cousin. He looked relaxed and energetic, as he handed over a canteen. "I just thought of something. Would you prefer poison? I don't want to be weird about this, but I think I would want poison."

The water helped refresh him and his body surged with his old strength. *Was I just dehydrated*, Eireden wondered? *Is that why I felt so weak*? It was possible, though not likely. He had been dehydrated on many battlefields—it came with the territory. Armor, by its very nature, tended to make a person dehydrated.

"I was thinking of starving to death actually—or better yet, eating myself to death," Eireden replied. "Send down a roast pig every morning until I burst." He was sad but not nervous over his coming death. His sadness was mainly for his scout and his family of sythei. They seemed to love him too much, if that was possible. "You won't hurt the fairies?"

he asked with a slight warning tone to his voice.

"I don't even want to hurt you, for goodness sake!" Eirowyth said with sudden savageness. "Why would I want to hurt them? This whole business...if only you hadn't run."

"I didn't..."

"Don't start in with that again..." Eirowyth said and then paused. He rode for a bit in silence before adding, "Look, I'm sorry about all of this. I know that I'm partly to blame. The Demorlaik was a nightmare and I shouldn't have laid guilt on anyone for running, even you. That was a mistake and I wish that I could take it back, but I can't. There is honor at stake. The highest honor."

"I suppose you are right," Eireden agreed. "It's funny, had we been in battle I would've given my life for you. Perhaps I should look at my death in that light?"

"Perhaps," acknowledge Eirowyth. He laughed suddenly. "Hurt the fairies? Remember how much trouble that one fairy of Ella's caused. I can't imagine having a hundred of them around here, especially if they were angry."

There was truth to that. The fairies in question rode upon Eireden's shoulders or circled him in swarms to the amazement of the people of Rhyoeven. Rumor of the outcome of the duel spread so fast that there was a crowd of people at the palace by the time Eireden came up. A lane had to be opened up before the condemned man could pass through. At the entrance to the dungeons he lost most of his fairy escort—only his family stayed. And when he got to the stairs leading to the lower ones where the smell turned men a shade of green Eireden demanded that the rest leave him.

"Go back to your grotto," he whispered to them, embarrassed that he was talking to a group of adoring fairies within earshot of hardened warriors. "Go live your lives and be happy. That's an order from your king." They cried as only fairies could and then touched him before floating up and away back into the palace.

The lower dungeons had changed quite a bit in the nine

days that he had last been in them. The cells that Furen had tunneled their way out of were under construction. The stone had been dug out completely to make room for full wrought iron cages. They weren't completed yet so Eireden was placed in the second cell. A minute later a stool and a rope were brought in by Rudyid.

"I'll see you on the other side, My Lord," he said as he left.

Eirowyth shut the door personally on him. "There will be three guards down here with you. Don't keep them waiting too long."

"It's a time of my choosing," Eireden replied.

The new king shook his head. "It's not. You had that option. While you are down here you won't be fed or given anything to drink. If you don't choose the rope you'll be dead of dehydration in three days. Like I said, don't keep them waiting."

He left.

Eireden immediately took up the rope, but it had a greasy evil feel and he put it back down again. He then went to the walls and began tapping on them, remembering the escape he had made with the dwarf's help. "Furen," he said. "Where are you when I need you?" But did he really need Furen? Escape shouldn't have been on his mind. His principles dictated that he should kill himself. He had been beaten in a duel of honor and to do anything but kill himself would only prove Eirowyth was right.

"I didn't run," he said obstinately. But he did—the memory came to him in a flash. There in the dark twisted boulevards of the Demorlaik he and his fellows had fought a nightmare battle. No matter the numbers that they slew there were always more of the fiendish creatures, bizarre things, things that were half man-half beast or dead things; animated corpses that knew no pain. These closed in time again and Eireden's numbers had dwindled with every passing hour until no more than five of his soldiers remained alive.

He then insisted that they run. "Cast off your armor if you must, but if we don't run we will never get out," he had ordered. They had run, but that wasn't dishonorable. It was only when they blundered into an ambush and he had fought his way free that there came the least dishonor. The remaining five hadn't fought free. They were surrounded by hundreds of the bizarre creatures. Eireden had hacked at them desperate to save his men, but quickly he saw it was too late and he had stepped back.

That little motion haunted him there in his cell. Was that what this was all about? He had stepped back and, with eyes grown wide by the horror he had witnessed, he watched his men as they were engulfed by the horde. He heard their shrieks.

Then he had run.

"That wasn't dishonorable," he insisted. "Where is the honor in being eaten alive?" *You stepped back.* "So what? There had been no chance to save those men." *You stepped back.* "Again, so what!" Eireden began pacing, in a fury, but what exactly he was so angry about, he didn't know.

"Yes you do," he whispered. "You stepped back because you were afraid. Yes, that was it. I was afraid. For that one moment."

But did that make him a coward? Did that mean he ran? "No. I would never judge another so harshly, so I won't judge myself any different." In truth he had been, if not afraid, than extremely anxious the entire time he was in the Demorlaik. They all had been, but they all had done their duty. With the thought of duty he looked again on the rope. That was his duty. He had challenged his cousin, knowing full well that victory or death were his only options—and he had certainly not won.

He went to the stool, but did not stand upon it. He sat for hours replaying every second of his duel, every move, every counter-move. Seeing now missed opportunities, but still not understanding the weakness that had grown over him.

Eirowyth had not cheated. There had been no lie in his words.

There had to be something. He had felt it in his sword arm first, yet he had used it almost exclusively so that was understandable to a point. Then his shield arm had grown feeble...then his chest and abs...and finally his legs. It made no sense.

"Does it need to?" he asked himself. No, it didn't. It wouldn't matter a hill of beans if he figured out what had gone wrong. It would change nothing. He had still lost, fair and square, and would still have to suffer the consequences. Eireden went to the door of his cell, wondering what the time was. How long had he been there in the semi-dark? The guards at the end of the hall had a lantern and he was able to get a little flicker of light from it. He smelled beef. It was dinner time or sometime after. Many hours had slipped away. He decided to wait a little longer, not wanting to disturb their dinner.

Those final minutes went by with amazing slowness compared to the hours that had flow along, but finally he stood with a long sigh. It was dehydration, or this. Taking the rope in hand he climbed up on his stool, attached the rope to the hook, and then settled the other end around his neck. His final thought was of Ella. He could still feel her in his heart. Then he kicked away the stool and dropped into darkness.

## Chapter 37

## Ella

Ella squinted up at Eireden through the fumes and the blizzard of falling and swirling ash. Again he had found her; that strange ability to track her had not left him. The idea was comforting to her in a way. It made her feel that no matter what, she would never be completely lost. Someone would know where she was, always.

But why was he here? And perhaps more importantly how was he here? He had fought a duel where the outcome could have only one result for the loser. "Did Eirowyth let him live?" she asked aloud. The Eirowyth that Ella knew probably wouldn't have; especially not a rival for the throne. And Eireden wasn't just any rival; he was in truth the king.

He wore all black; a smart thing with the utter filth of the Feylands. Only the shining hilt of his elf-sword gave any hint of color. Even the steel-grey of his eyes was hidden beneath his cloak which he wrapped around his face.

"Eireden!" she called in relief as he came closer. He cantered right up to her and then just as she put out her hand to him he kicked his horse on faster, drawing his sword as he did. What was happening? This was not making sense to Ella. She felt slow and stupid, watching without reaction as the man barreled down on the fey standing by the car. Thankfully, Aric and Alseya had their wits about them and their swords were out before Ella could even blink.

And a second later she not only blinked, but cringed back as well. A great gout of fire erupted from the outstretched hand of the man on the horse and swept over the two fey. They dove out of the path of the inferno and amazingly neither was hurt, though Alseya's cloak smoldered. The man on the horse leapt down and now Ella could see it wasn't a man at all. It was one of the burnt creatures that had ridden her and Eireden down on the plains of Rhyoeven weeks before.

Her mind screamed—*It's an elf!*

Though her mind screamed, her body reacted sluggishly and she took one slow step forward, disgusted at the sight of the elf. Was that what she would become? A horrid burnt fiend? Just then she remembered the black mark in the back of her throat. She remembered seeing how it had vined up from the hidden depths of her body. Had it progressed? Was she slowly turning into a creature such as the one before her?

The thought, the sudden fight, and the choking fumes left her standing on the road in a state of internal anarchy. She had a sword at her hip. It was the one she had carried out of the dungeons when they had made their escape from Rhyoeven. In a daze she drew it and started forward moving on weak legs. She watched as the elf came off his horse and attacked the two fey with such power and speed that Aric went down spurting blood from his chest in the first passage of arms. Alseya only saved herself by going on the defensive. In a blur of motion she spun with her blade, flashing, parrying every blow, yet giving ground step after step.

*What are you waiting for?* The sound of the voice in her mind jarred Ella into action. She knew why she had been so slow to react: the elf was too skilled—too strong. He was no simple goblin and Ella didn't stand a chance against him. She had hoped that Aric and Alseya would beat him, but that wasn't happening. They were losing and losing bad.

Behind the elf, Ella screwed up her courage and charged, however he sensed her coming and sent out a shockwave of air that struck her with the force of a tornado and sent her flying. She landed with a slapping sound in one of the quagmires and was immediately sucked in up to her waist. No amount of struggling helped to move her even an inch.

"Garris!" she screamed. "Help her." The old fey had shrunk back against the building at the first sign of violence and had done little else. At her scream he still did nothing, however the elf took notice of him. Blasting Alseya back with another explosion of air, the elf then went through a series of deliberate hand motions. This got Garris' attention and he stood up straighter with eyes wide—suddenly glittering knives flew at him. Ten or more streaks of metal honed straight at him, but at the last second they seemed to erupt into harmless feathers that spun in lazy circles to the ground. Garris had countered with his own magic.

And then Aric was back. Having healed himself in a flash he fought the elf with grim determination. Metal rang against metal and the colors of the fight were red and black streaked by silver lines as the swords cut the air. Aric was no match for the elf. Time and again his blade cleaved air instead of flesh, while his opponent showed his mastery of the sword. Turning aside attacks with ease he countered to lay open the flesh of the fey, once then twice and yet again.

Alseya came to his rescue, attacking from behind in a silent blur.

The elf seemed to expect this and turned from one opponent to the other with a simple pivot. He toyed with her, wearing a ghastly smile on his blackened face, while he slapped her around with the flat of his sword. She was undersized even more so than Aric was, and relying on her quickness got her nowhere for her speed was matched by the elf's. So desperate did her plight become that in less than a minute Aric had to come back into the fight though he still bled from wounds that he lacked the magical strength to heal.

The elf was stronger than both combined. The power of his magic; the strength of his arm; the skill of his sword and his unbelievable quickness was too great and they both went down within seconds of each other. Aric with a gaping hole in his shoulder and Alseya run through the midsection. The elf stood over them preparing to finish them off, but he took a moment to gloat.

He paused a second too long. Ella reached out with her mind and using her telekinetic power took the elf in body and flung him into one of the black creeping swamps. She then began working herself out of the sludge that held her. The strength of the suction was nearly greater than her powers and she had to rest from time to time with her head pounding. In his own muck, the elf was having the same issues and it seemed that they would be in a race to see who would get clear first.

"Garris!" Ella screamed when it became obvious she wasn't going to make it. "Heal them!" The fey had stood with his hands clenched to his chest, as if resigned to a fate of death. Now he seemed to wake and he darted to Aric's side. Blue light spread across the bleeding fey and for a moment the dead world of the Feylands held a touch of color other than black and red, but the light was cut short. From his pit of slime the elf cast a spell and out of his outstretched hand, more streaking daggers flew at the old fey.

"Look out!" Ella screamed. Garris was too slow. His counter-spell came a second too late and although some of the daggers morphed harmlessly into feathers two did not. They sunk into his chest and he slumped forward over the limp form of Aric.

There came a moment of quiet realization then: they were all going to die—she was going to die. It lasted only a second and then Ella went into a frenzy, straining with all her might against the tar like swamp. Mostly she used the strength of her legs, but after a moment she used her sword as an oar, pushing off the ground at the bottom of the bog. She refused to use the power of her mind. That was all ready fading from overuse.

A minute later the Den sword broke and she nearly stumbled face first into the muck. She put a hand out to keep herself completely out of it and there beneath her fingers was what felt like a rope. It was actually a root of a tree that had been torn up and burned, but still it served her purposes. Hand over hand she pulled herself out of the bog.

Falling face first onto the road, her breath raged in her

throat from her exertion yet she had no time to recover, the elf had made it clear as well. Staggering up Ella hurried to Alseya hoping to heal her enough for her to fight, but the gaping wound was too massive. She could tell the fey was beyond her feeble strength. Aric was as well. Not only did he have the shoulder wound, he bled from other injuries that she hadn't seen before.

In a trembling hand he held out his elf sword for her to take. "Run," he whispered. "Go... get in the car and go."

She could. It was right there with the engine still rumbling and Whip-wip's scared face pressed against the glass. The fairy pointed behind Ella. The elf was coming. A glance over her shoulder showed that he had just freed himself from his bog. There was still time; she could make it! If she got in right at that moment and gunned the engine she could make it!

*And where would you go?*

Indeed. The real question was where *could* she go that would be any safer than right there in the hell of the Feylands? Nowhere. She could be tracked by these elves without a problem. Nowhere was safe as long as they lived.

Ella turned from the car.

She was no damsel in distress. This she had decided a long time ago on her first day in the Hidden Lands. With a battle cry that sounded similar to the one Eireden had used on that same day so long ago, Ella charged her enemy. The cry's strength had been feeble and it only caused the elf to grin. They clashed swords.

A moment later she was on her back—disarmed, as the elf's sword crept toward her heart. She strained against him with all the strength of her mind and body, but the elf was too powerful.

## Chapter 38

### Eireden

The darkness of death was not complete for the Sun King. A flicker of light came to him, one that should not have been, one that confused him. He lay upon the floor of his cell as if waking from a long sleep. In a state of growing bewilderment he had to ask himself: *Is this death?* There was no way to tell. Having never been dead before he had to assume that it was.

Getting up, his armor scraped against the stone of his cell.

"Armor?" he said aloud, looking down at his plate-mail covered chest. "How...?" He had died in his tunic, but now he was fully armored just as he had been before his duel and what's more the armor had been completely repaired. And at his side was a sword. Eireden shrugged at this; death, it seemed, came complete with a sword. It also came with a black cube.

There upon the ground, next to the overturned stool sat a small black square of glistening ebony. He reached out to grab it but pulled his hand back, startled, as an image came into life above it. It showed Eirowyth's mother, the Lady Harowyth, standing in the king's chamber.

*"Your sheath is dirty!"* she admonished a person yet unseen. *"Since you were a boy I've been telling you to keep it polished if you ever wanted to be king and now that you are one look at you going around with it dirty. Here I shall clean it for you."*

The angle of the moving image changed and now Eireden could see his cousin unbuckling his sword belt. *"Thank you, Mother,"* Eirowyth said and then the image moved, following along after Harowyth as she went to her own quarters. With a wave of her hand the sword was instantly clean—the dirt had been illusion only. She then drew the sword. It wasn't the black sword of Ag-Raumon; it was the plain steel that he had fought Eireden with. A vial of clear liquid appeared in her hand and this she poured upon the blade. The liquid seemed to seep into it and when she was done the sword looked just as it did when they had dueled.

And the image faded to nothing.

"What? What was that?" Eireden asked the cube. A part of him expected an answer. He was dead after all and things were certainly different in the land of the dead. No answer came from the cube, but one did come from his own mind.

"I didn't lose. Harowyth cheated." It was a bitter realization, because in a way he did lose. He was dead and his honor was tarnished for all time. A second time he pressed the cube and watched the same image. Harowyth had grown strong in her magic. The illusion had been good enough to fool her son and the magic on the blade had not once stirred his senses. Placing the cube in the pouch at his belt, Eireden stood and stretched. Only then did he find that death was also painless.

Not only had his armor been repaired, he had been fully healed as well. This did not surprise him. What surprised him was that he had a body at all. He had been raised to believe that only his soul would survive after death. "It is what it is," he murmured, not really caring one way or the other. He left the cell that he died in, making his way to the source of the light. It was a lantern, as he knew it would be. The guards had huddled around it chatting quietly, waiting for Eireden to kill himself. Now it sputtered, running low and those same guards lay upon the floor.

He thought them dead at first, but closer examination discovered that they slept only. It didn't make sense, however he didn't bother to make sense out of it. To him, it just was—just like being healed and having a sword. Leaving them sleeping peacefully he went to the upper floor dungeon and discovered the remaining guards sleeping as well.

"Death is strange," he remarked, before heading up to the palace. Would he find everyone comatose? Or were there others like himself wandering around? "Maybe I am a ghost." Again he shrugged.

At the top of the stairs he looked left and right. To the left was the passage to the stables and the kitchens and to the right was the palace proper. He decided to go to the right, but something to the left caught his attention. Upon the ground far down the passage was a little green box. Right away he knew what it was.

"Riecie," he said hurrying to the little woven casket. It was hers all right. She lay curled in the bottom of it just as she had, but her pearl was missing. Further down the hall he saw another of the fairy caskets. For some reason they had been taken from his pouch and strewn about. After he collected it he saw a pearl glinting on the floor thirty feet away. Now he understood.

Somebody or something was leading him toward the stables. On the way he collected his little caskets and the pearls. Once there he found the late-night stable boy laid out on the floor in a deep sleep. Beside him stood a sturdy, dappled mare already saddled and upon her back lay a long cloak of the type messengers of the king wore.

Eireden was not quick to climb into the saddle. His "death" was more strange than he reckoned it would be. In fact he got the feeling he wasn't dead at all. He led the horse through the low arch at the entrance to the stables and stood staring into the city. It was late, but not too late—around eleven he guessed. People were out strolling along under the magical lights and this was entirely normal, which bothered him. What he had expected to see—if he were truly dead— were more people lying around sleeping. Why were these others not like his guards or the stable-boy? Why was it only people in his direct path who were out cold?

"Because you're not dead, fool," Eireden said to himself, coming to the easiest explanation. "Those people are out cold so that you can escape."

Someone had engineered this escape. If he had to guess he would say that it was his mother, Ilenwyth-Eden, who was behind it. Though she couldn't have acted alone; there was too much spell work involved even for one as powerful as she.

"But do I escape?" he mused. "Or do I go back and hang myself?" The choice wasn't all that hard.

Eireden threw the cloak over his shoulders and climbed up on the mare. He would escape, though beyond that he was clueless on what to do. Cantering down to the nearest gate with his hood pulled down low over his forehead, he barely begun slowing when a voice rang, "King's messenger!" The gate opened before him and he was off down the sloping road to the next gate without challenge. This second one proved just as simple to pass through. Again came the cry: "King's messenger!"

In a minute he was on the battle plain riding unhurriedly westward. His first inclination had been to ride southeast to Hildoeven, but he figured that was the direction most likely expected. Why he chose westward wasn't known to him for some time, until it dawned on him that Ella had moved into the west. Subconsciously he followed her still. His heart had not ceased to center on her, nor had its longing for her diminished in any way.

"Turn around," he growled. "There's nothing for you in this direction." The horse's ears twisted in little half-circles at his words and she slowed in confusion. Eireden checked the horse entirely and stood staring where the sun had set hours before. He was right—there was nothing for him in the west except heartache. "You could have had her, but you gave up her up," he said speaking to himself. In answer he sighed and turned the horse around only to stop mid-way. *Was there anything for him in any direction*?

No city of the Den would be a refuge. He had placed all that was left of his honor on the duel and had lost. Yes, he had an excuse now; however the little black cube with the moving images wasn't exactly ironclad proof of wrongdoing on Lady Harowyth's part. It was magic and could have been created through illusion, which meant the image could be false; not that he didn't believe it for a second. He knew the sly, disreputable mind of the lady's and there had been some sort of dwimmer-craft at work in his defeat.

But that didn't mean that others would jump to believe it. Without any other proofs, Eireden could expect only those nearest to him to take the images produced by the cube at face value. The people of Hildoeven would believe it, but what about the citizens of Avargard? Or Varisgard? Would they believe images presented by a former *gada* who had twice now escaped from the dungeons of Rhyoeven? Not likely.

What sort of options did that leave for Eireden? One more attempt at a duel? Eirowyth wouldn't allow it. In his mind he had fought and won. Also he would be the last person to believe anything that showed his mother in a bad light. This left Eireden with only one real choice: exile. He could go to America—the land of opportunity. And do what? Become a grocer...a gas station attendant...a janitor? He had little training that would be of any use in their corporate world. He could kill in a hundred different ways, but what use was that there?

The man slumped in his saddle and looked again to the west, towards Ella. What was she doing now? What was in the west? She wasn't back in Seattle—that was south and west. The only thing he knew that lay west was...

"She's in the Feylands," Eireden said aloud and then sat up straight. "I could go there." This was an idea. It was the only place that he could go in the Hidden Lands where the Den couldn't follow. He could live there. Yes, the goblins had a made a mess of it—burning the homes and trees, but that didn't mean he could clear away some the rubble and debris and start over.

Eireden kicked the horse westward, while in his mind he began picturing what sort of work would need to be done to start a farm. He was sure there would be tools available. After all every Fey home had their own garden and no self-respecting goblin would ever touch something that would indicate work, not if they could help it. But a farm would take time. How would he live in the mean time?

"The lake...and all those streams," he said. He could fish. It was something he enjoyed. "This could be alright...if not a bit lonely. Thankfully I have you," he exclaimed, patting his horse on the neck. "You could be my best friend."

The horse was non-committal on the matter of friendship, but she was a sturdy animal and the miles flicked by under her hooves. It was just before dawn that horse and rider came to the Forest of Mists. It hadn't changed and was still the second most frightful place Eireden had ever been in. Using his cloak he bound the horse's head against the intrusion of the illusions and set off at a brisk walk, leading the mare. Keeping his head down, he watched his feet as he went.

Even so the illusions came at him in all their horror. With a strength of mind that was without equal, he ignored the sights and sounds in his periphery and began singing. What came out was a love song and what he pictured in his mind was face that went with it. Eleanor Belmont. Yes, he loved Generai in his way and yes, he was intrigued by the exotic and beautiful Alseya, but he still loved Ella. There was no question of that.

And so for the five miles that terror washed over him, Eireden sang every love song that he knew and patted his distraught horse. The mare blew out noisily and balked from time to time, shaking in a perfect lather of fear. "It will be all right," he soothed through the cloak. "You'll see. There will be the sweetest grasses in the world for you to dine upon. Perhaps not in the abundance there had been. But still, as the only horse in the valley I have no doubt you will be able to eat to your heart's content. It's the trees that I'm worried about."

During his escape from the valley a month before he couldn't remember seeing any tree that hadn't been either in flames or hacked to the ground. Lumber wouldn't be much of an issue either way as the valley was surrounded by forest, but he just felt a pain in his chest at the idea of all those pretty trees gone.

When he finally emerged from the Forest of Mists that pain in his chest doubled and then doubled again. At the sight in front of him he had to wonder if he was still seeing illusions. The Feylands were a nightmare of death. He reeled from the poisonous chemical stench, while his eyes were assaulted by the reality of hell on earth.

"How...?"

How was such a thing possible? Not a single blade of grass remained. Nor anything green—not a leaf, or stem, or even the semblance of a tree remained. He would never have guessed that the tortured land in front of him were the Feylands had it not been for the fact that he had just traveled through the illusions of the forest. He stood almost in a daze until a twinkle of color caught his eye.

A flash of silver to his right had him turning in time to see Ella fall back to the charred ground with an elf astride her. Even from a quarter mile there was no mistaking his love, nor was there mistaking a mortal enemy. Unthinking, Eireden leapt into the saddle. The mare wanted to bolt and run away from the terror that gripped her, but Eireden would have none of it and he charged the horse straight down the hillside letting out a war cry and unsheathing his sword.

# Chapter 39

## Ella

The sword bearing down at her suddenly lifted as the battle cry raged throughout the valley. Ella knew that cry. She didn't need to turn her head to know that her Eireden was coming to *attempt* to rescue her. And attempt is all it would be. The elf was too powerful. He had fought three of the strongest fey alive and hadn't suffered a scratch while they lay stretched out on the ground, bleeding out the last seconds of their lives.

The pounding hooves of Eireden's horse came closer. The elf stood and gave a glance at this newcomer, before turning back to Ella. "Stay," he said. The single word was filled with such power that Ella froze in place. Her body went rigid with only her eyes having any capacity at movement. She strained with all her might and was just barely able to creak her head around in time to see the charge of Eireden culminate in the death of his horse. The dappled-grey went down with blood spurting from a tremendous wound in its neck. Nimble as always, Eireden leapt off and using the animal's momentum brought his sword down with greater power than any normal man could.

The elf made the mistake of parrying instead of dodging and the blow staggered him, though it left him unhurt. Eireden followed up that strike with another and another. The Den struck with all the savage might in his arms, blow after ringing blow. Ella saw what tactic he was attempting. It was basically the same one he had used in his fight with Aric. Eireden would use his physical strength to wear down the magical strength of the elf.

There was only one problem with this: the elf was just too strong. In her heart she knew that no man, even one as formidable as Eireden, could stand alone opposing an elf.

Gritting her teeth against the strain, she turned her head back toward the car. Not knowing that three fairies of Whip-wip's family had already died at the hands of the elves, Ella commanded, "Whip-wip! Help him, please."

Brave as always the fairy went to the door console and triggered the button that lowered the window. The little creature shot at the elf like a bullet. Streaking in, she exploded light square in his face and as she did Eireden switched tactics from dropping hammering blows on the elf to using sly finesse. The change caught the elf off guard and the tip of Eireden's sword slid under the plate of armor in the elf's side and went deep.

Then came a beautiful minute in which man and fairy worked together in unreal precision. Back and forth. Blade and shining light. Dancing in a rhythm. The light of the fairy lent Eireden an aura of purity and goodness, while the shadows it caused made the elf more sinister looking by contrast. Ella watched the battle in complete relaxation as the minute progressed.

And then the fairy grew tired and Eireden received his first injury, a penetrating wound in his left arm. There came just the slightest pause in their attack and the elf took advantage, whisking Whip-wip away with a huge gust of wind. Ella couldn't see where she went or if she was ok. She actually didn't try; she lay upon the ground still unmoving and unworried. Her mind was far away in her special garden—the one she had created with her magic for the trophy wife of the tech-millionaire back in Seattle. It had been a few weeks since she had to rely on her special garden in order to bring about the focused state of mind required for magic. Lately the magic had just come springing forth with ease and there had been no need for the garden.

Now her head thumped dreadfully and she had absolutely nothing left; so she went to her garden and breathed in the rejuvenating air, trying in the calmest of desperation to bring something—anything out of herself. Eireden was losing his fight, despite his size and skill. That outcome was almost pre-ordained.

"You were second only to Dahrain, weren't you?" Eireden asked, going back to the hammering that had been sapping the strength of his opponent. The elf took to using his speed advantage, avoiding the attacks, and delivering minor cuts that were beginning to take their toll on the big man.

"When I slay the great *Sun King* I will be second only to the master," the high voiced elf replied. "Dahrain was a know-nothing, big talking fool!"

"How many..." Eireden started to ask, but just then the elf riposted elegantly and with the last of his magic gained the upper hand and slid his sword through the man.

"How many are we?" the elf asked casually, still holding the sword in Eireden's belly. "Now just four, plus the master of course...but I plan on creating many of my kind." His eyes left Eireden as the man stumbled to his knees and went to Ella. The elf leered horribly.

Ella came from her garden then, and brought with her the slightest hope. She had scrounged only enough strength to cast aside the elf's spell that held her—which would gain her nothing whatsoever—so she didn't bother. Instead she looked for the slimmest opening. The elf promptly gave her one. As the man went to his knees, he slid his sword from Eireden's belly and went to deliver a final killing stroke. Bringing the sword way back, he seemed to want to cut the man near in two. However just as his ferocious blow came Ella used the last of her magic to divert the course of the sword and the devastating stroke went deep into the charred earth next to the man. The elf lurched forward surprised at the lack of resistance and Eireden, gripping his stomach with one hand, brought his sword around faster than sight could follow and took the elf's head off in one blow.

Immediately Ella was released from the spell and she jumped up not knowing who to turn to first. Despite their sudden victory there was no relief within her; she spun in place seeing nothing but red blood and lifeless bodies. Only the Den still moved. She took a step toward him, but he shook his head.

"No...I live," Eireden said. "They need your help more than I do." Despite his brave words, his face had gone paper white and he lowered himself down into the black filth that he had been fighting in.

Ella did as she was told. She went first to Alseya who still had her eyes open, though her breathing was very fast and light. "Alseya! Help me...I don't know what to do. I'm out of magic and...and everyone's dying."

"Go...to...the Sun King," the fey replied. "Kiss him."

"What?" Ella cried. "Why would I want to...Alseya! Alseya!" The fey's white eyes rolled back in her head. "Eireden! She's not responding. What do I do?"

"Come kiss me," he said, nodding slowly as if Alseya's idea had been a good one.

She blinked stupidly, clearing the ash from her blue eyes. Why would he want a kiss right then? Was he looking for a kiss good bye? "You're not dying. We'll get some help. I'll have Whip-wip..." The fairy was nowhere in sight and suddenly Ella felt dreadfully alone.

"Come kiss me. Hurry before you lose them," Eireden said. "You'll take my strength to heal them." That made more sense! Ella rushed to him and knelt down, but didn't know how to start. Were there magic words or a spell or... "Just kiss me," Eireden said, as if reading her mind. "Your soul will know what to do."

Ella bent to kiss a man who had once professed to love her and in a second found that his love hadn't weakened in the slightest. It had grown to dominate the sorrows of his heart with an emotion and strength that made her feelings for Aric seem like puppy-love.

That heart, despite the blood loss, was a sledgehammer in his chest that she could feel running, pulsating through her owns veins. He had great power—it was the raw unworked energy of a volcano that looked for any reason to explode. Ella felt that power course into her but it left just as fast. She had laid her right hand on his stomach just above his wound and now she was healing him, using his own strength.

After a second he turned his head gasping and listless. "That's enough...I'm healed enough. Go to the others." After he said this he went limp, unconscious.

When she stood, she swayed light-headed. The power of Eireden felt to be rising up out of her and she hurried to Alseya and knew what she had to do. She would have to kiss the fey. The power she had stolen had set a track within her, from her lips to her heart and she knew that if she attempted a normal healing she would lose too much of the power she had gained. Already it seemed to be evaporating.

Ella had never kissed a girl before, though this hardly counted. Alseya's lips were as soft as a butterfly's wing and when the power of the Sun King went into her, those lips became hungry for the strength of the man. After seconds only Ella had to pull back, feeling the new power diminishing—she wouldn't have enough left for two more healings.

"Thank you," Alseya said in a low voice. Just as Eireden, she was only partially healed and lacked any real strength.

"I only have the power for one of them?" Ella whispered. "Who do I heal?"

Garris spoke then, "You will heal the lord Aric. I have no wish to live. My world has ended—my people are homeless, defenseless, leaderless. We are weak. Alseya you were right and I was wrong. And...and I have what you were looking for here on my person. Please forgive me for hiding it."

Even as the two women stared the old fey closed his eyes and died.

Ella watched in horror and started toward Garris, but Alseya stopped her. "It's too late for him. He made his decision. Now, attend the living while you still may."

Feeling sick, Ella went to Aric and with the last of Eireden's strength she healed the fey, kissing him back into a semi-state of health. He didn't say a word, but blearily rubbed his lips—and then she was gone, stumbling around, trying to find Whip-wip in the light snow of hot ash that fell from the grieving sky. She found the poor fairy trapped in one of the muck pools, crying miserably. All four of her delicate wings were covered in a tar-like substance and were tearing as she struggled

"*Es ta! Es ta!*" Whip-wip sobbed: My wings! My wings!

Uncaring of anything else, Ella waded into the pool and fished the little thing out, though she was then stuck and was forced to call to Eireden. He came to her and pulled her to firmer land though he grimaced from his many injuries as he did. Whip-wip clung to Ella, shivering and refused for any of them to touch her. Eventually she went into Ella's pocket and after a time she began to throw out little black hunks of goo all the while she wept in misery.

"What are we going to do?" Ella asked after a time. The four were exhausted and no one seemed to have the energy to think. Alseya crawled on all fours to the body of Garris; she went through his pockets until she found a sheaf of papers. With her mouth slack and the foul air collecting unheeded upon her tongue, Ella watched as Alseya began reading the words. Strangely they were in the language of the Den. What was Alseya after? What had Garris exactly done that needed forgiving? The effort to ask was too much.

"What are we going to do? That depends on our friend," Aric answered when no one else would. "Did you happen to win your duel?" Eireden looked down and shook his head. This shocked Ella. How had he not won his duel? No one could out-fight him. If an elf couldn't finish him then no man could possibly.

"We are going to Hildoeven," Alseya said. "We need healing and time to think and to plan. They will take us in."

"I will take you there, but I cannot go myself," Eireden

said. He then gestured to Ella and Aric. "And neither can these two. They are fugitives even as I am. It would be different had I not lost my duel, but...it is what it is and now," he paused shaking his head. Taking out a small black object from his pouch he said, "I found out after that there was foul play involved...cheating by magic." An image sprung up from his palm, showing the Lady Harowyth doctoring her son's sword. Ella opened her mouth to protest and Eireden gave her a sad smile. "I know what you're going to say, however, this isn't proof enough. It could have been created through illusion. Not to mention I have twice accepted the rope. There will be no more chances; no more duels."

Alseya had watched with a strange look on her face. "Despite this, we are going to Hildoeven and you, my lord will fight for your throne."

# Chapter 40

## Eireden

The four gimped their way into the Ford with Eireden driving and Ella and Alseya sharing the passenger seat. Aric sat in the back with Elleni and the sad corpse of Garris-Unhi. The distance from the Feylands to Hildoeven was just under thirty miles which would have normally taken most of the day, but with the Ford it was just a little over three hours and that was with Eireden going as easy as possible.

It was noon when they turned off the road to drop off Alseya as close to the town as possible. Due to her insistence they decided not to leave the Hidden Lands yet and they made their way to a cabin that Eireden was familiar with in the forests to the east. On the way he quizzed Ella concerning the strange lady she had brought out of America.

"Your mother?" he exclaimed, turning with a grimace. There didn't seem much resemblance, except for the eyes, though with the woman being so dreadfully old and wizened it was hard to tell. "Well I guess, Aric, we were both right about Ella. That sure does explain some things."

"It doesn't explain how you can track me," Ella replied. "Or how those other elves can track me."

Eireden felt an odd feeling when she brought up the word 'elf'. Wasn't he supposed to hate her now? She was part elf—part her mortal enemy—and part so breathtakingly beautiful that he had to fight to keep from staring or touching her hand. He kept both his hands on the steering wheel as he edged the Ford through the woods, gently easing along a tiny trail. It was so narrow that time and again the forest reached out branches to mar the paint and set their ears on edge.

He also had to keep from sighing, so he spoke far more glibly that was usual. "Those elves that chased us to the gate suggested that you were related to them, remember? Maybe you and I are related somehow as well. Maybe that lady back there is a Den."

"Her name is Elleni Feyden," she said.

"Elleni Feyden? Well that certainly is a Den name."
Eireden slowed the car and took a better look at the woman.
She was awful small for a Den.

Aric spoke from the back seat. "Feyden is certainly made
up and Elleni is from the elvish *Elleney*. You should know
that."

"That could be, but it's also a pet name for Eliniesar,"
Eireden replied. "I've known two women with the name
Elleni. You are right about the Feyden part. There are no
Feydens in the Forbidden Lands. But wouldn't that be
strange if we were related? It would have to be distantly
since I can account for all of my cousins four times
removed."

Ella frowned at this. "I think it has to do with more than
just being related, otherwise there would be many Den who
would be able to track me. As far as I know you are the only
one. And then there's that intense feeling I get when I touch
you. It's like our..." She bit back the sentence suddenly and
her eyes went wide with sudden guilt. Eireden felt a guilty
rush as well which cleaved his tongue to the top of his mouth
and there was a long moment of awkward silence between
them.

Thankfully at that moment, Ella's front pocket moved a
little and a tiny, plaintive voice called out, "*Zooti*?"

"Oh my!" Ella gasped. "I'm so sorry Whip-wip. We have
some grapes left. Would you like one of those?" The fairy let
out a hungry: *Sis*! Gingerly Ella handed over a grape. "We'll
get you cleaned up I promise. Aric, is there any magic we
can use? That gunk is all in her wings. She looks like one of
those birds that they pull out of an oil spill."

"I'm certain I don't know what you mean by an oil spill,"
Aric replied. "Though about using 'magic' I should be strong
enough to help with this. Let us get to the cabin first."

It wasn't long before they pulled up in front of the cabin.

It was tiny and more rustic than Ella had anticipated. She stared at the single room and the one lumpy bed; Eireden could hear the unasked question in her mind: *where are you two going to sleep*?

"Let's heal our brave Whip-wip and then we'll figure out what we are going to do about your mother," Aric said, limping toward Ella. In her shirt pocket the fairy began to whimper. "I know it hurts," the fey told her. "But I'm going to fix that. Just relax and close your eyes. Relax...relax...as if you are falling asleep. Go to sleep...go to sleep."

When Whip-wip went limp Aric wiped his forehead, looking ready to pass out himself. He then went to one of the few chairs in the cabin and sat slowly down. "We need a knife. A sharp one."

Eireden drew his dagger which had a fine edge. Ella looked at it with concern. "What do you need a knife for? What we need is soap and water."

"We'll need those as well," Aric replied. "But first we have to cut these wings off..."

"What! No way!" Ella cried. "I can heal her. I have the strength at least for that. And if I don't have the strength you would help wouldn't you Eireden?" The Den felt hollow inside, except where the elf's sword had ran him through—that part was filled with pain. Still, he would give all that he had to save Whip-wip. He nodded to Ella.

Aric looked pained. "Her wings are shredded; there's no saving them. We'll trim them off—clean her up—and *then* heal her. She'll be good as new."

Ella sagged in relief at the explanation. She then went around exploring the cabin; she couldn't bring herself to be near when the fairy's wings were sliced off and when it came time to heal her she insisted that Whip-wip be mostly covered so she wouldn't have to see the damage done to her.

Whip-wip was indeed good as new and two hours later she woke refreshed, hungry, and ready for visitors, of which they had many. The first to arrive was Eireden's family of sythei. They came flying in through the open window and greeted them all with rapturous joy.

Next to arrive was Generai. Riding up on a blown horse that was near to having a heart attack, she rushed into the cabin and crushed herself to Eireden...inadvertently causing him to groan. Ignoring the others, Generai put all of her magical powers into healing him and he felt almost himself after. She then crushed herself against him a second time, weeping as she did.

"The entire town is abuzz," she said, wiping away her tears. "I came right away when I heard the news. The prince will be here soon as well. What happened? How are you alive? How did you escape? And why are you all so filthy...and what's wrong with her?" She asked this last pointing at Elleni, who stood frozen in her catatonic state against the wall.

Eireden did his best to explain. It was such a long story that just as he finished telling it the sythei came in with news that a large company of horsemen were on their way.

Minutes later a hundred riders came into the small clearing in which sat the cabin. With Prince Lienhart were most of his captains and many fey, including Feylon and Alseya who looked as fresh and beautiful as Eireden had ever seen her. The riders came laden down with supplies: food, water, clean clothes, firewood, and even tents. Some of the fey healed Aric and Eireden fully, while others carried the body of Garris-Unhi away and a third group stood around Elleni Feyden and discussed how to break her out of her trance.

When the tents were erected, and when the three had bathed and were dressed more appropriately they dined with the prince and his men, while fairies flitted about sampling what they would from plates and drinking from cups. Whip-wip stayed with Ella and very proudly showed off her newly repaired wings so that the gold and silver pattern glinted in the sunlight.

During the meal, Eireden talked for some time about the duel he had fought, how his strength had drained away, and about his escape. He then brought out the cube and soon the captains were crying out in anger. Prince Lienhart was just as outraged as any, but he held back his anger and said, "You know what Eirowyth will say? Whoever has the power to break you out of the dungeons also has the power to fake this. Milord, can this be faked through illusion?" he asked Aric.

"Yes it can be. An illusion can be of anything limited only by the imagination of the individual," Aric answered. "Though I believe this was real enough based on Eireden's accounts. The question comes to us: will all believe him and if so what do we do?"

"Some will believe him, some won't," the prince said. "Eirowyth will certainly not and he is the final authority in this matter as far as the Den are concerned."

"Should he not recuse himself?" Aric asked. "He is clearly biased in this matter. This has long been the worst failing of autocratic rule. By your own laws the king is above the law. He can make laws to suit himself and his word cannot be overruled. I would suggest that you adopt the fey's way of self rule."

The Den listened to this advice and eyed Aric with suspicion, while the fey nodded along. Alseya stood forth and said, "I would not follow Aric Anorian's words. Our way has shown itself to be weak. We are a dwindling people. We are a weak-minded people. We are a fearful people. We have lived in fear of the past for so long that our future is in jeopardy. This needs to change. I have spoken."

The fey, including Aric, appeared unruffled by this and only looked at each other in a calm silence. Eireden locked eyes with Alseya. She seemed to have much more that she wanted to say—to Eireden in particular. There was something in her opal eyes...

"He won't recuse himself," Lienhart said, interrupting

Eireden's thoughts. "I'm sure of it. I received a message from Eirowyth this morning. You are to be killed on sight, my Lord...and any found with you. He's not going to give you the chance at an explanation let alone a trial. Which leaves us in a terrible position. Our only choice is revolution."

"It's not revolution since Eirowyth is not the true king. I say we fight!" Captain Dorcen proclaimed to loud cheers from the men and whistles from the fairies, who looked for any excuse, no matter how misunderstood, to celebrate.

"Brave indeed are the men of Hildoeven," Eireden said. "But your bravery will not avail you against the walls of Rhyoeven. As much as I appreciate the gesture, we are far overmatched. To assault the city properly we would need ten times your numbers."

"That may not be out of the question," Lienhart said. "The day after the great battle I received a letter from your mother suggesting that military action may be needed. As well, just after the king's messenger departed this morning I received a second letter from your mother." The prince held out a letter for Eireden to read.

*My Lord, Prince Lienhart,*

*You, who have been ever loyal to the true king of the Den, are once again put to the test. A traitor—a man without honor—sits upon the throne. From the very beginning Eirowyth has lied about his cousin, and what occurred in the Demorlaik. Misplaced love stayed Eireden's hand when he should have struck him down and now misplaced trust has brought Eireden low. Pathetically Eirowyth used magic to win the duel between them. I have proof of this and proof of other dishonorable actions of the weak boy who claims the throne. My son has put his faith in your wisdom, Lienhart. The Den are too great a people to allow this wretch to claim the kingship. I, for one, would rather fight and die than allow it. I implore thee to gather all those loyal to the true king and wrest away that which dishonor and falsehoods have taken and corrupted.*

*Yours,*
*Ilenwyth-Eden*

Eireden read it slowly, twice, going line by line. He then read it aloud so the others would know its contents. "I will not do this," he proclaimed to the shock of nearly everyone present. "I will not start a civil war. There hasn't been one in all our long history. It's not how we do things."

This did not sit well with the Den. "You would have one so dishonorable be our king?" Captain Dorcen asked. "It is the Den way to put our honor before our lives. That will not change, not for you and not for Eirowyth."

"We do not know what part my cousin plays in this," Eireden said. "You saw the image. He knew not that his sword had been treated. In this at least he is innocent. What happens if he is innocent in other matters as well? I would not have thousands of my soldiers die only to find out that the man you claim is dishonorable had simply been tricked or used as a pawn."

This line of logic calmed the men considerably. "Then we do nothing?" Dorcen asked. "That seems outrageous to me."

"I did not say we would do nothing," Eireden replied. "However, for the time being, *you* will do nothing. Eirowyth will likely remove Prince Lienhart and you, Dorcen are the next logical choice. If you agitate too much against him he will choose another."

"And what will we be doing?" Generai asked. "Hopefully something that involves bringing Lady Harowyth to justice."

"As much as I would like to, Generai, we can't think we will be able to waltz right into Rhyoeven and have her arrested," Eireden answered. "Right now we have to find out if the image in this cube is even authentic. Can I count on the fey with help in this matter?"

Aric and a number of them nodded, but Alseya spoke up, "No you may not. Individuals may help you but as a people I think it wise if we decline. As I said before, we are weak, in a weak position. Can you protect us, Eireden? Running and hiding as you are, I don't think you can."

With eyes flashing in anger, Generai rounded on her. "How can you say that after all that he's done for you? He has saved the fey time and again!"

"He has, but someone has to speak for the fey," Alseya shot back. "Eireden can't. He's a fugitive. Prince Lienhart can't. He likely won't be prince much longer. So who will it be? Who can guarantee us protection?"

"No one can, Milady," Eireden replied.

"Exactly! No one can protect us. That's why we have to start looking at a new solution."

# Chapter 41

## Ella

What that solution was no one could tell. Nor could they tell what Eireden's solution was to dealing with his cousin on the throne. All they got from him was a renewed pledge not to begin a civil war. He insisted that the prince and his knights go back to Hildoeven for the time being, while Alseya demanded that the fey leave as well, though she stayed behind. Generai too remained and watched the fey woman like a hawk.

Ella wished that in some way she could help, but there seemed little that she could do. She and Aric spent the next couple of days ghosting around the cabin or taking walks in the wood. These weren't as pleasant as they could have been since Aric was in a pensive mood. Everyone seemed pensive. All save the fairies.

Whip-wip's family flew about having the grandest time. On the first day they lured a skunk into the cabin; the next day everyone woke to find adorable hedgehogs and scary looking porcupines dangling from the trees. The sythei were making a sport out of flying through them at the highest possible speeds and soon Ella had her hands full dealing with crying fairies with torn wings.

"It serves you right Whip-wip," Ella berated. "After all the trouble I went through to heal you the other day. And those poor hedgehogs! You will release them right away or else."

Whip-wip decided to test the *or else* and instead of releasing the hedgehogs into the wild she released them into Ella's bed where they curled up contentedly. Later that night as she climbed into bed Ella got quite a bottom full of needles and in the process nearly squished one of the innocent little creatures. After setting the animals free she rounded up the fairies, snatching them out of the air with her mind one by one. She dangled them from their own filaments. "Now how do you like it?" They didn't and with many tears shed promised to be good—the promise didn't last the night, but for the most part they kept their antics far from Ella and her friends.

In the evenings, while Ella exercised her mother, Aric read through the papers that Garris-Unhi had saved from the Feylands. Ella was interested at first; however the papers concerned little beyond family history, and in a way they were as dull as the timeline of the dwarves. One thing that did fascinate her was the incredible age of the papers. Some were over twenty-five thousand years old.

"How does it not crumble away? Is it magic?"

Aric shook his head. "You are as bad as the humans with your talk of magic. It is a skill in the paper process only."

"I didn't know," Ella replied a little miffed. "And I am human, for better or worse. So don't stop expecting me to act like I'm not. Alseya? Do you know a *magical* spell that might erase a person's memory? Not a little bit of it, mind you, but all of it?"

Alseya had been studying the image coming from the cube. "I am not familiar with such a thing," she answered easily. "Though why would you want to? To take away a person's memory completely would be to change them on a basic level. What makes you who you are, is based partially upon genetics, but mostly on your past experiences—your memories."

"I beg to differ," Aric cut in. "Sad to say it's your genetic make-up that will decide your personality. Take Eireden there. You can see much in him from both his parents: strong minded, decisive, sound morals."

"And take my mother," Ella replied. "She is not like this because of genetics. She's like this due to what happened to her. That's why I'm looking to erase her memory, Alseya. Can you help me?"

The white-eyed fey went to Elleni and looked deep into her eyes and then flinched away. Turning back to Ella, she said, "Maybe, though I'm sure I don't want to try. There is so much misery in this woman that it...it sickens me."

"Then all the more reason that you should try."

"Sad to say, I may not be that strong emotionally," Alseya replied. "I suspect that in order to alter a person's memory, you would need to dominate them mentally. Do you know what that means?" Ella shrugged and Alseya said with gentle warm words, "Please sit on that hedgehog. The hedgehog is soft, now sit."

A hedgehog that Ella had overlooked was just then waddling by and immediately Ella found her knees starting to bend. She was going to sit on the poor animal! How was this happening? She wanted to stop herself, however the very idea of not sitting on it was strange to her and caused her head to hurt. But she persisted; gritting her teeth and was able to stop herself in mid-squat—a very unlady-like position.

"You did well fighting my intrusion," Alseya said coming to help Ella up. "That was mental dominance. First I reached out with my mind and connected to yours. You try it...good...but back off a bit. That's better. You don't want to overpower a person right off the bat; it will spring their defenses faster. Make it gentle; make it easy. Do you feel the connection?"

Ella did; it was as if an invisible road or a pipe or conduit of some sort flowed back and forth between their two minds.

Without moving her lips Alseya asked, "*Do you feel my surface thoughts?*" Ella did. The fey's thoughts were upon Ella. She thought Ella was beautiful and sweet...but also dangerous. And then her thoughts strayed to Eireden and then a wall came down on that invisible road breaking the connection.

"You see with an open mind thoughts are easy to read and pick up, but you also noted how easily I cut that off," Alseya said. "That's why with a suggestion you go in so smoothly the person doesn't even know you've made the suggestion at all."

"But what does mental dominance have to do with memories?" Ella asked. "Or erasing them."

"Everything," the fey replied. "If you were open to me and our minds connected, I could suggest that you forget a certain memory and as long as the memory held no consequences you probably would do it without issue. However Elleni's memories are so dreadfully consequential that they have taken over her life and thus there would be a great issue not only for her but for myself as well. Let me demonstrate: remember when Whip-wip let the skunk into our cabin?"

"That was disgusting," Ella said, wrinkling her nose.

"Yes it was," Alseya said. "You just demonstrated why this would be a very difficult undertaking. I mentioned the skunk and your mind focused on it right away. That is something you cannot stop, no matter what. Now take your mother's situation. Consider the horrors will you need to dredge up from deep within her. And will she let you? I doubt it. Look at the extremes she has gone to in order to hide them from herself. Even if you do get past her defenses another question arises: will you be able to handle the memories yourself?"

"Why would I have to? They are her memories."

"Let me show you," Alseya said. Ella felt the fey reach out to her mind. This time her own immediately set up a wall, but it was reflex only. Ella lowered it and their minds were connected. "I will show you a memory of mine," Alseya said.

*A shout went up and there was a man on horseback—not a fey, but a man. He was tall and strikingly handsome with steel-grey eyes. He rode through the village like a gale. "The maug are upon you!" he cried as he flew past. More shouts came from behind and soon confusion and screams rose all around. The fey were pointing and she looked up to the hills to see goblins by the tens of thousands spreading out along the rim of the valley. They weren't charging down at them yet, they were preparing their trap.*

*Alseya turned first in one direction and then another and then a third as panic started to take a hold of her. More riders came through the village. "Flee for your lives!" the called out. Already metal could be heard ringing on metal. Fey ran in all directions. Alseya stood rooted while her head spun—and then the maug were on the edge of the village. She saw her mother running for her life, but a goblin came up unseen from the side and her mother was brought down...and then they were on her...*

The connection broke and Ella stumbled out of the cabin in tears. The memory had been real to her—the cries, the smell of the air, the hard look on Eireden's face. He had been riding to save her...not Alseya but Ella. She turned back to the cabin and there he was in the doorway. The sight of him sent a guilty shock through her.

"Don't go too far by yourself," he warned. "It's not safe."

"Oh, no. Of course not. I just needed some air. That was...too much. I see now why helping my mother is going to be harder than it seems."

Eireden came down the steps to stand near her and his unique aroma wafted over her. It wasn't the odor of pine like when she had first met him. It was something else; something comforting. "So what did you see?" he asked. "Do you want to talk about it?"

"It was the attack on the Feylands...the one I caused."

"Stop it," he growled. "You caused nothing. If it hadn't been you it would have been someone else. Likely someone nowhere near as pretty and certainly not as sweet. Aric is lucky to have you."

"Thanks," she said, relaxing as the vision faded. "I have a secret you might want to know."

"If it concerns Alseya and her feelings for me it's not exactly a secret," he said and then laughed at her expression. "Next you'll be letting on that Generai has a thing for me."

She started to say something but just then the scout came outside as if summoned by the sound of her name. "It's really starting to cool off," Generai said, staring up at the gauzy white blanket of stars above. "Come, take a walk with me before the evening grows too cold."

"Go on," Ella whispered. "You can't keep your fans waiting."

Eireden flashed a white smile and then called to Tissa. The tiny fairy rushed out of the cabin, hooting at the prospect of a walk. Watching them go, Ella felt the slightest twinge of jealousy, which she tried to dismiss, but it wouldn't leave her. The truth was Aric had been distant for some time now, a few days at least. If she had to pinpoint the last time she felt really close to him it was on the beach after they had seen the adventure film.

It seemed long ago.

"Will you take a walk with me?" Ella asked him, sticking her head back in the cabin. Aric sat at the kitchen table reading. By his expression she could tell that he would have rather kept at the reading.

"I'll go," Alseya said. "If you need company that is. I promise I won't show you any more of my memories."

"It's alright Alseya," Aric said. Getting up he stretched and ran his hands through his gold hair. "I've been sitting for too long."

"Whip-wip!" Ella called. The fairy frequently went with them on their walks but not always. This time she was curled up with in a mass of her brothers and sisters. In a display of fairy laziness she barely lifted her arm and waved goodbye. That jealous feeling still had a good grip of Ella. "Whip-wip! You can't tell me that Tissa loves Eireden more than you love me."

The guilt worked. Whip-wip disentangled herself and flew to Ella. "That's better," Ella said, but then the fairy crawled into her front pocket and began to snore loud and pointedly. "Maybe I should think about getting a cat."

Aric took her hand and they started walking north. The prairie was a few miles away and the view of the stars was unbelievable there.

"So what memory did you see?" he asked after a mile in silence.

"The attack on the Feylands from Alseya's point of view...her mother died right in front of her."

"I heard," Aric said grimly. "When you felt her memory was it altogether seamless with your mind? Did you feel her fear as if it was your fear?" Ella nodded glumly. He squeezed her hand reassuringly. "It'll fade...like my dream I had of you in the Feylands. It used to be so strong, but now everything about it is hazy. Even the feeling I had. I'm now sure that dream was planted. Other dreams of mine are still fresh and clear at least the ones I..."

Without warning Aric stopped talking and walking at the same time. Just on the edge of the forest shadows began to move toward them. They brought a great fear that radiated in the night. "Run!" Aric yelled, pushing her back. As if in slow motion Ella turned to run. She would get help—she would get Eireden. Or so she thought, but then the forest seemed to come alive around her. Branches turned supple and tried to wrap themselves around her. Roots shot up snaking about her feet.

She leapt over them and with a blast of her magic cleared the hurdles, flying twenty feet through the air. Ella landed in mid-stride. "Eireden!" she screamed in vain. There was almost no chance that he would hear; the Den and the scout had turned south and there was likely three or four miles between them.

She ran on avoiding the magically imbued forest, but she could not avoid the riders. Elves in black raced on her left and right, easily overtaking her. One of them sent out a shower of daggers—with her mind she swept them away with ease. They laughed at her and sent more and again she deflected them. She turned to run, but they cut her off racing their horses across her path.

In a second Aric was there next to her, breathing heavily, sword in hand. He immediately charged the nearest elf, swinging the bright blade. Whip-wip appeared out of nowhere blasting light at it, allowing Aric to slash open his face. Ella was weaponless and so she contested the elf with her magic. She was stronger than he expected and his sword arm was slowed by her power and he felt the sting of Aric's blade a second time.

Then the other rider was on her and she was forced to retreat from his slashing sword. So desperately was she backing away from the elf that when the forest roots reached up to grab her she went down, falling to her back. "Whip-wip!" she cried. The fairy reacted faster than any of her kind could and sped at the elf like a bullet—straight into a blast of flame that shot from his hand.

The sythei's scream tore the air, high and beseeching, as her gold and silver wings went up in a blaze. She fell to the ground with her hair and skin on fire. Ella's soul seized in her chest at the horror befalling her best friend, she reached out for the fairy with her mind to pull her back towards her, to heal her—but it was too late. The elf upon his black horse was there. He reared his mount and then brought the heavy hooves down upon the screaming fairy, crushing her like a bug. Silencing her.

Out of spite or hate the elf reared the huge horse a second time and crushed the still body into the dirt.

"Where is the King of the Sythei now?" asked the high voiced elf in malignant joy. Something broke in Ella's mind at the sight of the dead fairy. Her thoughts unwound and she fell back uncaring what would happen to her. A second later her world went black and it was the greatest relief to her tortured soul.

## Chapter 42

## Eireden

Eireden couldn't hear Ella scream his name. It was a physical impossibility for the Den to catch words that had drifted east on a gentle breeze. Yet he stopped in his tracks nonetheless. Beside him Generai asked what was wrong. He didn't know exactly. The feeling was hard to describe except to say that a great fear smote his heart and turned his stomach sour.

Without saying a word he began to walk back towards the cabin, going faster and faster—and then Tissa, who had been flying just in front of him, screamed before falling to the damp earth. Again Generai asked what was happening but he answered her not. Now he didn't walk, he scooped up the fairy and ran. Ella was in trouble. She was north of him when Tissa fainted, but as he ran back to the cabin her bearing began to change heading north and west.

Behind him the scout struggled to catch up, but she managed to keep pace enough to climb into the passenger seat just as he gunned the Ford into life.

"...said what's wrong?" Generai said. It was hard for him to understand her. The words went in and out of his consciousness barely leaving an imprint. Then they were on the South Stream road and racing hard. He could feel Ella closer now. With the road opening up on the prairie and the miles speeding by, he would catch up. He saw it in his mind: he would catch her in the next belt of forest.

Only as he crested a hill in the woods a downed tree blocked his path and beside the road an elf sat atop a dark horse. As Eireden slammed down hard on the brakes a fire erupted out of his enemy's hand turning the Ford into an instant inferno. Tissa and Generai screamed for all of a second and then the car banged up hard against the fallen tree.

"We have to get out!" Eireden roared. The fire had spread

and now was under the hood as well as above and there was no knowing if any of the gas lines had been ruptured in the crash. "This way," he called over the noise and grabbed his scout, pulling her from the car through the driver's side.

The second he was free his sword blazed into the night, but of the elf there was nothing to be seen and only a fading laughter could be heard. "You have to tell me what's going on!" Generai demanded, holding her sword in a shaking hand.

"They have Ella. The elves have her...and something has happened to Whip-wip. I don't know what, but I fear the worst."

"And what of Aric?" Generai said. Her eyes seemed mesmerized by the flames running into the sky. The Ford burned brightly, throwing long and spooky shadows out into the forest.

"I don't know," Eireden whispered. He then grabbed the scouts hand and began the long march back to the cabin. They turned aside from the road after an hour to follow back down the tracks left by the horsemen. There had been three of them. It was easy to trace them to the site where a fight had occurred. There was blood upon the ground and scorch marks in the trees, but no sign of Aric or Ella or...

"Oh no..." Eireden said, going to one knee. He felt as though he was going to be sick. The fairy Whip-wip, her wings and hair burned away, her body broken, lay trampled in the dirt. "Heal her...please just try," he pleaded to Generai.

"She's dead," the scout said in a quiet voice.

"I said try!" Eireden screamed at her. Generai flinched back and tears slid from her eyes to drop from her chin. She knelt with her hands above the fairy, but no blue light came to rescue the fairy from death.

"I tried," Generai whispered. "Her soul is gone...I'm sorry."

Tissa was inconsolable and clung to body of Whip-wip crying helplessly. Eireden carried them both back in the palms of his hand. As he walked it felt as though his hearing had become impaired. He seemed to lose the ability to hear Generai's voice or Tissa crying or even the crickets in the night. There was only a roaring static that filled his mind.

They found Alseya with sword in hand coming up the path Ella and Aric had taken. "*What happened?*" her lips asked—still no sound came through the storm of anger in the man. Generai told her and she blanched at the sight of the dead fairy. Now in real silence the three walked the last couple of miles to the cabin and when the door opened the fairies crowded around.

"Do you have a pearl? Either of you?" Eireden asked. "I need one badly."

"No, but you have one around your neck," Generai said.

Eireden broke down crying at this. He offered the pearl to his family but they refused. Eventually he took it off and laid it down next to the body. Whip-wip was so horribly crushed that it hurt his heart to look at her. "Can you make it look like...like she's just sleeping? With an illusion or something. I can't bear to see her this way."

Alseya did, which made his pain less and conversely made his anger even greater. It grew inside him so that he wanted to lash out and tear the cabin down with his fists. Struggling to hold it in, he went to the window and checked the time by the position of the stars. It was after one in the morning. "At sunrise I'm leaving for Hildoeven," he said and then went to bed not bothering to hear any replies. With his fury mounting, he couldn't sleep until his fairies brought a little grass casket to lay beside his pillow. Then anger left him completely and he sagged in misery and fell into a sleep of depression.

In the morning the fairies were subdued. They greeted the sunrise in an eerie silence and ate their breakfast so quietly that their tiny teeth could be heard chewing. Eireden placed the casket in his pouch and tried not to think about what lay inside. What wasn't inside was his pearl; that he found around his neck when he woke. He didn't question it. After laying Elleni on the bed and assigning two fairies to watch over her until he could get assistance from Hildoeven, the king of the Den strode out of the cabin with his face set in a hard mask. So tight were the lines of his face that no emotion could possibly slip out.

On the walk to the city Generai and Alseya strode on his left and right decked out in the trappings of war: armor and bow—sword and dagger. They walked in silence even as the king did, until they reached the battle plain and saw encamped upon it an army of two-thousand dwarves.

"Whip...I mean Easa-see? Fly ahead and find out what's going on," Eireden ordered. It wasn't necessary as horsemen from the town rode toward them almost as soon as they stepped foot upon the plain.

Two knights of whom Eireden was familiar came to greet them. "My King! We were just on our way to find you. The Prince Lienhart begs for you to hold council with him."

"I was on my way for the same purpose. Tell me, what of them?" he asked pointing at the dwarves.

"Why they are part of your Grand Army, your Highness," one of the knights said jauntily. The man's pleasant attitude grated on the angry king, but he forced a smile onto his face and encouraged the man to go on. "Along with them you command the army of the fey, the army of the sythei, and all three armies of the cities of Avargard, Hildoeven, and Tayoeven. Prince Jarlen of Avargard showed up unexpectedly at sunset, while Prince Thyon arrived this morning just after the dwarves."

It was a surprise to Eireden that any of them were here, but it was worth asking about the other two Den cities. "What of Wesgard and Varisgard? Any word on them?"

"They aren't joining either side, the cowards," one of the knights spat out.

That was at least better than them joining Eirowyth. "Ride ahead," he ordered the first knight. "Let them know

I'm coming. And you, ask the leader of the dwarves to join us in our council. Alseya you will speak for the fey?"

"I will, but you may not like what I have to say," she replied, eyeing him coolly.

Eireden didn't doubt it seeing as he wasn't in the mood to like anything just then. Next to him Generai glared at the fey. He put his hand on the scout's arm and ordered, "Say nothing. I am not King of the Fey. They are not mine to command as I please."

"They should be," Generai hissed. "For what makes a king? Have you not bled for them? Have you not sacrificed for them? Do you not care for them even as your own?"

"Would you like to visit your father while I'm in council?" Eireden asked, crossly. "Because if you cannot obey my simplest commands, that is where you'll be." Generai placed her hands on her hips and glared defiantly up at him. At this the King had to wonder if he did indeed have any power over this girl. For some reason tears again threatened to come. Were these for Whip-wip? Or for Ella and the misery she was probably in just then? Or were they for Generai—a girl who would likely never have her dreams realized. "I didn't mean it," he said. "I'm just all over the place inside. Please forgive me."

She nodded and remained silent like he had asked. They marched on and came before the gates. Alseya stared at a patch of ground in front of the walls. It was where the fairies had come in that great ball of light above the two of them. Their eyes met and the image of him kissing her flashed through his mind. Feeling a sudden flush of heat he shook his head to clear the image. Then they were through the gates and surrounded by the soldiers of Hildoeven who greeted the king with many cheers. The fairies that had been resting on them took off at this and went to be with their kind. Strangely he missed them immediately.

With an entourage of men they went to the audience chamber in the palace where they were greeted by the princes of the three cities, a number of fey, as well as the king of the dwarves: Furen Traganfel.

"What...what is this?" Eireden asked in shock at seeing his friend dressed in gleaming mail, wearing a golden crown upon his large head. All Eireden could think of, was what sort of mischief Whip-wip would be having at Furen's expense if she were there. Again he blinked back tears. "You are king? What kind flower was that? A magical one?"

"Aye! Indeed it was my friend," Furen said, patting Eireden on the arm in greeting. "It worked like a charm. The old king—my father-in-law—was so impressed that he stepped down immediately and now is in retirement. He's off hunting goblins even as we speak, the lucky bastard. So, where is the beautiful Ella? And that confounding fairy of hers? I miss those two more than I thought I would."

The tears were there again. All over a dead fairy! "They are the reason I'm here. Whip-wip is dead..." He had to pause and inside he raged: *She was just one damned, nuisance of a fairy!* After a second he went on, "Ella and probably Aric as well have been captured. They are once again in the dungeons of Rhyoeven." This had been a surprise to him when he awoke. He had thought for sure that it would be in the direction of the Demorlaik that his heart would orient on, instead it was Rhyoeven.

There was murmuring at this and then Prince Jarlen asked incredulously, "This is why you return? A dead fairy and a girl you used to care for? What of your kingdom? What of the fact that a base creature sits upon the throne dishonoring all of us? I did not bring my men to fight and die because of a girl."

When Eireden said nothing to this Alseya spoke up, "I speak for the fey as requested. We will not fight either. Certainly not for this reason. As much as I care for my kin Aric and the sweet girl, their two lives aren't worth jeopardizing the last of my people. As well we won't fight to remove Eirowyth. This is a matter for the Den to work out among themselves. To us, one Den king is as good as another."

This was such an astonishing thing to say that Eireden stepped back. His anger began creeping up within him, yet it was nothing compared to the seething rage writ upon Generai's face. The scout stormed toward Alseya with her hand upon her hilts. The sword was half-drawn before Eireden said, "Generai. Please come to my side." The scout flashed her grey eyes at the fey before turning back to stand with her king. "What of the dwarves?" he asked.

Furen shrugged. "I have come to renew my friendship with Eireden, true king of the Den. For too long our peoples have been estranged and distant from one another. Yet at the same time I am troubled just as the fey woman is. Why do we fight? Is it Ella I am fighting to save—just one girl? Or do we go to remove a villain from the throne? I received personal letters from the Lady Ilenwyth-Eden, a woman of high birth, begging for military assistance. This is why I thought I came."

Eireden paused before answering. His anger and grief made it difficult for him to think and now the doubt on everyone's faces undermined him in every way. Why were they all being so difficult? Why couldn't they fight for both causes? In his weakness he turned to his scout. He was sure she would always tell him what he wanted to hear.

"What about you? Do you question why we fight, though you know in what direction my heart lies?"

"I will fight thy enemies even if they are Den, if you so command. I am yours always," Generai answered. Her eyes held a maelstrom of emotion: fear, grief, love, anger, and yes, jealousy. But also truth. She would fight and kill her own kin if he called upon her to do so. He was king to her. He was the ultimate source of right and wrong. Was it too much for one man to have that power? Would she slay even her father, the candle-maker if he asked?

"I would not have you fight your kin," Eireden said to

her. "I will not ask any of you to fight your kin."

"Then how do you propose removing Eirowyth from the throne," Prince Jarlen said. "*He* will fight. He won't be stopped by notions of humanity. To him you are the usurper."

"This isn't about Eirowyth..."

"I will not fight my kin for a girl!" Jarlen interrupted, smashing his mailed fist upon a side table.

"And this is not about Ella," Eireden finished. "This is not a civil war as the fey suggested. This is our war against evil that we have been fighting for so many thousands of years. I see it now plainly as I haven't before. Our enemy, the elf Darhmael of the line Narvai is behind all that has befallen us. He benefits from our strife and only he has the power to maneuver us like pawns. How quickly came the call for rebellion? The blood was still wet upon the battlefield before you received letters from Ilenwyth—supposedly. Yet that is not my mother's way. She would never be so obvious."

"Nor would she have thought you would lose the duel with Eirowyth," Generai added. "She thought you beyond match against any Den...as did we all."

"And the way you escaped from the dungeons, so easily," Alseya remarked. "You practically walked out holding evidence against your cousin that is just muddied enough for him to discount, and you to believe."

"And look at where we are now," Eireden said. "We are in perfect balance. With the dwarves and the fey, and the sythei and the soldiers of three cities, I have a force that could take Rhyoeven. But at what cost?"

"At the cost of our ability to defend ourselves," Lienhart answered. "Yes we might win, however the death toll would be atrocious and it may well leave the capital without enough men to defend itself. Remember, the maug army was only partially destroyed. If we fight this battle, whatever may happen to the capital we can rest assured that Hildoeven, Avargard, and Tayoeven will be practically defenseless."

"So what do we do?" Jarlen asked. "With the elf pulling his strings Eirowyth will not listen to the reasons just laid out. And we can be sure that the elf won't just sit back and wait. If we don't go to him he'll come for us."

Eyes flicked around the room, until all of them once again settled on the King. "We attack...or at least that is what I want them to believe. Instead we are going to attempt a rescue mission. I will need volunteers, perhaps as many as twenty."

Prince Jarlen scoffed, "Is this girl really worth the danger you are putting everyone in?"

"The rescue effort isn't going to be centered on Ella or Aric," Eireden said. "It's Eirowyth that needs to be saved." This shocked the room and a fast murmuring swept around the tall ceilings and ran up the polished marble walls. "He is just as much a victim of Darhmael as all of us. Yes he might be weak minded but he is not evil."

Alseya cleared her throat. "You may attempt this, yet you do so without the fey. Only upon one condition will we assist."

Stepping forward, Generai drew her sword. She glared and hissed, "You ungrateful bit..."

Eireden held her back. "Generai, bite your tongue. Alseya, my plan will not work without fey assistance. I cannot save Eirowyth without the fey."

"I understand this," she replied. Her words were calm yet in her eyes the shimmering colors of the opal increased.

"And do you understand that if I don't, all of us here will likely be hunted down, imprisoned, or forced into exile?" She nodded but would not speak. Eireden realized that she had him over a barrel. "Name your price," he said.

"One thing only do I demand," Alseya replied. "To save your kingdom and my people I ask that you marry me."

## Chapter 43

## Ella

When Ella opened her eyes she felt a thrill of panic. Had she gone blind? Was she buried beneath the earth somewhere? The dark she found herself in was unlike anything she had ever experienced in her life. She felt suffocated by it, yet at the same time she began panting.

Ella tried to reach out into the black to get some idea what sort of place she was in, but her hands were chained together and another chain ran from her shackles to an iron collar about her neck. When she reached out she inadvertently caused her head to be thrown forward. A scream nearly broke from her lips. To scream was the last thing she wanted to do. What would such a sound bring out of the dark?

Holding her panic in check by the barest margins, she began to explore her surroundings. She was in a prison cell—an iron cage. She knew it was iron, just like she knew her chains were of the same metal. It grated on her inner sense of being; like nails on a chalkboard or chewing on tinfoil. The magnitude of the aggravation it caused was something she had never experienced before.

It dawned on her she was in a witch's jail. Ella tried to use her magic and instantly got a migraine. After rubbing her temples till the pounding ceased she then went through a self-examination and found that she wasn't in any way hurt. Another thing she found was Whip-wip's dud of pearl. It hung on its filament, as useless as it always had been. Just when she could have used some light too! As she fingered the fat pearl the filament broke and it dropped in her palm.

With her death, Whip-wip's magic was fading.

Ella kissed the pearl before putting it in the breast pocket the fairy had liked to ride in. She tried—and failed—not to think of Whip-wip, only the little face kept coming to her in the dark. The deep blue eyes, the silver and gold wings, her happy laugh...depression smote Ella and she began to cry. Though she tried to cry as quietly as possible she couldn't stop the sniffles.

"Ella?"

"Aric? Is that you?"

"At your service," he replied despondently. "Although I'm afraid that there is little service I can currently render."

"Where are we?" Ella asked in a rush. "Is this the Demorlaik? Can you tell? Do you know how long we've been here?"

"Slow down," he said. It seemed an effort for him to talk. His words were low and breathy. "We're not in the Demorlaik, thank goodness. We're in the lower dungeons of Rhyoeven and as far as I can tell we've been here about a day and a half."

"What's wrong? Are you injured? You don't sound like yourself."

"I am wounded, but it is little to worry over," he answered. "*They* certainly won't let me die down here." Ella knew who *they* were—the elves. The fey moved and his chains clinked against each other. He coughed weakly and said, "They'll keep us both alive, probably for far longer than either of us wish. But for now we are safe enough. We are bait after all."

She meant to ask him about what he meant by bait when his cough came again, rattling in his chest. "Do you have your pearl still?" she asked. "Try lighting it...it might help you. This dark is starting to get to me. It sort of feels like it's eating my skin."

There came a brief flash of light that lit up Aric. There seemed to be a hole the size of his fist running square through his chest. "Oh my God! Aric, we have to get you out of here. Do you have any..."

Just then footsteps could be heard in the dark, slow and steady as if the dark wasn't in anyway a hindrance. Ella backed away from the front of her cage as they came on.

"There won't be any escape, my dear."

She had been expecting a high voice like those of the elves, but this was soft and melodious. "Who are you?" Ella asked, trying to open her eyes as wide as they would go to catch even the slightest hint of shadow. The being allowed the tiniest light to come about his person, but it was enough to blind Ella who cringed behind her cuffed hands.

"You know very well who I am, Daughter."

She knew. In her gut she had known from the first footstep. She just hadn't wanted to admit it to herself. Darhmael stood before her, tall and elegantly slim. His clothes were of the softest velvet and were black and grey in color. His skin was perfect as she knew it would be—no discoloration or burns for him—while his hair was long and silken silver, but not like that of an aged person, rather it flowed nearly like liquid. And his eyes were deep and black and quite a bit hypnotic. Ella's mouth came open as she stared into them.

She could feel his mind connect with hers but so smoothly did he join that by the time she was aware, it was too late. There was no fighting that mind not with her feeble abilities.

"You are feeble now, but in time you will grow stronger," he said, breaking the connection. Ella sagged, feeling her muscles start to tremble. He could have killed her. While that connection had lasted, he could have stopped her heart and there was nothing she could have done to stop it. They both knew it.

Ella tried to rally. "Will I grow as strong as you or stronger?" When he laughed, she demanded, "What's so funny?"

"You don't understand him is what's so funny," Aric answered. "It is the way of evil. He will suffer none to rival him. Especially his daughter. This is common enough, just as he is."

Aric let out a sudden groan and in the low light Ella could

see that he was holding back a scream of pain by the barest margins. Darhmael was doing something to him. Her mouth came open to protest, but then her father turned to check her reaction. Was he looking for her to beg for him to stop? Would that put her more in his power? That was funny. He had all the power. He could kill or torture with impunity. There was nothing she could do...except remain true to herself. If her father wanted her to beg she would not beg. Ella spied a bunk she had not noticed in the dark and went to it and waited for the torture to stop.

"I thought you loved him," Darhmael said, releasing his hold on the fey. "I read it there in your heart as plain as day, but you would just sit back while he is in pain? Is that because you love another?" Ella started to count the links on the chains that bound her, trying her best to ignore the elf. Darhmael went on, "Should I name this hidden love of yours? He is the son of Eirolden, a man dedicated to destroying the elven people."

Ella's jaw clenched. Yes, she loved Eireden, but that was a memory gone and a time passed. She was dedicated to Aric. "My heart has many loves," she replied. "My soul but one."

"Poetic," Darhmael said. "A lie, yet a poetic one. You don't know the first thing about your soul. You don't know that I created it. Oh, yes...don't shake your head when you know the truth. I shaped your soul. I engineered it you might say. After thousands of years and thousands of tries I created you—perfect in every way."

"I am hardly perfect."

"Aric?" the elf asked.

The fey sat slumped against the iron bars shaking and dripping sweat. He nodded. "You are perfect."

"You are both blind," Ella said. "You are blinded by love, Aric. And you are blinded by conceit, Darhmael. I lose my temper. I can be cranky. I am sometimes needy or whiny."

Darhmael raised his eyebrows to Aric. The fey said,

"Yes, but in the perfect proportions. You are sometimes cranky or needy, but only so much as to make you that much more loveable."

"Exactly," the elf agreed, beaming at Ella. "A person can't be too perfect and remain accounted as a person. There had to be the tiniest flaws in your character and in your physicality to make you real."

This was all too much. A person couldn't be engineered this way. It wasn't possible. There were just too many genes and chromosomes that went into making someone who they were. A new possibility struck her however. "Am I...am I a robot? Or a magical thingy like one?"

"A magical construct that simulates life is called a golem," Darhmael answered. "And no you are not one. You are an elf...or half elf I should say. But you are engineered nonetheless, magically so. I have discovered that which lies beneath all magic. There are rhythms to the universe, frequencies that are unheard and unseen, but that are not unfelt. Have you ever wondered about the instant bond between mother and baby? Or even father and baby. Newborn babies radiate these frequencies—they demand love—it is their only protection. That same demand to be loved pours out of you."

"You created me to be loved?" Ella asked incredulously. "That seems rather mushy for someone so evil. Were you getting lonely in your cave? Did all the other evil dads have someone for the Father-Daughter dance and you didn't want to be left out?"

"Just the right amount of crankiness," Darhmael said with a touch of pride. "The answer is no to all your questions. You were created to be loved for two reasons. First, to protect you until your mission could be fulfilled. Back in America, were there ever any times you really felt threatened? I am betting not. The worst criminals would take one look at you and melt. I had to keep you protected until the circumstances were perfect. The second reason...is

...right...over... here." He trailed off and looked pointedly into Aric's cage. The fey dropped his head knowing he had been played. "Yes, so good Aric would bend over backwards to bring you home with him. He saw the prediction of the maug in the Feylands, but his love blinded him to any sort of common sense."

"Stop it," Ella demanded.

"No," Darhmael said simply. "This is too much fun. I showed him just enough danger for his protective instincts to kick in, but not enough to keep you away...after all, the Feylands could never be found could they? How many times did that justification run through your head Aric *Anorian*?"

"Plenty...too many times," he answered truthfully. "Yet all the while I told myself she wasn't the cause of the danger. I would look at her and see peril all around her, but she wasn't the threat. She was good through to her soul. I—I can't believe you made me love her." This last he said with an accusing tone.

The words stung Ella more than the heavy chains digging into her wrists did. Darhmael only smiled. "Don't blame me. I only created her. You are the one who couldn't control his emotions. You're an embarrassment. Would you like to know what the other fey really think of you?"

"Please, stop it," Ella asked more gently this time. "He already tortures himself with this more than you ever could." Darhmael did stop, but he turned toward her and she guessed it would only be a second before he started in on all of her failings. Quickly she asked, "What are those burnt creatures? And how do you get them to follow me?"

Darhmael laughed. "Now you act the part of the daughter! Looking for a bedtime story?"

"Just curious," she answered. "You can't start explaining a diabolical plot and then leave off with the story half told. That's just evil."

"I will tell you since I'm feeling magnanimous," Darhmael said. "Those 'burnt' creatures as you call them are your kindred. Experiments in the reproductive process that had gone awry, but were too valuable to destroy. They are half-Den, which I assumed would be favorable; I was wrong. They have a love-hate relationship with themselves—mirrors drive them absolutely crazy. As to why they can sense you, remember those frequencies I mentioned? Everyone emits them all the time, but they are of such limited power that they dissipate after a short distance. What I did with you was boost their strength and limit their focus. You emit eight distinct frequencies, one for each of my progeny, and one that I reserved for myself."

"Then how did...?"

"Don't interrupt!" Darhmael snapped. "Each frequency can only be sensed by one individual. It is encoded when they first pick it up—I got the idea from penguins of all things. It has always been assumed that the mother penguin can find her single chick out of thousands by sense of smell. This is wrong; the chick emits a frequency that only the mother can hone in on; it is singular to her. No other penguin can tune in to it or there would be mass confusion. You see the brilliance?"

Ella nodded. "Yes, I do and I suppose it is brilliant," she said in all honestly. Yet for all its brilliance there had clearly been a flaw. The one frequency reserved for himself had been stolen by Eireden, probably on that very first day that she had met him. He had grabbed her wrist and she could remember the eerie calm that had come over her then. She should have been afraid of him, but just...

"Why are you feeling so magnanimous?" Aric asked breaking in on her thoughts. "It can't be because of us. You could have snatched us up at any time."

"It's not every day that you can sit back and watch your enemies destroy themselves," Darhmael said, grinning wolfishly. "The son of Eirolden is coming to claim his throne and he will, but at the cost of his kingdom. No wars are ever so vicious as civil wars. Brother against brother. No matter who wins, both will lose."

"He's coming?" Ella asked breathlessly. A spark of hope crept into her soul. Eireden had proved time and again more capable than Darhmael gave him credit.

"Yes and he might even rescue you," the elf replied. "He and his men will just have to climb the heights of the plateau under fire, and then scale fifty foot walls guarded by five thousand soldiers. The slaughter will be magnificent, but just as they start to fall back retreating, the gates will magically open for them. That's when the fun will really begin. Savage fighting from house to house—the horror of battle magnified a hundred fold, made all the worse because no one will really know who's fighting who. Then will come the fires, and who will put them out? Not the soldiers; they will be too busy fighting. How many women and children will perish?"

Ella was about to scream at him when a man-at-arms came down the hall. He was a Den in chainmail, except at his side he carried a fanciful sword. "Your Highness, *his* army has arrived!" he exclaimed in the strange high voice of one of the burnt elf creatures.

Darhmael smiled broadly and then turned back to Ella. "It won't be long now and I should be going. Those fires won't set themselves you know. However I'm in a bit of a quandary. I am party to a secret that I don't know if I should let out of the bag. Maybe you can help me." Ella shook her head, no. Whatever he had to say wouldn't be good. Darhmael ignored the headshake. "I knew I could count on you. Here it is: I know this girl who is about to get married; only her husband to be has had a change of heart. It turns out he doesn't love her nearly as much as he thought. The question is do I tell her?"

Aric had a change of heart? Aric didn't love her? When had that happened? Ella's eyes went back and forth between elf and fey. "Aric?" she asked.

"He is right, Ella," Aric said after a long silence. "My love isn't genuine...how could it be? It started as a lie and it only grew because of the way you were...engineered." He said the last word distastefully, as if it was a slime he wished to rid his tongue of. She could feel his revulsion coming through the semi-dark.

"Don't do this, Aric!" Ella cried. The cry not only came out of her voice, it came out her soul. She ignored the elf and gripped the bars. "Darhmael is only trying to hurt us. He's trying to drive us apart. I am still me, regardless where I came from. I am not asking how you were born, because I don't care. I love you, not because who your parents were or any of that. I love you because of who you are."

"Ella, that's not really fair," Darhmael said. "You don't question his parentage because Aric is fey. But what does he see when he looks at you? He sees nothing but a human. He thought he was getting the greatest of all prizes: a good elf! But oops, you're nothing of the sort. All you are in his eyes is a dirty human. Now I really have to go, good-bye." The elf left and took his meager light with him.

Ella's mouth came open and hung there uselessly, while her eyes turned slowly to Aric. He wouldn't look up.

# Chapter 44

## Eireden

Eireden's army spread out onto the battle plain of Rhyoeven at the first light of day. He had marched his fourteen-thousand soldiers as hard as he could through the night, fearing that time was against him. The longer he allowed Darhmael to prepare for every contingency the less likely Eireden's surprise would succeed.

"We will offer battle on the plain, first," Eireden told his captains. "Given our numbers they'll certainly turn it down, which is precisely what we want, however they will come out to parley. That's when we have to be ready to make the switch."

The hope was that Eirowyth himself would come out from his nearly impregnable walls to discuss terms. If he did then he would be snatched immediately—in clear violation of the standards of just warfare—and Eireden and a select few would ride back under guise of illusion to hunt the remaining elves and free Ella and Aric.

The hope was misplaced and Eirowyth did not come. Captain Rudyid and twenty sturdy knights rode out of the main gate in precise formation.

"Easa-see time to go," Eireden said, reaching out and touching the fairy for luck. There were nine others on the fairy's team—the most disciplined among them, which wasn't saying all that much—the King touched all of these as well. "Please, be very, very, careful."

Turning the color of the sky, the fairies flew off. Their job was to locate Eirowyth and if at all possible the elves. The elves would be very difficult to find. They too would be under cover of illusion and with their power no simple fairy would be able to penetrate it. For that reason the fairies were under orders to find the soldiers that were acting different from the rest, those that spent time alone or who showed even the slightest magical ability. Eireden's heart was in his throat watching them go. It was like sending children into danger.

"Do not fret so," Alseya said. His bride to be had barely left his side in the last twenty-four hours. "If we lose here today, their lands and lives are forfeit. They know this. They will do their part." Her soft hand reached out and took his hard one in hers. She did this often which made Eireden uncomfortable. He was in a military situation after all and handholding was generally frowned upon, but more than that it caused Generai pain.

His scout seemed on the verge of fainting and had throughout the long ride. Her face was so white it seemed bleached and her eyes would lose focus from time to time and she would stare at nothing. Sometimes she would sway in her saddle or droop over the head of her mount. When this happened everyone would look away until she righted herself.

"Not before the battle," Eireden said, pulling his hand away.

"Not before the battle—*dear*. You probably should practice," she suggested, making light of a difficult situation. He tried to smile only it sat crooked on his face. He had known from the moment he saw Ella kiss Aric in the Theater of Ancestral Concordance that he would never marry the woman he loved—that he would have to 'settle'. And he was sure that Alseya was settling as well.

*"My people are weak. I have spoken these words prior to this and now I will do something about it," Alseya had said in Hildoeven the day before. "The fey are made up of individuals and because of this we are, if not divided, then perhaps disjoined. It is not our way for one to command another even in the face of extinction. We are leaderless, rudderless. We are in need of a king and Eireden has proven himself a good man. He has bled for us and sacrificed for us. He cares for us as if we were his very own." She looked at Generai when she said this and the scout's eyes went wide*

*hearing her own words come back to haunt her.*

*"If we are to have a king then let it be one of our own,"
Feylon Darania announced to the general agreement of all
the fey present.*

*"Fine. Let the new king of the fey come forth and
command us," Alseya had shot back. None of the fey budged.
They only looked back and forth from one another
wondering who it would be. "The only one among us who
could be king is currently in the dungeons of Rhyoeven, yet
were he here he would not take the kingship either. It is not
the way of the fey."*

*"But he is a human!" one called out. "We know Eireden
and he is lordly and wise, but what of the next king, or the
next?"*

*Before speaking Alseya took a deep breath as if to steady
herself. "The next king will be half fey and half Den." She
then turned to Eireden and looked meaningfully into his
eyes—she wanted to have his baby. Eireden was as shocked
as all of them and could not seem to form words.*

*Generai stepped forward thin lipped and quivering. "Aric
said that was impossible. He said a joining of man and fey
was...impossible," she said again for lack of a better word.*

*"Aric was wrong," Alseya declared. "He based his words
on a racial bias that is common to all the fey. Simply put we
see ourselves as far more evolved or advanced than you. In
his view it would be like procreating with a monkey." The
Den grew angry at this. Alseya held up a hand to silence
them. "As I said, Aric is wrong. A dying species cannot
logically claim superiority over one that flourishes. And
besides I have proof that the joining of our races will
enhance both. Ella Belmont."*

*"She destroyed the Feylands," another fey called out.*

*"That is hardly truth and all of us here know it," Alseya
said. "She is as strong as an elf and just as beautiful, but she
also has the facility of the humans to not only command
others, but to care for them as well. And there is another*

*example in both our histories. The Den king who ruled as Feyden at the death of Feireden was a half-fey. Your great ancestor, Feylon was his mother."*

*"You can't know that," Feylon replied.*

*"Here are the words of Darania herself attesting to this— 'I willfully bind myself to this Den king for in him I see our only hope and salvation'," Alseya said, producing the sheaf of papers she had taken out of the Feylands and reading from them. "She foresaw weakness not only in the fey, but also in the humans and looked to Feireden. It was their union that kept the Den from returning to their homelands across the ocean when the war against the elves ended. Without them the humans would have butchered us."*

*The room quieted as each realized the truth. Eireden saw it too. As well he saw in Alseya's eyes that she would not budge from her decision: the fey would not help him if he would not marry her. "In my culture it is not right for a woman to propose to a man," he said. Generai let out a long sigh of relief that pained his heart. He refused to look at her. Instead he stared into the opal eyes of Alseya—she was beautiful and delicate, with perfect tiny features. "Will you marry me, Alseya?"*

How Generai had kept from fainting he did not know, though he was sure that it had been a near thing. "Please stay here," he asked again. The scout had demanded to go with the strike team into the capital, saying she would never leave his side regardless of his orders. "Remember you said: command me? Now I'm commanding you."

"And now I'm changing my mind— don't command me!" Generai said with her arms crossed. "If she is going then I am going." There was no use arguing the fact that since Alseya was the strongest fey it made sense for her to come and that, as just a scout, it made sense for Eireden to choose someone other that Generai . He would have liked to pick another dwarf. There would be two coming along with Furen and both were robust and extremely capable looking.

"In the Den culture, when the queen dies what becomes of the king," Alseya asked, pleasantly ignoring the presence of the jealous scout. "Can he remarry?"

"You aren't married yet," Generai said under her breath.

"The king can remarry," Eireden said, after poking the blonde scout in the ribs. "Though you should be asking if the queen can remarry. You will likely live thousands of years longer than myself...but you will have to save the question for later. Here they come. Button it up!" he shouted to his command. Immediately the Den and their allies came to attention, all save the fey who simply quieted and looked curious at the detachment from Rhyoeven.

The fairies also failed to come to attention. Like a great flock of sparrows they wheeled and danced above the riders in a dark cloud. Disciplined, the men of Rhyoeven did not turn their heads up to look at them. They came on keeping in perfect formation. Eireden was disappointed so few had come. It would mean that there would be only twenty of his men plus himself against an entire hostile city and four elves. It was the elves that worried him.

Rudyid and his men came to a halt within ten feet of the king and then stared in stony silence. The whole prairie went still and quiet. Even the fairies flew away, off to the right. A full thirty seconds passed and still no one spoke in the one sided battle of wills. Having been schooled by Eirowyth, Rudyid refused to speak until the king spoke.

At forty seconds a fey two rows behind the king said, "The main illusion is up." Rudyid's eyes went wide and he began reach for his sword but then the detachment from Rhyoeven began falling from their saddles.

## Chapter 45

## Eireden

"What the...?" Rudyid asked, glassy-eyed. All around him his men were slumped in their saddles or laying in unkempt puddles of armor beside their horses.

"Time to sleep," said a soft-spoken male fey in the most soothing tones. He came through the line of men and caught the captain just as he fell.

Eireden jumped from his horse in a rush. There would not be much time. The fey had covered them all in one large illusion. From an outside perspective it would look like the two groups were still just sitting on their horses staring at each other.

"Let's go!" Eireden yelled. "Match up as best as possible. Lienhart that man there, take his shield...Furen, you and the dwarves split up. You can't be side by side." The twenty soldiers and fey of the strike team chose among the sleeping men of Rhyoeven those whom they would impersonate. The closer they came in size and armor the easier it would be on the fey. Secondary illusions would cover all of them, making them appear as part of the detachment.

As this went on, men in the second ranks hurried forward and drug the sleeping soldiers away while others leapt onto the horses so recently abandoned by the strike team—these men would be covered in illusion as well.

The whole switch took less than thirty seconds and then Eireden sat staring at an exact replica of himself. Beside him Furen eyed his counterpart and said, "This is so strange. I never noticed what a big head I have." Low laughter came from around them.

"Button it up," growled Prince Jarlen.

A fey voice called out, "We will drop the main illusion in three...two...one."

Eyes flicked around, but no one moved. Eireden— looking exactly like Rudyid— gave the tiniest bob of his head. The man across from himself, a man with steel-grey eyes and a scar running along the side of his face spoke as if reading from a script, "I have come to take my throne back; by force if necessary. Tell Eirowyth that I will meet him in a duel in ten minutes or I will attack in fifteen."

"This is your course?" Eireden/Rudyid said in a low voice, playing his part just in case.

"It is," said the man.

"Let's go," Eireden replied as part of his rehearsed script. He turned his mount and rode away, but went slowly so that the detachment could form up properly by twos. Seconds later the fairies rushed by in a great twittering mass. The king kept his face forward even as the fairies banked and swept back in among them and then Easa-see buzzed by whistling a message: *Eirowyth in the battle tower*.

The battle tower was the highest point in the capital. From it one could see the entirety of the plains surrounding the city. That Eirowyth was there was not unexpected. Neither was the next message: *There are eight with him*.

"Damn," Eireden said under his breath. "Eight in the tower." This he said in a whisper and it was carried back all the way to the rear of the formations man by man.

Along with Eirowyth there were eight other men in the tower...how many of these were elves disguised by illusion? If all four were there in one place the fight would be sharp indeed. And he would have little chance to speak to Eirowyth...how would that turn out? Would he listen to reason? Any sort of reason? Only time would tell.

"Button it up," growled one of the soldiers in Prince Jarlen's voice. Eireden glanced back to see one of the soldiers veering off to the left. It had to be one of the dwarves!

"Relax your hands on the reins," Alseya suggested. "There's no need to grip so tightly. I promise you the horse won't let you fall. Just relax. Look in the direction you are riding."

*Oh boy*, thought Eireden. Maybe the dwarves weren't such a good idea.

Under the fey's tutelage the dwarf got his mount back in line and it stayed there—thankfully—until they reached the lower gates of the city. These thronged with angry soldiers.

"We fightin'?" some asked. "Traitors!" others yelled out across the plain. One soldier called out, "Hey Griffy, you forget how to ride?" This was followed by good-natured laughing and more ribbing followed. Eireden hurried his mount along faster...if the dwarf answered in any way they'd be in trouble right off the bat.

Whichever dwarf it was kept his cool and they made it up through the second gate without issue. Once there they ran into a problem in the form of Captain Terwyth, a large belligerent man. "They bluffing or what? I mean that can't be serious about attacking, it would be a slaughter."

Eireden cleared his throat and then grabbed it for a second as if it pained him. "They're serious," he said in his best impersonation of Rudyid. He didn't think he sounded too much like the captain but Terwyth didn't seem to notice.

"You are joking? They want to fight? That is incredible! Everyday this world seems more turned around than the last. How could they want to fight? Does Eireden not care about his people?"

Captain Terwyth kept pace with the formation, walking along briskly. At this rate he would follow them right up to the tower, which wouldn't do at all. Anyone watching the illusioned dwarves dismounting would think they were drunk. "Who knows? Maybe you should go look to your men. The...uh, king will be on edge when he hears the news."

"What?" Terwyth asked. "What do you mean, my men?"

Eireden blinked at this. The last he had heard Captain Terwyth commanded a regiment of the First Guards. Had something changed? Had he been promoted? He must have been. No captain of men would answer the way he had. "I meant your old regiment. I worry things have fallen off since you left." After he said this Eireden held his breath while his hand went to his sword hilt.

"You know they have," Terwyth said, shaking his head in dismay. "Belacud knows nothing of discipline! I better go check on them. Tell the pri...the king I'll be right up."

The man strode off and Eireden waited precisely ten seconds before spurring his horse into a canter. He feared anything more would dump the dwarves onto their round heads, but he wanted to get up to the battle tower as fast as possible. From behind came dwarvish cursing and the soft tones of the fey coaching them. Thankfully for the most part the streets were empty. The Den were at their battle stations.

The battle tower sat atop a low hill near the center of the city. It rose two-hundred feet in the air and could command the view from all around. Of the eight men at the top of the tower at least four would be scouts acting as signalmen one on each side of the building. Two more would likely be runners, again scouts whose job would be to ferry messages back and forth. But who were the other two? He couldn't worry too much on that. They could be anyone or just look like anyone. For all he knew there were four elves up there...and twenty men wouldn't be enough.

Dismounting at the base of the tower he ordered, "Remember, there will be no killing of Den if at all possible." When the last of the dwarves clambered laboriously down they marched in only to be stopped before they climbed a single one of the many steps. In the entrance chamber were ten scouts and the captain of the scouts: a woman named Adinai.

"What's the word?" she asked. Adinai was powerful in her way, and the combined strength of this many scouts would not make overcoming them easy or quiet. Could he risk subduing them?

"We fight," he said loudly. "And we do not wish to hurt any, but unfortunately there will be blows." He then cocked his head pointedly at the scouts ranging around the room. Some of his "soldiers" just stood there staring at him. These he guessed were fey and were clueless as to what was about to happen. The remainder spread out.

Adinai watched this with an odd expression. "These men shouldn't be here. Their stations are..."

Eireden punched her in the jaw, felling her with the single blow—despite the fact that he pulled the punch at the last second. Screams erupted from the scouts and a few weak spells sprung into being, but for the most part the scouts were defeated without incident. "Tie them up," Eireden ordered. "I want two knights and two fey down here. Generai you remain as well, in charge." He hoped that would mollify her somewhat, but when the scouts were bound and hidden away and Eireden led his men upwards she followed along after.

"Take down our illusions," Eireden commanded, ten minutes later when they neared the top of the tower. "I want to know who is fighting on our team. When we get to the top there will be a scout on each side of the building. I want a pair—one knight and one fey, to overcome these. When you have, converge inwards on any elf that's in sight. Lienhart, you will take on Eirowyth. Try not to engage him, just keep him busy. I will go after the first elf that we identify. Jarlen will take on the second if there is one, and let's pray there is not. The rest of you find an opponent and subdue them as fast as possible."

Eireden knew he wasn't a match for a full powered elf. If there was more than one elf their chances of victory were slim. "It's going to be chaotic up there..." he began, but then a bright light flashed up from below. The stairs ran along the walls leaving a long drop in the center of the tower. Everyone stared down for all of a second. "To the top!" Eireden ordered.

If the group he left at the base of the tower were fighting there was nothing he could do to help. His mission was upwards not down. Drawing his elf-sword with a ringing flourish he charged the rest of the way up and surprised a scout who was just coming to investigate the source of the light. She screamed and fell back before him. He could have killed her easily, but could not bring himself even to wound her. Instead he pushed her down and raced onto the rooftop.

There, with a shocked looking Eirowyth, was his mother—the Lady Harowyth, and the fey Mayata. They were standing with a gaggle of scouts overlooking the southern plain where the allied army was drawn up.

"Where's the elf?" Eireden cried out to Alseya as his men started to pour onto the roof and battle the scouts. At first she didn't see him. The fight was an instant swirling melee with soldiers going in every direction. Alseya spun slowly searching, while beside her Eireden gripped his sword anxiously. The elf's illusion, coupled with his natural camouflage made him nearly impossible to spot. And then she pointed at the white-haired fey. "It's Mayata!"

The warning came too late for Prince Lienhart. He had pushed his way to Eirowyth while ignoring Mayata altogether. Just as he passed him the elf dropped his illusion and shot a great gout of fire over the man, burning and cooking him within his armor. The screams were enough to stop the battle in place for a span of seconds. But then Feylon went to douse the fire. She threw a bubble from her hand that grew in the air until it came down in a wave over Lienhart—and then just like that the fight recommenced.

It was a hodgepodge of separate battles with swords slashing and spells flying everywhere. Eireden charged the elf, needing to get close enough for his sword to make any difference. The elf threw off his illusion surprising Eireden with his beauty. He wasn't one of the burnt creatures. Instead Darhmael was tall and had an aristocratic air about him. He enjoyed flame.

Just as Eireden closed in on him another torrent erupted from his hand. Eireden had expected this and bringing his shield up he threw himself to the side. Still the fire was like liquid. It ran over his shield and down his arm; he was forced to throw the shield away to keep from going up in flames.

"Is this the preliminary to your attack?" the elf asked. One of Eireden's soldiers charged the elf. Darhmael picked him up using the power of his mind. Grunting with the psychic effort he threw the man off the tower. Despite the danger, Eireden watched him spinning until he hit the ground—then he was up and charging again. "I see you didn't learn his lesson," Darhmael commented blandly.

Eireden felt himself suddenly gripped by an unseen hand, and he was lifted into the air just as the other soldier had been. He knew struggling would be useless so instead he hurled his sword at the elf. Instantly he dropped. The elf couldn't throw him and block the sword at the same time.

"Very nice!" cried the elf. "I haven't had a worthy opponent in so long. But...you are out of swords." Again came the grip and again he was lifted, only this time he was thrown. Tossing armored men, especially those as big as the Den were, couldn't have been easy. Eireden didn't fly nearly as high as the other poor soldier and so when he stretched out his hands in desperation his fingers caught in the hair of Harowyth who was stepping down on the throat of one of the fey.

Instantly they fell together in a heap. She was like a viper, even caught unaware as she was. Before they had completely stopped tumbling a dagger appeared in her hand. She drove it into his face. Turning his head saved his eye, but still a dreadful slash opened up and blood poured down. She raised the weapon a second time and he kicked her violently in the midsection; she fell away, gasping. Eireden sat up, blinking the blood from his eyes.

The battle ran the gamut like a mural. Furen raged at the top of the stairs against unseen opponents trying to get up to the roof. The other two dwarves were fighting the elf, while Jarlen was going toe to toe with Eirowyth. Bodies were everywhere. Some were knights, some were scouts, some were fey. There were more bodies than there should have been. Right in front of him were seven scouts in various stages of consciousness and even more were fighting Alseya and Feylon on the other side of the roof.

As he got to his feet, he looked at all the scouts and wondered: *Could fairies even count?*

The pressing dwarves were being helped by two fey and this caused Darhmael to finally draw his sword. He was a master of the blade and the four were butchered before Eireden could even find a new sword.

Snatching one from an unconscious knight, Eireden came on quick not wanting to give the elf even a second to recover his magical power. "Why does your army just sit there?" Darhmael asked parrying the Den's attacks with ease. "With Eirowyth so engaged now would be a perfect time to storm the walls."

"There will be no attack," Eireden replied trying every trick, every possible maneuver, every ruse to get past the guard of the elf. He felt like a child.

"No attack?" the elf asked. It was clear he was disappointed; in fact he was furious. With a wave of his hand he threw Eireden backwards knocking the wind out of him. "Finish him," Darhmael said, but to whom he spoke Eireden didn't know. Just then a soft hand gripped his forehead and the flash of a dagger came. It laid his throat open from ear to ear and blood poured down into his windpipe.

## Chapter 46

### Eireden

Eireden fell back and his head lolled grotesquely due to the mortal wound. Above him glared Harowyth with an evil glint to her eye. "That's for leaving my husband to die."

The world went grey and it was hard for him to see that Harowyth's glare turned to surprise as blood erupted from her stomach. A sword tip came out the front of her and then disappeared again as she fell away from his vision. And then Alseya was there along with Generai.

"Heal him," Alseya ordered. Blood covered her white clothing, but whose it was there was no way to tell. "I will take on the elf."

Generai grabbed her arm. "I'll fight the elf!"

"You can't! He's too strong."

The scout shoved Alseya away and then bent to kiss the dying lips of the king. Eireden couldn't feel his body, but he could feel Generai's lips. No kiss had ever been so divided between love and pain. He could feel both coming from the girl and both were mighty rivers within her—they gave her strength without hope.

"The men of the Den find their worth in battle," Generai whispered. "The women find their worth in how much they can sacrifice before they can't give anymore...I wish you could've loved me." Standing she turned so that her blonde hair flared in the morning sun. She wanted Eireden to see it—to know where she was. Alone Generai charged the elf who had just tossed another fey to her death off the top of the building.

Swords clashed bringing a sharp pain in Eireden's soul. The scout could last seconds only and her death would tear him apart inside.

A frantic Alseya dropped to her knees next to the king and a blue light spread about him. Even before he had finished healing Eireden was up, desperate to save his scout.

Darhmael toyed with her and she bled from new wounds. He could kill her at any time, and those few left alive on the roof knew it. Eireden was barely up before he felt the power of the elf once more.

With one hand Darhmael casually battled Generai and with the other he sent Eireden flying toward the edge of the tower—and then a soft body leapt upon his. Alseya clung to the Den in desperation hoping her slim form would be enough to keep him from hurtling to his death. In this she was wrong—the elf still had great power. Yet the extra weight slowed them down enough so that as they flew off the tower Eireden was able to catch hold of the low railing that circled the building. There they dangled, Alseya hanging from his cloak with a frantic grip, inadvertently choking him.

Darhmael took a step back so that he could watch when Eireden fell and there would be no doubt that he would fall. The elf, using his mind alone began to pull Eireden's fingers back, one by one.

Generai saw this and went berserk. She hacked and hacked at the elf with all that she had left, but Darhmael coolly riposted with the elegance of an artist. Eireden saw the counter thrust coming a mile away, but then again so did Generai. She was no fool. She welcomed the blade and instead of cringing or pulling back she practically threw herself upon it.

And did she scream and whither in her death as Darhmael hoped? No, she clawed her way further onto the blade, so that she was practically nose-to-nose with the startled elf. Gripping his stylish black outfit with hooked claws, she embraced her death like a lover—eagerly she drove forward into his arms. The move surprised the elf and off-balance as he was, leaning back over the edge; he fell with the scout still on him.

"No!" Eireden cried. He wanted to turn away, but his eyes betrayed him and watched the pair fall. The elf used his magic and pushed the limp form from him and at the last second before they thudded into the earth Darhmael flared up and alit softly upon the ground. Generai didn't. She hit with a sound that would haunt Eireden's dreams for weeks to come and lay there unmoving.

He stared and stared until from below him, swinging gently back and forth from his cloak, Alseya said, "Your cousin. He remains unfought." She then climbed up the man with the dexterity of a monkey. He climbed up after, painfully. The roof was a horrific sight. Bodies and blood were everywhere. Of his strike force only Furen, Feylon, and Alseya remained on their feet and that was just barely.

Eirowyth stood with the black sword of Aug-Raumon poised. He had slain Jarlen and had watched the remainder of the battle recovering himself. He seemed very much fresher than Eireden who still had blood leaking into his lungs. His partially healed wound was becoming less healed with every passing second.

Eireden looked around for a sword, but then thought better of it. Generai's death had been too much for him—she had not died for him, she had died because of him; because he couldn't love her. "I did not come here to fight you, my Cousin," Eireden said. "I came here to save you. There is still much good you can do."

"I...I am good," Eirowyth replied. Confusion plucked at the muscles of his face and he couldn't seem to decide how to comport himself. He tried anger. "You are the traitor and the coward!"

Eireden produced the black cube and displayed the image. Eirowyth went a shade of green as he watched it. He then brought out his own cube. The image of this one showed Eireden in the Demorlaik. It had been doctored— changed through illusion. The images were spliced so that Eireden looked to be a coward.

"Both of these cannot be correct," Eirowyth said.

"They can actually," replied Eireden, logically. "As well they can both be false. Which leaves us where?" Eirowyth shrugged staring around at the dead and the dying.

Eireden looked down on the body of Harowyth, cold and stiff. He dropped the black cube next to her bloodstained hand and ground it under his heel. "It leaves us with you up here battling alongside an elf. In this I do not blame you. He has been playing us as the fools we are."

His young cousin considered this for a while. "If I discount what I see on this cube, you are still you, Eireden, King of the Den." He crushed the cube as Eireden had. "If I discount it then I am the fool. I am the one who has been blind to what should have been clear before. I knew there was something wrong when I battled you. I knew it, yet I...I basked in the glory of your defeat. I knew you were no coward, yet there was the throne calling to me."

He paused and swallowed hard. "It was my mother. She wanted so badly for me to be king. Even when I was young she would sneer at you." His words were a whisper. Wiping his suddenly damp eyes, he snarled, "It wasn't right! Look at this! Look at what I've done."

Bodies were everywhere. Alseya and Feylon were going to each giving the last of themselves to keep who they could alive. Furen had stopped battling and had wandered away from the stairs. A number of soldiers from Rhyoeven were standing there watching, listening. Among them was the scout Adinai and Captain Terwyth. Upon seeing them Eirowyth almost gagged. He recovered himself though his face remained alabaster.

"*We* weren't played for fools...only I was. I was the fool. This is yours," Eirowyth said, holding out the black sword. Eireden didn't see it. Instead he saw death in his cousin's eyes. The day's killing was not done and the young man did indeed prove the fresher. He turned for the ledge and leapt off before Eireden could catch him.

# Epilogue

## Ella

"Are you sure you wish to stay here? I mean it's rather cramped and I get up very early. They'll have you at the palace for certain and it's much nicer. With servants and everything. They'd even have you at the palace in Rhyoeven."

Ella shrugged at the man. "I'd be lonely there. I'm afraid I'd be lonely anywhere but here. I never had many friends here, but she was my best friend, while I had her."

Tears came to the candle-makers eyes and he turned away and inspected a wall. Taking his thumbnail he scraped at something completely inconsequential but very important all the same. "She talked about you. Said you was the sweetest girl on two legs. Said everyone loved you." He turned back and his eyes were bright red and still damp.

A shrug started to come but Ella forced it away. "That's just the way I was born, I guess...so what do you say? Would you like a roommate for a while? I don't eat much and I can help around the place. And you can teach me how to make candles."

This made him smile—everyone always smiled at Ella when she wanted them too. It was just the way she was born.

"You can stay as long as you want," the candle maker answered. "Come; let me take your things." There wasn't much. Just some clothes and the short sword the candle maker's daughter had given her a long time before. With her magic, an unbridled force within her, she could have picked up both the candle maker and her case and brought them up to her room. Instead she allowed him to take the case that held most of her things.

Ella's greatest possession, a large gaudy pearl, she kept in a locket around her neck. This she had the habit of touching when the least thing upset her—she had touched it frequently since she had been released from the dungeons by a weary dwarf. She had demanded to stay in the pits, but Furen had carried her out despite her tantrum.

Aric left her.

He felt he had been tricked into loving her is what he said. But that wasn't the real reason he had left. She knew the real problem; she was part human. She was *less than* in his eyes. Every time he had looked upon Elleni Feyden his love for Ella had withered just a little bit more. Ella had felt it slip away in those final days—tick, tick, tick like a clock ticking down on a bomb.

And who could she turn to?

Not to the candle maker's daughter, she was dead.

Not to Whip-wip, she was dead as well.

Furen had left in a great parade of dwarves, decked out in flowers by loving fairies. Ella had cried at that, but then again she found herself crying over all sorts of things.

She couldn't turn to Feylon; the lady fey had grown cold since her son had disappeared. And she definitely couldn't turn to Eireden. The king found every excuse not to see her after the battle. It hurt terribly, but it was worse when she did see him. He was clearly trying to hide the love he had for her, but whether he was trying to hide it from himself or Ella or Alseya it hardly mattered— he was stiff and awkward and avoided looking into her eyes. He didn't smile when she was around—the one person she wished would, didn't.

Strangely, the only person she did grow closer to in the weeks after the battle was Ilenwyth-Eden. The mother of the king took a special interest in Elleni. She was in Rhyoeven even then, still as catatonic as ever, but was at least being looked after properly, while a cure was being sought.

"You'll stay for the wedding?" Ilenwyth asked. "For me? There'll be no family on the groom's side if you don't. I'll be all alone. Besides I have a dress for you that will positively make Alseya look like a cow in comparison to you."

"I'll go to the wedding, but I won't wear that dress," Ella said. "And I can't stay in the palace any longer—or the city for that matter." Oddly the fey did not assign the least blame to her for her part in the destruction of the Feylands, but the citizens of Rhyoeven eyed her with suspicion and for what she couldn't tell.

Had it not been for that promise Ella would have gone back to America already. The Hidden Lands had turned out not to be the adventure she was looking for. Adventures were only good if everyone lived happily ever after and as far as she could tell no one was living happily ever after. After the wedding, which she was sure would be one of the most painful experiences of her life; she would leave the Hidden Lands and not look back.

"Which room?" the candle maker asked. There was no smile now, his lips were drawn tight. He had two dead daughters and two empty rooms.

"Olawe's."

He held back the tears until he closed the door, but with Ella's hearing there was little that she missed. She certainly didn't miss the whistling of a fairy. At midnight on that first night, Tissa, whistling a jaunty tune wiggled between the shutters and after saying a quick hello asked, "*Issa Whip-wip?*" Translated: Where's Whip-wip?

This hardly made sense since Whip-wip had been dead a month. It took some time to figure out that the scattered brained little thing wanted to know where Whip-wip's pearl was. "I have it here," Ella said touching her locket. "But I'm afraid I'm not going to give it to you. You'll have to find another."

"*Swirrp, El-a, swirrp,*" Tissa said, tugging on her hair.

"Come here? Come where? I said I wasn't giving you the pearl."

Tissa was so insistent that Ella allowed herself to be led out of the town, though she dragged her feet. The moon was full and bright, yet Ella did not care for it. It was too bright for liking. She was in a darker mood and embraced the shadows.

"Is this about a poor 'needy' fairy who's going to beg for my..." Ella stopped as she realized where Tissa had brought her. Ahead was the clearing where she and Aric had been captured—where Whip-wip had died.

"I'm not going in there," Ella said through sudden tears. Just then the woods all around seemed to come awake and begin to move. Shadows danced but what they were Ella couldn't tell.

*"Swirrp, swirrp, swirrp,"* Tissa sang.

"No! I'm not going in there. This isn't a game!"

*"Swirrp, swirrp, swirrp, swirrp, swirrp, swirrp,"* Tissa insisted. "Ees gud."

"It's good? Are you sure?" It didn't seem good. Regardless Ella walked forward slowly even as the movement intensified around her. There were many little things shooting about, but they stayed in the shadows.

Tissa brought her to the very spot where Whip-wip died and then tugged her down on her knees by her hair and sang: "*Issa Whip-wip?*" The fairy then pointed at the locket.

"Fine, you can have the pearl," Ella said and then clicked open the locket.

Beneath the high full moon, the pearl sat in the polished silver, shining away. Finally after all this time the dud of a pearl was shining—but then the shining grew into radiance and Ella cringed back. With all the light she saw that she was surrounded by fairies, there were thousands. They were dark and the pearl was light—they grew still and the pearl moved. It jumped a little, and then some more, and now a crack ran along its outer shell.

"Shell?" Ella asked aloud in amazement. Realization struck her: the fat gaudy pearl wasn't a pearl at all and had never been one. It was an egg and from it something emerged.

The End

*

Author's note:

The story continues with To Ensnare a Queen, but before you run off to the bookstore to snatch up your copy could I ask a favor? The review is the most practical and inexpensive form of advertisement an independent author has available in order to get his work known. If you could put a kind review on Amazon and your Facebook page, I would greatly appreciate it.

Peter Meredith

To Ensnare a Queen:

Separated by chance and fate, Eireden has to give up on finding love with Ella, instead he must watch helplessly as his kingdom is destroyed one city at a time. His enemies are vast in number and skillfully led, but they have no chance against the mighty fortress city of Rhyoeven…or do they? Eireden begins to suspect he has been maneuvered into trapping himself exactly where his enemies want him.

Not wanting to be anywhere near Eireden when he weds another woman, Ella thinks she is leaving the world of magic and swords behind her, but by accident she comes across another fugitive from the Hidden Lands. However this fugitive is very much planning on returning and when he does he plans on bringing back something that can end the war in a flash.

## Fictional works by Peter Meredith:

A Perfect America
The Sacrificial Daughter
The Apocalypse Crusade War of the Undead: Day One
The Apocalypse Crusade War of the Undead: Day Two
The Horror of the Shade: Trilogy of the Void 1
An Illusion of Hell: Trilogy of the Void 2
Hell Blade: Trilogy of the Void 3
The Punished
Sprite
The Blood Lure: The Hidden Land Novel 1
The King's Trap: The Hidden Land Novel 2
To Ensnare a Queen: The Hidden Land Novel 3
The Apocalypse: The Undead World Novel 1
The Apocalypse Survivors: The Undead World Novel 2
The Apocalypse Outcasts: The Undead World Novel 3
The Apocalypse Fugitives: The Undead World Novel 4
The Apocalypse Renegades: The Undead World Novel 5
The Apocalypse Exile: The Undead World Novel 6
Pen(Novella)
A Sliver of Perfection (Novella)
The Haunting At Red Feathers(Short Story)
The Haunting On Colonel's Row(Short Story)
The Drawer(Short Story)
The Eyes in the Storm(Short Story)